NEW DIREC⊥⊥∪⊥∖∪

Spring 2006

"The thing is to get the nonconforming stuff in print when it is written and not fifteen years after."
—James Laughlin, founder of New Directions

WORLD BEAT:
International Poetry Now from New Directions
Edited by Eliot Weinberger

A celebration of contemporary poetry from around the world, *World Beat* opens with Octavio Paz, and ends with Nicanor Parra. In between there is poetry by the young Albanian Luljeta Lleshanaku, the exiled Iraqi Dunya Mikhail, the controversial Israeli Aharon Shabtai, the Caribbean poet Kamau Brathwaite, the Mexican poet Homero Aridjis, two Chinese experimentalists Gu Cheng and Bei Dao, the Japanese avant-garde poet Kazuko Shiraishi. There's Inger Chritensen from Denmark, Gennady Aygi from the tiny country buried deep in the heart of Russian, Chuvashia, the Swede Tomas Tranströmer, and Canadian Anne Carson to name a few, plus the Americans Susan Howe, Michael Palmer, and Robert Creeley. $14.95 pbk. original

TERRESTRIAL INTELLIGENCE:
International Fiction Now from New Directions
Edited by Barbara Epler

Terrestrial Intelligence is a collection of the best new groundbreaking fiction recently published by New Directions. Included are stories by the premier Latin-American writer Roberto Bolaño, the German author W. G. Sebald, the Russian enfant terrible Victor Pelevin, the astonishing Japanese/German writer Yoko Tawada. We've included Antonio Tabucchi from Italy, Javier Marías from Spain, Yoel Hoffmann from Israel, Leonid Tsypkin the Russian Jew whose work had to be smuggled to the West, the world-renowned Muriel Spark, and the new South-American phenomenon César Aira from Argentina. They are just some of the diverse writers selected for this anthology.
                                                  $14.95 pbk. original

Please send for free complete catalog.
NEW DIRECTIONS, 80 8th Avenue, NYC 10011
INDEPENDENT PUBLISHER SINCE 1936
                                        www.ndpublishing.com

CONJUNCTIONS

Bi-Annual Volumes of New Writing

Edited by
Bradford Morrow

published by Bard College

EDITOR: Bradford Morrow
MANAGING EDITOR: Michael Bergstein
SENIOR EDITORS: Robert Antoni, Peter Constantine, Brian Evenson,
  Micaela Morrissette, David Shields, Pat Sims, Alan Tinkler
WEBMASTER: Brian Evenson
ASSOCIATE EDITORS: Jedediah Berry, J. W. McCormack, Eric Olson
ART EDITOR: Norton Batkin
PUBLICITY: Mark R. Primoff
EDITORIAL ASSISTANT: Justine Haemmerli

CONJUNCTIONS is published in the Spring and Fall of each year
by Bard College, Annandale-on-Hudson, NY 12504. This issue is
made possible in part with public funds from the New York State
Council on the Arts, a State Agency. NYSCA

SUBSCRIPTIONS: Send subscription orders to CONJUNCTIONS, Bard
College, Annandale-on-Hudson, NY 12504. Single year (two volumes): $18.00
for individuals; $35.00 for institutions and overseas. Two years (four volumes):
$32.00 for individuals; $70.00 for institutions and overseas. Patron subscription (lifetime): $500.00. Overseas subscribers please make payment by
International Money Order. For information about subscriptions, back issues,
and advertising, call Michael Bergstein at (845) 758-1539 or fax (845) 758-2660.

Editorial communications should be sent to Bradford Morrow, *Conjunctions*,
21 East 10th Street, New York, NY 10003. Unsolicited manuscripts cannot be
returned unless accompanied by a stamped, self-addressed envelope.
Electronic and simultaneous submissions will not be considered.

Conjunctions is listed and indexed in the American Humanities Index.

Visit the *Conjunctions* Web site at www.conjunctions.com.

Cover design by Jerry Kelly, New York.
Original cover art: *Gustave Courbet's Sister Regards a Paul Klee* (1929) by
Kenneth Rexroth. Wax, varnish, and silica on board. 23½ x 17¾ inches. Reproduced by permission of The Kenneth Rexroth Trust. Copyright © 2006. Private
collection.

Available through D.A.P./Distributed Art Publishers, Inc., 155 Sixth Avenue,
New York, NY 10013. Telephone: (212) 627-1999. Fax: (212) 627-9484.

Printers: Edwards Brothers

Typesetter: Bill White, Typeworks

ISSN 0278-2324
ISBN 0-941964-62-0

Manufactured in the United States of America.

TABLE OF CONTENTS

SELECTED SUBVERSIONS
ESSAYS ON THE WORLD AT LARGE

Edited by Rikki Ducornet, Bradford Morrow, and Robert Polito

*   *   *

SPECIAL PORTFOLIO:

EDITORS' NOTE

THE ESSAY ASSAYS. It tests and tries the world through a cascade of nuanced ideas. It provides a map to a place one has heard about, perhaps dreamed about, but not yet visited. It offers the reader access from an unforeseen angle to an experience perhaps already known intimately, but not quite from the same experiential pathway, or neuropathway, that the essayist has traveled. A good essay analyzes from new perspectives, and it radiates with itineraries. It weighs (*exagium*, among its etymological forebears, is a weighing). It compares. Illuminating perplexities, sometimes creating perplexities, it makes arcane connections at times, delving into eccentric spaces, probing anomalies. It often changes, even subtly, how one thinks. An *essai* is a trial. It is a medium of analysis whose end result is to change things, to alter, *assai*. Because it is meant to be revelatory, is meant to make an assault on certitudes, it is by its very nature subversive.

One need only recall the verbal ingenuities of such writers as Montaigne, Browne, Burton, Swift, Johnson, and others who authored the great, canonical "nonfiction" (to use *that* silhouette of a word, which says what it is by saying what it isn't) to be struck by how formally attenuated so many contemporary essays can be. What we have attempted to explore here, to assay, are the possibilities of the form beyond the genial declarative sentences that conspire to become the polite essay. We have gone for a range. If some of the essays don't seem to be essays, think of them as assays. And see where they lead, noting their sometimes deliberately different gaits.

The Quay Brothers are pioneering assayers, too, and though their final medium is film, we are pleased they have offered us a chance to prowl around their verbal workshop. Reading their scenarios gives us a rare opportunity to produce a Quay film in our heads. Or, that is, to try.

—Rikki Ducornet, Bradford Morrow, Robert Polito
New York City and Denver, April 2006

7

Three Essays
John D'Agata

ESSAY ABOUT IT ALL

IN CHINA, THE BODY of a turtle is earth, and the shell of a turtle is heaven, and a turtle can live for ten thousand years. In Taoist philosophy, the number ten thousand symbolizes infinity. In the Bible, it is two thousand more years than the world has even existed. "And torture one word ten thousand ways," John Dryden wrote in sixteen seventy-eight. In English, the word *myriad* is an adjective meaning "numerous," but in its earliest incarnations as a noun from the Greek it literally represented the number "ten thousand." Which is the number of cells in the human body that signal a heart to beat. Which is the number of civilians found in Nanking in the Ditch of Ten Thousand Corpses. Which is the cost in dollars of the oldest bottle of scotch sold at auction. Which is how many monkeys at how many typewriters in how many years it would take. Human consciousness, Jung said, is a room of ten thousand whispers. In *Ten Thousand Dreams Interpreted, or, What's in a Dream*, the ten thousandth dream that the author interprets is about zoological gardens: "To dream of visiting zoological gardens denotes that you will have a varied future. Sometimes it seems that enemies overpower you, and yet at other times you seem to stand in the front rank of success. It also means that you will gain knowledge by traveling to foreign countries." Jerusalem is called the City of Ten Thousand Memories. Vancouver is called the City of Ten Thousand Buddhas. Manhattan is called the City of Ten Thousand Journalists. Shanghai used to be called the City of Ten Thousand Flags, but when officials issued a new law in nineteen ninety-four that banned all laundry from being hung outdoors, the city's trees and balconies and utility poles went bare, and now Shanghai is not known for being the city of anything. In London, there is a fictional museum called the Museum of Ten Thousand Things, which was founded in eighteen thirty-five and in which is exhibited "the Wall of Clarification," a fifty foot–long list of every known color's name. In nineteen twenty-

8

one, the Katmai National Park in Alaska experienced a volcanic eruption that opened hundreds of steam vents in a previously unpopular area of the park, which rangers now call "the Valley of Ten Thousand Smokes." There are ten thousand lakes in Minnesota. There are ten thousand islands off the Gulf Coast of Florida. Alfred Bryan once wrote upon seeing the Grand Canyon: "I am ten thousand cathedrals in one." The Hill of Ten Thousand Ages in Beijing was the summer palace of the empress. In the Forbidden City in China there is a Garden of Ten Thousand Springs. And at the temple where Confucius is said to have died there is a Ten Thousand Fathom Wall. In Japan, at the Kasuga Grand Shrine, there is an annual festival called "the Night of Ten Thousand Lanterns," during which candles are lit on a river in honor of the country's dead. The Martyrdom of Ten Thousand is celebrated by Christians on March eighteenth, the day on which the emperor Diocletian set five hundred tigers on three hundred Christians. According to the Koran, ten thousand is the number of Muslims it took to liberate Mecca. During an election in nineteen ninety-seven, officials in India claimed they received ten thousand ballots from local gods and goddesses, which registrars ultimately decided to count because the right to vote in India is based on land deeds, many of which are signed over to deities for luck. Isis was known as the Goddess of Ten Thousand Names. Ten Thousand Angels is an American chain of Christian bookstores. MIT's gospel choir is called "the Ten Thousand Tongues." Ten thousand, according to astronomer Francis Drake's famous equation— $N=N*f_p n_e f_l f_i f_c f_r$—is the number of intelligent civilizations we can assume are sharing the universe. The Vietnam War has been called the "War of Ten Thousand Days." There were ten thousand gay men killed in the Holocaust. (There were twelve thousand six hundred lesbians.) General Patton's fifth regiment was called "the Army of Ten Thousand Men." Harvard University's fight song is called "The Ten Thousand Men of Harvard." In nineteen fifty-six, John Cage abandoned a project he tentatively entitled "the Ten Thousand Things," for which he planned a series of individual arrangements that would have totaled ten thousand individual measures. "I Was Born Ten Thousand Years Ago" is an American folk song from the nineteen twenties: "I saw Satan when he looked the Garden over / And I saw Adam driven from the door / And behind the bushes peeping / I saw what he was eating, / And I swear I'm the one who ate the core!" According to the Federal Bureau of Investigation, ten thousand dollars is the most common amount of money that is offered by the families of kidnapped children. It is the number of Americans in a recent census who identified their race as "vampire." It is how many fleas were caught by the trap that holds the Guinness World Record for "World's Most Effective Glue Pad." It is the largest printed bill in United States currency. It is the size of the fine an American pays for traveling illegally to Cuba. And it is the amount that one received in nineteen seventy-four—before the recent appearance of *The Million Dollar Pyramid Starring Donny Osmond,* and before the earlier appearances of the "Two Hundred Thousand Dollar Pyramid," the "One Hundred Thousand Dollar Pyramid," the "Fifty Thousand Dollar Pyramid," the "Twenty-Five Thousand Dollar Pyramid," the "Twenty Thousand Dollar Pyramid," and the "Fifteen Thousand Dollar Pyramid"—on *The Ten Thousand Dollar Pyramid Starring Dick Clark,* a game show in which your challenge was to guess what phrase your partner was trying to describe without the use of that phrase.

ESSAY ON WHERE IT'S FROM

On that evening of his sunset, Edvard probably left his house by five o'clock to hear the scream. Down the block on Pilestredet around the corner to the tram, or down the block on Pilestredet by foot to Karl Johan, he would have passed the place that's now a bar called Edvard's on the corner, and then the one with pizza called Edvard's Oven Fresh, and then a store across the street called Scream If You Like Sweets! He could have cut through Grazing Place, where every citizen could keep cattle, and then walked across a bridge that linked the city to its shore. But Edvard says he liked to walk—"I need to walk to think"—and knew a longer path up Ekeberg Hill and through its forest. It was eighteen eighty-three, and it was very likely August. Up the hill from Kristiania he passed couples stretched on blankets, dozens of slanting bodies on the city's Lovers' Lane, and then he reached the forest once the meadow hillside leveled, and then he walked inside the woods, despite his father's warnings. "There is evil there," his father said, "long forgotten curses from Norway's pagan past." Edvard turned nineteen that year, and was living still at home. He would have needed his dad's permission to have been out past six thirty. He would have needed to miss his dinner, retired early to his room, established two days earlier that he was feeling rather ill. He would have needed three years earlier to have had rheumatic fever, and needed twelve years earlier to almost die on Christmas day. Then he would have needed a low window he could climb through. There was a gray straw hat he wore "every single day that I knew him in Kristiania, from the time that he was fifteen until he left home for Berlin," according to a memoir by Edvard's closest friend. He would have needed that straw hat. Some good walking shoes. The light wool brown coat that all middle-class boys wore. He would have needed forty minutes to pass through Ekeberg's forest and would have needed to understand its ancient pagan history, the thousand-year-old practice of bringing infants here to die, digging narrow graves over which boulders were then laid so that the child didn't suffocate but rather starved to death, a practice that was so common by the early eleventh century that St. Olav, the Christian bishop who arrived to baptize pagans, wrote a letter to Norwegians enforcing three new Christian laws—"There shall be no more folk singing in God's northern kingdom, for these are not the sounds our Lord and Savior wants to hear. . . . There shall desist immediately all the eating of horsemeat. . . . And because all Christian lives begin with Holy Baptism, no longer may any child be left exposed if it's unwanted"—the last of which proved so controversial for the pagans that one decade later, in the famous Gulathing's Law, a revision was applied in which "no healthy child may now be exposed, except if his heels are in the place of his toes, whose chin is turned around and connected to the shoulder, the neck upon his breast, with the calves on his legs turning back the wrong direction, his two eyes on the back of the poor child's hands . . . and seal's fins . . . a dog's head. . . . The child must be brought to the forest, therefore, and buried where neither men nor cattle ever go," a condition that was actually not uncommon at the time, for, as Jenny Jochens explains in *Women in Old Norse Society*, the low-valleyed villages and high walls of mountains confined the majority of Norwegians to their homes, "forcing upon the culture a certain amount of inbreeding . . . thus resulting in increasingly deformed infants at birth." He would have needed to know the phrase "I christen thee at random, Jon or Johanna," the spell St. Olav wrote to ward off any *utburd*, the wide-eyed, pale, and hairless ghosts of Norway's exposed children, thin hairless shrieking souls who haunted Ekeberg's forest, looking for their parents. He would have needed to know that night, if one mistook him for its father, clinging to his back with a black and gaping jaw, that the only way to rid oneself at that point of an *utburd* was to convince the child to kill itself, and bury it again. What he wouldn't have needed to know, during his walk here as a teen, was that his childhood friend in fifteen years would shoot himself in Ekeberg. Wouldn't have needed to know, once he had reached the other side, looking down now from the hill that edged the city's shore, that his sister would be committed, that he would never visit her, and that eventually she would die along the city's shoreline, through the forest, down the hill, in a loud and red asylum, from which the screams that were heard were so consistently high-pitched that local residents soon forgot it didn't house the slaughterhouse. Wouldn't have needed to know that this view he now walked toward would eventually be the city's most famous for postcards. Wouldn't have needed to see, as he brushed off the forest leaves, the stone marker that the city would never place upon this spot, commemorating where Edvard first felt that he was hurt. Wouldn't need the bench that's there, the one turned the wrong direction. Wouldn't need to cross the highway, where there are no crossing walks, approaching the metal guardrail, which no longer is a railing. Wouldn't need to glimpse below to where the tracks are running now to the service road, the power grid, the industry of concrete ports and forklift trucks and corrugated terminals to Unicon and Exxon and BP and Shell. Would only need the evening now. A slow dusty shuffle down the hill, around the rocks. Would only need his parents dead. Favorite sister, younger brother, older sister to be dead. To help bleach their bloody sheets to light brown mottled spots with urine. He needed to hate his father. Love with fear his smiling mother. He needed to kiss a boy before he ever kissed a girl, and then to go on living without anyone to kiss. He needed someone saying that he'd invented something new, that he had felt an ancient emptiness at the center of the world and then gathered up that emptiness into something that had borders, a face, the chance to see what was wrong, he needed someone saying that God was not in every detail, that God was sometimes in experience, someone to write letters to, from whom he could get letters back, take train trips with, and snuggle with, and then never to have met. He needed earth, ten million years ago, to rumble from the bottom of its ocean floor a mountain, a four-thousand-acre island in Indonesia called Rakato, one of thirteen thousand islands in the narrow Sundra Strait on which he needed Krakatoa, a mountain on the mountain, a volcano whose eruption in fourteen ten BC was said to have caused tsunamis that were so big they sank Atlantis, a volcano whose eruption in five thirty-seven was said to have clouded skies so thoroughly that summer that it snowed in Rome in June, that crops in Europe failed, that floods appeared in deserts, that wandering Mongolians, retreating from the weather, fled with tribal families west into Eurasia, ended the Persian empire, and started modern Islam, a volcano that locals called the "pulsing heart of all the world" to once again erupt with so much power in this year that on August twenty-fifth, the week proceeding Edvard's walk, it practiced an eruption at five thirty in the morning, then practiced at six forty, then eight twenty-one, then ten, ten fifty, midnight, and one, and then finally at three thirty on August twenty-sixth it erupted with a force that razed one hundred sixty villages, killed forty thousand people, burst so loudly that radiometrists have called the mountain's blast the second-loudest noise ever heard by human beings, sending out concussive waves seven times around the world, and exploding up a mile high, and then exploding out: blanketing the atmosphere with two hundred twenty-seven million tons of new debris, over two thirds of the island's entire rocky mass, dust that drifted across the earth so thoroughly and fast that by August twenty-eighth British offices in Delhi were reporting having seen a bank of yellow clouds at night, by August twenty-ninth they were orange in Madrid, and by August thirty-first they had mixed with moisture over London from where a cold front pushed the dust and rain westward over Norway, where the evenings were still sunny, and the dust caught more than light. He only needed to look up. For Lord William Rayleigh, in the English countryside that night, to wonder while on horseback why at sunsets colors changed. The lord was studying chemistry and physics at the time, and soon would win the Nobel Prize for discovering ancient argon, a noble gas that never reacts to other gases in the air, never changes or combines, and therefore cannot die. "It is this gas," the lord explained, accepting his Nobel Prize, "that allows us to imagine the deep stretches of earthly time, inhaling today the very same particles of the gas that Aristotle, Galileo, and Newton once exhaled. . . . Oh, how many great ideas has a single atom thus inspired?" The lord made several notes on how sunsets work and why, developing that night a new theory regarding color, evolving it eventually into the Rayleigh Scattering Effect, the founding principle of which explains that light must pass at sunsets diagonally through the sky, and therefore only displays those colors with long wavelengths—the yellows and the oranges and the many kinds of red—that which Edvard saw as blood, and the lord determined why.

ESSAY YOU DO NOT GET

Apparent Suicide at Las Vegas Casino. Apparent Suicide Claims Young Tourist. Apparent Suicide at Vegas High School. Apparent Suicide. Apparent Suicide. Apparent Suicide. Apparent Suicide. AWOL Soldier Kills Himself, Leaves Note for Bush. Body Discovered, Suicide Suspected. Bodies Discovered in Suicide Pact. Boy Named Suicide. Boy Remains Stable after Suicide Attempt. Boy Watches Father Kill Brother and Self. Candidate in Sex Scandal Shoots Self in Court. Cause of Death Suicide. Coroner Rules Suicide. Coroner Says Inmate Hanged Self with Laundry Bag. Couple Found Dead in Murder-Suicide. Couple Found Dead in Motel Suicide. Cross-Dressing Burglar Commits Jail-Cell Suicide. Death of Boy, Twelve, Ruled Suicide. Defense Says Note Left after "Suicide" Song Lyrics. Desperate Man Commits Suicide. Detention Center Suicides Hit Las Vegas High. Devotion Ends in Vegas with Death and a Suicide. Distraught Cabby Kills Himself by Ramming City Hall. Elderly Couple Dies in Mobile Home Suicide. Escaped Convict Kills Himself. Ex-Judge Kills Himself. Ex-Marine Kills Himself. Ex-Patient Kills Himself. Ex-Player's Death an Apparent Suicide. Father Discovers Daughter's Body in Apparent Suicide. Friends Say Boy Tried Suicide Twice. Gunman Kills Himself at K-Mart Warehouse. His Second Attempt at Suicide Apparently Successful. Hospital Blamed in Suicide. Hotel Jumper Kills Himself. Human Remains a Suicide. Insurance Pay-Out Denied to Suicide Victim's Wife. Jackpot Winner Suicide. Las Vegas Man Commits Suicide. Las Vegas Man Commits Suicide. Las Vegas Man Commits Suicide at Ex-Girlfriend's Apartment. Las Vegas Man Talked Down from Ledge, Shoots Himself at Home. Las Vegas Man Shoots Self and Dog. Las Vegas Pharmacist Commits Suicide. Local Teen Commits Suicide. Local Teen Commits Suicide. Local Teen Commits Suicide. Local Teen Commits Suicide. Local Teen Commits Suicide. Local Teen Commits Suicide. Man Commits Suicide as Police Surround His House. Man Commits Suicide in Stranger's Apartment. Man Commits Suicide at Strip Hotel. Man Commits Suicide on Grounds of Estate. Man Crashes Car Then Kills Self with Knife. Man Dies after Leap from Stratosphere Hotel. Man Found Hanging in Naked City Motel. Man Kills Family Then Commits Suicide. Man Kills Himself When Parole Office Calls. Man Leaps to Death from Top of Mirage. Man Shoots Football Player Then Kills Himself. Man Shoots Wife, Commits Suicide at Laundry. Man Who Killed His Mother

14

an Apparent Suicide. Metro Sergeant Suicide a Shock to Precinct. Missing Man Found Dead from Apparent Suicide. Mississippi Tourist an Apparent Suicide. Montana Tourist Commits Hotel Suicide. One Dead of Suicide in Caesar's Palace Lot. Nevada Leads Nation in Suicide Rate. New Jaycee President Commits Suicide. Police Respond to Leap from Flamingo Hotel. Police Officer with Gambling Problem Commits Suicide. Robber Commits Suicide. Stalking Suspect Suicide. Taxi Driver Dies When Lights Himself Afire. Travel Agents Dead in Double Suicide. Two Teens Dead in Ritual Suicide. Utah Tourist Commits Suicide. Vogue Owners Killed in Murder-Suicide. Weapons Enthusiast Goes Out in Blaze of Gunfire, Coroner Rules Example of "Suicide by Cop." Young Actor Dead in Las Vegas Suicide. Young Actor's Suicide in Las Vegas Hotel. Young Actor Kills Himself. Young Actor Kills Himself. Young Actor Kills Himself. Young Actor Kills Himself. Young Actor Kills Himself in Las Vegas Club. Young Actress Dead in Las Vegas Hotel. Young Actress Kills Herself. Young Model's Suicide a Lesson for Teens. Zoo Visitor Kills Himself in Front of School Group.

In a Glance

Joanna Scott

ISABEL ARCHER STOPS SHORT just beyond the threshold of the drawing room and briefly observes her husband, Osmond, and Madame Merle absorbed in conversation. The flash of perception is unsettling. Though the scene appears harmless, Isabel feels that she is detecting the presence of something that is supposed to remain hidden. And then it's over—"the thing made an image, lasting only a moment, like a sudden flicker of light."

Clarissa Dalloway loves to see the sky—at dusk, at dawn, at dinner between people's shoulders or out the window on the night of her party. She parts the curtains. She glances out. To her surprise, an old woman is staring straight at her from a room across the way. Clarissa is fascinated. A moment later the old woman puts out her light, her room is enveloped in darkness, and the clock starts striking the hour. Clarissa tells herself she "must assemble," and she returns to her guests.

Faulkner's Darl, having set the barn on fire, watches Jewel against the backdrop of the flames. "For an instant," Jewel is lit by moonlight. "For an instant," Jewel looks out through the flames, "through the rain of burning hay." And "for another instant," the coffin Jewel is carrying stands upright while the fire falls in "scattering bursts" upon it.

For an instant, the sudden flicker of vision proves infinitely fascinating—again and again, from moment to moment and page to page. Why?

We drove south on Route 17 between slopes dusted with snow, beside winding creeks laced with thin ice. The day had started out glittering and cold, but the sky grayed with cloud cover near the trout town of Roscoe, and by the time we reached Route 87, a heavy rain was falling.

In the hotel in Stamford, we rode the elevator up to the fourteenth floor, to our room overlooking the rail line and I-95. Parting the

16

drapes, we saw the traffic clogged in the southbound lanes. Then the phone rang, and we turned away from the window.

Later, we met up with relatives, ate dinner in the hotel restaurant, teased and endured teasing, and, at the end of the evening, we watched helplessly as our teenage niece got stuck trying to push her grandfather in his wheelchair through the hotel's revolving door. The comic crisis lasted only a moment—our niece was able to nudge the wheelchair forward and put the door in motion again, and she delivered Grandpa safely to the curb beside my brother's car, where we all said our good-byes and promised to gather again soon.

The next morning we drove through a freezing rain to the Cross-Bronx Expressway. We missed the turnoff for the FDR Drive and had to continue across the tip of Manhattan and down the West Side Highway. We spent the afternoon in the Metropolitan Museum, following the circular route of the Fra Angelico show, looking at saints dancing in paradise, martyrs being separated from their heads, the damned gesturing futilely. Between the shoulders of other visitors we saw a red-eyed Christ who, crowned with thorns and empowered by infinite melancholy, seemed to have conquered the mortal urge to blink. We continued on, past light searing the hands of St. Francis, the blessed gathering in expectation, the magi kneeling in adoration.

With the paintings behind us, it was the blood-rimmed eyes of the suffering Christ that lingered in memory. The more I thought about it, the more I came to feel that I wasn't sure what I'd seen. I wanted to look again at the painting, but by then we were near the exit of the exhibition, and our daughters were restless. We wandered across the hall to the cafeteria. After a quick lunch, we left the museum and drove back across the park. We deposited the car in a garage on West Eighty-third and checked into the Excelsior.

On Sunday morning we wobbled along the icy sidewalk and across the street to the Natural History Museum. We bought tickets, climbed the stairs to the third floor, wandered past displays of reptile bones and fossils, and marveled at the two Galápagos turtles, one dull-eyed and motionless, the other stepping across the pen with great determination, its elephantine legs bowed beneath the weight of its shell.

We stood in the line for the exhibit. We gave our tickets to the guard. We filed into the darkness of the hall. We watched the people in front of us lean forward to get a better look at the first object on display. We reached a table that was theatrically lit by spotlights.

On the table was a small pedestal. Attached to the pedestal was a nineteenth-century handheld magnifying glass that had belonged to Darwin. We took turns glancing quickly, greedily, through the magnifying glass at a dragonfly pinned to a board, until the momentum of the line pushed us forward. And that was that.

Glitter of ice along the shore. Red-eyed Christ. The legs of a turtle. A dragonfly wing. When we glance out the window of a hotel room at the traffic creeping miserably through a winter rain, we perceive only part of the scene. When we glance through the glass panels of a revolving door at a girl trying to push an old man in his wheelchair, we see a fragment of the whole image. The door revolves another notch, and the two of them are outside. What have we noticed? What have we missed?

Aldous Huxley, writing in *The Art of Seeing* about selective perception, emphasizes the importance of memory to vision. Without memory, the raw material for the physical world, "the visual sensum," would be impossible to process. Without memory, perception would be incoherent. It's a common-sense description of the process of vision, and it sounds a lot like experiential accounts of language acquisition. In both cases, early experience provides the basis for interpretation. If I'm going to make sense of the word *cow*, I need to compare it to preceding encounters with the word. And if the ribbed wool near my hands is going to distinguish itself as the red sleeve of my sweater, it needs a precedent: another sweater perceived at an earlier point in time and another equivalent red.

We have different strategies for refining our visual ability. We might gaze at something, squint at it, watch it, do a double take, or pick up a magnifying glass and study the minutia of an object. We look inside the frame that defines the boundaries of a scene. We note the way edges create shape and contour. Light illuminates, and shadows often revealingly obscure.

We see partially, limited not just by the field of vision but by the abundance of detail. To see carefully, we need to keep our gaze fixed on a set of images. We stare. We return to scenes recorded with videos and photographs. The harder we look, the more we tend to see.

Given the complexity of vision, it's difficult to account for the power of a glance—that momentary and unrepeatable flicker of vision. Unlike other forms of looking, a glance is experienced in the space of time between two heartbeats. We don't have time to consider how we might preserve the memory. Often, we don't even realize the significance of what we're seeing until long after the experience.

Yet ideas and emotions are nourished by glances. Fragments of images are revived and reinvented with fragments in dreams. Glances set thought in motion. Glances seize our interest when we're least prepared. What Isabel and Clarissa and Darl see in an instant would not have the same power if these images were observed at length.

When we close our eyes and the whole scene before us disappears from sight, the majority of details disappear from consciousness. We forget much of what we've just been looking at. Yet we're able to understand what we see because of our extensive memory of images, acquired through visual attention that registers what are commonly described as *central* and *peripheral* aspects of the visual field. Even with a glance, we manage to store in memory more than we notice, and we experience a degree of recognition, both conscious and automatic, with every new image.

The kind of glance that amplifies awareness often sparks a strange sense of recognition, offering a mysterious echo of a forgotten expectation. At the same time, it casts the image as new, fresh, odd. A resonant glance offers us an image that is at once familiar and unfamiliar. We might not even realize the significance of the encounter at the moment, but a powerful glance comes back to haunt us. Like the glass of Darwin's magnifier, a glance can provide us with an uncanny sense that we have seen more than we could ever see intentionally. We haven't just observed the threads of color in the wing of a dragonfly; we've been picturing what Darwin saw. Ignited by the spark of a glance, we see imaginatively.

With the sense of touch, we can identify textures, contours, and pressure. With our nose and tongue, we detect the diffusion of chemical substances. Our ears absorb mechanical energy through sound waves. Important information is conveyed through all the senses as the human brain combines separate elements of sensation into ongoing experience. But it's through vision that we orient ourselves in a room or a landscape. By observing details of color, distance, and edge, we're more confident as we move through the world.

It takes about eight minutes for the photons from the sun to reach the neural tissue at the back of the eye. And much of that light escapes our vision. Some of the photons collide with particles of matter, giving up their energy, and disappearing—which means I can't see beyond the brick wall of my neighbor's house or through the trunks of trees. Other photons are diffracted in the thick atmosphere, the rays scattered by small airborne particles, turning the sky on this winter morning a flat gray, dominated by a blend of indigo and violet. This is February daylight in western New York State: not just partial, not just diffracted, but also paradoxically bright, the light reflecting off the smooth surface of the snow-covered lawn.

Despite all those photons bounced, refracted, and absorbed, a portion of available light does manage to reach the sclera of my eye and pass through the small window of the cornea and through the even smaller aperture of the pupil and from there through the eye's lens to the rods and cones of the retina, triggering a series of biochemical reactions that send information to the brain. In its physical aspects, the process of vision involves measurable transformations. Like plants fed by the nutrient products of photosynthesis, we're nourished and changed by light.

We learn how to look deliberately, scanning the visible world for danger, for beauty, for food, for mates, for the answers to our questions. Following the logic of evolutionary biology, the single-chambered eye is sufficient for the jellyfish, giving it the ability to sense the shadow of an approaching predator. A complex eye, however, is an advantage to the hawk, which has to spot the mouse in the grass hundreds of feet below. The more intricate structure in the eye expands perception through what scientists describe as "increasing directional sensitivity." While we can't match the visual acuity of hawks, we're much more capable than jellyfish at identifying spatial relationships and differentiating between distances. As long as sufficient light reaches the retina and it is registered in the brain, we see more than we need to see—this in spite of all the lost photons. And in order to separate consequential objects from distractions, we learn to ignore the details that are irrelevant to our current purpose (I'm looking at these words, not at the cap of my pen) and to cultivate a habit of indifference (I don't have to think about what I'm not noticing).

The physical structure of the eye provides its own defenses against the world's distractions. The more sensitive the compound eye is to light, the lower its visual acuity. Nocturnal animals need high sensitivity to register limited light; their acuity is weakened as light intensifies. For humans and other diurnal animals, increased acuity corresponds with decreased sensitivity. With our particular ratio of rods and cones in the retina, we can tolerate a wider range of light than the animals that search for food at night, but we can't see as well in the dark.

Until recently, the hardware of the human eye was thought to be consistent, with each eye containing approximately 120 million rods and seven million cones. But according to research reported in the October 2005 issue of *Neuroscience,* the number of color-sensitive cones in the retina varies wildly. Using laser-based optics to map the topography of the inner eye, scientists have discovered a ratio of variation from person to person that could be as high as forty to one. While your retina may be packed with cones, my retina might have very few.

If these preliminary findings are accurate, they show that though most of us perceive color in similar ways, the initial stage of perception is strikingly different. Optics scientist David Williams proposes that the difference "points to some kind of normalization or auto-calibration mechanism" in the brain. Despite the variations in the light receptors of the eye, at the back end of the process the brain is balancing and normalizing colors. Thanks to this quick electrical work in the brain, I don't doubt that the green folder on my desk is dependably green and the red folder is red.

Whether the action of looking is lengthy or brief, perception is rapid fire. The brain can calibrate familiar colors that are observed with a glance or a long gaze. And yet the physical differences in the eye could be a factor that distinguishes the glance from other forms of looking. Generally, a person can increase his memory of the visual field by studying it with care, over an extended period of time. But after we glance at something, we tend to be unsure about the details. Even if we need only an instant to process vision, the more time we have to look, the more certain we can be about what we're seeing. Paradoxically, a scene we perceive at a glance tends to be remembered both with sharp clarity and as a fractured jumble. What has been seen so briefly, with a flash of intensity, lingers as a vivid, partial memory, intense yet uncertain.

If the uncertainty provoked by a glance serves a strategic purpose by causing us to pause, restraining immediate response and saving us (we hope) from impulsive mistakes, it also makes us more aware of the solitary nature of vision. The incomplete and puzzling mental image produced by a powerful glance reminds us that what we see is not necessarily what others see. While concentrated attention sharpens perception and extends the period in which the brain can make sense of the image, the impact of a glance tends to catch us by surprise. In contrast to other forms of deliberate looking, a glance is cast in a moment of evasion or indifference, and the impact is felt when we're least expecting to be roused.

The face of a stranger inside an express train passing through the station; a hand reaching into someone's purse on a crowded bus; a squirrel darting away from the front wheel of a car; the squinting eyes of a stranger; the kiss of lovers seen through the window of a taxi; the gleam of a peculiar red in one painting displayed among hundreds of others; bodies trapped inside the glass compartment of a revolving door. These are the sorts of images that interrupt the pattern of visual experience we've come to take for granted. They rise intrusively, emerging from the blur of life and disrupting our effort to make sense of the world's variety. There we are, looking for something else entirely, and the scene flashes by—or we flash by it. And then it's gone before we realize that we want a closer look.

The glance reminds us of the potential power of vision and at the same time makes us think about its limitations. When some piece of the physical composite takes on unexpected significance, we long to return and extend perception with a voracious stare. But the glance is over; the image that survives in memory is partial, its relation to the rest of the scene is uncertain, and we're left wondering about its meaning. The stranger on the train—who was he? I think I might have recognized him, not because I've met him before but, rather, because I apprehended him immediately, intuitively. Yet I can't be certain that my knowledge is accurate, since I only saw him at a glance. Uncertainty makes the experience feel more solitary, and in my solitude I seize on the mental fragment of the image and try to expand it with details. But memory fails me—I can't remember more than the fragment, and I can't repeat the experience since the train has already sped past.

So I find myself imagining what I might have discovered if I'd been able to stare at the man, to study him, to ask him questions, to reach out to him. Before I'm even aware that I'm imagining, I've interfered with the memory, making it more than it was, or less, or something else entirely. It is difficult to differentiate between the recollected image and the imagined version, and I become more aware of the odd subjectivity of perception. How many middle-wavelength cones do my retinas really contain? It shouldn't matter. But since my attempt to return the partial image to reality and calibrate it more fully has failed, I have to wonder if anyone else saw what I saw, in the same way, with the same intensity. Unable to determine the exact relationship between the real connection of the image to its context, my overly enthusiastic imagination takes the fragment of the recollected image and animates it with associations, creating something newly significant, more elaborate than the memory and intensified by the desire to revive the original image in order to compare it to this new, imaginary occupant in my mind.

In *Visitation*, a short silent film made in 2002 by Nathaniel Dorsky, the screen fills with a bold stroke of green. A moment later, the green becomes a wavering blade of grass. The grass is subsumed by black. The black fills with a ruddy patch, and the patch expands into the flesh of a hand. The tumble of images continues through the film, each unique image arising with perplexing clarity before it joins some recognizable context. It's as though the sequence enacts the work of the mind, with perception and imagination combining to create new meaning with new images.

After a vivid sight has been snatched away, or we've turned away, we imagine how the fragment retained in memory might exist as a part of a whole. By putting a partial image apprehended at a glance in an unreal context, the brain adds a new dimension to the process of visual perception, giving us the potential means to see the elusive mysteries that exist beyond and within the visual world. Sometimes it can feel as though we've suddenly and momentarily caught a glimpse of what's invisible. And the familiar, forward motion of time seems altered.

Say you're walking along Greenwich Avenue in the evening. You cast a bored glance at the window of a diner. Through the plate glass you see a man and woman sitting rigidly, another man with his back to you, and the server in his white hat and jacket reaching beneath the counter. You might deem the scene irrelevant as you pass along the street—you have other things on your mind. But unexpectedly, a fragment of the scene remains insistently in memory. You've already turned the corner onto Sixth Avenue, but you find yourself thinking about the red of the woman's dress and the orange of her hair against the background yellow of the diner's wall. There she was. Here you are. You walk along, thinking about the woman, her companion, the man with his back to you, the yellow of the wall. That mesmerizing yellow. The woman's orange hair.

There's no reason for you to keep thinking about the diner. But you think and think and think about it, wondering about the woman, the men, their lives, their futures. In its remembered version, the fragment of the scene exists in utter silliness, unchanging in its visual aspects and yet forever available to the possibilities offered by your imagination—with its potential for imaginative elaboration captured by Edward Hopper in his painting of the scene.

Where Nathaniel Dorsky's *Visitation* shows us how imagination works upon fragments of images, extending them into their contexts, putting them back in time, Edward Hopper's *Nighthawks* shows how something perceived at a glance is felt in retrospect at a strange remove from reality. Motion abruptly stops and the context disappears when an image perceived at a glance becomes significant. Inside the frame of the precise recollection are fragments of shapes and colors, the stillness enhancing the mystery, reminding us that though we can't know more than we've seen at a glance, we have the ability to imagine beyond what we know.

Light illuminates, but it also blinds us. We close our eyes when vision is painful. We learn in childhood to look away from what we don't want to see. Eventually, we learn to look without seeing. We become so inured to visual experience that we have to keep adding to the clutter if we're going to see anything at all. Or maybe we become so capable at orienting ourselves in a complex visual environment that we become skillful at isolating what we want to see from the blur. Either way, understanding depends upon our powers of selective perception.

In 1932, M. von Senden published his first edition of *Space and Sight*, a study of visual perception in the congenitally blind who had their vision restored by surgery. Citing hundreds of successful operations, von Senden describes a uniform pattern: the first experience of sight for a patient who'd been blind from birth was painfully disorienting. Many of the patients, trying to defend themselves against the "passive influx of visual impressions," chose to close their eyes.

Von Senden quotes Mesmer, who, after operating on a girl in Vienna in 1777, reported that the girl was so uneasy with her new vision that she wanted to recover her former blindness. According to another Viennese surgeon, Beer, who performed fourteen surgeries between 1783 and 1813, "Among the most remarkable psychological phenomena presented to my observation in all patients so far operated upon is the rapid and complete loss of that striking and wonderful serenity which is characteristic only of those who have never yet seen." To a man who saw for the first time after an operation in London in 1840, "everything appeared dull, confused, and in motion." To a girl who saw for the first time in Lincoln, Nebraska, in 1928, images appeared as "a lot of different kinds of brightness," without shape or distance.

Von Senden acknowledges that these experiences of acquiring sight for the first time can never be fully understood by a normally sighted adult. But he proposes as a comparable experience "the situation in which we have found ourselves in noticing that, lost in thought, we have reached the end of the road without having any recollection of even the smallest detail of the route."

Without some reliable store of relatively similar experience, vision would be overwhelmingly disorienting. Since we learn to interpret by the process of association, we come to depend upon the perception of resemblance. Recognition is a comfort. We're reassured by our routines that there's nothing new to see. We drive along a road, forgetting to look at the world. We turn on the news and wait for the weather report.

And then—the flicker of light. Suddenly. Oh, what a surprise! For an instant. The shock of a glance. It wakes us up. By catching us when we're unaware, it makes us more aware of what we haven't seen before. Time stops. We stand on the threshold of a drawing room or across from a stranger's bedroom or in front of a burning barn. We look through a window at the rain, at traffic, at ice fringing a creek. We watch a girl and her grandfather through the glass panes of a revolving door. Whenever we experience the aftereffects of a powerful glance, we have to struggle to make sense of something that doesn't quite fit the patterns we've come to think of as familiar. And yet at the same time there's often the feeling of unsettling déjà vu. Recognition is an important component in the fleeting apprehension of an image. But it doesn't seem to be the same reliable feeling associated with predictable patterns. Rather, it's a kind of recognition that illuminates familiar perceptions in new ways.

Joanna Scott

A glance heightens perception of the details of an image and at the same time provokes us to guess at associations that are outside the scope of vision. We start to think about the past. Or the future. Or our connection with the symbolic possibilities. Quick—look—there—oh!—what was that? It's gone already. We find ourselves reviving the intensity of the experience in memory. Struggling to remember what we just saw, we imagine that we're there again, experiencing the spark of perception, looking with the kind of absorption that we can't sustain for longer than an instant.

Between blinks, the strange seems familiar and the familiar strange. As confidence falters, imagination springs into action. Even while we notice less than is visible, we see more than is possible. Components of motion are illuminated in a flash. Fragments become suddenly vivid.

And yet the speed of a glance isn't necessarily its defining characteristic. Vision cast quickly might be described as a glimpse, a peep, a fleeting look, a peek. One of the important elements that differentiates the glance from these other brief forms of seeing is the angle of approach, its sideways relationship to the visual field.

A stroke in cricket, when the bat is swung at a slant, deflecting the ball to leg, is a glance. A *glancing angle* is the angle between an incident beam and the surface, such as with the angle of an X-ray. An archaic meaning of glancing connects it to insinuation. The Middle English *glenten*, from which *glance* is derived, means to move quickly sideways or to strike obliquely. The synonym offered in *Webster's* first definition for the verb form is *ricochet*. A bullet glances off a stone wall and smashes a window, or a small flat stone glances lightly across a pond. Introduce light into the subject, and the example comes from Malcolm Lowry: "Light from the setting sun glanced off the oil tanks."

The kind of glance that makes a piece of the world abruptly vivid depends for its effect, like these other types of glances, on our sideways, oblique relationship to the object. It can be a redirection of the angle of vision that lets us notice a particular set of details in a crowded scene. We stop looking ahead for a moment and cast a glance to the side, and this is when we notice the pickpocket's hand slipping into the purse. But even if we're not actually looking sideways, the experience of a glance often involves some unexpected quality of reflection, with light sparkling or glinting off the surface,

26

giving the fragmented scene a shimmering quality as it's perceived and an unearthly quality as it's remembered.

This is how some important memories remain in mind—like ripples on a pond reflecting moonlight, like bullets shattering glass, or even like passing gibes, which sting because they contain some slanted kind of truth. The shimmering, glinting, slanted world. We look at it straightforwardly, and we don't have to see the distractions. We look at it obliquely, and the distractions become newly significant. Even though a glance is quick, it lasts long enough to change the way we look at what is there, waiting to be seen.

I happened to be in Venice at the beginning of Carnevale. I saw a woman wearing a hat in the shape of a three-masted ship with blue sails. Through the masts and strings of the ship I saw the streaked marble wall of the Salute. Beside the woman wearing the ship, a man in a blue-feathered costume held out his arms to let the cloth flutter in the wind.

Walking along the Zattere in the evening, I saw wobbling columns of light stretching across the water of the Guidecca Canal. Early in the morning, I looked out the window of our apartment to the Rio Terra di San Vio and saw a woman in a green coat limping across the paving stones.

There's something about a glance—the way it blends processes of thought, enhancing memory, grounding imagination. I remember seeing raindrops disappearing into the thick, green water of the canal, leaving behind ringlets on the surface. And I remember seeing a boy in the Bar di Dino shake cocoa onto his cappuccino, coating the foam with brown. The boy was wearing a parka and ski hat. Actually, I'm not sure about the ski hat. But the powdery cocoa staining the milk foam—I remember this, along with the bowl of sugar packets and the fingers of the *barista* holding the saucer as he set it on the counter.

From the glanced scene to the memory to the account with words, significance is derived and then savored, or projected and then derived. Meaning comes mysteriously to images we never intended to notice. Perception, memory, and imagination nourish one another, and at the same time they steal and transform.

A dog shivered on its leash inside the door of the supermarket on the Zattere. A wide orange peel floated beneath the Accademia Bridge. A man dressed as the devil wore a mask with red cheeks plumped by the curve of his grin. The old woman on the *vaporetto* who scolded my daughters for resting their feet against the lip of the bench squinted as she shook her finger.

Ci dispiace, Signora.

We took the Number 20 boat to the little island of San Lazzaro; the monk stood with his back to us as he unlocked the door to the chapel. Later, I hurried after Jim, my husband, through the cold rain and into Santa Maria dei Miracoli, where I noticed the broken thumb of a marble angel. The next day, we stared through the grille over the window of Signor Constantini's glass shop. Somewhere in Cannaregio, my younger daughter ran ahead of me through a narrow *calle*, her arm raised, holding a pink umbrella. Near San Marco, my older daughter emerged from behind the curtain of the Sisley dressing room, wearing a blue sweater.

Do you like it?

It's beautiful!

Memory takes me back. That's a lie. Memory reminds me of the distance between here and there. Imagination takes me back. That's another lie. Imagination, in balance, reminds me that here is not there.

Here is enriched by what is not here, the present is enriched by the past, and our active minds come up with all sorts of crazy things when we imagine what could be. However sensual perception mixes and combines the details around us, we concoct a lively other world in our minds, a mix of memory and possibility. And when we collect details from oblique perspectives, when we cast those quick sideways looks and notice what we otherwise would have missed, when we catch the light reflecting off the water at an unexpected angle, we get to experience the intense interplay of meaning and mystery that comes from agile thought. We step into life as we step out of the train station in Venice. It's Carnevale. Everything around us is worth seeing.

A History of Religions
Geoffrey O'Brien

1.

"WHAT MATTERS," HE WROTE, "is not what things people think but the circumstances under which they think them." So one should not write essays but rather works of fiction involving characters motivated to write essays. But aren't all essays already written by fictional characters?

2.

He could not precisely recall when it was that the two of them decided to study, entirely under their own auspices, the origins and progress of religion; to understand religion thoroughly—its history, that is, the real things that happened on earth in its name—perhaps so as to exorcise it as thoroughly. He did remember that the enterprise had ended, if not badly, at any rate quite far from its ostensible goal.

3.

He could not recall precisely when they decided they wanted to learn about everything as if for the first time. To desire to explain everything, or to feel that everything was explainable, or at least to feel that if the explanation had been knowable they would not have been entirely surprised: this seemed natural, indeed irresistible. One morning he muttered to himself, as if it were the long-sought solution to a mystery: man is an explanation-seeking animal. And took the trouble to write it down.

"The gene that makes the infant insistently ask, 'Why?' seems not to make him press for a more rigorous answer than might be invented on the spot. . . . The question then being whether there is a gene for doubt."

4.

Can you remember when you began to know that you were living in a medieval world?

Medieval is when you make it up from one day to the next, from one town to the next. Go down the road and a different history operates. Every town has a radius. In the gaps between radii are the zones where things get lost, waylaid.

5.

To envision a history of religions. No religion; only religions. A history of incompatibilities. Crease marks, overlaps, torn stitches.

6.

She told him that she wanted to give up everything—her job, her apartment, her books, and go to Rwanda to offer her services as some kind of paramedic in the wake of the massacres. He wondered if this was not a sort of madness.

7.

He read a best-selling account of the Ebola virus, in which a vision was conjured up of an airborne form of the virus infecting large urban populations with stunning speed. It interfered with his sleep and made other considerations seem trivial.

8.

"What is sacred is tangled." In the lush world of multiple gods meanings are abundant and overlapping. The keepers of scattered shrines perpetuate alternate narratives. All histories are local. An odd-shaped stone memorializes a god's visit. Signs like spiders demarcate off-limit zones. "What is sacred is almost garish." "What is sacred is faded." "What is sacred is almost black." Dusty space preserved in jungle hut.

A beautiful title: *The Eternal Ones of the Dream.* Later he learned that the Freudian psychologist who had written it committed suicide.

The name of a god is murmured. . . .

9.

Sinners on their pleasant mornings imagine a pagan world.

"We had bodies then!" Or the image of it, refracted through Gautier, Louÿs, Flaubert, Anatole France: of oiled and perfumed bodies in smoky light, accompanied by the drone of reed flutes.

The Nile. Mud, serpent, library.

Can you remember when you first began to know that you were living in late antiquity?

10.

In late antiquity dreaming of the sandy plains of Plato. Sentences that are to be scaled, walked across, slept in.

Apertures in a winding rocky watchtower admit light.

A grain of clarity. It is possible to measure.

Ancient Mediterranean, seascape of lost Ionia. As if that geography were made of those ideas, rather than the other way around.

Where there is only presence. Saved from corruption.

11.

It was already becoming medieval. The light decays along the trade route. The young man traveling through a strange town in the border region spies on women turning into vampires. It is the world of Apuleius where any misfortune is plausible; you can speak the wrong language, practice the wrong custom, get invited to the wrong dinner party, lose your physical form. Remote approximation of credentials among social sets far from any imaginable center. The Balkans in late antiquity. A cowboy movie with no actors that anyone would recognize. No dictionaries: gestures as approximations of glossary.

31

12.

Dispersed and contradictory genealogies. Border world of Thaïs (transfigured whore) or Thekla (tortured martyr). Bodies changing. Sentences describing bodies changing. Burning of sentences describing bodies changing.

Manuals of physical forms, physical behavior, physical punishments. The orgy and its distorted double, the tribunal.

They make systems and destroy systems. Make lists of them and burn them. Cutting edge of orthodoxy: a grammar of the world. Destruction of idols, more gradual disappearance of pagan philosophers. Augustine logically demolishing logical holes of paganism to make way for his new brand of illogic.

History trampled and after a thousand years partially reconstructed. A medieval world is one in which you start always at the beginning. Begin by assembling dispersed materials. Or finding out where they are. Or what places are said to exist.

Build on a basis of random distortions. Correct on a basis of rumor.

There can be no history because they have already changed it. The book consists of nothing but rewritings.

Mostly scraped off. Almost nothing not discarded in the process.

As for the motives for preserving . . .

This human prose—because made with blood and flesh—and bone certainly—grand history of storytelling that must obscure its own origin in order to exist at all.

History of concealments that reveals by obscuring.

These are potent enzymes, which digest prophecies.

Amid the immensity of the local.

This is war.

13.

Scattered body parts restored to life and wholeness by word magic of Finnish shamans.

In the dark forest . . .

To think that some British guy in the nineteenth century simply made up The Rapture.

14.

The emergence of animals with unusual brain capacity—able to generate and (to a degree) retain thoughts—and subsequently their taking over an entire planet.

As if earth should be all hive or all anthill or all interconnected network of prairie-dog burrows.

On whose walls would be hung pictures of what had been displaced or exterminated.

A planet of trophies.

15.

The trial comes when the sun goes down.

It is hard to be willing to become a child again. Learn new names for things and imagine a new history of the world, hidden until now. Free online offer from the World Institute of Eschatology (over four hundred thousand branches worldwide). The most ancient truth is always cracking open for the first time ever.

Fire.

It's self that discovers where it is, self transformed, self purified, self ripped apart and replaced by a new self, self shared with other like-wise ripped-apart and reupholstered selves.

It begins to happen in the special meeting place, which can be any crypt, field, housing development.

"That's where it's at, / It's all happening / Down in the basement. . . ."

The evil children, the insouciant children, the defiant children, the indifferent children: it happens among them, as they begin to find themselves. As in an ancient savage German ballad concerning thorns, snakebites, marks of violation: "Years ago when we were children . . ."

16.

When they were young, in the middle of the twentieth century, as early as the fifth or sixth grade, they took it that they understood the dynamics of political and religious persecution—so thoroughly they could play at it, reenact the show trial, the persecution of sorcery, the sessions of HUAC or the Spanish Inquisition. The heretic imprisoned, like Joan of Arc or the Bolshevik of Koestler's *Darkness at Noon*; the heretic recanting, inwardly reversing himself; the young prosecutor fearing his own desires, egged on by fear to merciless rigor. To see through one's own inability to see through one's motives: like savoring the wall of a membrane.

What need to imagine what one has already been. . . .

Guards and prisoners. This was just after the war that was kept hidden. Or that would have been, had it been possible.

The Witchcraft of Salem Village (a children's book written by Shirley Jackson) served as a primer in hysteria and persecution for sixth graders, to be acted out in school hallways. Diabolist games of late childhood feeding off medieval arcanum obtained from the local library.

Knowledge of the dark. Knowledge in the dark.

17.

Street people in dreams move through walls to take possession of locked apartments.

A friend decided one night that she would give her money away to the poor. Her husband arranged quickly to have her held for observation in a psychiatric ward. As who would not?

18.

In their enthusiasm to roam the fields. Tear their clothes, or gather in the woods at night singing hymns, waiting for a fire from heaven. See them, at a later time, put on special clothes as they prepare to poison themselves into another dimension. Group suicide in suburban chambers. A motel room as a space capsule.

We know them. Have dreamt of their fanes and caves, detention barracks and choir schools, neighborhood enclaves where they conspire against the unpersuaded, weeping in a rage that is like joy.

Afterward neither weeping nor raging but settling into a spic-and-span calm.

19.

The others make appalled war on devil worshippers. Rage and confusion of the villagers.

In the perfect ecstasy of fear become what one fears.

Religion and its double: which is the demon disguised as preacher or monk, devil who can quote scripture to his purpose, temptress in Grail legend disguised as holy woman so that by slipping her gown off (the crisis endlessly arrived at of a certain medieval literature), she can unleash erotic torment on emotionally unprepared questing knights.

No way to tell them apart but by secret sign or inward whisper, here where any sign may be counterfeited. (Slip among them by flashing the mark of the spider. . . .)

20.

Intuiting that it must be for some sacrament that the blood of movie posters is spilled. Mexican wrestlers against the vampire army, the strangler's curse. Children satanically abused on milk cartons. The horror of hidden driveways.

Living below street level that year—amid the fear of toxic industrial waste and harassment by street gangs—the milk cartons were like leaflets slipped under the door, designed to spread panic.

The memory of an age of witch trials remains grainy, a smeared photo of what was never really shown in clear light. In those days, psychological theories of recovered memory took the place of such manuals as the *Malleus Maleficarum.* Isolation rooms of convicted serial abusers. Conversion experiences at backwoods police stations. A schoolteacher imprisoned for torture sessions of which no trace can ever be found, enacted in the preternatural brevity of a rest period. "They fly, they transform themselves into a variety of creatures."

Tape-recorded confessions in which syntax itself had been wedged open so that nothing could impede the flow of incriminating detail. A language consisting of nothing but incrimination, of self-incrimination.

Can you remember when you began to know you were living through the transition into a different era, of which (you asserted resentfully) you had not been warned? Can you remember anything at all?

21.

A family of killers live on the beach and make sacrificial fires at night. They drive off in their campers toward dawn. To aspire to be one of them, or to live in dread of them. Plot their extermination in a remorseless and well-planned campaign similar to the ancient raids on apostates. Mountain hideouts under siege by episcopal armies. South American religious colony to which the torture of prisoners was farmed out under the former regime. The burned compound of the Old Believers in Waco, or in Mussorgsky's opera.

"But this already happened. . . ." Or has only begun. The burial of the future in the resurrection of the past. Wheel turning in reverse, that fearful creaking sound.

At Qumran, death penalty for apostasy while in a state of demonic possession. The preacher Pat Robertson calling for the assassination of the president of Venezuela on television. Underground Christian sects doing murderous battle with each other in rural China. Eastern Lightning (it sounds like a brand name for street heroin) posits a Chinese woman as the already returned Christ.

The spooked become demons, the cowed become spies, the state is corrupted by superstition, books are burned or buried, doctrinal study camps are established for children and parents alike, with guest visits from government officials to let the instructors know how warmly their activities are appreciated. . . . Flowers are strewn along the path. . . .

I hear a voice murmuring in an easygoing drawl, "Now what are you getting all fired up about?"

I made it up. I confess. Patched it together out of these fragments lying around. *But they are everywhere.*

22.

Final monotony of an imagination in love with catastrophe.

It is so tedious in the abyss. The only charm it has is from a distance, where its striations and crevasses acquire a certain abstract beauty.

This is nothing, this is fancy, the mere effluvium of much reading in old chronicles and wayside pamphlets, seasoned by the occasional intercepted radio broadcast. Or a remote recollection of scary dungeon scenes from drive-in movies, with cult members in cloaks chanting hymns to Satan while the sacrifice is readied, or Knights Templar risen from the dead out of mossy crypts.

Except that all these chronicles and movies only reflected much darker realities. What has happened is without exception worse than what has been imagined. . . .

37

23.

That the Twin Towers at the moment of their destruction will look finally (in some unimaginable future imagination) like the illustration in an old *Children's Book of Bible Stories* showing the walls of Jericho tumbling down at the sound of Joshua's trumpets.

To have grown up in Troy, with its history, its traditions, its sense of permanence.

The great burnings, seared into archaic memory. Antimonuments. They provide a place for permanent absence.

Troy, *mon amour.*

Investigation into the Death of Logan
Michael Logan

IT IS A MATTER OF military record concerning Major Donald Gordon Logan, that he shot himself with his own gun in Vietnam. This is the record. BUT: Everyone who knew him from his parents, his relatives, and all of his friends and fellow military officers say: THIS IS IMPOSSIBLE. He was a brilliant officer; much decorated and on his way up the ladder toward his lifelong ambition—serving his country, married to the girl of his dreams, four wonderful children. I watched him hold and play with the children. Affection and pride shown on his face and from his eyes. He had volunteered for this duty as a guided Missile expert in Vietnam because it was his field of expertise. These are not the marks of A suicidal person. A photograph made of him, not long before he went to Vietnam is included in this Manuscript.

> —Dorothy W. Bertine, Logan Document L-3, *The Bertine Family: Descendants and Allied Families, A Genealogy*, January 29, 1992. Note: Dorothy Bertine was my great-aunt, sister to my grandmother Logan, self-proclaimed family historian and mythologist. Her family genealogy publication, *The Bertine Family: Descendants and Allied Families*, included an insert regarding my father, Major Donald Logan, and his death in Vietnam circa 1963.

Michael Logan

In 1963, the American advisory command began experimenting with small field lie detectors for use by Vietnamese troops on Vietcong suspects.

—Malcolm W. Browne, *The New Face of War*, 1965

Dear Mr. Logan,

I did serve as an advisor to the 21st Infantry Division and was assigned where Major Donald Logan was assigned.

I was not present when your father was killed. He was actually found by a Captain Gus Teller. Captain Teller after finding your father came and notified me. We immediately notified CID and they should have all the records of his death . . .

—Letter to Michael Logan from former military police advisor Donald Whitmarsh, IV Corp, Can Tho, South Vietnam

There is no Captain Teller mentioned or deposed in the Army's report "Investigation into the Death of Logan." I would like to meet Captain Teller, especially if he is now retired from the CIA.

•

He was a police detective thirty years; before that, he served in Vietnam. Wirily built into a stressed weld job—these guys always surprise me when they appear wearing glasses. I petitioned him to review the Army's "Investigation into the Death of Logan" official documents. After his examination, we met to talk. I am hoping for inconsistencies revealed, malfeasance, someone to help reopen and prosecute the case against the Army. If he was teaching at the police academy, he said, he could use these documents as a textbook case for a course in suicide.

The detective told me stories. In one, a couple married decades are leaving the house to run errands. The husband starts the car, tells the wife he forgot something in the house, and reenters it. After a long wait, the wife calls his name in the front vestibule and receives no response. She finds him in the bedroom, her picture held to his heart, a gun dropped out the other hand, and suicide blood pooling. Admittedly, she is not a mental health professional, but she never saw him in such a sentimental pose before.

7 July 64
Dear Pat,

I have just learned of the death of Donald by reading the list of deceased members of the Army Mutual Aid Assoc recently received.

I saw his orders in the *Army Navy Journal* when he was sent to Vietnam, but have had no contact with any one from over there . . . If I had had my way or had known that they were considering sending Don to Vietnam I would have interceded. He was too smart a young man to have his talents wasted in a place like that when an infantry foot slogger would have served equally as well . . .

I remember very dearly our days at Fort Bliss and if you ever had any question about my thoughts of Don ask for a transcript of his efficiency reports.

Please tell me if you have any problems at all that I can help with . . .

                Sincerely,
                Col. (ret) Julian S. Albergotti

•

February 29, 1964
PO Box 176
Grapevine, Texas

Dearest Dot and George:
We received your letters and the information on Donald. Bill had a lengthy conversation with the boy from San Antonio. He was home last weekend. It was obvious that he had been trained not to talk, Bill said, but there are a couple of things of interest he did say. About the suicide angle, he said that the government frequently would use that to prevent an investigation. If a person dies any other way, someone else has to be involved and so there is always a starting point for an investigation. But with suicide, there is nothing or no one to start an investigation with.

The only way he said you would ever find out

41

```
more information surrounding the incident, would
be to keep all newspaper clippings on Viet Nam --
especially the papers around that date. He said
the only way to find out anything would be to
contact a civilian. He said you would never
find out from the government. He said sooner or
later there would be civilians miagrate to this
country from over there who would give you the
information you desire. Bill has started saving
newspaper clippings on events there. This is not
much to go on but we didn't expect it would be
easy ...
```

—Letter to Dorothy Bertine from her sister-in-law, Wayna

He began his business career in advertising but soon found his interests to be in electrical engineering. In this field he served in the capacity of research, executive and manufacturing manager and as a consultant on many top-secret projects for private industry and the military. . . . His field was electronic controls. How many projects of a secret nature he worked on is not known but see Logan Doc. L2 for more information by Frank Jr.

—On Frank Gordon Logan Sr., father to Major Logan, *The Bertine Family: Descendants and Allied Families, A Genealogy*

•   /

```
When Wayna got into her final illness a house
keeper threw away the clippings!
```

—Letter to Michael Logan from Dorothy Bertine

Donald had a lifelong interest in the military and as a child played military strategy games with all kinds of logistics and maneuvers with his toy soldiers and equipment. His Uncle George remembers him as a serious but humorous child full of interesting questions and desire for companionship of an older uncle who was a "college man." Since he went to Admiral Billard Academy early in life he always had a military bearing. "He won numerous academic honors and awards in high school and was President of his freshman class at the U.S. Coast Guard Academy, New London, CT. After three years at the

Coast Guard where he served on the sailing ship "Eagle" and other vessels he resigned to enter R.O.T.C. Officer Candidate School, advance[d] courses, from which he graduated. He took the Regular Army exams and became an Officer. He received accommodation medals after EVERY ASSIGNMENT HE HELD IN THE ARMY. He was the ranking officer at WENTWORTH MILITARY ACADEMY IN LEXINGTON, MO., after his return from Germany and the ROTC UNIT IS NAMED IN HIS HONOR. Served in the 'FOUR HOUR ZONE in Germany' in the Army of Occupation in the 1950's, as guided Missile Expert at Fort Bliss, El Paso, Texas, and at Fort Sill, Oklahoma. He was much liked and respected in the Army. Many senior officers remarked that Don would have had an outstanding and brilliant career, as he was special as an officer and as a person. He went to Vietnam as military advisor to the South Vietnamese under programs initiated by the Kennedy Administration. Promoted to Major just before departure to Southeast Asia, he died in Vietnam on August 23, 1963." (Pat's words.)

He is recorded to have killed himself with his own hand gun! Yet, his best friend and fellow officer who had joined him in this voluntary mission stated to his wife and in public that Donald never carried a gun, in fact never owned one, not even when he was in the "four hour zone" in Germany. His expertise was with weapons that one does not carry. This does not sound like a suicidal person.

> —Dorothy W. Bertine, Logan Document L-3, *The Bertine Family, Descendants and Allied Families, A Genealogy*

In the margin to my father's copy of *The Tragedy of King Richard the Second*, read at the United States Coast Guard Academy, he wrote:

This play is probably not a tragedy but rather a historical play.

Michael Logan

MAJOR DONALD G. LOGAN, PROPOSED SECURITY STATUS AND REVIEW:

1). Assassinated by VC for political reasons in Can Tho. To remain classified pending periodic, 10-year interval review by both U.S. Army and CIA.

2). Killed In Action. Suicide report fabricated to prevent mission declaration. KIA status to remain classified pending next review, scheduled 2010.

3). Murdered by U.S. Army sponsored operative. Mission rationale, event description: TOP SECRET. No review until 2050 *at discretion of CIA and JCS.*

4). Despondent, hounded by military strategy books, obsessed with T.E. Lawrence, peasant cruelty, anonymous child death, fear of laying bloated and dead in the swamp for days—suicide complete. Declassified immediate.

```
I am on the staff of the 21st (Vietnamese)
Division, South of Saigon. The advisory team
here [Saigon] is large and lives extremely
well. I leave later today for Can Tho and will
finish this there.
```

```
Tue evening:
```

```
Arrived in Can Tho at noon and finally married
up with all my luggage. My roommate here is a
Navy Lieutenant and a submariner! How about
that. Doesn't practice his specialty here by
the way. I'll write again soon.
```

Love,

Don

—Letter to his parents from Major Logan, August 6, 1963

Yeu and quy are capricious, often wicked supernatural beings, capable of doing unguarded humans great harm. Of all these beings, however, none is so malevolent as the tinh who villagers claim use a variety of tricks to induce their intended victims to open their mouths, whereupon the tinh draw out their souls, leaving them insane.

—*Village in Vietnam*, Gerald Hickey

Dear Mr. Logan,
Yes, I was the Advisor to the VN Province Chief of Can Tho in
1963; however your Father and I did not serve together and I
do not recall him or know anything of his death. Surely wish
I could have been of help and I wish you success in locating
someone who served with your Father.

> —Letter to Michael Logan from former U.S. senior military advisor
> John E. Mathis

•

...I realized once the first letter was complete
that I have some other documents from the time
of my father's death which may, or may not, be
of interest. I furnish copies of them to you
for clarification and edification of what I
have already stated. One is personal data and
military information compiled by Don's father,
Frank G. Logan, Sr., in an attempt to learn
more of his son's death from government
officials contacted on his behalf. The second
is a letter from my Aunt to her brother,
Archie, who attempted to learn more about Don's
demise from military men who flew in and out of
Saigon via Hawaii, where he was stationed at the
time. It does make reference to the fact that a
local undertaker had made an investigation of
the body which did not reveal a gunshot wound
to the head. I asked my mother about this.
It took her twenty years to remarry, these
remain difficult issues to discuss with her,
but her response was this: the body was shipped
to New London, Conn, to the aforementioned
undertaker's. Inside the metallic casket was a
sealed, glass container which held my father's
remains. The inspection the undertaker made, to
which he signed an affidavit, was a visual one
because of the nature with which the body was
packaged by the military. (I'm sure there are
reasons for this, the intense heat of south
Vietnam being one) But it doesn't seem possible

that one could hide a bullet wound to the head from a mortician, even if it were only a visual inspection.

I just wanted to clarify these matters. Thank you.

—Letter to former U.S. MAAG-Vietnam advisor Bill Laurie from Michael Logan

•

Patent Number 2,362,650, "Gun Controlling Apparatus and the Like," granted November 14, 1944 to Frank G. Logan, Sr.

This invention relates to an improved electromechanical system for actuating an object or apparatus which cannot itself be moved conveniently or rapidly directly by the operator to a desired position with a high degree of accuracy. One of the important applications is to the control of a gun for rapidly bringing it in position for hitting an objective. The invention is applicable to the movement of heavy guns of large caliber and also to small guns now manually moved with some difficulty by the operator in his effort to secure rapid and accurate aiming of the gun. Another object is to obtain a comparatively high degree of accuracy in the aiming of the gun or the positioning of the controlled apparatus ... another object is to insure that the parts will be dependable under severe shocks and jars and not likely to get out of order.

•

If suicide was in fact the case, I would like to believe that he was exposed to some atrocity so unimaginably terrific that only a person in that sort of hell could explain the need for self-destruction and the accompanying relieve from the nightmares. He deserves this benefit of doubt based on the investigations' repeated claims that no motives appeared evident by

anyone who spent time with him in Can Tho. Then
again the entire investigation report could be
bullshit. Knowing the truth, no matter how ugly,
would certainly help to free my mind but given
the apparent contradictions in the statements
the truth will probably never be known. It
appears to be a powerless situation.

> —Letter to Michael Logan from Donald M. Logan

He writes: "...unimaginably terrific" instead of "unimaginably horrific."

One suspects that should they ever be faced with such a choice, men might very well give up women before they gave up war.

> —*On Future War,* Martin van Creveld

A college professor and students, including my sister, travel to India to study and practice. She becomes extremely ill there. The extent of her flirtation with death is not fully known until she returns home. She told me, in talking to several Vietnam veterans, she discovered that a particular spider's bite in Southeast Asia was a noncombat cause of death. The venom caused victims to become paranoid, delusional, and ultimately suicidal. No one remembers the name of the spider.

Don arrived in Saigon where he had briefing
etc., and is now stationed south of there. He
is pleased with his assignment and thinks it
will be interesting. Will enclose his address,
as you may like to have it ... It's nice to be
home again with my family and friends, but we
are so very lonely. Don left on July 20th, and
do we miss him. I guess in time, we'll adjust
to the situation, but a year seems like eternity
at this point ...

> —Letter to the Bertines from Patricia Logan, Major Logan's wife,
> August 1963

Michael Logan

Taking all these factors together, it appears that you have penetrated the dimension in which this mongrel parlance is spoken, and have a grasp as to why so many former counterparts, both Occidental and Asian, feel as they do. I remember thinking, way back in early 1975, while in my final months in VN, that it was not simply the VC (such as remained) and the NVA regulars from the north that opposed us, but in fact the entire world, whether by complete indifference or vindictive hostility. By 'us', I mean those US and VN who did give a damn, who did have a reason—a well articulated one—for following their deepest beliefs. It is a bit unsettling that not only your own country, but also the rest of the entire world, is not on your side. Loneliness is an understatement.

> —Letter to Michael Logan from former U.S. Army advisor Bill Laurie

He mentioned no names of people in his letters. However, his wife received a letter dated a few days before his death which speaks of his plan to learn the Vietnamese language under the tutelage of an interpreter attached (probably) to the head quarters company of the 21st Division.

> —Data and Military Information Re: Major Donald G. Logan. Furnished by his father, Frank G. Logan Sr., Annapolis, Maryland, in pursuit of an investigation into his son's death, 1963

I found him. He is a doctor living in the western United States, possibly still practicing. He tersely replied to my first letter and refused my follow-up interrogatories. In August 1963 he was a medical corps flight surgeon and captain newly assigned to MAAG (Military Assistance and Advisory Group)-Vietnam, Can Tho. Ronald Schemm was the U.S. Forces M.C. doctor called to the death scene to pronounce the man dead and later signed Logan's certificate of death and the statement of medical examination and duty status. The latter concluded death was from "Gunshot wound through the brain." He checked the form boxes stating the individual "was not under the influence of alcohol or drugs" and "was mentally sound."

There were approximately 1,445 Army MAAG field advisors stationed in Vietnam by August 1963. Others must also have had nuclear weapons clearances. Logan's big secret hasn't heard boo from any of these guys.

In *Dispatches*, Michael Herr overhears U.S. officers at a Saigon Army hangout under the influence: ". . . and for backup, deep in their hearts, there were always the Nukes, they loved to remind you that we had some, 'right here in-country.'"

•

It was during his first class year that Don became outstanding in his all around performance. He was appointed battalion commander by a board of the faculty. He earned varsity letters in football, fencing and track, while at the same time he earned honor academic grades for the entire school year. At graduation he was awarded the cup for greatest proficiency in Naval Drills; the Alumni Loyalty award for evidencing the greatest interest in the welfare and progress of the school; and the Sarah M. Palmer Character Award, presented to that member of the graduating class proving himself the best influence for good throughout the year. This is the first time a battalion commander has won the Sarah M. Palmer cup. The Superintendent has given permission to quote from a letter written by him to the Commandant of the Coast Guard when recommending Don for entry into the Coast Guard Academy: "I consider Mr. Logan one of the finest young men ever to attend this school. If my son should develop the abilities and character of this young man I would indeed be proud of him."

Don took the entrance examinations for both Annapolis and the Coast Guard Academy, and was successful in passing both examinations. He has chosen the Coast Guard Academy.

Rarely does the *Wheel Watch* eulogize a Billard graduate, particularly a recent one. It is felt, however, that the splendid record maintained throughout a six-year period by Don Logan cannot go into the files without notice.

—*Wheel Watch*, the official newspaper of Admiral Billard Academy, Naval Prep School, New London, Connecticut, 1948

My brothers Donald and Steven and I read Michael Herr's *Dispatches* so many times we could recite passages verbatim. We considered getting tattoos with the quote: "Vietnam was what we had instead of happy childhoods." But we verbalized it so often the writing lost its danger. As much Nam war as we read, nothing quotes better than a scar.

Michael Logan

So we knocked out fire hydrants and totaled cars, scared of and thrilled by speed and its instant demise. Fell off roofs. Put cigarettes out on our skin to make cheap tattoos and tore joints open in fights. Punched walls and broke arms, hands, and feet, some faces. Lit undeveloped woodlands on fire. Had our teeth knocked out. Steven danced on chimneys drunk and shot pneumatic nails into future arthritis. And we found out, in the end, nothing matches a combat war scar.

You may have hit the nail squarely on the head with your comments about nuclear weapons and the US still not wanting to acknowledge the deployment of them to SV. Donald was well trained in both conventional artillery and tactical guided missiles. In 1963, nuclear warheads were deployed in both media. As background, Donald had played an important role, at Fort Bliss, Texas, in writing the Army Field Manual for the Nike missile ... This was eventually mated with the Ajax missile to make a formidable nuclear carrying weapons system. (Someone back then was in love with Greek God names). Donald could have been somehow involved with such a weapons system.

—Letter to Michael Logan from Frank Logan Jr., brother to Major Logan

•

Added by Reviewing Authority:

It is the opinion of the Surgeon General that subject was mentally unsound at the time of his self-destruction. Such mental unsoundness was not due to own misconduct.

> Date: 3 Oct. 63
> John A. Bowman, Capt., MC, SGO
>> —Final reviewing authority postscript to Army death of Logan investigation

. . . I was assigned to USMACV Advisory Team 40 at My Tho, RVN, I served with Tm 40 from 12-62 through 12-63. We were training the ARVN to fight a conventional battle such as the Korean War rather than a counterinsurgency which is actually what we were involved in . . .

It became evident after Ap Bac on 2 January 1963 that the ARVN were not up to the effort. A dear friend of mine, Capt. Ken Good was KIA at Ap Bac, I was his RTO that day. He's listed several lines above your dad on panel 1E of the wall. I'll relate a story that in many ways illustrates the difficulty of the war we fought. We had hired a team barber at My Tho, he was with the team long before I arrived. He was a local Vietnamese and cut everyones hair in the team, we paid a dollar a month. The VC hit the compound three or four times a month, an after each attack we would go out in the morning to collect the dead and weapons. Usually some VC would be hung up in the barbed wire that surrounded the compound. Because bodies tended to decay rapidly in the hot climate we would burn the VC sappers out of the wire with flame throwers. After an attack in March we found our team barber hung up in the wire, he was local VC. We never knew who they were or where they were. After a while it became very difficult to trust any Vietnamese. It is very hard to train and advise troops you don't trust.

> —Letter to Michael Logan from former U.S. Army advisor Patrick J. Donovan, Oct. 26, 1993

Dear Senator Dodd:

This replies to your October 25, 1999 inquiry on behalf of Mr. Michael J. Logan, who requests that the investigation into the death of his father be re-opened.

Michael Logan

The report of investigation concerning Major Donald G. Logan's death was reviewed by senior investigators of the Deputy Chief of Staff for Operations, United States Army Criminal Investigation Command (USACIDC). This review concluded that the investigation established sufficient evidence to believe that Major Logan committed suicide by shooting himself . . . This, in conjunction with the witness' observations upon entering the latrine, as well as the autopsy protocol supports the conclusion that Major Logan's wound was self-inflicted. This command declines to reopen the USACIDC investigation.

—Office of the Staff Judge Advocate, November 30, 1999

We searched the Records of the United States Army, Vietnam (Record Group 472) but were unable to locate any information regarding the history of your father's unit. The 21st Infantry Division was aided by MAC-V Advisory Team #51. The Military Assistance and Advisory Group records do not cover Military Advisory Team unit histories.

We regret that we cannot be of more assistance in this matter.

—Letter to Michael Logan from U.S. National Archives

Section 11 of Form DA 66 is titled "Investigations and Clearances." Major Donald Logan's form has two listings beneath the title:

NAC Completed 14Oct52, 4A, SECRET
SPH 1May55 cmpl 04Oct58

The *St. Louis Post-Dispatch* front page of April 5, 1956, contains a photograph of two men, John H. Garwood and Frank G. Logan. The caption reads: "Major part of typical magnetic amplifier that will be used in automatic pilot unit for controlling flight of Vanguard rocket into outer space being inspected by Frank G. Logan, vice president and general manager of Vickers Electric Division. Watching at left is John H. Garwood, assistant general manager of [the] concern. Testing instruments and other electrical equipment are on the bench."

The story text followed:

The automatic pilot for controlling flight of the Vanguard earth-satellite rocket, from its launching point on Florida's east coast to an altitude of approximately 300 miles, will be built here by Vickers

Electric Division of Vickers Inc., a unit of Sperry Rand Corp., it was announced today.

Plans for Project Vanguard, which is under auspices of the United States Navy, call for launching a series of man-made satellites from the Air Force Missile Test Center at Cocoa, Fla., in the International Geophysical Year from July 1957 to December 1958.

Announcement that the St. Louis concern would design and manufacture the flight-control device was made at Baltimore by the Navy and the Glenn L. Martin Co. of Baltimore, which is prime contractor for the three-stage launching vehicle intended to project the satellite into its outer space orbit . . .

Garwood and Frank G. Logan, who is vice-president and general manager of Vickers Electric Division, said they were not at liberty to give details concerning the contract. They could not say how many automatic-pilots would be built, what they would look like or when they were to be completed.

The automatic-pilot will be quite small, however, and the heart of it will be a magnetic amplifier. This device is akin to the electronic or vacuum tube in many respects, but has the advantage of being extremely rugged and shock-resistant, with a long life span. It amplifies weak signals or impulses and translates them into action.

CIRCUIT INVENTING

Logan is the inventor of a series of self-saturating circuits, which made the present-day magnetic amplifier possible. Most major manufacturers of magnetic amplifiers in this country are licensed under Logan patents held by Vickers Electric Division.

Grandfather Logan, Royal Canadian Air Force uniform, circa WWI.

Michael Logan

September 18, 1963

Dear Dorothy and George:
Am sorry it has taken me so long in getting
this note off. However, I am way behind in
everything.
  The children are doing well in school and seem
to be enjoying it. They keep me quite busy.
  As to your letter, I can't add much that
Father [Frank Logan, Sr.] has not already
written to you. Don's BOQ was in Can Tho. He
did write that most of the time he spent in
the field, and was only in Can Tho a few days
a week. As for names of people there, I don't
know any either . . .

> —Letter to the Bertines from Patricia Logan

•

I have never seen rain like they have here. It
comes very suddenly and hard. A little like the
thunder showers we ran into a couple of times
on the Pennsylvania Turnpike. This part of the
country is made up mainly of rice paddies and
is very wet anyway. About this time of the year
I don't see why it doesn't sink completely under
water. One of the airstrips has a sign on it
"Elevation + 1 foot (dry season) – 1 foot
(rainy season)." It must be very nearly true.
So far I haven't been out on it much and
probably won't be . . .

> —Last unfinished letter to Patricia Logan from Major Logan, August 22,
> 1963

My father's personnel records contain Form DA66. Section 9 lists
Military Occupational Specialties. Logan's listed specialties include
Fire Control Officer, Radar Officer, AFA Unit Commander. The
penultimate listing is "Nuclear Wpn Empl."

So I began with three propositions. Firstly that irregulars would not attack places, and so remained incapable of forcing a decision. Secondly, that they were unable to defend a line or point as they were to attack it. Thirdly, that their virtue lay in depth, not in face.

—Section underlined by my father in his copy of the book *Revolt in the Desert*, by T. E. Lawrence

At a Connecticut bar ordering beer, rock noise bludgeoning. He enters the side door swarthy and bleak, three others with him. I ask if he knows the time. I can smell blood. Though I don't know him I know him. Without a word, he pumps out my eyebrow blood to the bone with a right, hard uppercut. I lurch back, clearing twenty feet of glass liquids off the bar top. The fight ends with him in my headlock. I don't know the steps in between. My hand is blue swelling, the sound is the slow metronome of my rust drops hitting boot toe. I'm crushing his windpipe. I can feel his dense muscles even as he is strangely limp. Two of his friends are holding my forearms, saying the police will be here soon, you'd better let go. My brother Steven is bleeding from the corner of his mouth. I look back and see another face, body twisted over crumpled legs. We climb into Steven's blue Firebird parked only a few yards from the bar front entrance. He is talking, but I hear only echoes, until I realize he's conceived a plan. There is still skin with bone inside. He is going to drive through the building front and bar area, exploding mass and territory, before reversing out. Just as Steven starts the car, two state police cruisers pull in, spewing and rewinding red light; my brother instinctively switches from first to reverse. Dawn returns the glaze to transparent glass windows in our separated emergency-room cubicles, medical staff bent over their reconstructive work on us.

You have to remember first that Donald was
doing what he loved. He had planned from his
very great youth to be a military man. He
loved the "military strategy" approach. He had
a great mind. His was a challenging world. It
is entirely possible that the real story is
something really great. A Plan that was in the
making for that area that he was carrying out.
Something that he would do, even with sacrifice.
It is also possible that someone else was
supposed to pick up the pieces in case it fell

55

apart, and they did not do so. Who will ever
know? Even if he could have known the end from
the beginning, it is possible that he would have
done as he did. Men do those things when what
they do is what they love.

—Letter to Michael Logan from Dorothy Bertine

**Patent Number 2,685,292, "Device for Overcoming
Effects of Shock," was filed on May 11, 1943, and granted
September 18, 1945, to Frank G. Logan Sr.**

Most controversial of all is the practice of torturing prisoners, generally with electric shocks or smothering with wet towels. Murder and
torture have been standard accessories to Viet Cong tactics for years.
Prisoners often are killed outright or tortured to death. Troops on
both sides are fond of beheading their enemies to get grisly trophies.
It is a war in which no quarter is given on either side.
America, deeply involved as it is in the Vietnamese conflict, has
inevitably become involved in the "dirtier" sides of the war. U.S.
advisors generally are somewhere around when prisoners are taken,
and often witness ugly things.

—Associated Press, March 25, 1965

56

Michael Logan

The main object is to provide simple and inexpensive means for overcoming the effect of mechanical shocks or jars by maintaining the energization of the magnet during such shocks and thereby avoiding an undesired deenergization of the magnet.

—Shockproof Electromagnetic Relay, patent 2,481,431, filed by the inventor, Frank G. Logan Sr., August 10, 1943

•

Upon arrival he identified himself in a friendly fashion and his Military bearing, poise and apparent self-assurance caused me to evaluate Major Logan as one officer destined to do well in this or any duty. He informed me that his last three years were in ROTC at Wentworth Military Academy. I had several dealings with this school while stationed at Ft. Riley and was informed that only a most outstanding officer was accepted in any capacity there. This is certainly indicative of past performance of subject officer.

On 22 August 1963, I conducted a staff visit to Chuong Thian Province with Major Logan accompanying me to check Civil Guard/Self Defense Corps operations. At the time he requested that we coordinate together such visits within his zone of duty. My impression of him at this time was that he seemed as usual, quiet, reserved, business-like, getting right down to the subject at hand. He seemed to work well with the people visited.

During the return trip little conversation was possible due to chopper noise. He did mention the poor protection and lack of tactical advantage of most Self Defense Corps posts, where the triangular set up was not mutually supporting, provided little protection from any type of weapon fire and the presence of women and children inside offered further restrictions . . .

—Exhibit M, Statement of Major John D. Howard, U.S. Army Investigation into the Death of Logan, August 26, 1963

The Trumpeter, the newspaper of Wentworth Military Academy, announced another new staff assignment, the appointment of Lt. Col. Boyd F. Walker as professor of military science, in its September 13, 1961, edition. "A graduate of West Point, he also did postgraduate work at the University of Michigan, majoring in Latin American

57

affairs. During World War II, he served in various capacities with the Anti-tank company, 382nd Infantry, 96th Division, in the Philippines and Okinawa campaigns. After the war Colonel Walker served first with 172nd Infantry, 43rd Division in Germany, first as battalion commander and then as regimental executive officer. Later, he served as 43rd Division G-2 (Intelligence), and held a similar post with the 5th Division. Following his stint in Germany, he was assigned to Korea where he was Deputy G-2, Headquarters, Eighth Army. He came to Wentworth from Hawaii where he was executive and Plans Officer, G-2 at Headquarters USARPAC [U.S. Army Pacific Command]." Walker was one of the ranking officers my father petitioned successfully to have his orders changed from Wentworth Military Science instructor to Vietnam active duty. The two had become, as mentor to young officer, friends.

•

In his retirement he continued to work on ideas and was exploring an unusual type of timepiece before his death.

> —Frank Logan Jr., writing on Frank G. Logan Sr., *The Bertine Family: Descendants and Allied Families, A Genealogy*

PENTAGON TO REVIEW 11 'SUICIDES'

The deaths of 12 U.S. servicemen ruled self-inflicted by the military are being reviewed by the Defense Department's inspector general after families contended that the investigations were bungled.

Among the cases under review is the 1991 death of Col. James E. Sabow . . . The Navy concluded that Sabow, 51, shot himself in the head with a shotgun after he was suspended for allegedly using military planes for personal trips.

Sabow's brother, J.D. Sabow, and widow, Sally Sabow, say he was killed because he had threatened to expose what he knew about allegations of drug trafficking on aircraft at El Toro. Forensic experts hired by the Sabows said the shotgun blast blew away the colonel's brain stem, instantly ceasing all breathing. But they found that he had breathed blood into his lungs for four to five minutes.

The blood in the lungs, and a contusion on Sabow's head, led those experts to conclude he had been knocked unconscious, then shot minutes later.

Sabow's fingerprints were not found on the shotgun or on two shells in it.
—Associated Press, 1993

Several things may have contributed to this kind of a report of his death. We were not officially at War with North Vietnam. Cabot Lodge was there that day in an attempt to find a place of reconciliation between the South and the North Vietnamese governments. Any assistance which the United States rendered to the South Vietnamese was unofficial and purely voluntary. The exact nature of Donald's official capacity there is not clear, as is proper for all negotiations of this kind. There was much unrest not only between the North and South Vietnamese for political control, but also between the Buddhist and Catholics for religious control, and persons were killed in riots daily. The news was filled with acts of violence. For the United States to have recognized the death of an officer in the line of duty by a foreign source would have required some kind of action. To do that at this time would have interrupted the negotiations. What kind of a secret mission Donald was really engaged in, will never be made public. The real answer will never be known. But: To put this kind of report on the record of such a fine young man is nothing short of heresy and sacrilege. Time has not softened this blow.

We do know that some others had the same report of death of their dear one when they were sure that it was a false report. One man from the Rio Grande Valley was so reported. His family pulled strings all the way from the Congressman to the Bishop but could not get it changed. Since the Catholic Church in the Rio Grand Valley would not bury a man in their church cemetery who had committed suicide, the military was forced to bury him at Arlington Cemetery. A travesty.

These comments are meant to honor a fine young man who Served his Country with all his heart and who deserves better treatment at the hand of it[s] citizens. Since it is difficult for his immediate family to take this public action, I am assuming the responsibility of refuting the official record. May this writing in some way serve to blot out the official record and restore him to his rightful dignity.

—Dorothy W. Bertine, Logan Document L-3, *The Bertine Family: Descendants and Allied Families, A Genealogy*

Continued:
Debriefing Report on Insurgency in the Mekong River Delta of Vietnam
By Colonel John P. Connor, US Army
Senior Advisor to IV Vietnamese Corps
1 February 1963 to 1 February 1964

VI. UNIQUE CHARACTERISTICS OF INSURGENCY IN THE DELTA

3a. Vietnamese and VC look alike. There is no more difference in their appearance than there is between Republicans and Democrats . . .

e. Physical Condition of US Advisors. The conditions of combat in the swamp are so exacting physically that only those US advisors who are able to operate under severe physical and mental duress for extended periods should be ordered there. I have had one Major advisor commit suicide, one Major and one first lieutenant evacuated for emotional troubles, and the condition of several others is such that they would not survive more than a few days in the swamp; therefore, I keep them at the Corps Headquarters. While I realize that this is not a Special Warfare problem, it is nevertheless a real one which needs immediate solution. The requirement that officers coming to Vietnam pass a complete physical examination is a good one but it has no teeth in it because it is not enforced. In my own case, no one checked to see (1) if I had taken the examination or (2) whether I had passed it. I know of no other officer whose examination was so checked.

IV. CONCEPTS FOR COMBATING INSURGENCY

. . . e. An added concept is the imposition of a curfew. Anything that moves between 2000 and 0500 will be engaged as a target. To be effective, the curfew must be enforceable throughout the delta. This is not now possible.

From concluding section to death of Logan investigation:

"There is no doubt that he did, in fact, commit suicide and apparently made the decision sometime between 2220 hours, 22 Aug 63, and 0450 hours, 23 Aug 63."

Michael Logan

SUICIDE AND ASSASSINATION WATCH

New York Times Headlines, 1963:

7/24/63:
Nun Plans Suicide

7/25/63:
Vietnam's Embassy Denies Any Officer Desertions Here

8/21/63:
Crisis in South Vietnam Deepens as Diem Forces Raid Pagodas; US Sees its Troops Endangered

8/23/63:
US Phone Lines Cut

8/24/63:
There were reports of increasing bitterness against Americans, who are being held responsible by the population for permitting the Government to take anti-Buddhist actions.
 . . . Those who have committed "subversive acts" will be court martialed, the broadcast said . . .
 Vietnam appeared to be sealed off—no cables, no phones, and no flights . . .

8/24/63:
Saigon Reports Six Killed in Red Attacks on Hamlets

8/25/63:
Nhu Asserts US Is Being Deceived:
 "Suicide as an anti-Government tactic is a 'camouflage' of political motivation," Mr. Nhu declared. The government is impotent in the face of such "'diabolically clever tactics.'"

8/28/63:
Anti-Suicide Squads on Patrol

61

Michael Logan

He was extremely neat and orderly in his personal life and in the conduct of his work. There was considerable evidence of plans for future staff visits and preparation of long term plans with regard to his assignment.

—From U.S. Army Investigation into the Death of Logan, "Line of Duty and Misconduct Status"

SOME SAY MILITARY TOO QUICK TO LABEL SOME DEATHS SUICIDE

The military may have bungled investigations into the deaths of 40 soldiers by labeling them suicides when evidence suggested some of the soldiers were killed, the *Philadelphia Inquirer* reported.

The investigators misquoted witnesses, failed to perform routine forensic tests and lost or destroyed evidence in reaching their conclusions, the paper reported yesterday.

Spokesmen for the Army, Navy and Air Force investigative offices defended their work as thorough and professional. But a former Air Force investigator said it is often easier for the military to label a death suicide.

—Wire service newspaper article, 1993

Frank turned heaven and earth with everyone he knew. They all said, 'all we know is what the report says.' It ruined his life. Donald would not want you to let it do the same to you. He was a gentle man of courage.

—Letter to Michael Logan from Dorothy Bertine

Whatever the fuck happened in the darkness before the dawn in Can Tho, Vietnam on 23 August 1963, will stay in the darkness.

—Letter to Michael Logan from Donald M. Logan

When the societal context of life was unbalanced, a Vietnamese family often withdrew from active civic engagement into isolation until the natural order reasserted itself. Withdrawal, in this case, was a reaffirmation of higher values, a tacit nod toward the cyclical nature of time and refusal to be a perverse distortion in the midst of chaos.

Give and Go
Diane Ackerman

ROLLING OVER ASTROTURF to his feet, the ball caught willowy Beckenbauer midstride. He corralled it with an instep and tapped it on the run, keeping it snug as a new moon in orbit as it skidded along on the leash of his momentum, and three victory-mad men in yellow raced after him, their faces tense and feet snatching. In they piled. Trapped, he quibbled with the ball for a moment, caged it in his legs as if it were a brussels sprout caught in a wire whisk, then waltzed it among the players as cheers poured from the open vat of the Giants Stadium crowd. Gyroscope faultless, he spun around to face each attacker in turn, bluffing and feinting, a grin on his face. Then he spotted a door jarred open in the maze of legs and fled through it, leaving them before they knew how he had gone. Running from a zone of sunlight into one of shadow, he seemed to grow more substantial over those few steps, and the ball he dandled at his toe moved less easily, as if resisting him.

Then he stopped, quivered, recouping all the energy he'd just used, and, spreading his arms to balance on an invisible beam, he stroked the ball away from him and into the sunlight, paving the air with a long dusty arc. When it fell at the feet of a man who was just running into the open downfield, he smiled, put his hands on his hips, and seemed glad for once not to be running after it, to have this moment to himself. Hundreds of times I'd seen him do this regal, inconspicuously agile thing, pulling the ball to him for a few magnetic moments, in which his idiom was uniquely his own, a way of phrasing with the ball at high speed, or debating it through the legs of three frantic players, then releasing it charged with a new destiny that only he could have devised.

When he turned, I saw his neck wet with sweat just under the hairline, where beads clung to the curls at his nape then dropped heavily to the grass. He had cropped his curly hair even shorter since the last game, as his only defense against the barbaric heat of American high summer. In the center of his white shorts, at the outside of his thigh, the characteristic notch in the fabric hung so still you could have laid a sextant's course by it.

Downfield the ball moved into play, but I kept my binoculars on him, watching, studying, searching his face. What could I find there? Under his bony forehead, his eyes looked sphinxlike, half in shadow. Overhead, the sun was an irregular wick in a desert sky, whose heat the metal stadium bowl just magnified. Rain would have been a mercy. He turned to look at the crowd. What was he thinking? Did he see them as individual faces or as an organic swarm? Under the hot, greenhouse sky, the crowd chanted *Cosmos! Cosmos!* as if to lidless creation. Did that form a pool of noise or an eerie, single instance in his memory? He turned his face back to the play, as if to another thought, another measure in the tempo of the game. Did he perceive the game's rhythm as something uncontrollable he was part of, or could he change it by himself? Did he feel the possibility of that change like a switch he could throw, and wonder in the milliseconds when intuition became action which rhythm to choose, at last skying the ball downfield to the feet of a striker, gauging it so well that it spent its energy completely by the time it landed dead at the striker's feet?

Only yards away from him, the ball was still in play, and I watched his face follow the action like a gunman tracking a clay pigeon just before he fires. What was he tracking? The ball was no longer with him. It was the idea of the ball that hadn't left him. In his mind, he was tracking it, sliding his boot under it so smoothly it was lifting into the sky, not straining into height like a rocket, but gingerly, as if to say, there are things on this earth that fly, there are nearly weightless things, there is something invisible life can produce. Not only things like itself that live, and not only bare, mute objects, serums, or art, but invisible things—forces, propulsion, motion, thought.

I wondered: Could he be thinking any of this? Had he thought it even in the midst of play, when lulls were like unsealed envelopes collecting time? Suppose he stood still when the ball fell toward him, suppose he watched its path shorten in the air and then drop like a piece of fruit at his feet, a succulent apple off a Bavarian tree, suppose he watched it on the green turf here in New Jersey while the crowd roar blurred, suppose he stood over the ball, considered the crowd, considered the onrushing men, suppose his right leg didn't cock back from the knee and kick the ball as it always had before, suppose he just looked at the tallow sky and the stubbly Astroturf beneath him and felt the sun as palpable as the hand of a blind girl spelling his name out on each leg?

As I watched through binoculars, my eyes groped to focus, the stadium noise disappeared, and I became private, in the visual turrets as if in another room, the way a child, hiding its head, believes no one can see it. I felt spellbound and all alone in the grandstand, watching dark eyes below the visor of his bony brow. How long I had been obsessed with soccer I couldn't say, time vanished so swiftly into the well of my obsession. First the present stole along with all its delicate upheavals, in which a minute was a multitude, and I could count the separate rugged beatings of my heart. And then suddenly a year had vanished, not *passed* slowly as a caravan or been preserved frame by frame in the memory, but vanished, as if canceled, had never been. This shimmy in time's fabric puzzled me about life; that though one could give oneself with diabolical precision or voluptuous revelry or emotional daring to a moment that seemed wide and limitless as the tundra, soon enough it would race away and be unrepeatable, erasing itself as it fled.

I had been obsessed with soccer for nearly a year, ever since I saw a match on television at a department cocktail party of the sort I went to out of boredom, only to find a greater boredom awaiting me. Roaming through the house, I heard loud, antic voices from the den and, opening the door gently lest I interrupt some clandestine meeting, I was amazed to find three men energetically watching a broadcast of the European Cup Finals, Czechoslovakia versus West Germany. Without understanding exactly what I was watching, nonetheless I became enraptured by the elegance, sheer power, and changing patterns of the game. The field was a single green moment in August, on which beautiful men ran like ancient hunters, wild eyed, with quarry at their feet, hazing it, coasting, punching it toward the net. Without taking his eyes off the screen, a man made room for me on the sofa; laughing, I took a handful of popcorn from a bowl on the end table and settled down for a look-see, and what I saw possessed me. The ball passed from one foot to another among the maze of players, leaping like an electron from shell to shell, tactic to tactic, in the larger unknowable strategy of the game. I was not aware of the men as merely lissome beings caught up in only another tournament. I was smitten by the ceremonial violence I saw unfolding, the long drawl of a single run, the cutting-horse swivels and quick starts, the rhythmic eddies of clustered players, the organized alarm: all apropos of the white ball and all within the unimpeachable white lines of the field. I got up and sat closer to the screen, looking through its glass as I might into an exposed brain. When I watched Hans Beckenbauer gathering the urgent rhythms of the field with his acute, threshing legs, a mental depth charge went off inside me. I couldn't name what it was, but that silent wonderful concussion happened every time I watched a top-flight game from then on. Something about the rhythm of the mind, I thought, but that was as far as I could focus it. The main thing was the unexpected tonic of the spectacle. It was like falling into the well of a profound attention. That was it. How else could I explain parties and meetings foreshortened so I could run home to catch an important game on television? How else explain my sudden passion for soccer books and my subscribing to three juvenile soccer magazines? Somehow, without warning or my planning it, it extracted from me my complete attention; I had fallen ill with a gorgeous disease, which I didn't know about until the symptoms were full-blown.

My friends and colleagues found my soccer mania inexplicably strange, a whim that, if chosen to shock, merely showed how much of a grandstander I was, and, if serious, proved I was even odder than they imagined. So had my oceanic phase, my flying phase, and that perhaps least understandable phase, during which I spent one winter hooking rya rugs in biological patterns seen through a scanning electron microscope: amino acids, bladder, prostate, brain cells. For me, there was nothing to explain; it was all so simple. Each part of life willy-nilly suggested the rest, revealed so much about the large, unknowable texture. Just as you could peek through any keyhole on any of the many doors leading to a grand ballroom and see the same interior, but from different angles—the brocade chair cushions, the resiny floor varnish, the chandeliers cut to look like crystal crowns, the wrought-iron plant stand from which Swedish ivy cascaded—I sensed that the passionate study of any moment of Creation would teach me more and more about what it meant to have once been alive on the planet, to have been mortal, to have had a probing, contrary, stubborn, exhilarating, nomadic, treacherous, self-amazing mind. Soccer could tell me all of that, I thought, as ballet could, or physics, or horse trading, or stamp collecting, provided I gave it my rapt, undiluted attention, provided I fell in love with it so deeply I became aware of all its subtleties. Those I would add to what through thought and sense I already knew, other views through other keyholes, and somehow it would homestead another corner in the limitless estate of my curiosity about what it meant to *know* something, to *want* something, to *be*.

67

Those who knew me thought my heart a pushover; surely it was fickle to be swept away by any panaching fancy. But my obsessions were poignant and solemn, so much so that it embarrassed me to admit it; thus I went along with the smirks and banter. Who would believe a summer spent in men's locker rooms was a mystical obbligato? As for the fancies, they might lose my attention at some point by passing, but the questions they tantalized me with would never pass, not even when I did. But it was true, at some point the fever would break, and control of my life would return to me again. New planets would be found and cataloged, and that would excite my imagination, but never with the soul-drenching attention I gave to astronomy when I was in that well of attention, during which the drabbest morsel of information could hone my sense of wonder to a needle edge. I had done my tour of duty there, and it had taught me *all I was able to learn from it* about mortality. And when I had distilled what I could from it, I let it drop, walking away, people thought, because I had accomplished my immodest goal and collected another field of experts and expertise. In truth, I had merely come to the end of that hamlet; when a subject ceased to teach me, it released me. Nor was it enough to behold a subject, I needed to touch and be touched by it, to make love to it, to become its life, to take it into my body and create something dysgenic and beautiful from it that would illuminate us both. Maybe it's this simple: my need to transform life both trapped and freed me, made me weak and vulnerable as an avalanche.

Time out. Beckenbauer disappeared behind another player, a fullback who was built like a draft horse and yet always ran with his hands hanging limply from his wrists, as if they'd been broken or were marcescent leaves. Beckenbauer never did; his hands poised at different attitudes like a tightrope walker's, and when he outdribbled players, feinting this way and that, he seemed to be casting spells. His balance had a complex choreography. The Bulgarian had a coarser and rougher technique, and so it was doubly strange to see his hands hanging limp when he crashed into someone, and almost sickly, delicate, as he stole the ball away and raced downfield.

I set my binoculars on the table in front of me, the white formica that curved around the press-box window. A player was down at the other end of the field, one of the visiting team's young defenders who had been tripped from behind. The referee stopped play, even though half time was only seconds away, and signaled the team's physiotherapist onto the field. In the press box, three tiers of journalists relaxed. Some lit cigarettes, and others got up to stretch. Though they couldn't risk sharing their night's copy, they found things to talk about. Chitchat in several languages filled the smoky enclosures. Occasionally, they watched the TV monitors suspended above them for close-ups of the boy's writhing and the physio's laying on of hands, over which ran a repetitive account by the play-by-play and color commentators hired by the team.

I noticed that my reflection, warped by the curved glass, split into a ghoulish blend of primary colors so vibrant it was like looking at my exposed circulatory system. When, finally, patterns began to form behind it—the game resuming—I was glad to dive through the apparition, back into the swirling, perfect flow. I lifted my binoculars, and pulled Beckenbauer nearer and nearer, until I held him in a clear tight focus once again.

The Pete Townshend Fragments
Rick Moody

IN JANUARY 2003, THE BRITISH police turned up, on a list of visitors to a Web site devoted to child pornography, a name belonging to a certain significant "rock star." This was in the course of Operation Ore, an FBI-initiated undertaking, one that had swept into the international criminal justice system a great number of persons both eminent and unknown, all over the world, many of them involved in activities that were not going to turn out felicitously for them.

I read the item first in a gossip column. It was one of those blind squibs in which it's not clear immediately who the unlucky individual is, but soon will be. Indeed, the identity of the "rock star," as the tabs would have it, was quickly revealed by the *Daily Mail*, and this celebrity surrendered thereafter to Scotland Yard. The musician in question was Pete Townshend. Townshend is best known, of course, as the principal songwriter and the guitar player in the British rock-and-roll band called the Who. Much horrible publicity ensued, of the sort that regular citizens like you and me can't begin to imagine. The British tabloids make the American tabloids look timid in their zeal to bait and torture, and in this matter they performed according to type. No doubt Pete was miserable leaving the house for a while. It's fair to assume his career was in some doubt.

Pete's explanation, as much of it as he has given over the years, makes clear that he did, in fact, give his credit card number to the Web site in question.* And yet having investigated Pete and his claims, the authorities proffered no charges, and Townshend was free to go about his business.

---

*"From the very beginning, I acknowledged that I did access this site. . . . I accessed the site because of my concern at the shocking material readily available . . . to children as well as adults, and as part of my research toward the campaign I had been putting together since 1995 to counter damage done by all kinds of pornography on the Internet, but especially any involving child abuse. . . . The police have unconditionally accepted that these were my motives in looking at this site and that there was no other nefarious purpose, and as a result they have decided not to charge me. I accept that I was wrong to access this site, and that by doing so, I broke the law, and I have accepted the caution that the police have given me."

The fact that Pete was not prosecuted is reassuring, insofar as fans need to be reassured. The matter, that is, is closed. It probably *ought* to be closed. Except that Pete, in his Pete Townshend way, suggested in the course of defending himself that anyone who was uncertain about the degree to which he was preoccupied with the abuse of children should look into the *work*. To my knowledge no one has given the work the requisite sustained look, and so I have undertaken to do so myself.

Why bother with the Who now? Their best work is long behind them. They are perhaps the quintessence of classic rock dinosaurs. Pete hasn't been a terribly convincing rock personality since, well, "Eminence Front" on the mostly dismal *It's Hard* album (1983). Since then he has released some inconsistent solo recordings and dabbled in musical theater.

Well, for me the reason to bother is that the Who was the first rock-and-roll band with whom I was completely obsessed, beginning at about age thirteen, when the film of *Tommy* came out. I knew a little bit about the band before that. I remember hearing "I Can See for Miles" on the radio in the late sixties. At that point, I didn't really pay much attention. In fact, the route to the Who for me was through teenybopper music. The catalyst was none other than Elton John. Before the Who, I was primarily interested in Elton John, of whose catalog I had purchased a couple of albums. I had therefore heard the recording of "Pinball Wizard" that Elton had made for the *Tommy* soundtrack.

Tommy, the film, didn't venture near New Canaan, Connecticut. Or that's how I reconstruct it. But since I was unable to see the film, I made do with the *Tommy* soundtrack album. Among true aficionados, the Who's own recording is considered far superior, but I loved the film soundtrack. This is how it goes sometimes. You find your way to the inferior work first. The updated arrangements on the soundtrack recording, with all the synthesizer parts, sounded strange and novel to me. And trying to imagine what the film would look like just from hearing the songs—this was an activity that filled the better part of a couple years.

About the same time, *The Who by Numbers* was released. I suppose I got the *Tommy* soundtrack at the end of eighth grade. And not so

Rick Moody

long after, I purchased *The Who by Numbers* on one of my weekly record-buying excursions. This is a highly improbable album with which to enter into the story. For one thing, it has almost none of the keyboard razzle-dazzle that Pete made use of on the *Tommy* soundtrack. Also, unlike *Tommy* and its sibling *Quadrophenia* (which had immediately preceded the *Tommy* film), the recording in question has no conceptual apparatus. It's just an album of songs. In particular, very, very bleak confessional songs. Most of the arrangements are rather simple. It's the Who as they sounded best, a little bit acoustic, a little bit electric. Roger Daltrey wasn't yelling a lot; he was *singing.* And despite the abundant melancholy, there is a little bit of whimsy around the edges, too. In short, *The Who by Numbers* is an agitated, British-invasion version of a singer-songwriter album.

Something about the record rang true. I was away at school by then, and I wasn't having an easy time. It was my first year in private school, after a lifetime in public schools in the suburbs. Many of my classmates at boarding school had been through the various "country day" academies of Connecticut, or the private school system of New York City. They seemed to know each other well. They had social skills I didn't have. They all dressed alike. They all summered in the same locales. In this rather difficult social environment, I became besotted with rock and roll, as boys do, and the songs on *The Who by Numbers,* like "Slip Kid" and "How Many Friends," songs about the difficulty of living a happy and contented life, were exactly the kind of soundtrack I required.

I suppose the quality I was responding to when I was a fervent believer in the Who was Pete Townshend's honesty. It was abundant on *The Who by Numbers.* The rumor I heard was that when Keith Moon, the drummer, first heard the demos for *The Who by Numbers,* he wept. It's a record that seems as though it could easily inspire this sort of passionate response. True, there is the country throwaway, "Squeeze Box" ("Mama's got a squeeze box she wears on her chest, and when Daddy gets home she never gets no rest"), which is delightful, full of double entendres, and cheerful the way the Who were during the fertile interval of the midsixties when they recorded "Substitute," "Pictures of Lily," "Tattoo," et al. I always thought this part of what they did was moving and indisputably great, and I still do. Nevertheless, when I was lonely and woebegone, *The Who by Numbers,* with its surfeit of misery, inspired allegiance in me, and because I felt great allegiance, I bought everything I could get my hands on. I was an adherent, as regards the Who. By the next year, I

72

had *Who's Next, Quadrophenia, The Who Sell Out,* the aforementioned singles compilation, a couple of Roger Daltrey and Entwistle solo albums, and of course Pete's neglected masterpiece, *Who Came First,* his album of devotional songs.

Do any of these songs have anything to do with child abuse? Did I understand the Who songs this way? What is the vision of familial care and psychological socialization that we find in the early Who songs? Well, there is "I'm a Boy," whose first verse runs: "One girl was called Jean Marie / Another little girl was called Felicity / Another little girl was Sally Joy / The other was me and I'm a boy." In the chorus, the unhappy narrator of these aforementioned lines has it even worse, apparently, since his "ma won't admit" that he's a boy, he's a boy, he's a boy. From the same period, there is "Pictures of Lily," about onanistic pursuits, in which a young man is fixated upon pin-up images given to him by his paterfamilias: "Pictures of Lily made my life so wonderful / Pictures of Lily helped me sleep at night / Pictures of Lily solved my childhood problems / Pictures of Lily helped me feel all right." Taken as a pair, these eccentric pop gems give a much different view of male psychology from the sort you might have found on the Stones or Beatles releases from the same period. In fact, even the minor Who songs from the midsixties have their share of dark forebodings. We have the cheerful divorce anthem, "A Legal Matter." We have the childhood beatings administered in "Tattoo": "My dad beat me 'cause mine said 'Mother,' but my Mother naturally liked it and beat my brother / 'Cause his tattoo was of a lady in the nude / And my mother thought that was extremely rude." And so forth.

The family as construed on *Meaty, Beaty, Big, and Bouncy,* their album of early singles, would seem to be a rather, uh, dysfunctional landscape, even if the Who songs are understood as occasionally comic, with their French horn solos, their three-part harmonies and childlike melodies. And I'm not even scratching the surface of "Substitute," with its obsessional fraudulence. Or "I Can't Explain," in which skepticism about romantic language makes it impossible for love to take root. Nor am I lingering over the dark lyrics of Who bassist John Entwistle, author of, e.g., "Boris the Spider" and "Heaven and Hell."

If there is not outright child abuse in the abusive and dysfunctional psychic environment of the early singles by Pete Townshend and the Who, we have only to wait for *Tommy*. In that album, we find exhibits A and B of the child abuse theme, "Uncle Ernie" and "Cousin Kevin," two excerpts from the second act, more or less, of the infamous *rock opera*.

Cousin Kevin, according to the story, is mainly given to physically torturing young Tommy Walker. In the film, at least, he's quite glam, quite sexually ambiguous, and the torture does seem to have a patently sexual cast to it. "Uncle Ernie," which follows, is even darker and more psychosexual: "I'm your wicked Uncle Ernie / And you won't see or hear me as I fiddle about." "Uncle Ernie" is the more transparent of the two tunes that deal with the subject under consideration here, and in the film Keith Moon plays Uncle Ernie with a manic depravity that genuinely disturbed me the first time I beheld it. These songs *are* unequivocally about abuse, and they are about abuse in a way that does, it seems to me, have the ring of conviction, perhaps more so when one considers that they were written in a period rather more permissive and freewheeling than the historical present.* Only problem is: Pete Townshend didn't write either of them! John Entwistle, the bass player, wrote both "Cousin Kevin" and "Uncle Ernie," in his mock horror style, also on display, e.g., in "Boris the Spider." It is perhaps interesting to note, however, that Entwistle's parents, like Pete Townshend's, divorced when he was still a very young child. He, too, was raised by his grandparents.

Tommy Walker, according to the well-known if thin narrative, is a war baby, like the members of the Who themselves. He's born during or just before the Blitz,** and the story depicts the period from that military assault until the social upheavals of the late sixties. It's as though the entire span, including the counterculture, was one gigantic sham, in which even the most lofty attempt (Tommy's) to try to convert the broken and misguided is doomed to backfire.

In this light, it's sort of amazing that *Tommy* was considered a wide-eyed document of the *haute* psychedelic period, since, like one

---

*Townshend in *Mojo*, February 2006: "Roger had always expressed an absolute disgust of somebody that would sleep with an underage girl. And I'd often say to him, 'Well, how do we know if we've slept with underage girls? You started having sex with girls when you were sixteen, so how do you know?' So it's very difficult to be absolutely black and white and cut and dried about it."
**Ken Russell's film features a moment in which it lingers over the cages that some residents of London slept in during the war, and it's just one of many overpowering images in the film.

of the Who's best-known songs "Won't Get Fooled Again," it's arguably just as skeptical as it is faithful. (There's an opera-within-the-
opera, too, "Sally Simpson," which offers an even more dire narrative about the perils of rock messianic fervor.) Unless, of course, the
thing that rescues, the thing that promises escape, is the music itself.
Not the lyrics, but the music. The principal claim for the greatness
of *Tommy* is its structure, actually, is the way an entire story is
stretched out on the four sides of the LP, including an overture and
instrumental portions, including reprises and leifmotifs. Music is the
thing that enables Tommy's story to offer some kind of transcendence. It's not what the Who *say*, but *how* they say it.

Still, is it possible that *Tommy* is a cryptoautobiographical document about Pete's own abuse and the way in which he was rescued,
through the sonic liberation of rock and roll? You could make the
case. It may be why, as a narrative, it's a mess—because the author
was concealing and revealing at the same time. It would be hard,
even impossible, to think of *Tommy* as conclusive about this autobiographical interpretation. If it works at all,* it's by reason of clever
pop songwriting and great playing by a band that was nearly at its
peak as an ensemble. They could have been singing about traffic in
central London and it would have sounded just as overpowering.

So: I don't actually like *Tommy* that much myself. As far as I'm concerned, it created more problems than it solved. Pete is free to do
whatever he likes, of course. The more free he is, the more I admire
him. Yet the conceptual baggage hanging around his neck from
Tommy was considerable. After *Tommy*, Pete, whether he wanted to
be or not, was an Artist. This is evident not only on the windy and
out-of-control *Quadrophenia*, whose story never gets off the ground
at all, but even more transparently on such solo suites as *White City*
and *Psychoderelict*. Pete's a brilliant writer of pop songs, as good as
they get, but after *Tommy* he doesn't much *want* to be a writer of
pop songs anymore. That's where the trouble starts. He made a name
for himself in this band, possibly one of the ugliest, most acrimo-
nious bands ever, a band where everyone involved seemed to dislike
one another, where the drummer was so drunken and depressive that
they had a hard time keeping him alive. The lead singer resented the

---

*And not everyone thinks it works. It recently turned up on a well-publicized list of
the worst albums ever made.

guitar player and Pete, who was by no means blameless, who responded by exerting more control rather than less. They all resented
him for it, and in the interpretation I'm formulating here he disliked
himself, too. He made his name in this band, but that didn't mean he
couldn't outgrow it.

Tommy might point to some explanations for the Townshend
kiddie-porn debacle, but I just don't think it's a complete diagram
for Townshend's character, not as I'm constructing him. Though
perhaps one earlier song is, namely the track called "A Quick One
while He's Away." It's a rash assertion, but I happen to think "A
Quick One" is one of the best rock-and-roll songs ever written. I like
few pieces of music on earth as much as I like this song. It's ridiculous, hilarious, clever, and then, in the last three minutes, trans-
portative, generous, even numinous.

"A Quick One," the way the lore is told, was written after an
assignment by Kit Lambert, who managed the Who at the time.
Lambert, a fan of opera, had been challenging Pete to write a longer
piece of music. It took Kit's birthday party to bring about the right
circumstances. They dashed off this suite of songs for the celebration, but short of material for the *Happy Jack* album, they also committed it to tape.

The studio recording is not bad. But you would never get to the
heart of the song if you only listened to the studio recording. There
are at least two superior renditions of it floating around.* The first is
on the *Rolling Stones Rock and Roll Circus*, which, according to
legend, is the reason that the Stones later refused to release that particular television broadcast. The Who were *too good*. However, as
Pete points out on the DVD release of *Rock and Roll Circus* (he
is as engaging and garrulous as ever on the *extras* portion of the
disc), a more likely interpretation is to be found in the fact that Brian
Jones was on the point of leaving the band. In fact, *Rock and Roll
Circus* was the last performance of Brian Jones with the Rolling
Stones. There's something ghostly and heartbreaking about Brian
whenever he turns up in the footage, and this would be reason
enough to suppress it.

The Who play "A Quick One" in the released version of *Rock
and Roll Circus*, and nothing else, not one other song, and it's an

---

*Actually, now there's a third, a live version on *The BBC Sessions*.

amazing performance, justifiably renowned. They are completely at ease, confident to the point of cocksure, and they hurtle through to the last three minutes like no one on earth could touch them.

Yes, a good version, to be sure—in front of Stones fans, no less— but it's not the rendition you should listen to. The one you should listen to is the recording of "A Quick One" from the expanded edition of *Live at Leeds*.

But wait, before I talk about that, I have to tell you about taking my mother to see *The Kids Are Alright* back when I was in high school. This, in fact, was when I first saw live footage of "A Quick One." I was home for some vacation, Christmas probably. I think my mother and my brother, unencumbered by other family, decided to go to the movies, and somehow my mother agreed to see this documentary about the Who. It was playing at the mall in New Rochelle. How horrible. I can only think of moments like this with shame. Why on earth did I try to persuade my mother to listen to the music I liked? For example, I remember sitting her down one day, when I was in tenth grade, saying, in effect, *Look, if you want to know something about how I live, you're going to have to hear some of the music I listen to.* For example, I remember playing her "Heroes," by David Bowie, and I remember playing her some Roxy Music, and I can remember when, at the tolling of a telephone, she rushed from the sofa to get away from me and my apparently endless capacity for reminding her to listen *really carefully* to the guitar solo. I wish now that I had not taken my mother to see *The Kids Are Alright*. She didn't like it, and the mall in New Rochelle was always a deadening place.

And yet what I remember my mother saying about *The Kids Are Alright*, in her attempt to say something favorable, was that the sections about Keith Moon were moving to her. And this is an interesting thing to say. In my recollection, we saw *The Kids Are Alright* just after Keith Moon died. This may be completely factually erroneous, and it may be that we saw it just *before* Keith died, but let's say that it was after, for the sake of the argument, and that's why Keith seems spectral in the film, like the prankster counterpart to Brian Jones. Because he's not long for the world. In *The Kids Are Alright*, whenever the camera is on Keith, he can't stop himself. He tears off Pete's shirt in one television interview, he starts taking off his own clothes, he won't stop unless the camera cuts away. In one sequence, Keith is being interviewed, while at the same time being whipped by a bemused and scantily clad dominatrix. There are also scenes in which Moon is interviewed by Ringo Starr. Ringo asks him about the other members of the band, and though Keith attempts the class-clown responses, there's a desperately sad quality to how hard he works the game. This is a guy who, at thirty-one years old, is about to overdose on a medication designed to keep him from drinking.

Many people in my mother's family had drinking problems. My grandmother, for example, died of cirrhosis. My uncle had a drinking problem. My grandfather was no slouch. I have a drinking problem. My sister drank too much. And so forth. I imagine that my mother had and has a particular sensitivity to this question, and I imagine that even though she hated the music in *The Kids Are Alright*, maybe she saw the spectral, ghostly Keith Moon, halfway to his eternal resting place, and recognized a sad predilection she had observed close up.

Of course, Keith isn't the only doomed character in the film. John Entwistle, for example, died a couple of years before the writing of this essay of a cocaine overdose. He was in a hotel in Las Vegas. He had two hookers with him. John says very little in *The Kids Are Alright*, though there is a funny passage in which he tries skeet shooting on the grounds of his estate, using gold records as targets. He can't seem to hit anything until he uses a machine gun of some kind. And apparently Entwistle used actual gold records for this sequence.

If John isn't enough, there is Pete in the film. In particular, I find it sort of harrowing to watch the footage of the band from Shepperton Film Studios. The production notes indicate that there wasn't much good footage of the Who playing "Baba O'Riley" or "Won't Get Fooled Again," two of their best-known tracks. As a teenager, I felt no hesitation in liking "Baba O'Riley," even though the "teenage wasteland" sing-along chorus of the tune would seem to be full of venom for the very thing the song does, which is to constitute community through the *anthemic*. I loved the song. And I probably still would, had I not heard it a hundred and ten thousand times. Anyway, the Shepperton gig was convened to film these songs before five hundred or so invited guests, and the performances are loose limbed and fun, if a little bit jaundiced. Pete, in particular, does some kind of deranged Sufi dance during the parts of "Baba O'Riley" in which he does not play, and when the camera closes in on him for his portion of the bridge, "Don't cry / Don't raise your eye," he sort of botches the lines at first. His own eyes are red and he seems—well, to me he seems a little fucked up, or heartbroken, or something. He's half in the song and half out of it, even though it's kind of an easy song. There's something unsettling about the whole thing, like he doesn't want to do this anymore. And apparently he did not. These days, Townshend says that the creative period of the Who ended with *Quadrophenia,* and that was four or five years before the Shepperton gig.

The Kids Are Alright introduced me to "A Quick One" live, and this was later supplemented by the stunning *Live at Leeds* rendition, which I first heard in Wes Anderson's film *Rushmore.* The original release of *Live at Leeds,* in 1970, mostly had chestnuts on it like "Substitute" and "Summertime Blues." It did not, until it got expanded in 1995, feature "A Quick One." In *Rushmore,* the big last three minutes of the suite are used to galvanizing effect during one of Max Fischer's bad spots. I bought the *Rushmore* soundtrack (mainly to get hold of the Faces tune at the end, "Ooh La La"), and it was then that I first heard the *Live at Leeds* recording in all its glory.

The story of "A Quick One," such as it is, concerns a woman whose husband goes off to war (like Tommy's dad) and who then takes up with another man (just as Ann-Margret did with the creepy Oliver Reed in the film version of *Tommy*), in this case a man called by the epithet Ivor the Engine Driver. The entirety of "A Quick One" is divided into vignettes, e.g., an a cappella section in close harmony that makes clear that "her man is gone," a *b* section in which the band gets involved and during which the heroine is revealed to be bereft, grief stricken, and, apparently, quite comely (since she comes from a town "famous for the little girls"). The *b* section is followed by a *c* section sung together by Roger, John, and Pete, in which the town seems to suggest that it can comfort the heroine in her time of sorrow. In the *d* section, which forgoes the peeling rock tones of *b* and *c,* Ivor the Engine Driver is introduced, via some amazing drumming by Moon, and a country-and-western bass part. John, who plays Ivor, sings: "He told you he loved you, he ain't no liar and I ain't either / So let's have a smile for an old engine driver." From here we cut away to the missing husband in *e,* who will soon, soon, soon be home. Throughout, in the *Leeds* recording, the Who are trying to amuse one another with interruptions about the characters in the story (Keith yells, "Dirty old sod!" when Ivor the Engine Driver is first introduced and Pete says deadpan, "Come on, old horse," during the C&W section, etc.). Their collective ease and joy about the material is manifest. The whole proceeding may seem like a joke, of course, since the music is occasionally parodistic, and the characters' names are ridiculous, and Pete plays the girl's role (or so he says during the introduction in Leeds), but suddenly, toward its close, "A Quick One" *is* about some variety of sexual abuse or statutory rape. The heartsick heroine is seduced by the much older engine driver, thinking her husband is gone for good, only to find, as in *Tommy*, that he who may have been lost is "only late." To put it more succinctly, the *f* section brings back the chiming guitars, and we get the girl's tearful confession to her man, now returned to her: "Am I back in your arms? / Away from all harm?"

And this prompts the part of the song that is germane to these investigations*: "I missed you and I must admit," the little girl guide sings, "I kissed a few and once did sit / on Ivor the Engine Driver's lap, and later with him / had a nap." Now the band locks into a classic one-four-five chord progression, with Roger, Pete, and John all singing—John in falsetto descant—and the lyrics of reply from the husband consist only of the words "You are forgiven!"

In all honesty, it's hard for me to listen to this section of "A Quick One" without weeping. And I listen to it pretty often. My feeling, and I admit it is a lofty feeling, is that Pete, in this moment, has somehow managed to channel something like a God's-eye-view of absolution. Here is the ineffable something or other that *Tommy* rarely manages. Pete has figured out how to render compassion for the easily tempted of the world, if just for a split second, has looked down on them and has seen how flawed his fellows are, how broken, how innocent, how careless, and has announced, as the song does, that we are all absolved. In fact, Pete even says so, at the end, to the audience—"We're *all* forgiven!" And I always believe him.

Is this big ending (actually, it's *two* endings, because the song ends once and then everyone comes in a second time with the refrain) the

---

*Let me not overlook here the passage where all three singers sing the word "cello" over and over again for a while. Apparently, the band was eager to have cellos in this spot but were told that there wasn't money in the production budget.

work of a guy who was sexually abused as a child? And who is preoccupied or even obsessed with issues of sexual abuse? Or is it the work of a pedophile himself? Maybe Pete had or has no access to the memories of his childhood abuse. Maybe he is experiencing so-called recovered memory syndrome. Except that recovered memory syndrome is somewhat discredited these days. Actually, it's a little hard for me, personally, to believe that Pete has the syndrome so designated. I incline toward the view of Frederic Crews (as articulated in an article in *The New York Review of Books**) that if it were so easy to forget trauma, why is it that the vast majority of survivors of the Holocaust, e.g., do not seem to have forgotten any of it at all? Crews writes, in reviewing Richard McNally's treatise on the subject, *Remembering Trauma:*

> It makes no sense . . . to count forgetfulness for some "aspect of the trauma" within the definition of post-traumatic stress disorder, because normal people as well as PTSD sufferers get disoriented by shocking incidents and fail to memorize everything about the event, even while knowing for the rest of their lives *that it occurred.* Likewise, it has never been established, and it seems quite unbelievable, that people can be haunted by memories that were never cognitively registered as such [italics mine]."

On the basis of the big ending of "A Quick One," it's easier for me to understand Pete as someone who has equanimity for both victims and, well, perpetrators. The victims, though they may treat themselves horribly later on, do not need to be forgiven for much. We do have compassion for them and for their problems. Therefore, the repetitions of "You Are Forgiven" are not designed exclusively for the victims. The girl guide is forgiven for her willing participation in the abuse/betrayal, as is the engine driver. In fact, we are *all* forgiven.

There's another way to look at these questions. The victims of trauma sometimes do have Stockholm Syndrome; they sometimes do identify with the perps. Accordingly, it's possible that Pete, even in this incredibly triumphant moment, is somehow working out both his identification with those who inflict childhood abuse, *and* those who somehow tragically cooperate with it, as the little girl guide does. The issue is complicated.

---

*March 11, 2004.

Rick Moody

Recently, I read an interview Pete did with *Rolling Stone*,* from the period when the Who were touring again. Pete said some inexplicable things. For example, he said that he was only doing the tour for Roger Daltrey ("I agreed with Roger that, in order to keep him amused this year, we should go back to New York and play a couple of shows"); he said that he didn't care what the audience thought about licensing the Who songs to corporate advertisements ("Who fans will often think, 'This is my song, it belongs to me, it reminds me of the first time that I kissed Susie, and you can't sell it.' And the fact is that I can and I will and I have. I don't give a fuck about the first time you kissed Susie."). And he said some stuff about bisexuality, when confronted by the reporter. Pete, in his Pete Townshend way, seemed to feel like he had to try to answer all the questions. But what was the point? According to the interviewer, Danny Fields (former manager of the Doors) had on occasion referred to Townshend as his "on-and-off boyfriend." At this revelation, Pete became singularly combative, said over and over that he couldn't remember, said he might have been drugged, said it was the sixties and, as such, it was a time of great social and sexual experimentation. And finally he went wild with rage, or this is my characterization:

> To actually say that we were boyfriend and girlfriend! Boyfriend and boyfriend. I don't know what he's fucking talking about. [*Louder*] And this is it. This is the fucking thing that stinks about this whole fucking thing of doing a fucking interview with fucking *Rolling Stone* magazine in the first place when I don't need to! . . . The tour is sold out. I don't want to talk about my work. I don't want to talk about the Who, I don't want to talk about any of this shit. . . . I just don't know what Danny is talking about. I know that I spent a night in his house. I don't remember much else about it. You know, I did not go out with him. He is not my type.

This is the Pete Townshend that I really loved and admired in the seventies. Completely unpredictable, completely impulsive, but totally human and sympathetic. Because what he is saying is, well, he's being contemptuous of *Rolling Stone*, and this is a credit to him. *Rolling Stone*, even in the seventies, was contemptible, and when you compare its fiery rhetoric back in the sixties with its

---

*July 2002.

devotion these days to teenybopper pabulum and Cristal-swilling celebutantes, you can only conclude that it has fallen far. Actually, the magazine has never met a corporate trend to which it wouldn't genuflect immediately. When Pete admits that he doesn't give a shit about talking about his work, when he's dismissive about the Who, when he says how much he loves John and Roger, you totally believe that he does love John and Roger, *and* that he doesn't give a shit about the Who. It's the mix of registers that feels most honest. He's evasive about the bisexuality issue, tries every circumlocution he can come up with, and then he says that Danny Fields was "not his type." So what's the truth exactly? Did he sleep with Danny Fields? I don't really care whether he did or he didn't. In fact, I wish he *had*, since protestations of heterosexuality are so unsatisfying. My recommendation is that no one should ever again protest or attest as to their fixed sexuality. However, Pete doesn't exactly create a climate of reliability, on the child pornography issue later, when he says: "I'm fifty-seven, I've got a young girlfriend, I'm not gay. I'm not interested in men. I don't think I ever really have been. I've had a high sex drive all my life, which has actually been difficult sometimes to reconcile with some of my spiritual aspirations."

Similar provocations grace the pages of *Mojo*, the British music magazine, in a recent issue devoted to the Who.* Townshend remarks, for example, about Bob Dylan:

> There was a richness around us which was totally and purely and entirely our own and you have to look at Scorsese's Dylan movie to see how lost some of those older rockers were. Dylan's rock and roll was silly rock and roll, he couldn't play rock and roll, he's never been able to play rock and roll. Not only that, but the band he hired to play rock and roll was Ronnie Hawkins's old fucking backing band! He was dead meat, he was gone. . . . We were working with something new and pure and refined.

Wow! Bob Dylan was dead meat! We should all be so badly decomposed! And the Band is "Ronnie Hawkins's old fucking band"? Nicely outrageous, these observations, but he couldn't really believe them, and when mounting the apology on his Web site it was

---

*February 2006.

apparent he didn't.* Later, in the same issue of *Mojo*—and despite having written at least one song lionizing Keith Moon (rightly so)— Pete took a few shots at Keith, saying, e.g., that "he was a giant of a man in so many respects, but in other respects he was a fucking tick on the back of the Who. No one's got the guts to say it . . . but it's true."

Townshend also touched upon the pedophilia charges** as well as his own childhood abuse. As in other published remarks, he managed to be both oblique and elsewhere forthright about his experiences. For example:

> A lot of the people I was talking to when I was writing this book [his autobiographical account of his abuse], and people that I was helping to deal with recovery, had suffered when they were evacuated during the war. And the idea emerged that about a year or two before the war had ended, this message went out that we were going to lose. And there were all these people that had the possession of all these beautiful young children, and they started to abuse them. Because they thought the end of the world was coming, and nobody would give a fuck.

This outline of wartime history certainly seems a bit precarious. Beyond anecdotal accounts, I'm not sure there's voluminous support for Pete's historical suppositions, and this is a frequent trope of Townshend the interview subject. Friends are adduced as evidence of this or that assertion.

Later, when Townshend placed himself within the confines of his sketch of wartime history, he seemed to do so with more emphasis on poor parenting than outright abuse:

> Then I'm born right at the end of the war, May 19, 1945, the week Albert Speer is arrested. It's just bizarre, the idea that they [his parents] then have to go on and live their lives. . . . To be a child at that time, you're saying to your parents, I need Mummy and Daddy, and they're going, "Fuck off!"

---

*"I was trying to show how over here in the UK in the early sixties we looked at the old guard of 'white' rock and roll (even Elvis) as being almost 'washed up.' I know it sounds crazy now. We still worshipped the old guard: Eddie Cochran, Elvis, Buddy Holly, the Everly Brothers, Ricky Nelson, all of them. But people like me believed R&B artists (and only the black ones like Chuck Berry, John Lee Hooker, Bo Diddley, and Jimmy Reed) were the ones we needed to emulate. It seemed to me . . . Dylan was groping in the dark. . . . Dylan doesn't need my puffs, but neither should he or the Band be subject to slurs I didn't intend to make."
**Mojo.

because they're traumatized. So many of my generation experienced that kind of neglect.

Further on, in *Mojo*, I came upon the one spot where Pete Townshend has been absolutely clear about his understanding of his childhood: "When I talk about abuse [after the war] I'm not talking about sexual abuse, *which I experienced*, I'm talking about postwar neglect. . . . I'm talking about the fact of the matter. My dad, after the war, chose to go and play Germany for a year. He stayed with the band, the Squadronaires, and as a result I never saw him [italics mine]."

This is moving and sad. And as someone also separated from his father for several months (in 1970) because of legal wrangling, I can sympathize with the kind of loss that Pete is trying to get at. Still, the logic feels muddled to me. It may be that the logic is muddled because the editors of *Mojo* have muddled it themselves. But part of the confusion also comes from the fact that the revelation of Townshend's sexual abuse is tucked into some rather passionate ranting about the war and its aftermath. Because of the way the sexual abuse is left unexamined, the remark has the effect of suggesting that it is the wartime history that has made the indelible mark on Pete Townshend. He is forthright about having been sexually abused, yes, but he is much more forthright about the neglect of his parents, and the scars of the war itself.

Maybe it is simply that Townshend as an interview subject is just extremely unfocused. He has trouble with taxonomies of abuse because he has trouble prioritizing in general (earlier in the interview, e.g., he says of Roger Daltrey, "He respects my lack of boundaries and lack of ability to live in reality"). *Abuse*, the word, seems to stand here for varieties of experience, and Pete doesn't always make clear which way he's using it. Having been absolutely clear above, he then backs away from the subject.

It's unsettling to think about Townshend's life in that aftermath of the abuse charges: "I thought, it's going to be impossible for me to live—do I have to think of some way to kill myself?" It would take enormous confidence for someone who was in his position, as an alleged pedophile, not to feel devastated by the press to the point of paralysis. However, I'm just as interested in the *end* of his further remarks,* which are broadly indicative of the way Townshend

---

Mojo.

communicates to the press, and in public generally: "I was frightened, and I think it's the first time I've felt that kind of fear and panic. I did an interview with *The Guardian,* and I said that if I'd had a gun I would have shot myself. It was pulled out as a headline, and I don't think it's true."

If he *did* say to *The Guardian* that he would have shot himself, how can it not be true? And yet at the end of the quotation he says just this, that it was *not* true that if he had a gun he would have shot himself. These two perceptions are mutually contradictory. But this is how Pete seems to use the interviews he gives, and how he uses writing in general. He doesn't think ahead. He thinks intuitively. When he contradicts himself, he contradicts himself. He will apologize later, if need be, or he will allow the contradictions to stand. Townshend lacks, perhaps entirely, an editorial function where his mouth is concerned, and this allows for great, expansive answers to questions, but it also allows for answers that are tangled, paradoxical, or contradictory.

I sort of want to know more about Pete's grandmother, about the period of his real or imagined child abuse. This is a fascinating autobiographical subplot for those who are interested in such things. I will sketch out what is in the record. His parents were both living. They were separated, as indicated above, only to reconcile later. During the separation, Pete was sent to live with his grandma Denny, and here's his account of it (from 1995):

> I was a postwar kid. I grew up with parents who came out of the end of the war with a great resilience, excitement, and big ideas, and I got left behind for a while. My parents split when I was very young, and I was sent to live with my grandmother, who had just been dumped by a very wealthy lover. She was in midlife crisis. She was my age today, and I identify very much with this woman who had to look after me. She ran naked in the streets and stuff like that. She was completely nuts. She was a very strict woman and I hated her. . . . I had two years with her before my parents realized that they'd left me with someone who was insane.*

Pete relocated to his grandmother's house when he was four, and by all accounts he was not exaggerating about her mental state. I've

---

*Quoted in *Behind Blue Eyes: The Life of Pete Townshend,* by Geoffrey Giuliano (Cooper Square Press).

read descriptions that feature *word salad* (the verbal gibberish of psychotic people), as well as pointless street searches for lost objects, etc. His grandmother also left him alone a lot. When she wasn't leaving him alone, she was berating him.

The particulars of the unstable grandmother are among the things Pete has forgotten over the years, and in his words it was only when his mother was writing *her* autobiography that he inquired about the gaps between ages four and six. His mother, Betty, was also unconventional in the area of familial relations: "She was very, very seductive. . . . Mum was always surrounded by crowds of men. She had plenty of money, was on her own a lot." The stories of Betty Townshend don't improve later on. For example, here she is commenting on Pete after his father's death in the 1980s*:

> At Cliff's funeral, we all got steaming drunk, and Peter and I made a pact to go on the wagon. I was doing great for two years and didn't touch a drop, and then a very dear friend of mine died. I went to pieces and hit the bottle again. But Peter has managed to keep off it. He is a very strong person and just has the occasional glass of champagne.

Wouldn't this situation with his biological mother also amount to a kind of abuse? But what kind of abuse are we talking about? Most often, when he has described the trouble with his grandmother—and one finds this especially in the aftermath of the child pornography investigation—Townshend uses qualifiers to describe the nature of the abuse. He says he "believes" he was sexually abused by his grandmother, or otherwise backs away from factual accounts. "I cannot remember clearly what happened, but my creative work tends to throw up nasty shadows—particularly in *Tommy*." And yet interpreting inductively from nasty shadows can be risky. I have one friend who was repeatedly abused as a child. She has one *very clear memory* of the sexual abuse, and only later did the most damaging memories of several years' worth of abuse surface in her recollection, landing her pretty quickly in a psychiatric hospital. Should we take Townshend at his word, and accept that something grave and soul slaughtering took place with his grandmother, despite his lack of clarity?

*

---

*Giuliano.

87

If so, if he was abused, the music was compensatory, was redemptive, so I don't want to overlook some technical analysis of Townshend the musician in this anatomy of his life. For example, it's worth talking about how Pete plays or played the guitar and about his singing, as these relate to his biography and character.

For example, Townshend thinks he's a *bad* guitar player, and that may be true, if by playing badly you mean he doesn't play like Eric Clapton or Jeff Beck. And it's true he is not a phenomenally melodic guitar player. In fact, the one interesting thing about his guitar playing is the strumming, the open chords. Also the volume. Pete is all about the open chord played through the original Marshall stack. I guess that the Who were among the first people to use actual Marshall stacks, and that Pete and John Entwistle helped design these Marshall stacks, in order to facilitate, among other things, the way Pete manipulated feedback on his guitar. This is especially satisfying on early songs like "My Generation" and "Anyway, Anyhow, Anywhere." The big open chord, with lots of feedback, is a thing of violence, a force of nature, and perhaps an engine of *forgetting,* and it is a recognizable aspect of the Who, so much so that when Pete was really trying to escape from the Who, one escape strategy was to build the songs around keyboards (as he frequently does on *All the Best Cowboys Have Chinese Eyes*), or to confine himself to playing the acoustic guitar (which he did in the late eighties because of his hearing problems).

There is also the visual part of Pete's guitar playing, the windmilling, the jumping up and down with the power chords. I have only seen them play live one time, to my shame, and it was late in their career. Pete was only jumping up and down now and then, in this particular show. Compared with the guitar playing of others, with, e.g., a Keith Richards, or an Eric Clapton, this is an anarchic way of playing, and we can observe this even without lingering over the habitual smashing of guitars, which may have been, at a certain point, a Vegas move, a bit of ritual destruction that was giving the people what they wanted, but which *began* as an earnest and heartfelt enactment of rage and frustration. The destruction suggests to me nothing so much as the anthropologically chronicled destruction of the Kwakiutl natives: whichever clan managed to destroy more of their *own* property won the war.

How does the guitar playing of Pete Townshend serve as evidence—or lack thereof—with respect to the allegations about Pete and the pedophilia, etc.? It doesn't serve at all. It serves as an engine of forgetting. Or suppressing. Playing guitar is the place where all the controversy about Pete Townshend, all the provocative nonsense that he has said on occasion, is completely set aside and the perfect, primitive value of whatever rock and roll once was is apparent to anyone within range. Pete Townshend, no matter his condition, was not a god, was not anything but a *man* when he played guitar, but if so, yes, he was the best that man had to offer, strumming thirty-second notes faster than almost anyone else could do it, and using his thumb on the low e-string, so that he always had a big fat bass note on the bottom of the chord, using amplification so that he right-eously fucked up his hearing for ever after, bobbing up and down in the air like he was trying to get himself to coast on the sound waves coming out of the amplifiers, a great guitar player, who did as much, if not more, than the better practitioners of guitar craft, in terms of advancing the instrument. Playing guitar is about surviving, playing guitar is about overcoming, playing guitar is about distracting, in great waves of distortion and feedback, from the problems out there in the world, or playing guitar is about distracting the player from the past.

The Smothers Brothers Show is a good visual example of this transformative aspect of the guitar. The Who's appearance on *The Smothers Brothers Show* took place on September 1967, a couple of months after they played the Monterey Pop Festival. I guess I was too young to stay up to see it, which is why I saw it instead in *The Kids Are Alright.* This is the footage that opens that film.

The Smothers Brothers program was a true example of late sixties television. Which is to say: it was manifestly political but was still a television show. The script called for the Who to thrash around to backing tracks of "My Generation" (the vocals were cut live) at the conclusion of which they would smash up a bunch of equipment, and *fast*, because you only had so much time on television. Then Pete was going to smash Tommy Smothers's acoustic guitar. Normally, when they were doing it onstage, in live performance, the band took their time about the destruction of property. But you couldn't spend ten minutes busting shit up with the Smothers Brothers; the sponsors wouldn't go for that.

"My Generation" is absolute anarchic brilliance. It's one of the greatest rock songs because of the big ending, the squawling of guitar feedback. Well, also the drum fills. Toward the end of the Smothers

Brothers tape, it's quite lovely to see Pete start jabbing the neck of his guitar into the amplifier, after which casually, like he'd done it every day, he began destroying his guitar. What could be better? But that's still not the interesting part; the interesting part has to do with the drummer, Keith Moon, who is busy executing his rolls, until the smashing-things-up portion of the song. Now it's said that Moon put a bunch of explosives in his bass drum, and somehow the prank didn't quite work like it was supposed to do, because it wasn't until after the song that the explosion detonated. It's an incredibly violent song anyway, and with Pete rushing through javelining his amp and smashing his guitar, that's plenty, but suddenly a ferocious *bang* and then lots of smoke and shit go flying everywhere, and nobody does anything! It's like nothing at all has happened, and that's when Pete smashes up Tommy's acoustic guitar, and there's this shot of him, standing in profile next to Tommy, and the look on his face is sort of arresting. It's the look of the lion who has just devoured his prey, the look of the felon caught in his felony. I remember someone describing to me Bill Clinton's appearance when he first had to address Congress after the Lewinsky affair came to light, and I suppose I somehow associate that look with this look, the look of pure power and remorselessness. The even more amazing part is that Pete, later on, dated the beginning of his hearing loss to this moment. So in spite of the fact that he was twenty-three, skinny, and beautiful in a feline way, he was, just then, completely deaf, from a drum-kit explosion. Here he was at the peak of his powers, celebrating mayhem, menace, destruction, and yet at the same time he was really beginning the self-slaughter but good.

Having described the brilliance and animus of Townshend the guitar player, I think it's important to try to talk about Townshend the singer a little bit, too. Because this was a crucial aspect of the Who sound, and it's sort of why I still like them a lot. If Roger Daltrey's voice, the baritone, drawing heavily from blues singers and R&B/Motown, was all about the masculine hubris of the Who ("They're all WASTED!"), Townshend's voice, especially in the earlier days, was exactly the opposite. Roger is "I'm Free," "Won't Get Fooled Again," "The Real Me," the signature songs of the Who. Pete is "Sunrise," from *The Who Sell Out;* "Blue, Red, and Grey," from *The Who by Numbers;* or "I'm One," from *Quadrophenia.* Pete is a high tenor, a white Smokey Robinson, with a nice, controlled vibrato. No pitch problems. He could have been a great country-and-western singer.

This is a reductive model, of course. There have been moments in the history of the Who when they effectively exploited reversing Roger and Pete (Roger's winsome side is even more persuasive because of his machismo elsewhere). But I think the general principle is sound: the quality best expressed with Townshend's instrument is *vulnerability.* "I'm One" is a good example. It's one of the rare finger-picking numbers in the later Who output, and as such it's perhaps reliant on "Behind Blue Eyes" as a forerunner, though not to its detriment. It's also got a big helping of the bruising self-criticism that Townshend has saved for the songs he sang himself—"Ill-fitting clothes and I blend in the crowd / Fingers so clumsy, voice too loud." The band passages where Townshend's lead guitar also comes in to muddy up the pristine surface conceal the vulnerability beneath a roar. But it doesn't quite do the job. He's still twisting in the breeze, which is part of why the song has lasted.

"Blue, Red, and Grey" is possibly the best example of this vulnerability I'm describing, and Townshend, who rarely plays this song, has said uncharitable things about it. True, the refrain, "I like every moment of the day," *does* sound like a man trying to talk himself out of a really dark spot, and yet in the third chorus, when he moves to the top end of his range, there's a great restraint and understatement evoked that actually make the song do *more,* ache more, than most of the rock-oriented compositions on the album.

The same compelling vulnerability is much in evidence on Townshend's first solo album, *Who Came First.* Townshend originally released the collection in order to preempt bootlegs of the songs, which had appeared on three limited-edition devotional albums for followers of Meher Baba. While the motive may have been professional,the songs are anything but careerist. The album includes a couple of nakedly arranged standards, "Content" and "I Look Around and There's a Heartache Following Me," which have a remarkable power considering how uncharacteristic they are for the writer of "My Generation" and "Won't Get Fooled Again." Townshend, on these pieces, sounds like a torch singer, like the rock-and-roll alter ego of Nina Simone or Dolly Parton. Then there are two leftovers from the aborted *Lifehouse* film, which appear here in their demo versions. And, most memorably, there are two stunningly beautiful ballads, "Sheraton Gibson," a folksy piece, written under the influence of Bob Dylan, about Pete's touring miseries, and his setting of one of

Meher Baba's prayers, "Pavardigar." The singing on these latter pieces is so full of soul and, in the case of "Pavardigar," spiritual awe, that it's impossible to think of this work in the same way you would think of the unpredictable and menacing band in which the author more often plied his trade. When I was fourteen and first purchased *Who Came First*, I knew nothing about gurus and very little about spirituality. I wasn't even baptized yet. But the record still made me cry.

Which is to say what exactly? About his singing? It's to say that if the guitar playing of Pete Townshend somehow operates as the infernal engine that transports its player, its practitioner, above and beyond a difficult childhood and its traumas, his voice is the part of the operation that expiates the crimes and excesses of his guitar playing. If only you heard Pete Townshend singing, if that were your only opportunity to encounter him, you would think he was an incredibly gentle and sweet guy.

And yet, just in the way that Brian Wilson at a certain point apparently felt that singing the falsetto part in the Beach Boys was somehow undignified, Pete seems lately to feel that this high part of his range, his lonesome vulnerability, is somehow too easy. You can see how primal this perception might be, given what we know about his biography. The falsetto and the high tenor are just not *masculine* voices. For example, Pete, in rationalizing a new song theoretically to be included on the upcoming album he's going to make with Roger Daltrey,* has repeatedly observed that an artist in his sixties should sing with the voice of a *man*. But I suspect the issue is not where, in what clef, a man should sing. Pavarotti, also a tenor, has never been accused of being a sissy of a singer. Maybe the issue is more properly *at what cost so vulnerable?* What's it like to feel so close to permeability, as open to the whims of the world as the Pete Townshend of *Who Came First?* Like a twig in the breeze, or like a cork in the ocean, as Wilson sang in one of his later Beach Boys compositions.

Is the lonesome, vulnerable tenor of Pete Townshend the voice of a guy evoking the traumatic episodes of his past? And how to square this with fits of rage that you encounter in any précis of Townshend and his work (like at Woodstock when he says, "Fuck off my fucking

---

*To be released, according to the press, in 2006.

stage" to Abbie Hoffman; or Long Beach Arena, 1971, when he says to the audience, "I'll tell you fuckers something! All right, now listen! Now just fucking listen, and *shut up*, right. Either sit down, or stand up, or lay down, or do something but *shut up*. This is a fucking *rock-and-roll concert*, not a fucking tea party"), the outbursts of violence (as when he punched out Ronnie Lane, already ill with multiple sclerosis, in the studio during *Rough Mix*, as when he hit Keith in the face with a guitar for being late to a gig). And what about the hideous, condescending liner notes to *Maximum R&B*, the Who box set, when he's practically giddy about how much he dislikes the band, when he seems contemptuous of anyone who shelled out for the box set? How to square this with a voice of such gentleness and vulnerability?

I have so far omitted the most defensible part of the output of the Who, viz. the album known as *Who's Next*. Let me redress the omission briefly. That album cemented their status as rock dinosaurs, and spawned some quite good automobile advertisements. At one time, I loved *Who's Next* so much that I had the liner notes memorized. Everything. The engineering credits. The record label information. Memorized. I would spit out the entirety of the back of the album cover whenever it came up.

Some description of the origin of *Who's Next* is therefore in order. It's an album of songs, which, as I have said, is what the Who did best, and what Pete is best at, despite what he may feel these days. And yet the album began as a *concept*, after the rather grand impact of *Tommy*. Specifically, the concept was called *Lifehouse*, and it had to do with the Who occupying some kind of film studio set and allowing themselves to interact with the fans directly. The conceptual apparatus of *Lifehouse* has always been on the hazy side, notwithstanding the fact that it spawned a raft of excellent songs, most of which either ended up on *Who's Next* ("Baba O'Riley," "Won't Get Fooled Again") or on Pete's solo album *Who Came First* ("Let's See Action" and "Pure and Easy"). These are *all* great songs, that's indisputable, but what are they about really? One biography of Townshend describes *Lifehouse* as a "full-length film script about life in a programmed totalitarian society on the verge of collapse, where people wear 'experimental suits' and are fed through test tubes."*

---

*Giuliano.

93

This description is enough, yes, to engender mixed feelings about the fact that *Lifehouse* never came to fruition. At one point, there was a million dollars in seed money from Universal Pictures, but perhaps Universal was a little wary of the climax wherein a "guru figure" demonstrates how rock music will enable the masses to achieve spiritual bliss.

And skepticism about the *Lifehouse* project is undiminished by Pete's insistence recently that *Lifehouse* predicted the Internet. This is a theme in Pete's online journal, this long-ago prediction, and he mentions it from the stage of Royal Albert Hall in 2003. Of course, it's largely irrelevant who, if anyone, "created" or "predicted" the Internet. In contrast, what is of interest is art. The *Lifehouse* concept involved the band playing live on their film set for two weeks solid, with the audience free to come and go throughout. Now, *that* is art of a particularly meaningful kind. It's the sort of art, the sort of concord between audience and artist, that made "The Who Cares" such an appropriate and oft-deployed slogan later on. Yet this preliminary stratagem was overburdened with *ideas*, about totalitarianism, about everyone playing one note together (cf. "Pure and Easy") until a glorious cacophony would ensue, which would culminate in "nirvana."

One wonders what the other members of the band thought of this. Roger Daltrey was wont to refer to Townshend's guru, Meher Baba, as "Ali Baba," on occasion. And Keith Moon was pretty clear about getting bored playing *Tommy* during the years when the band toured relentlessly in support of its material. If the rest of the band were skeptical initially, the first rehearsals didn't help. Finally, throwing open the doors and inviting in anyone who passed by apparently resulted in audiences composed mainly of the intoxicated and indifferent. In one memorable rehearsal, Townshend roughed up a guy who charged the stage.

A consequence of the resultant collapse of the *Lifehouse* project was Pete's "nervous breakdown." I have no idea what this phrase means. And I say this as someone who, to my chagrin, is not unacquainted with mental-health professionals. I have no idea what "nervous breakdown" means. It is not a genuine clinical diagnosis. I don't know if it's Townshend himself who uses the term. Or if doctors of the time inclined toward this quaint and old-fashioned pettifoggery. "Nervous breakdown" does, and ought, refer to a psychotic break on occasion. The features of a psychotic break are obvious. Visual and/ or auditory hallucinations, inability to distinguish reality from hallucination, and so forth. And according to the *Mojo* article about *Quadrophenia* this *is* what happened: "Pete suffered a massive anxiety attack of such intensity the people in the room morphed into 'frogs or some strange creatures.' Later, he was told he'd tried to jump out of the window, but was restrained. What really hurt him, Pete said later, was the fact that his friend and mentor [Kit Lambert] had referred to him out of earshot as 'Townshend.'"*

"Nervous breakdown" can also refer to nervous collapse, or exhaustion, which should be plausible, and is a time-honored explanation for strange turns of events in the lives of rock-and-roll musicians. It's not hard to imagine that Pete was exhausted from the relentless touring and high-profile performances that came the band's way in the wake of *Tommy*.

Still another interpretation of "nervous breakdown" might be the cycle of alcohol abuse and withdrawal. And given the period under scrutiny, late sixties/early seventies, it's not hard to imagine that there was some of that going on, though Pete did not embark on harder drugs until much later. Whichever way you parse the term "nervous breakdown," however, the collapse of *Lifehouse* brought about the *Who's Next* sessions, and perhaps the loudest and most unbridled music the band ever made. People adore this album, I imagine, not just because the sound is great, and the keyboards are used in inventive ways, but partly because it emerges from the despair of losing control of *Lifehouse,* because it comes out of giving up on the late sixties, giving up on idealism, on unworkable or impracticable idealism. That's why "Won't Get Fooled Again" is at the end, and why the last line on the album is "Meet the new boss / Same as the old boss."

To put it another way: even though Pete, by the time of *Who's Next,* and thereafter, had come to the end of his youthful ability to bear up under the worst circumstances, and even though the fissures were beginning to show in the band, they did take this opportunity, this failure, and make great art from it. Unlike, e.g., *Smile,* the lost Beach Boys album, whose tracks, when scattered around in later albums, felt orphaned and curiously diffident, *Lifehouse* seems better, at

---

*Mojo.

least to this listener, when sundered from its apparatus. Townshend's self-release, not long ago, of a six-volume edition of the pieces from the project, as well as a "greatest hits" single-disc volume, called *Lifehouse Elements*, feels palpably like rationalization ex post facto. It did not improve the reputation of the lost masterpiece. Ditto his attempt to write a novel that deals with similar material.* The action of this novel seems to mix palpably autobiographical musings with more quasifuturistic stuff about computers and the Internet and music, to no great effect.

Yet this does offer me a brief moment, despite not caring whether Pete predicted the Internet, to praise the way the man uses technology. Part of what makes me still kind of adore Pete Townshend is the variety and simplicity and diffusion of his interests. On the Web, for example, you can find his blog and his self-composed profile. He lists his age (sixty) and his interests, and his industry ("arts"), his taste in fiction (he likes anything by Paul Auster and Siri Hustvedt, as well as Michael Chabon), and video footage of him in the studio and around the house. This same tenderness, the aforementioned vulnerability, is barely concealed beneath his occasional outbursts of egomania ("What is well known is that I am a rock star"). It's a complicated stew to be found there, but it's a human one.

Quadrophenia, the somewhat misbegotten album that succeeded *Who's Next*, ornate in its production and overblown in conceptual armature, just isn't going to come in for much attention here. I think the story of *Quadrophenia* is rather hard to follow, if in fact there is a story at all. Mostly it seems to be about mods and taking speed, or mods and rockers clashing while taking speed. The big production number at the end, "Love Reign O'er Me," is too cloying for me, and the songs that Pete devotes to the other members of the band (with the exception of "Bell Boy," Keith's song) feel as though he wasn't up to dealing with tensions in the organization directly. There are rather lovely and astonishing moments on *Quadrophenia*, but I still don't listen to it very much.

After *Quadrophenia* came *The Who by Numbers*, which I have mentioned, and that was in turn followed by *Who Are You?* which is mainly noteworthy for being the album the band made right before Keith Moon died. It had a good photograph on the cover, and for a brief period, I personally tried to *dress* like the Pete Townshend in

---

*This recently self-published novella, *The Boy Who Heard Music*, is available on the Web.

this photograph. It didn't work. Meanwhile, just as I was getting acclimated to that rather lackluster album, Keith Moon passed away. At which point the Who, as a useful entity, as a band of four distinct personalities balanced the way certain chemical compounds are balanced, collapsed, never to be made right again.

It's fair to say that there were a lot of other problems, besides the band, besides Keith: Pete's own drinking, his hearing loss, his refusal to tour, the creative corner they had painted themselves into, etc. It wasn't just that Keith died.

And yet, for my part, I started to get impatient with the Who. Everything about the next album, *Face Dances*, seemed ill advised to me. The name was ill advised. The new drummer, Kenny Jones, who seemed fine when he was with the Faces, seemed metronomic and dull when attempting to fill in for Keith. I kind of like the pop throwaway that became the hit from the record, "You Better You Bet." But the rest of it? Forget it.

In the case of *It's Hard*, their last studio album, I don't think I've ever heard it all the way through. I tried a couple of times, but except for "Eminence Front," there just didn't seem to be a reason. The material feels desperate to me, uncertain. Was it uncertain because of the people involved? Or uncertain because of history? How can you be ambitious enough to make *The Who Sell Out*, and then careless enough to make *It's Hard*? I bought a vinyl copy of *It's Hard* on eBay a couple of years ago, when I had a turntable again, and even then, in a nostalgic moment, I was impervious to its charms.

One song from this sunset period of Who releases concerns a certain rather distasteful sexual compulsion, and so it bears mentioning. I don't happen to like the song in question,* although the bass part is lovely and serpentine in the 1997 remix. But I like the description of how it came to be written. It's worth pointing out that in this same period Pete was apprehended (in Switzerland), having crawled drunkenly into a bear cage. There were other colorful incidents. It's against this backdrop of addictive illness that he came to write "How Can You Do It Alone?"

> I was actually going up Holland Park Road and I wanted a
> cigarette, I didn't have a light and it was about two in the

---

*From *Face Dances*. The quotations on the subject come from www.thewho.net/linernotes/FaceDances.htm.

morning, and this guy came out of the station and I asked him for a light and he looked very afraid and he stepped back and I said, "Listen, all I want is a light from your cigarette" and he said, "Oh, all right." He opened his coat up and got a lighter out and before he'd known what he'd done, he was completely naked underneath, with the trousers and the string, he was a flasher! He'd obviously just come off the tube doing a bit of flashing. He saw that I saw that he was naked and that I knew what he was up to. I looked into his eyes and he looked into mine and the shame in his face! I felt like saying to him, "Listen, don't be ashamed. I don't give a damn." Then I was walking up the street and I thought I should have asked him, "How do you do it all on your own? How do you live that solitary . . . How do you get your kicks?" Because that's more alone than masturbation. So I started to explore that idea and that turned into the song.

In view of my ongoing attempt to try to ascertain what kind of shadows play over Townshend with respect to the issues of sexual abuse, this incident gives a glimpse of a younger, less strident Townshend, one much more tolerant of libidinous ambiguity, here confronted with a variety of paraphilia that is analogous to pedophilia, if less traumatic. Townshend is *not* judgmental, is *not*, for example, trying to ascertain if the "bit of flashing" just performed was performed before an underage audience. Nor is he running in the direction of the nearest pay phone to have the flasher apprehended. He's rather sympathetic to the kind of anguish that is apparent in the face of the perp.

Pete's solo recording career was, at the time of *Face Dances*, beginning to take off. Everything changed for him thereafter, and quickly. Even Pete's *singing* changed dramatically on the somewhat inconsistent solo albums. He became a better singer. There were vast improvements in the area of basic pop craft. And the solo albums were more tolerant of the balladry in the Pete Townshend output. He didn't need to play as much electric guitar. He wasn't so hell-bent on the rock posturing that hemmed in the Who in the late seventies, the cock-rock section of the songbook. And some of the parts of his character that didn't seem to win over many converts in the band were given full flower when there was no antagonist for him.

Maybe it was because he had fewer antagonists that in this period he made some rather infamous and ill-interpreted remarks in an interview. He declared that "inside he was a woman."* Moreover, he refused to say that he wasn't a transvestite, and refused to repudiate the rumors about his gay experimentation. No doubt the mooks of Madison Square Garden, and other arenas across America, that is to say Who fans, would have misunderstood these remarks, had they paid much attention, unless they had learned by now to consign his more outlandish quotables to the file marked Pete Shooting Off Mouth.

Still, the process of individuation makes things rise to the surface. The longer one is busy about the game of creativity, the more twists and turns assert themselves, and that's why on the first of the somewhat inconsistent solo albums, namely *Empty Glass,* you get a song like "And I Moved." Perhaps because of the remarks above, this tune, and one other song on *Empty Glass,* really set tongues wagging.

Pete's notes said that "And I Moved" was first written for Bette Midler. Why Pete would be writing a song for Bette Midler, who first got her start in the bathhouses and who was very gay identified, is unclear. But this is what he says. Maybe he intended to have gay themes in the song *because* it was for Bette Midler. In any event, since it was composed for a woman, it needed to have a narrator who was passively, or let's say receptively, engaged in a sexual encounter with a man, and thus the feminine imagery: "And I moved / And his hands felt like ice exciting / As he laid me back just like an empty dress / And I moved / But a minute after he was weeping / His tears his only truth / And I moved / But I moved toward him."

It never occurred to me that this song narrated a gay sexual encounter until very recently. I thought of the song as having a spiritual theme. The song does appear on *Empty Glass,* after all, and the title song on that album, "Empty Glass," quotes from Ecclesiastes, while the chorus ("My life's a mess / I wait for you to pass / I stand here at the bar / I hold an empty glass") uses thirst as a metaphor for spiritual longing. Moreover, this Pete Townshend was an alcoholic, even kind of *looked* like one on the album jacket, and so it's fair to say that the empty glass of the title might be thought of as some kind of allusion to addiction and alcoholism, and as an insightful person

---

*Giuliano.

once remarked, "Alcoholism is a low-level search for God." So when I thought about "And I Moved," a song I loved and felt like was a big improvement over the music he was making with the Who, at the same time, I thought it was about being ravished by a spiritual master.

How frequently in black music are spiritual longing and carnal longing one and the same? Look at almost anything by Aretha Franklin or Al Green. And isn't it the case that *love* for God in the Christian tradition (just as potently elsewhere) gives us a model for a kind of theological ravishment that is patently, well, homosexually themed, at least if you are a Christian male. We're all Teresa in ecstasy, we're all being ravished by God, at least if we are spiritual adepts, and so "And I Moved" can just as easily be taken for a narrative of "moving toward" the will of God, and in a way that is just as orgasmic as what Teresa appears to be feeling in Bernini's depiction of her.

What about "Rough Boys" then? It was the hit from *Empty Glass.* There was even a rather primitive video of it. It seemed to have something to do—like "Who Are You?"—with an old rock-star type of a guy encountering young turks of the music scene. It is dedicated to the Sex Pistols (as well as to Pete's daughters). But it does have the lines: "Rough boys / Don't walk away / I very nearly missed you / Tough boys / Come over here / I wanna bite and kiss you." And the subsequent verses would not exactly reassure the portion of the audience given to homosexual panic.

Pete, of course, says the two songs are not about homosexual longing, and then elsewhere he kind of says maybe they are. He is not conclusive on the subject, as, in fact, he is inconclusive about many things. To what degree is memory even a useful tool in talking about the songs, because, as Pete has rightly observed on occasion, after a point the listeners begin to seize control of the songs and assert their own interpretations. And once the songs belong to the listeners, he is no longer able to mandate the way in which they are understood. Thus, though Pete says that he was not rooting around on child pornography Web sites with any prurient purpose in mind, and though Roger Daltrey has himself said he doesn't believe it, and though I don't believe it either, and though we know it's a huge political mistake to assume that just because someone is bisexual or omnisexual or whatever it is that Pete is, it doesn't mean that it's not possible to believe that he is, at the very least, a little reckless. And willing to climb into a bear cage.

In the midst of his solo career, Pete also became, for a time, an editor at the venerable British publisher Faber & Faber. He became, that is, kind of bookish. What publishing house could have been more bookish than T. S. Eliot's onetime employer? Moreover, in the midst of this bookishness, Townshend (in 1985) published a book himself, entitled *Horse's Neck*. It's a collection of short stories, some of them patently autobiographical, some of them more veiled. Quite a number have a lot to do with the problem of being very well known and lionized in the bizarre milieu of rock and roll.

There is some lean, muscular, and completely effective prose writing on display in Townshend's collection. He reads mysteries, I have heard, and I find faint traces of Chandler in his unadorned but self-assured sentences. Furthermore, he doesn't shrink from disturbing or unsettling material in the book. Men are creeps in *Horse's Neck*, and they are creeps with a lot of desire. They are lecherous.

One of the stories goes even further than this, however, and deals very explicitly with the sexual abuse of children. It's called "Tonight's the Night," after the rather dreadful song by Rod Stewart. "Tonight's the Night" is written in the third person largely from the point of view of a person named Pete. Let me try to summarize the story briefly.

The Pete character in the story is staying in California with someone called "the Baron," apparently a Kit Lambert stand-in. The Baron and Pete, at the outset, are shooting the breeze with a "pretty, spicy girl." In fact, the Baron is holding forth to the others about his rather precocious sexuality, which, according to his recollection, was fully operational from age three: "The mums and dads could go dancing while babysitters ran up and down checking the kids. I poured all my mother's perfume down the sink one night. I called the nurse (she was kissing her boyfriend on the bench outside). She came in and I could feel her heat."

Pete and the "spicy" girl hit it off, and much discussion between the two ensues. She expatiates upon her favorite song by Rod Stewart: "Here's where she gets it! He sings about her spreading her wings—you know what that means?" Not long after, Pete effects his seduction of the woman in question. Beyond her physical beauty, it's unclear what the attraction is, but Pete is smitten. Next morning, after he drops her at her hotel, he and the Baron revisit the previous night's delights, with Pete recounting at length the woman's story: "At eleven years old she had a promising bosom and early periods. Her father ran off with his assistant nurse. Her mother moved her own lover in, a crazy stud of twenty-five who worked as an occasional logger in the hills."

Soon enough, the young heroine, in this story within the story, is visited in her room by the "crazy stud." The consummation is not instantaneous, or Rod Stewart–style, owing to the fact that the stud, among other things, was "very big." Further uncomfortable details are included in the conversation between Pete and the Baron: "She said he felt like a horse. She learned how to get him off. She would be completely drenched." After much precoital fumbling over the course of weeks, the stud/logger kidnaps the spicy girl *for three years,* making her his sexual slave. She serves in this capacity until she's fifteen. At this point, the Baron, intrigued, asks Pete what it was like making love with the girl, and Pete answers, "She was really big, you know, down there. Enormous. It embarrassed me."

When the girl returned to her mother after three years in captivity, no one made any kind of "fuss" about her kidnapping. In fact, it went undiscussed: "The logger never touched her again and none of them ever mentioned it."

Five years later. The Pete character is in the middle of a bad spell with his drinking ("He was trying to give up the booze, taking all kinds of pills and vomiting a lot, seeing little stars and using sleepers to keep himself from being bored") when the girl suddenly reappears. In some kind of trouble. "I met this guy in L.A. He had a kind of ashram. I joined it." However, her guru has abdicated his position, and only keeps in touch with followers *telepathically.* In fact, the telepathic guru somehow keeps the girl imprisoned. Pete asks how he can imprison her if he's far away, in Houston, to which she replies, "He comes in the guise of a little boy from down the street." Just as Pete is about to intervene, she rings off.

Next day, the Baron brings news that the woman has been "accused of kidnapping some twelve-year-old boy. She's been doing bad things to the kid."

"Tonight's the Night" then includes an odd postscriptus, which I need to include in its entirety:

Pete finally got himself straight about a year later. He quit the
booze, quit the casinos, and the Baron went home to England.
Pete decided to close the Nob Hill apartment and put it up for
sale. Clearing it up he came across a magazine full of naked
people. He was about to throw it into the trash when he recognized her face. She was with a very big man. She was holding him in one hand, and her little Cindy doll in the other.
The photograph had been taken in a dentist's chair.

There's so much that's disturbing about "Tonight's the Night"
that it's hard to find a preliminary handhold. The use of the third
person is disturbing, for example, because it means to remove the
author Pete Townshend from the character Pete, at the same time as
it confuses the issue.

Similarly, the relationship between Pete and the Baron is confused.
Pete is said to be a "singer" and the Baron his "manager," but their
relationship is a lot closer than that, and their conversation verges on
the ambiguous throughout. This is made more transparent in the
fact of the triangle between the Baron, Pete, and the girl. The girl is
a piece of currency that is exchanged between them in the course of
the story. She doesn't even get to have a name.

The story-within-the-story of the life of the "strawberry blonde,"
as she is also known, is a grueling tale of sexual abuse of children. It's
not some episodic story, where a drunken parent appears in the bedroom; it's systematic, ongoing violation, for three years of this girl's
life. Even in a more permissive social environment (the rock-and-
roll underworld of the seventies and eighties), it's a shocking story.
Certainly, it would be difficult to write such a scene, a scene that
accords this violation its proper weight and seriousness. Townshend
is not a sophisticated fiction writer, and it shows. We have *none* of
the girl's misery in his version of the story. Moreover, the girl's story
is recounted to the Baron *after* Pete heard it from the girl, which suggests the possibility that she told him about the abuse and yet he
nonetheless managed to make love with her without significant feelings of complicity in her rape.

The traditional therapeutic equation, that sexually abused children abuse others in turn, is given an affecting treatment, in the
person of the little boy (her "guru") with whom the "strawberry
blonde" carries on at the end of "Tonight's the Night." It occurs to
me, with respect to this therapeutic equation, to ask, however, if
Pete (the author) is identifying with the "strawberry blonde," or with
the Pete character. The "strawberry blonde" is sexually abused, as

Pete sometimes says he was, and she abuses the boy in turn, as Pete was believed to have done, briefly, by the authorities. Is he that kind of abuser? Or is he the Pete *character*, who, in a period of alcoholism and rather dubious morality, sleeps with an obviously disturbed woman, and even seems to fall in love with her after she tells him the story of her shattering abuse. Is he the codependent trying to rescue the broken child? Or the broken child himself? And is either of these people, savior or victim, free from the inclination to abuse in turn?

All of this becomes even more unsettling in the light of the post-scriptus at the end of the story. Obviously, it seems to suggest that the "spicy girl" was sexually abused by her own father (a dentist) as well as her mother's lover, and the presence of the doll in the shot, in a magazine "full of naked people," further suggests some kind of ongoing sexual abuse of children to which she was party, perhaps over the course of many years.

This systematic abuse is intrinsic, is central to the story, and it implies one last question to be asked of "Tonight's the Night," and that is the question of the ownership of the magazine in which this nude photograph of the "strawberry blonde" appears. Pete the character is closing up the apartment in Nob Hill, in order to sell it. Is it not his apartment? Is not his responsibility for its sale an indicator that he is responsible for its contents, too? And does he not then own the magazine in question? Is the magazine not manifestly devoted to child pornography or, at least, to simulations of child pornography? If Pete has finally got himself straight, are we meant to understand that this child pornography, or simulated child pornography, is a legacy of his active alcoholism? If it is *not* Pete's magazine, then to whom does this magazine belong? And if the magazine doesn't belong to Pete the character, well, is it not possible that it belongs to Pete the author? Is it not possible that the author Pete is attempting to get the character Pete to throw the magazine away *for him?*

One song that I revere completely, despite its being from the inconsistent solo period of Pete Townshend's career, appeared on the album after *Empty Glass* entitled *All the Best Cowboys Have Chinese Eyes*. There are a number of moving songs to be found on that album, in fact, including "Slit Skirts" and "Stardom in Acton." But the song I mean to pursue here is "The Sea Refuses No River," which title, according to my researches, derives from an early seventeenth-century English proverb.

I'd been kind of indifferent to *All the Best Cowboys* when it first came out. Despite its sterling moments, the record *is* uneven. But when I got out of the psychiatric hospital in 1987, when I was suddenly in bad circumstances myself, I wanted to hear *All the Best Cowboys* again. Because, I remembered, Pete had been trying to put an end to his own period of excess. In my recollection, the songs had that self-critical quality that I needed, which I sought out in other albums during my rehabilitation, like *Astral Weeks* by Van Morrison.* I liked Warren Zevon then, too. Warren Zevon had done his time in the detox mansion.

Above all, one particular song on *All the Best Cowboys* went into heavy rotation and that song was "The Sea Refuses No River."

It starts with electric guitar, harmonica, and some glockenspiel (he nicked the idea, I think, from Bruce Springsteen), and it starts right in with the litany of Pete's crimes. "I remember being richer than a king / The minutes of the day were golden / I recall that when the joint passed round / My body felt a little colder." Soon, the melody rises into the refrain, according to the "gospel in the choruses" strategy that Springsteen used back in the day: "The sea refuses no river / And right now this river's banks are blown / The sea refuses no river / Whether stinking and rank / Or red from the tank," etc.

You can imagine, against a backdrop of domestic difficulty, with Pete's wife having already tossed him out and taken him back, that the earnest wish of the chorus was not simulated. Furthermore, there's a spot in the song when Pete (and it was maybe the last time he was able) truly *keens,* "The sea refuses no river, remember that when the beggar buys a round!" It still makes me shudder with recognition, no matter how many times I hear it, and here's why: because nobody, no addict, is *deserving* of another chance, another length of rope. We're more undeserving than almost anyone. And yet every now and then an addict or criminal does get redeemed, despite his or her lack of merit. Thus "The Sea Refuses No River" captures as few songs have, "We're polluted now but in our hearts still clean," or, at its close, "The sea refuses no river / and the river is where I am."

It ends with a recognition of failure and desperation, and it ends big, and when it ends, with some incredibly generous acceptance of

---

*Which Lester Bangs, in a celebrated essay, said was all about pedophilia.

the damned, it's hard for me to believe that Pete Townshend, who knows himself here as he has rarely known himself (since perhaps, *The Who by Numbers*), is the sort of guy who would launch a single-handed vigilante operation to entrap users of child pornography. He just doesn't seem like a crusader for justice.

And there is evidence to the contrary: the Who recorded a public service announcement about the dangers of smoking when all four members of the band smoked, and Pete made passionate antidrug comments in the British press while drinking heavily. On the basis of his past record as a moral crusader, one would have to admit to feeling that he's a much better negative role model than a positive role model for young or at-risk persons. He knows much better how to feel isolated, alienated, alone, broken, spiritually impoverished, and compulsive than he knows how to be upright and morally correct.

When I was done listening to *All the Best Cowboys*, I was done with Pete Townshend for a good long spell. Ten years maybe. I heard a couple of songs from *White City*, but no one could make me listen to *The Iron Man*, and when I saw a video of a staged version of *Psychoderelict*, his last solo album of new material, I felt an inability to relate happily to the work of the guy I'd looked up to so much in my teens. And I can scarcely bring myself to touch on the Broadway theatrical known as *Tommy*. I saw it once, and I went to it, I think, out of longing for the period when *Tommy* mattered, not out of a faith that this was going to be a memorable experience.

Long about 1999, the three surviving members of the Who got together to do something that Pete had done himself a couple of years prior. They played one of the Neil Young Bridge Concerts. The Bridge Concerts take place in the San Francisco Bay Area, and they're benefit events for a school that serves the needs of children with autism and related disabilities. The Bridge Concerts are usually acoustic and they are often freewheeling and star studded, for lack of a better term. For some reason, I was eager to hear the three surviving members of the band play live together, which they had done irregularly in recent years, and eager to hear them play some old material. I actually watched the gig on the Internet, which was harder back then. I was on dial-up, so it was kind of stop and go. Still, there was something so unpretentious and graceful about the performance that suddenly all the slick nonsense that had disappointed me about the Who in the eighties was forgotten.

Chief among the successes of that particular gig was a new version of an old familiar Who tune, "The Kids Are Alright." The Who have done a lot of really great charitable work for teenagers (they donated a million pounds to a London clinic for teenagers with cancer), and this may have prompted them to turn up at the Bridge Concert in the first place. When they sang "The Kids Are Alright," in addition to incorporating Roger on the guitar (almost unimaginable), they also added a big improvised section toward the close where Roger and Pete traded recollections of their own childhoods. At this gig, the ad-libbed portion felt genuinely spontaneous, and patently directed at the Bridge School students themselves. The strange ominous repetition that Pete favors in the extended section of the song, "I know the kids are alright, my kids are alright, your kids are alright," seemed awkwardly sincere in its early iterations.

In the years since, and especially in the aftermath of the child pornography charges, the *new* version of "The Kids Are Alright" has become predictive of Pete Townshend's problems in a way that does make the charges against him look suspect. Only, that is, if you had some good reason to feel that it was possible for children to be unsafe would you go on at such length extolling the virtues of *safe children.* Either he has a reason to feel strongly about it, or he's a bald sentimentalist. I'm just not willing to go that far yet. Townshend is only sentimental when he feels deeply, if that is not oxymoronic. And he feels most deeply about the things he knows from personal experience.

The ultimate irony in the Townshend pedophilia case became apparent in August of this past year, when a former expert witness in the Operation Ore prosecutions wrote a lengthy demurral in the *Sunday Times* (of London) alleging significant prosecutorial mistakes in the course of the pedophilia investigations.* The allegations are of mistakes so systemic and so thoughtless that they certainly do undermine the supposed accomplishments of the operation:

> In information given to Interpol and in sworn statements submitted to British courts in 2002, Dallas detective Steven Nelson and US postal inspector Michael Mead claimed

---

*A reprint of the article can be found on the Computer Crime Research Center site, http://www.crime-research.org/analytics/1453/.

that everyone who went to Landslide [the Web site where the illegal material was said to be available] always saw a front page screen button offering "Click Here (for) Child Porn." . . . But what passed almost unnoticed eight months later was that after British police and computer investigators had finally examined American files, they found that the "child porn" button was not on the front page of Landslide at all, but was an advertisement for another site appearing elsewhere. . . . The real front page of Landslide was an innocuous image of a mountain, carrying no link to child porn.

In fact, according to at least one expert cited in this article, it was actually rather difficult to get from the relevant Web site to a child porn archive: "There was 'no way' a visitor to Landslide could link from there to child porn sites, according to Sam Type, a British forensic computer consultant." The bulk of Landslide-related sites was for ordinary adult-type sexual material, and in some cases the sites were not sex related at all. The Web site shut down in 1999, as well, so by the time the arrests took place for in some cases inadvertent or fraudulent use of the supposed child porn sites, the offenses were so outdated that it's possible alleged pedophiles could not remember the events they were being charged with.

Other celebrities were caught up in this investigation, like Robert Del Naja of Massive Attack, who, like Townshend, had his charges dropped after a month. The commander of British forces in Gibraltar, David White, was accused in the course of it, and he committed suicide, like thirty-three others, rather than face the trial proceedings. Names were routinely leaked to the press (as in Del Naja's case), so that the cases could play in the court of public opinion before the trials, thus making it extremely difficult for the innocent, of whom there were clearly a number, to get a fair hearing.

If, under these circumstances, Pete Townshend really did manage to access child pornography, he must have worked diligently to do so. His statement on the subject admits to visiting the site, but it's more than possible that the public statement was arranged with the investigators in order to assure that charges would be dropped. If, under these circumstances, Townshend did enter the site *for research*, as he further claims, one can only wonder at the poor decision-making involved in his efforts. It was a really bad idea. And why use your credit card to do it? Pete?

*

In the end, therefore, I don't know whether Townshend is a pedophile or not. And it's obviously impossible for me to know, and, in fact, it's impossible for anyone to know, save for Pete Townshend himself. If the dark tones of child abuse are shadowed forth in his work, which is undeniable, it is impossible to tease apart the experience of having suffered childhood sexual abuse and the guilt and remorse about having committed some of it. The two are so close as to be almost indivisible. As to what we ought to think of his work in light of the investigation, the answer to that question is obvious: his work is what it is. It is either bad, or good, or outrageously great, entirely apart from his sexual peccadilloes or the lack thereof. If we hounded every rock-and-roll musician who had a tendency to morally dubious excesses, we would have no rock-and-roll musicians. I might recognize being disappointed in the person of Pete Townshend, should it ever come out that he did what he was accused of doing, but I make a distinction between this and the work. I don't give a fuck, in fact, about Pete Townshend's personal life, not when I am listening to "My Generation" or "A Quick One," "Blue, Red, and Grey" or "I'm One." I care only about his voice, his guitar, and his songwriting talents. What if it turns out that, yes, he was falsely accused? In that instance, the work more than survives, it glitters with the sheen of triumph over adversity.

If we can never know about that moment when Pete was logged on to the offending Web portal, we can know quite a bit about him besides. For example, we know, I think, that Pete Townshend is a mass of contradictory material. Pete Townshend is a rather electrifying guitar player who likes to write Broadway show tunes; Pete Townshend has a gentle high tenor voice that he often uses to sing about very masculine, even occasionally aggressive songs; Pete Townshend is a person of great garrulousness who emulated an Indian guru who never spoke; Pete Townshend is an ardent heterosexual who has had any number of homosexual experiences; Pete Townshend is a committed family man who is involved with a woman twenty-five years younger than he is; Pete Townshend is a person of keen humility and significant arrogance; Pete Townshend is a person who has written pop songs of great tenderness and who has purposefully hit fans and friends and band members with his guitar; Pete Townshend is almost always in the public eye and has been for over forty years, and yet he writes best about loneliness; Pete Townshend is both physically alluring and homely; Pete Townshend is both spiritually thirsty and breathtakingly cynical;

Pete Townshend is deeply romantic and has written very few genuine love songs; Pete Townshend is deeply serious, but the most effective period of his work was his most humorous period; Pete Townshend is incredibly complicated, hard to figure out, evasive, and yet he's also completely open and one of the most accessible popular musicians in the world. Pete Townshend was raised in a jazz-playing family, but helped invent British invasion rock and roll. Pete Townshend has claimed to be a socialist, but he cooperated with Margaret Thatcher's antidrug crusade. Pete Townshend wrote his best songs about being young and is now sixty years old. Pete Townshend may have done some horrible things and he may not. Pete Townshend may have been charged with certain horrible crimes he did not commit. Pete Townshend may have committed other crimes we know nothing about. He loved his wife and wrote memorably about her, and they divorced anyway. He wrote great songs and flabby, uninspired songs. He tried a lot of new things, and many of them did not work at all. A mass of contradictions! An exasperating and erratic person! Changeable! Mercurial! Impossible! Despite this, or perhaps because of it, Pete Townshend does *not* seem different from most people you might meet, in terms of his irreducible complexity and his emotionally finicky moods. He's obvious, deep, human, impenetrable, sometimes dull. Despite everything that's happened, he's a representative man.

Which is why we loved his songs once and will again. He's one of us.

A Simple Metaphysics
Robin Hemley

> It is this kind of question that Photography raises
> for me: questions which derive from a "stupid" or
> simple metaphysics (it is the answers which are
> complicated): probably the true metaphysics.
>
> —Roland Barthes, *Camera Lucida*

ONE REASON PHOTOGRAPHS speak to us is because of their very muteness. We who cannot be quiet feel compelled to listen to them. We can't resist interpreting love photographs because of their lack of resistance to interpretation, from the most documentary photo to the most stylized. Photographs cannot defend themselves, and even the image that seems to tell the starkest tale—say, a photograph of the liberation of Auschwitz—can be denied, reinterpreted, reinvented. Only those who were at Auschwitz or their liberators can speak for the photo, can say this really happened and was not staged for the camera or otherwise manipulated by the photographer. Once all the eyewitnesses have died (and of course, eyewitness accounts are often less definitive than photographs), then we only have our own moral certitude to fall back on, at least if we're relying *only* on the photograph for documentary evidence, and not other types of records. Photographs are witnesses, but not foolproof ones. The stark Civil War photos of Mathew Brady showing bloated corpses were in some cases staged. One dead Confederate sniper was photographed in one picture with his head turned away from the camera and his rifle by his side. In another, he faced the camera and he still clutched his weapon. Other pictures of Brady's were staged in an even more theatrical way—he posed live soldiers as dead ones at the Battle of Bull Run. Is there anything wrong with this?

All peopled photographs are theater, even those that are candid. Portraits, snapshots, documentary photos, stylized or self-conscious artistic photos, certainly authors' photos—all theater of a kind, some more theatrical than others, but by their very nature, their muteness, their stopping of time, they constitute an ambiguous kind of drama. John Berger, writing of the "language of appearances," claims that

111

Robin Hemley

Dead Confederate. Circa 1861.
Photograph by Mathew Brady.

images tend to "cohere" and so when we see a photo of a baby at its mother's breast our memories and expectations combine to create an idea of this baby, both particular and generalized. This is in part why the photo of a complete stranger can move us. Through memory and expectation, we supply a kind of mininarrative. I'd call it theatrical rather than storylike or even cinematic because of the static quality of the photo and the set of the theater stage, but for other reasons as well. The fourth wall in theater is the audience. The fourth wall in the photograph is the viewer, who in turn becomes an actor in the drama. I'm not writing here of series of photos—a different matter entirely because they provide movement, at least for the duration of the series, a continuity, a sense of the future, if not the past.

In Method Acting, the actor constantly attempts to understand her role by investigating the motivations of her character. In a person-centered photograph, the viewer is as much concerned with text and subtext as an actor is. What does the photo say through its appearances and what does it *really* say? The viewer in this case steps into the photo and becomes the actor for a moment in the minidrama, based on memory and expectation. Susan Sontag says we can never fully comprehend or sympathize with the pain of others, but in fact

112

we *can* sympathize or photos would not have such power. Our own experiences matched with the expectations of our own deaths make the famous images of the Vietnam era so powerful: Eddie Adams's photo of the South Vietnamese general executing a suspected member of the Vietcong on the streets of Saigon, Nick Ut's famous photo of the napalmed girl fleeing down a road, Malcolm Browne's Buddhist monk sitting serenely through his own immolation. I've seen these photographs grouped as a series as well as stills, but the stills hold far more power than any series of photos. Television, because it moves, allows the viewer a moral passivity that a photograph does not allow. By stopping the flow of time, the viewer is forced to step inside the photo and complete it, supplying his version of the past that preceded this moment and an expectation of the future. For this reason, these Vietnam photos had as much if not more to do with turning the public against the war as news broadcasts beamed into America's living rooms at night.

Some of this might seem anti-intuitive: documentary photography as inherently theatrical, a staged event in many respects, even the most candid and seemingly unrehearsed shot. I'm framing this as a kind of theatrical collaboration between photographer, subject, and viewer, in which one is producer (the photographer), one is director (the viewer, and sometimes the subject), and two become the actors (subject and viewer). The drama takes place at the crossroads of experience, expectation, and imagination. The experience upon which the drama is based has long since disappeared and what is left is an interpretation, a production of the original.

I wrote a book on the Tasaday people of the Southern Philippines, a group who, when they were "discovered" in 1971, were heralded by the world media, including *National Geographic,* as an authentic "Stone Age tribe" living in complete isolation from the outside world. Photos of this small band of twenty-six men, women, and children from the rain forest graced the covers of many magazines for a couple of years before the government of the Philippines closed down the forty-five-thousand-acre reserve it had granted to the Tasaday and few people gained entrance for the next dozen years or so. Then, in 1986, a Swiss freelance reporter hiked into the Tasaday rain forest and met a very different group from the one first encountered in 1971. While in 1971 they had been photographed in caves wearing only leaf loincloths, sometimes displaying stone tools, now they wore blue jeans and sports T-shirts and carried guns. The Tasaday supposedly told the reporter through a translator that the whole

113

Stone Age thing had been a hoax, that in fact they were simply a group of farmers who had been bribed to dress up as cavemen and pose at the behest of a powerful Philippine government official.

Never before has photographic evidence been used so dramatically to prove one point or the other, that the Tasaday were either real cave people living a Pleistocene-like existence or a bald hoax. As it turns out, neither is an accurate representation of the Tasaday, but the former was more accurate than the latter, which itself turned out to be a hoax. An overreliance on documentary photography and the persistent belief that photographs don't lie plagued the Tasaday question. Part of the problem lay in the fact that each photograph, pro-authenticity or pro-hoax, was a staging of a minidrama that the viewer completed in his own head, based on his own experience, expectation, and imagination.

The chief photographic chronicler of the Tasaday in the early days was John Nance, a Vietnam War photographer who became the Associated Press bureau chief in Manila. In due course, Nance quit his job with the AP, wrote the best-selling *The Gentle Tasaday*, in 1975, was tarred and feathered by the hoax proponents in the 1980s, and now quietly runs a nonprofit organization for the group, who still live in what little remains of the rain forest in the Philippines. Over the years, he has taken tens of thousands of images of the Tasaday, from the early seventies to today. His earliest photographs show the Tasaday at their caves dressed in leaves. His latest show them riding motorcycles. All these images speak loud and clear in the language of appearances, but depending upon one's own knowledge of the Tasaday case and one's own experience, the drama being conveyed can swing radically. When I was first starting my book project in 1998, I visited Nance in Portland, Oregon, and viewed an exhibit of his Tasaday photographs mounted at the Portland Art Museum. Nance supplied the captions to the photos and visitors recorded their thoughts on the exhibit in a guest book. Those who knew nothing of the Tasaday case but saw only Nance's lovely images of cave people frolicking in mountain streams tended to write equally romantic comments:

The first two walls blow you away. Then civilization hits.
But let's be hopeful, though. Really a wonderful experience.

I love the smiles on the Tasaday people. So beautiful.
Much appreciation.

114

Those who knew more of the story tended to respond differently:

This whole exhibition is a hoax covering up a larger hoax.

One of my favorite Nance photos shows two Tasaday men, clothed in leaves, squatting on the dirt floor of a cave and flanking a third man who is working a stick to make fire. A naked toddler stands beside them, looking on curiously. Without a caption, without any knowledge of the Tasaday, this photograph would still be shouting in the language of appearances. We would enter into the picture and become actors in the drama—our first impressions would be truest because the longer we analyzed it, the more difficult the role.

Tasaday in cave. Circa 1972. Photograph by John Nance.

Despite our resistance to romanticizing or exoticizing other people, we would most likely do just that, then our skeptic sensors would fire up and we'd pull back from the photo to assess it more dispassionately. Who are these people? Are they actors? This wasn't really taken ten thousand years ago, after all. Should I laugh at this photo so that I won't play the fool?

Another photograph I possess shows the Philippine government official at the center of the Tasaday hoax controversy, Manuel

Robin Hemley

Elizalde Jr., a millionaire aristocrat of Spanish and American background. Elizalde was the gatekeeper of the Tasaday and, among other things, had a reputation as a sexual omnivore. Persistent rumor had him having sex with everyone from imported Spanish beauty queens to mountain tribal women, including the Tasaday. The pro-hoax documentaries tended to use what I call the "tribal maiden" photo to illustrate the drama of Elizalde as deflowerer of rain-forest virgins. The photo shows three people leaving a helicopter. In the foreground is a tribal maiden, giggling as she brushes her hair lightly with a hand. Even though the rotor of the helicopter has been stilled by the shutter of the camera, we can imagine the wind tousling her hair. Behind her, young Elizalde departs from the open cockpit—he's wearing a yachting hat, dark glasses, and smoking a cigarette. His right-hand man, the T'boli tribal chief, Mai Tuan, holds the door of the helicopter open. Behind the helicopter stands a lone tree, its branches a spindly fan. If you have any familiarity with the Philippines and its tribes, you will recognize the young woman's garb as distinctly T'boli, with its designs like the peaks and valleys of a mountain range, and less obviously because it blends in with her shirt in the photo, the belt made of hundreds of brass bells that T'boli women use to ward off evil spirits. What we're witnessing is an

PANAMIN photo of Elizalde, Mai Tuan, and unknown woman.
Circa 1971. Photographer unknown.

116

ambiguous moment, a drama that can have one of many outcomes. The version I was told by one of Elizalde's longtime associates was that the woman's sister had been Medivac-ed by Elizalde and the woman had come along for the ride. This was her first helicopter ride and she was both exhilarated and terrified by it. Completely plausible. In one of the hoax documentaries, it became something altogether more ominous. Dark music grew in intensity as the photo flashed on the screen and the narrator said terrible things about Elizalde. Nothing specifically was said about this photo, but it was used to illustrate Elizalde's predatory nature. Was it taken out of context? Yes, but so has every photograph ever shot been taken out of context. The moment passes and context is lost.

Look for your lost mother in photos taken of her, as Roland Barthes tried in *Camera Lucida,* and you will sort through dozens, maybe hundreds, before you "rediscover" her, the authentic her, the way you remember her. For Barthes, it was an image he calls the Winter Garden photo, and that he describes but refuses to reproduce for the reader. To do so would be a betrayal of his relationship with his mother and this particular picture, offering up an illustration that would illustrate nothing. The viewer would merely see the photo as "an indifferent picture, one of the thousand manifestations of the 'ordinary.'" But one of the chief delights of photographs is just this, their confounding natures, the fact that we often want them to open up a keyhole to history, to authenticity, when they only open up a keyhole to ourselves.

Photographs are inexorably linked to our desire for authenticity. Take, for example, the crowds at the Louvre that I saw last summer hovering around the *Mona Lisa,* taking photos above their heads, hardly aiming, as though the *Mona Lisa* were a starlet and they were paparazzi who might turn their fuzzy snapshots into millions of dollars. To anyone without a camera at the Louvre, the scene, undoubtedly repeated every minute the museum is open, feels ridiculous. To anyone with a camera, the lure of authenticity must seem as irresistible as the gravitational pull of a dead star. Don DeLillo captures this type of moment marvelously in *White Noise* when his protagonist visits the "most photographed barn in America," the quintessential American barn, so photographed that no one sees the actual barn anymore, but simply its representation. Of course, such encounters are about symbolic possession, but they're also about drama. The quadrillionth photographer of the *Mona Lisa* seeks to be part of the drama of the *Mona Lisa.* The *Mona Lisa*

Robin Hemley

People looking at the *Mona Lisa*, Louvre. 2004. Photograph by Dave Munger.

becomes an actor in the drama he creates of the day on which he viewed the *Mona Lisa*. Such photos hold no allure for anyone besides the person who took them and perhaps his immediate family. In the language of appearances, the idea of the *Mona Lisa* is so general that it can no longer be particularized except by the person who took the quadrillionth photo of it. But the photographer is happy. He looks at his photo and enters for a moment into the photograph of the painting. He steps from the chorus to leading man for a moment. His role has been elevated for a moment above the rest of the visitors thronging the famous painting. The camera here becomes a tool of anxiety about the photographer's place in the world.

Susan Sontag attributes too much power to the photographer when she writes, "To photograph people is to violate them, by seeing them as they never see themselves, by having knowledge of them they can never have; it turns people into objects that can be symbolically possessed." The inherent moral rectitude of that statement fascinates me, though Sontag wasn't arguing *against* such "violations." She was merely illustrating a point. Still, invasion is what Americans tend to fear most, whether national, personal, economic, cultural, or moral. Cameras: another way to invade. Another reason for guilt. But cameras are amoral really and so are photographs—the

118

more possibility there is for "violation," the more a subject *invites* a photograph. Drama (in both the large sense and the drama of a particular photo) is what we thrive on and photographs simply set the stage, so to speak. The key of course is the word "symbolically," though we're apt to forget symbolism when we feel violated and possessed in actuality. Strictly speaking, no one is ever violated by a photograph or possessed by one. Photographs neither violate *nor* possess the subject. If they could, then we would only need to use the camera once or twice in our lives and that would be enough.

It *is* true literally that a photograph shows a person a self she never sees. As we know, but don't necessarily process when we look in the mirror, the reflection we see is a reversed image. Recently, a photographer told me that when he was first starting out, he sometimes took portraits of people who hated the way they looked in photos. As a solution, he started flipping the negatives, and invariably the problem was solved and the client felt comfortable again with the self he saw.

When we talk of violation, we forget that the subject is often in control of the photograph. In a studio shot, the customer has the right to accept or reject, to pose as she wants. The same holds true for nearly every smiling tourist photo ever taken. Here, the subject symbolically possesses the camera if not the photographer herself. Far from predatory, the camera becomes a tool of the actor's trade.

The biggest act is the formal portrait. I love to study them, from the stacks of anonymous nineteenth-century portraits you can find in antique stores to my own family's portraits through the years to my own author's portraits on the books I've written. My mother had an author friend in New York, Ursule Molinaro, who refused to allow photos of herself on her book jackets. My mother thought Ursule didn't want her soul snatched away, but I think she was simply being smart. My own jacket photos cause me nothing but shame now, so clearly do I see the Idea of Author I was trying to portray, and badly, with each successive book. As time passes, the subject of a portrait will invariably come to regard it as the expression of a failed role. "I was so young then!" "I can't believe I wore my hair like that!" "Who did I think I was fooling?" David Shields in *Remote: Reflections on Life in the Shadow of Celebrity* slyly illustrates the act of the formal portrait in a section titled "About the Author" in which he places his book-jacket photos side by side, instantly parodying himself while simultaneously redeeming himself by the very self-awareness this juxtaposing of selves implies.

Robin Hemley

When I was writing *Nola: A Memoir of Faith, Art, and Madness,*
my memoir of my sister, who suffered from schizophrenia and died
at the age of twenty-five, I consciously inserted photographs into the
text as I was writing the book, and formed the words around photos.
This was 1997—the ability to do this on one's computer and not
immediately run out of memory (no pun intended) was a relatively
recent innovation. For me, the photograph was as much talisman as
evidence. The photos I used were as much magical evocations as
illustrations or authentications. I wanted some essence of the people
I had loved to infuse me and the words I wrote about them. I wanted
to reach back into the past and snatch them, carrying them into the
temporary haven of the present. I wanted to comfort and be comforted, trouble and be troubled, and in large part, it worked. Berger
calls the language of appearances "oracular." And it was true for me
that these photographs spoke in an oracular manner, sometimes
faintly, sometimes in ways that needed interpretation.

Time elevates memory in the same way that time elevates photographs. A fixed memory from childhood fascinates us more the older
we get. Sometimes we have no idea why the memory survives—it's
not necessarily an important moment, maybe as simple a memory
as stepping off a bus at the age of five and looking up into the sunlit
branches of a tree. What is remarkable about that moment? Perhaps
nothing except that it has survived. Perhaps more, but it's there that
the writer needs to investigate, contemplate, burrow. We need to
learn how to speak for the fixed images of memory.

As Akiko Busch points out in *The Uncommon Life of Common
Objects,* digital photography works as memory does because it edits
and erases in the same manner as memory. The memoir and the
digital photograph actually share a great deal in common—the digital photograph employs a kind of willful selectivity and invention
that mirrors in many ways the memoirist's process. A child in a wad-
ing pool in the background gets erased because she doesn't fit the
program of the photographer or the program of the memoirist, either
for aesthetic reasons, reasons of privacy, or reasons of psychological
sensitivity.

Two images that leap to mind from my memoir and from memory are a studio portrait by the famous New York photographer Aaron
Siskind taken of my mother in the late 1940s, and a photo of my
sister at age ten or eleven, sitting on a fire escape, hand on chin, looking up as though contemplating heaven. Few photographs could
seem more stylized than these. My mother, in her early thirties,

looks every bit the glamorous author, as she wanted to be, and my sister, the aesthete, as she wanted to be. The photo Siskind took of my mother—an author's photo for her first and only novel, published in 1947, was clearly not a violation by Siskind, nor an attempt to possess her or see her as she didn't want to see herself. In essence, it was an advertisement of her, a refinement of how she wanted to be seen, making her not only an object, but a product. My sister's photo, much less refined, was also an interpretation, meant to be read in a certain way.

Not long ago, I was chatting with some acquaintances when one of them asked simply what a face is. The question took us by surprise—it seemed an odd, obvious question and at the same time the type of thing too easily taken for granted. Well, it's the place we like to keep our noses, mouths, and eyes, of course. Everyone present took the bait and stammered, trying to describe what a face is rather than simply what it does. I don't remember what most of the answers were, but I remember someone saying that a face is a mask. I knew *that* wasn't the right answer. At best, the face is a lot of masks, not simply one. A mask is a representation of a face and so when someone calls a face a mask, they're saying in effect that a face is a representation of a face that is a representation of a face, ad infinitum.

By now, it should be clear what I think a face is. Simply a stage on which desire and emotion play. The camera produces a number of dramas upon this stage, each a separate performance.

In trying to understand why some images fascinate and others don't, Roland Barthes devises an eccentric yet appealing method for explaining his interest or lack of interest in a particular photograph. It's what he terms the *"punctum"* and the *"studium."* The *studium,* as Barthes explains it, is a photo or a part of a photo that holds a kind of dispassionate or historical interest for the reader. The *punctum,* by contrast, is what fascinates us, though "fascinate" is too mild a term. What wounds us, the wound of the photo, is the way Barthes phrases it. A photo of three soldiers patrolling in Nicaragua is all *studium* to Barthes because, in the background of this photo, we see two nuns crossing the street. The elements of the photo are easily grasped, too easily, and so it merely exists for Barthes but holds no interest. Another photo shows a gathering of smiling kids in Little Italy, 1954. A presumably toy gun is pressed by someone taller and older to the temple of one smiling boy's head. Here, the *punctum,* the wound of the photo, for Barthes is not the gun, but the boy's bad teeth. It's a detail, a tiny shock. In another photo of Queen Victoria on horseback, she's all *studium* to Barthes while the kilted groom holding the bridle is *punctum*. Don't try to understand this concept rationally, because it's not meant to be rational but a reaction, a private reaction.

He writes of one photo: "Here is Queen Victoria photographed in 1863 by George W. Wilson; she is on horseback, her skirt suitably draping the entire animal (this is the historical interest, the *studium*); but beside her, attracting my eyes, a kilted groom holds the horse's bridle: this is the *punctum*; for even if I do not know just what the social status of this Scotsman may be (servant? equerry?), I can see his function clearly: to supervise the horse's behavior: what if the horse suddenly began to rear? What would happen to the queen's skirt, *i.e., to her majesty?*"

It's easy to explain in different terms why Barthes was so fascinated with this photo, leaving aside the *punctum* and *studium*. Barthes neglects to describe the expressions on the faces of Victoria and her kilted "groomsman." Hers is bland and blank. His is intense, intent, guarded, guarding. He looks as though he will reach through the mists of time and throttle you if you dare approach the queen. And, indeed, he *would* do so if he could. While Barthes does not know the identity of this man, I do. His name was John Brown and he was the subject of the 1997 film *Mrs. Brown*, starring Judi Dench and Billy Connolly, about the devotion and dependence Victoria and Brown had for one another. One look at Brown in this photo and you're mesmerized. All *punctum*. But a plainer, less fanciful way to view our interest in the photo is in its elaborate staging and the inherent drama that it suggests to the viewer whether or not the viewer knows anything at all about John Brown or even Queen Victoria. Billy Connolly must have studied this photo for the role—in the film he was able to perfectly capture Brown's expressive intensity.

In John Berger and Jean Mohr's book *Another Way of Telling*, Swiss photographer Mohr makes the point that we want photos to tell us what they're about, but they can't, so we speak for them. Mohr takes five photographs from his archives, and shows them to a disparate group of people, asking them to essentially caption the photographs, to speak for them.

Some of the photos are more easily deciphered than others. A girl seemingly biting her doll is indeed biting her doll. But a young man floating among tree branches is only a photographer trying to get a better view of an antiwar demonstration in Washington, D.C., in the early seventies. A man with his arms spread wide is a Turkish worker in a German factory trying to get the photographer's attention. The supplied explanations dismiss our interest in the photos' narratives. If we remain enamored of them, it's most likely because of their formal composition, the visual coherence of the photos. But the photos that are most haunting narratively are the two outside my normal ken at least, one of a figure asleep on a giant pipeline and a group of twenty-five or thirty men from India or Pakistan, dressed in T-shirts for the most part, staring solemnly at the viewer. In these two cases, the explanations provided by the photographer are just as intriguing, if not more, than those I might supply with my imagination. The photo of the Indian men is actually a photo taken in Sri Lanka of a group of men who are listening to a presentation about the benefits of vasectomies. No wonder the grim expressions! Yet Jean Mohr tells us that thirty of them—that seems the entire lot— signed up immediately to be sterilized. The other photo is of a boy outside Bombay lying on a pipe bringing water to the city; the pipes are cool and he's done it to escape the heat. To someone in Bombay or Sri Lanka, these photos might seem utterly pedestrian and the photo of the young man in the flowering tree truly exotic. We can't control what appeals to us in a photograph; though a photo often makes public a private moment, it still remains a kind of private visual correspondence between the photo and the viewer. What the viewer brings to the viewing—imagination and his/her private associations and memory—can't necessarily be rationally explained.

One of the many reasons W. G. Sebald's novels are so fascinating is the way he blurs the boundaries between the aims of authentication, illustration, and evocation in the photos with which he peppers his narratives. The black-and-white photos of the eastern shore of England in *The Rings of Saturn* seem like illustrations at first, but illustrations to what effect? The photos for the most part depict the most ordinary scenes, largely unpeopled. The photographs in his work confound our expectations of what a photo should do (Barthes, I'm sure, would see only *studium* in Sebald's photos) *and* what a novel should do. Photographs illustrating a novel? Doesn't that make it nonfiction? Despite or because of their ambiguous natures, Sebald's photos have on the reader the same *talismanic* effect that the photos I used in *Nola* had for me. They are meant to evoke not an exterior landscape but an interior one.

I am interested in what I might refer to as the *telesma* of the photograph, more than its *studium* or *punctum*. A photo can be all *studium* as in Sebald's washed-out landscapes and still possess *telesma*.

These photos seem magical in their ability to transcend time or in their complex, sometimes contradictory evocations of the human drama. The *telesma* is that talismanic aspect of the image that draws us into it. The photo that possesses *telesma* doesn't ward off evil spirits per se, but time and mortality. It invites us, even traps us, in some place between ambiguity and awe. It is that which astonishes us. "In themselves appearances are ambiguous, with multiple meanings," writes Berger. "This is why the visual is astonishing and why memory based on the visual is freer than reason." Some photos possess *telesma* close to the surface, almost bubbling out of them. Some require a little investigation before you discover the *telesma*. The first photograph ever taken, in 1823, of a table setting, has *telesma*— there is something undeniably magical in its being the first. The powerful photo of John Brown and Queen Victoria is another. John Nance's photos of the Tasaday have it, but here's something curious. If you disbelieve in something magical, it loses its power. It ceases to astonish. If you believe a photo of Mathew Brady's Civil War dead was staged or that the Tasaday were a hoax, your skepticism will likely, though not necessarily, diminish the photo's *telesma*. A new window of *telesma* might open up for you as you imagine the scene of the soldiers posing as dead on that long ago afternoon, some of them dead in similar attitudes not long after, and all of them long since turned to dust. Similarly, in a portrait, its very staginess creates its own *telesma*, especially as time passes and the role the actor played in the portrait seems ever more pathetic and vulnerable. And what of purposefully staged artistic photos, such as those of Cindy Sherman and other artists whose work plays with melodrama and movie moments? These photos are cultural talismans of a kind—for me, they are curious, even remarkable in their effects of simulation and satire, but I can't discern the *telesma* in them. Their very pointedness, the fact that they speak so unambiguously in the language of appearances, robs them of *telesma* for me. Another way of putting it: the drama of such photos seems exhausted.

Other photographs may be granted *telesma* by the viewer, may be salvaged from becoming "an indifferent picture, one of the thousand manifestations of the 'ordinary.'" While photo captions often try to fix meaning in a photo in a way that is ultimately futile and unsatisfying, writers of imagination do the opposite. They create a mix of image and language that can take the blandest photograph and turn it into a talisman against the very forces of banality and mortality with which photographer and subject and viewer all struggle.

One does not even need the photograph itself to grant it *teles-ma*, but simply the memory of the photograph. Take, for example, Barthes's own description of the unrevealed Winter Garden photo.

Alone in the apartment where his mother had died, Barthes one day sorted through photographs of her one by one under the light of a lamp, scouring each picture for a glimpse of the person he had loved, gradually traveling back in time with her. And then he discovered a photograph unlike all the others. The faded sepia print showed his mother when she was only five years old, standing with her seven-year-old brother on a wooden bridge in a glassed-in conservatory:

"He was leaning against the bridge railing, along which he had extended one arm; she, shorter than he, was standing a little back, facing the camera; you could tell that the photographer had said, 'Step forward a little so we can see you'; she was holding one finger in the other hand, as children often do, in an awkward gesture. The brother and sister, united, as I knew, by the discord of their parents, who were soon to divorce, had posed side by side, alone, under the palms of the Winter Garden. . . ."

In this photograph, Barthes at last discovers his mother, in the distinctness of her face, the docile place she has assumed beside her brother, the innocence of her face and gestures, what he refers to as a "sovereign innocence."

Here, Barthes's language becomes a reliquary for the image. Barthes has granted the photograph *telesma* in his lovely evocation of it and need not reproduce it for us because he has fixed it in our minds the way he wants us to see it, with the same reverence and magic it contains for him. It's no coincidence that commentators on photography continually speak of magic when trying to understand the photograph. "The oracular nature of appearance," as Berger says, "a magic, not an art." "Prophecy in reverse," says Barthes; "the magic of the real," Sontag calls it.

In Lawrence Sutin's *A Postcard Memoir*, he illustrates this idea of *telesma* in a fashion completely different from Barthes's search for his mother. In this book, Sutin uses images from his vast collection of nineteenth- and early twentieth-century postcards and uses them in ways they were certainly never meant, as touchstones for meditations on his own life. The reproduced postcards and meditations, side by side on the page, are not explanations. Through his words, Sutin sees the subjects of the photos in ways they never could, and, more important, sees himself through the photographs in a way he perhaps never could without them.

From *A Postcard Memoir* by Lawrence Sutin.
Date and photographer unknown.

Once a photograph has been taken, it's not inviolable. It's not the end of the story. The photo from another era seems to carry a drama within it, but the exact nature of that drama often remains opaque. The word "reliquary" strikes me as just right in trying to understand this. The bone of a saint by its very nature possesses *telesma* but without the reliquary to contain it, what's to distinguish it from any other ordinary bone? Sometimes, a photograph alone serves as a reliquary for human experience. Sometimes language alone serves as a reliquary. And sometimes by employing both language and the image, another form of reliquary is created. Transcendent magic and mortal drama. These are the cornerstones of human existence, and it is at the confounding intersections of the two where the photograph haunts the photographer, the viewer, the subject, and this writer.

Two Essays
Ned Rorem

WHAT DOES MUSIC MEAN?

I'VE BEEN LIVING WITH MUSIC all my life and still don't know the answer to this question. Surely music's the most immediately persuasive of the seven arts—can any of the others make us weep, or fall in love, or recall the past? Yet *how* does music do this? Is the ear more sensitive than the eye? Or is it that our whole body is affected, as when we are moved to dance? Mendelssohn said: It's not that music is too vague for words; it's too precise for words.

But if music can be proved to have concrete meaning, it's only music with *words*, not the notes, that is the proof. For words are symbols of specifics like "tree" or "rain" or "Tuesday," or even "and" or "but." Chords and phrases are possibly symbols, too, but of what? Music cannot depict "yellow" or "spoon" or "Jennifer," much less "perhaps" or "if." If a composer writes a nonvocal tone poem with a programmatic title, we envision the action, but only after having read the program. The music means only what the composer tells us, *in words*, it means. Play *The Pines of Rome* for an unalerted listener and tell him it's *The Fountains of Rome*, and he'll be none the wiser. Play *La Mer* for the same listener, and say it depicts three times of day, not at sea, but in Paris: Les Halles in the morning, a slaughterhouse at noon, and a dance hall in the evening. Again, he'll be none the wiser.

True, certain vast generalities seem recognizable through music: Love, for example, or Death, or Weather. Yet, the concept of Love as expressed through swooning strings stems from Wagner; before him the convention was more sedate, as with Monteverdi, then Schubert; after Wagner the convention turned coarser, as with Shostakovich's naughty trumpets in *Lady Macbeth of the Mtsensk District* or Ravel's scorching *Boléro*. As for Death, the minor mode did not signify sadness even two centuries ago (witness "God Rest Ye Merry, Gentlemen"), while the major mode in ancient Sparta was banished for its lasciviousness. Only Weather seems inarguably representable in music, and that's through onomatopoeia: a gong stroke *is* thunder, high piano tinkles *are* raindrops.

In music's so-called abstraction lies its power, especially when combined with theater. A slow score can bog down a scene at the racetrack. Fast music might make a courthouse scene seem silly. Music can weaken a strong script, strengthen a weak script. . . . Years ago, a piece of mine called *Eleven Studies for Eleven Players* was choreographed by several companies. It was fun for me, if not especially revealing, to watch lithe bodies doing the obvious—leaping to the lively sections, writhing to the mournful sections. Only when Martha Graham put her hand to the same music did I realize the potential, indeed the need, for the juxtaposition of mediums. In one movement, where the music goes mad with breakneck brasses blasting, she had a male dancer simply stand silent, moving his head ever so slightly. In another movement, where the slow tempo scarcely budges, she had a female dancer gyrate hysterically. Martha's imagination lent a whole new sense to my score, and by extension to her choreography, simply by going against the music.

To state that all music is abstract, all painting representative, and all literature concrete is to state the obvious. Sure, they can be joined, as in song and dance, and thus shift their sense, to some extent. But they are not mutually inclusive. After all, if the arts could express each other, we wouldn't need more than one.

ON DAVID DIAMOND

Many laymen hold the notion that so-called Creative Artists, even famous ones, are all suicidal alcoholic misfits. But for every Rimbaud or Mussorgsky or Pollock, each of whom died young, there are scores of sober artists who are not especially colorful as personalities; their color is saved for their work. Might one argue that artists are the best adjusted of citizens? They know what they want to do, are able to do it, and are appreciated for doing it, without wasting time on eccentricities. Yet one may also argue that they are the only humans who resist generalities.

For example, David Diamond. While being a prolific first-rate composer, he was in many social ways a mess.

He had the saddest eyes I've ever seen. I saw them first in 1944, when I was twenty and David thirty. He was sitting with his friend,

the painter Allela Cornell, while she sketched dollar-portraits of pas-
sersby in Washington Square. I had long heard about him: his morbidity, his profuse gifts, his unapologetic homosexuality, his public
obstreperousness. Now here he was, looking as if the world were at
an end. A few months later, Allela killed herself, leaving to David an
apartment above a garage on Hudson Street. There he lived for the
next seven years, until the Serial Killers took over our musical world,
whereupon he moved to Italy.

During this period I was close to David in a master-pupil arrangement. I worked as his copyist in exchange for lessons in composition
and orchestration. I did score-&-parts of the Third and Fourth
Symphonies, the Second String Quartet, and sundry smaller works,
mostly songs. As his copyist in those precomputer days I was accountable, after the fact, for each note in relation to itself and to the
thousands of surrounding notes. As his student I was accountable,
before the fact, for each sequence of notes that I would pen. David's
years with Nadia Boulanger had shown him acute communication
through both words and music. To this day I recall his every syllable:
he taught me to write *perfect* music. (As to whether that music
could breathe and bleed is beyond anyone's control.) He was my
deepest influence then, both socially and musically.

David dazzled us all with talk of his dear friends like André Gide
and Lana Turner, Maurice Ravel and Greta Garbo. If fact and fantasy
were confounded, the results was nonetheless intriguing.

Like his friends, the texts for his two hundred–odd songs were
diverse, ranging from the Bible and Shakespeare through Shelley and
Joyce, to cummings and—yes—Marilyn Monroe. These songs were
immediate: they "spoke," were diatonic, prosodically immaculate,
and were featured on every American singer's program back in the
days when American singers deigned to perform in their native
tongues. His nonvocal music, including ten string quartets and
eleven symphonies, was highly formal, eighteenth-century in structure, contrapuntal, even fugal. And though he composed no performed operas, he wrote a great deal for the dance, especially Martha
Graham; for six movies, when Hollywood used real composers; and
for the theater, where, nightly for a year, he conducted his own lavish
score to *The Tempest.* Otherwise he earned a living teaching, and as
a violinist in Broadway orchestras.

He was world famous before turning twenty, a favorite of Kous-
sevitzsky, Dimitri Mitropoulos, Munch, and Bernstein. After the
eclipse in the 1950s, he experienced a resurgence on returning from

Europe. He taught for some time at Juilliard, then retired to his native Rochester, where he died in June 2005, four weeks short of his ninetieth birthday.

If David was his own worst enemy (assaulting conductors at rehearsals, getting assaulted by sailors at midnight), he was also gentle and compassionate. In 1945 he was responsible for the publication of my very first songs. Forty-three years later, when my parents died, he sent me these words: "...I can write about death and dying, but find it difficult to talk about. Your words, 'so now they're both gone,' tell me so much of what you have passed through. But what extraordinary human beings they were! I truly feel I respected them more than anyone else, more than my own parents, more than Dimitri...."

By this time the wild life was behind him, as it was behind all of us who survived. The reasoning went: Anyone can dissipate, but only we can write our tunes. And David Diamond's greatest work lay just before him.

He was a swell cook, too, even with his strong death wish. Already at nineteen he wrote a song to a John Clare text that begins:

The world is not my home, I'm only passing through.
My treasures and my hopes are all beyond the sky....

Yet his greatest treasure—the vast catalogue of expert music—remains here on earth forever.

—10 November 2005

Hobart's Brushes
Honor Moore

ON THE WALL NEXT TO the cabinet where the scrapbooks are kept is a photograph of my paternal grandfather and his two brothers, each dressed up, jacket, starched collar, necktie, each reading a book. Though the room is hung topsy-turvy with photographs and paintings, the boys are quiet, concentrated. Two of them sit in straight-back chairs at a round oak table, a third in an armchair in front of a shoulder-high oak shelf crammed with books. It is the 1890s in Chicago; the address is 2922 Michigan Avenue.

The middle brother was named Eddy, and after being widowed, he married his secretary, whose nickname was Pug, and they bred and raced thoroughbred horses. I remember Pug at my grandmother's eightieth, dancing the twist.

The youngest brother was my grandfather Paul, who, in the words of his oldest son, my banker uncle, "never did much work." He died of alcoholism and Lou Gehrig's disease in his eighties, an inscribed photograph of President Eisenhower in his library where the

hinged double-depth shelves held leather-bound rows of Tennyson, Dickens, Browning, and Scott.

The eldest brother, Hobart, died at twenty-three.

Of course I never knew Hobart, but because I share his initials, I inherited his ivory hairbrushes, "HM" carved in swirls across their concave oval surfaces. They are men's hairbrushes, straw-colored bristle sunk into the ivory, and I keep them on my bedside table.

When I got the brushes I was eleven, and all I was told about Hobart was that he was dead. I don't know when I learned that he died of tuberculosis in the famous sanitarium run by Dr. Trudeau at Saranac Lake, but recently I found out he married barely a year before his death: "She knew he was dying, but they were in love." Her name was Ruth Emmons and later she married again.

The scrapbooks are kept at the place in the Adirondacks where my family goes summers; it's inaccessible during the winter. Last August, hours passing, I paged through the large, heavy books, allowing my eye to move across black-and-white photographs, letters, clippings, telegrams, greeting cards that brought back color, voices, heat, even smell.

I inherited the hairbrushes when my great-grandmother, Hobart's mother, died at ninety-six. I felt privileged to have them. For a while, I also had Hobart's desk, but in the flotsam of moves, it came to belong to one of my sisters. I knew what to do with the desk, but I felt confused by the brushes. My hair was so thick I couldn't use them and also the HM belonged not to me but to a dead man about whom no one ever spoke. Who was Hobart? I didn't care. I wanted jewelry. I wanted a carpet. I wanted beauty. Once I let a Popsicle melt on one of the brushes, and the ivory absorbed the color of cherry. I stored them for seven years in that condition, and when I retrieved them bleached away the cherry stain with Clorox.

The cabinet was built specially. My mother began collecting and pasting in 1944; the original leather bindings had initials and dates, but in the late 1960s when the leather began to disintegrate, my mother rebound the books in navy blue buckram, doing away with initials and dates, making do with years: 1947, 1951. There are references to the scrapbooks in letters my parents wrote during their first year of marriage: "Quigg's letter is scrapbook material, don't you think?" After my mother died in 1973, my father kept up the project, but only fitfully. After he died, several more cartons were shipped. In one of them was an old scrapbook kept by his grandmother, my great-grandmother and Hobart's mother, which chronicles the life she had with her husband and sons, a past I had previously seen only in the photograph of the three boys that hangs on the wall next to the scrapbook cabinet.

When I begin looking, the zoom sticks on the digital camera I've brought to photograph, and so at first I default to written description: starched collar, necktie, each reading a book. . . . But then I remember my laptop has a camera in it. I press the button that says "Capture."

And I am outside, across the street. Michigan Avenue! I pull in close and even though there's no color, it's like seeing. An enormous three-story row house that looks to be brownstone, columns at the entrance, two large trees out front, ivy crawling up the facade.

Inside, my great-grandmother sits in the corner of a large Victorian sofa, her left hand holding a white handkerchief, that arm extended along the top of the sofa, her right hand in her lap. She is wearing white, or what looks white in the photograph. Her face and head do not match in any way the flounced glamor of the dress, the cinching of her trim and youthful waist. Her dark hair is gathered on top of her head, and she wears wire-rimmed glasses. Her neck seems oddly nonexistent, her head too small for her body.

And yet I see the generous intelligence and warm curiosity my father so adored. When she was widowed in 1923 at the age of sixty-five, Adelia, called Ada, came into her own, traveling around the world on a leased yacht called *Alacrity*, another time flying in two small planes, the second one for her luggage. In a photograph taken in Egypt, she sits on a camel, her entourage also mounted on camels, a crowd of bedouins gathered around them on foot, beyond them the pyramids rising. Men of her generation—gentlemen looters—brought home artifacts from distant places but my great-grandmother put up money to build a museum at Corinth. When I knew her, she was in her nineties, fragile and transparent as a doll. There she is on the window seat in the living room of the huge white house where they spent summers north of Boston, her smile beckoning as she reaches for a great-grandchild fifty years after the awkward sofa in Chicago.

Pulling back from the close-up into another photograph, I see the sofa was in a parlor: enormously high ceilings, that same sofa, elaborate Victorian lamps with shades of milk glass, a brass chandelier with seven gas lights englobed with etched glass. In the corner is the mahogany rocker my father shattered, falling across it in a hallucinatory leap from his deathbed. But now my great-grandmother moves to another chair and her husband, my great-grandfather, sits in a chair next to her. She has a book in her lap.

Turn and face the fireplace, dark marble, a mirrored, enclosed mantel, oval-framed photographs.

Of whom I can't make out.

They left this house for New York in 1903 when Illinois tax law became disadvantageous to my great-grandfather's business. He leased a train and moved his entire office and household, work uninterrupted, ticker tape running, stenographers typing. In New York, still in partnership with his brother, another Hobart who remained in Chicago, he bought and sold companies. Is 2922 Michigan Avenue still there? If not, what replaced that tree-lined row of ornate, almost garish houses?

A vitrine with three shelves, the small landscape above it in a wide gilt frame, a bouquet of peonies flopping from a thick crystal bowl.

The music room, its curved bay window, the indentation forming a hollow large enough for a fortepiano with sheet music on it, an upholstered piano bench whose ends flip up like the roof of a pagoda. On the floor there's a bear rug, the animal's face turned to the music. Polar or grizzly? Hard to tell which, but when Great-Grandfather was a young man, he lived in the West.

134

I am most taken by a photograph in which one of the brothers turns as if to climb the stairs. His hair is carefully combed and he wears a suit, his hand posed on the banister, the angle of his climbing leg almost mimicking the slant of the second flight of carpeted stairs as it switches back and heads up. Let's say it's Hobart, heading already into the mysteries of wildness with which I associate his final illness. Along the narrow dirt road, the trees on either side arching over like the ceiling of a cathedral so what's ahead looks like a tunnel. I haven't been here before, the mountain darkness frightening and thrilling, the train shuddering and thundering to a halt especially to let us off, a man who knew us waving a red lamp in the cold night air.

But here in the attic of the house where Hobart spent his childhood—the safe oak-paneled house on Michigan Avenue—the third-floor eaves make a slanting ceiling, a brass double desk lamp with milk-glass shades illuminates the round oak table, a fenestrated bookshelf extends the entire length of a wall. Books. Books. Books. And above the shelf framed photographs hang on a bare wall in careful groups.

My computer sequences the pictures so that a photograph of a slightly older Hobart interrupts the Michigan Avenue interiors. He wears a jaunty cap and grins into the camera. Get into the boat! he seems to say. So alive! You can see why Ruth Emmons married him.

The death of Hobart introduced his brothers to sadness and loss. In a photograph from a later scrapbook, my grandfather is about forty, his face seems stern, even forbidding, but as I keep looking, I see his eyes are sad beyond measure—by which I mean his gaze fixes me and teaches me more about him than I remember knowing while he was alive. For sixteen years, we were alive at the same time, and so I say that I knew him. But I remember no conversation. He never went outside, and that worried me. He just sat in the library all day, a bourbon in his hand. The sound was ice clinking against glass.

Tell me about Hobart.

He had tuberculosis.

I know that. But what else?

He fell in love and she knew he was dying but they married anyway. Her name was Ruth and she married again a few years after he died.

Was Hobart the star of the family? A lost light?

Eddy was his mother's favorite, I think. He made her laugh.

Hobart takes walks at Dr. Trudeau's and boats on Saranac Lake, which is the body of water you see behind him in the lively photograph. In another, dressed nattily in his cap, tweed jacket, and striped tie, he stands with three buddies. The trees are tall white pines and the sky is nearly white.

Then I see a photograph that shocks me. Thirteen women and men, all of whom seem to be in their twenties, bundled up, posing in a glassed-in room. Caught in the staring gaze of a honey-haired woman wearing an enormous hat, it comes to me that this is the sunroom at the sanitarium and that these striking young people are all dying. They wear fur coats and look solemn, despondent, theatrical. Is that dark-haired young man crushed in the posing group my great-uncle? Is that look on his face a smile of protest, of irony, or the simple discomfort of being photographed?

The black and white, the shadows, the beautiful faces of the unidentified dead. Did Ruth, Hobart's fiancée, visit him at Saranac, wave at him through the glass? She could not have been with him when he died, but I picture her there nonetheless, wearing white, her hand resting on his hand, his so pale it's almost transparent.

When my grandfather grew up, sportsmen traveled to the Adirondacks to shoot. Deer and birds. And to fish for trout and quananiche, a fish that was obsolete by the time we inherited the guest book, its pages ruled with columns headed Brook Trout. Lake Trout. Quananiche. Deer. Pheasant. When you sign, you enter the number you've caught or shot of each. Our place, which is a hunting and fishing camp my grandfather eventually bought with five friends, was near the hospital at Saranac Lake where his brother died. No one ever considered a connection. Eighty years ago the trip from one to the other must have taken the better part of a day, but now you drive from one to the other in forty-five minutes.

In a black tin document box among the scrapbooks is an algebra paper of Hobart's. "Excellent," the teacher wrote. Also in the black tin box are letters of condolence from Yale classmates and fraternity

brothers, in packets tied with string. I think Hobart will jump toward me from where he sits on the dock or step out of the crowd in the glass room. He's going to make me laugh.

When my great-grandmother was an older widow, she gave her collection of Chinese paintings to Yale in Hobart's name, and in the name of Eddy, who also died young. By now the collection has been in the Yale museum for more than fifty years. I have never seen it, but when my father died, I inherited *A Study of Chinese Paintings in the Collection of Ada Small Moore* by Louise Wallace Hackney and Yau Chang-Foo, a massive illustrated volume. My father had inherited his grandmother's collection of Babylonian cylinder seals— carved cylinders the size of a bullet, a cigarette, a lipstick, carved from jade, obsidian, quartz—that you roll across wax like a rolling pin. An impression of what is carved on the cylinder appears on the wax—an Assyrian battle, for instance, horses and warriors in profile and in step. The longer your strip of wax, the longer the procession of warriors, the rotations multiplying numbers and also duration and therefore time.

The collection was sold, broken up, and my father took the income while he was alive and after he died left the proceeds to Yale. The Metropolitan Museum, to which he had lent it for decades, was chagrined.

You collect and collect, the objects animated first by your desire, then after your death by love of you or the respect someone has for your memory. Keeping what you leave is a way to keep you. But eventually the desire or love or respect for memory is diluted by the force of the present. Wherever they are now, those cylinder seals no longer bring to mind the woman in a flounced dress sitting with her husband, founder of a fortune now also dispersed, on a settee in Chicago, the woman who chartered a yacht called *Alacrity* or flew around the world in two small planes with her old school friend Miss Enders, and paid for the museum at Corinth.

For decades the ivory brushes remained intact, but sometime during the years after I bleached away the Popsicle stain, I dropped one and broke off a piece of its edge. It makes me sad to look at it. Lost and broken things. The rocking chair my father shattered, all that's left of that Chicago parlor. The necklace from India of spiky gold beads dotted with rubies, the jewelry I inherited from that great-grandmother stolen when I was eighteen, in an airport. Why didn't my mother lock it up? Is there no end to what pulls us under? Everything we leave behind losing meaning as time moves forward, its dinosaur tail thrashing behind it, careless, nonverbal, unseeing?

The Thing About Life Is That One Day You'll Be Dead
David Shields

DYING JUST A LITTLE

WHEREAS BOYS WANT to be superheroes who dominate the world, anorexic girls retreat from the world and sexuality. Adolescent boys are trying to become strong and aggressive, but anorexic girls are trying to become weak and fragile. Anorexia, the feminine flip side to masculine violence and heroic fantasy, comes directly from pubescent peer pressure. Teenage girls develop anorexia in specific response to sex changes. Girls become anorexic because they're trying to meet a cultural ideal of extreme thinness and/or desexualize themselves. They don't want to develop hips and breasts, and they're afraid of their bodies getting fat. The anorexic girl—wasted, tired, not menstruating, her secondary sexual characteristics slowed by poor nutrition—thus delays her entry into adulthood.

A superstition among "primitive" peoples: if a woman touches a cadaver, she'll stop menstruating.

Ninety percent of anorexics are female. Seventy percent of women say that looking at models in fashion magazines causes them to feel depressed, guilty, and shameful. Ninety-five percent of people who enroll in formal weight-reduction programs are women. Ninety-eight percent of women gain back the weight they lose by dieting. Women regard themselves as fat if they're fifteen pounds overweight; men don't think of themselves as fat unless they're thirty-five pounds above the national average. Eighty percent of people who have part of their small intestines removed in order to help themselves lose weight are women. Fifty-five percent of adolescent girls believe they're overweight; only thirteen percent of adolescent girls are actually overweight. Anorexia has the highest fatality rate of any psychiatric illness. Eleven percent of Americans would abort a fetus if they were told it had a tendency toward obesity. When asked to identify good-looking individuals, five-year-olds select pictures of thin people. Elementary school children have more negative attitudes toward the obese than toward bullies, the handicapped, or children of another race. Teachers routinely underestimate the intelligence of the obese and overestimate the intelligence of the slender. Obese students are less likely to be granted scholarships. Anorexics often grow lanugo, which is soft, woolly body hair that grows to compensate for the loss of fat cells so the body can hold in heat. Anorexics have many of the physical symptoms of starvation: their bellies are distended, their hair is dull and brittle, their periods stop, they're weak, and they're vulnerable to infections. They also have the psychological characteristics of the starving: they're depressed, irritable, pessimistic, apathetic, and preoccupied with food. They dream of feasts.

"I've heard about that illness anorexia nervosa and I keep looking around for someone who has it. I want to go sit next to her. I think to myself, Maybe I'll catch it."

"One of my cousins used to throw food under the table when no one was looking. Finally, she got so thin they had to take her to the hospital. I always admired her."

"I'm embarrassed to have bulimia. It's such a preppy disease."

"I don't care how long it takes. One day I'm going to get my body to obey me. I'm going to make it lean and tight and hard. I'll succeed in this, even if it kills me."

"To have control over your body becomes an extreme accomplishment. You make of your body your very own kingdom where you are the tyrant, the absolute dictator."

"Look, see how thin I am, even thinner than you wanted me to be. You can't make me eat more. I am in control of my fate, even if my fate is starving."

"I get lots of compliments. My friends are jealous, but I've made new friends. Guys who never considered me before have been asking me out."

"I hate to say this, but I'd rather binge than make out."

"In all the years I've been a therapist, I've yet to meet one girl who likes her body."

I'm in my midtwenties. Before taking off her clothes, she says she needs to tell me something: she has herpes. Madly in love with her witchy bitchiness, I find occasional enforced celibacy insanely erotic, the way a chastity belt glamorizes what it locks out. We wind up living together, and as we fall out of love with each other, her herpes becomes a debate point between us. She suggests that we just get married and then if I get it, I get it, and who cares? I suggest she at least explore some of the possibilities of which modern medicine avails us.

For a multitude of reasons, the two of us didn't belong together, but what interests me now is what, for lack of a better term, a free-floating signifier the virus was. When I was in love with her, it eroticized her. When I wasn't, it repelled me. The body has no meanings. We bring meanings to it.

As psychologist Nancy Etcoff says in *Survival of the Prettiest*, "In a context where only a king can control enough food resources and labor supply to eat enough and do no physical labor so that he becomes fat, prestige is conferred by signs of abundance. A thin person is a person too poor to afford the calories, and maybe one who does so much physical labor that she cannot keep weight on. When poor women are fat (because junk food is so cheap and available, and they are less educated about its hazards and unable to afford expensive healthy foods), then it's in to be thin and dietary restraint and physical exercise become prestigious."

"I can't stand fat women," a thin woman says. "If one of them has been sitting on a chair in a coffee shop, or on the bus, and there's no other place to sit, I won't go in there or sit in that place."

"It's like watching a death's head," another woman says about a fat woman at the market. "The co-op ought to pay her to get out of here. Who can go home to a good dinner with that in mind?"

Laurie and I stage monthly dieting competitions. Neither of us is overweight; neither of us is stunningly thin. "Want a second helping?" "I made some banana bread for you." What's going on here? We're each saying: you're beautiful; I, though, am wanting; I will do anything for love.

Fasting frees one from carnal needs and desires, prepares one for visions and trances. Moses fasted forty days before receiving the Ten Commandments. Jesus fasted forty days before his enlightenment. Medieval saints (mostly women) fasted to demonstrate their purity

141

and holiness, and if their fasting appeared to continue far beyond normal human bounds, it was proof of God's grace. By controlling their breathing, nuns in ancient times were able to stop menstruating and limit their need for food.

Fasting is a constant for the female saints. In the thirteenth century, Margaret of Cortona said, "I want to die of starvation to satiate the poor." Thérèse of Lisieux died of tuberculosis in 1897, just short of her twenty-fifth birthday. As she lay dying, bleeding from her intestines and unable to keep down water, she was tormented by the thought of banquets. Gemma Galgani died in 1903—also of TB, at twenty-five. She dreamed of food. Would it be all right, she asked her confessor, to ask Jesus to take away her sense of taste? Permission was granted. She arranged with Jesus that she should begin to expiate, through her own suffering, all the sins committed by priests. For the next sixty days she vomited whenever she tried to eat.

In 1859, an American doctor, William Stout Chipley, published an article describing a condition he called "sitophobia," fear of food. In 1868, William Withey Gull, an English physician, first mentioned anorexia nervosa; in 1873, he delivered a lecture on the disorder. The same year, a French doctor, Charles-Ernest Lasègue, published a long article on what he called "hysterical anorexia." Lasègue described the following symptoms: menstruation ceases, thirst increases, the abdomen retracts and loses elasticity, constipation becomes obstinate, the skin is pale and dry, the pulse is quickened, the patient tires easily, and when she rises from resting often experiences vertigo—all of which are still associated with anorexia.

In the late nineteenth century, a tepid appetite was proof of a woman's delicacy and elegance. A young lady who admitted to a hearty appetite would be said to "eat like a ploughboy" and would be the object of sneers and jests. Victorian women, even when they became mothers, were admonished never to demonstrate their hunger. If they did confess to hunger, they were expected to yearn only for light, sweet, delicate morsels and not for meat, which was thought to stimulate sexual desire. For a woman to enjoy a slab of roast beef was to suggest a baser nature that she was not supposed to acknowledge in herself.

In 2004, Hilary Mantel wrote, "Why do women still feel so hounded? The ideal body seems now attainable only by plastic surgery. The ideal woman has the earning powers of a chief executive, breasts like an inflatable doll, no hips at all, and the tidy, hairless labia of an unviolated six-year-old. The world gets harder and harder. There's no pleasing it. No wonder some girls want out. Anorexia itself seems like mad behavior, but I don't think it is madness. It is a way of shrinking back, of reserving, preserving the self, fighting free of sexual and emotional entanglements. It says, like Christ, *noli me tangere*. Touch me not and take yourself off. For a year or two, it may be a valid strategy; to be greensick, to be out of the game; to die just a little; to nourish the inner being while starving the outer being; to buy time. Most anorexics do recover, after all. Anorexia can be an accommodation, a strategy for survival."

In *Cymbeline*, Imogen apparently dies when she's about fifteen. Her brothers, Guiderius and Arviragus, stand over her grave and chant a dirge over what they think is her lifeless body inside her coffin: "Golden lads and girls all must / As chimney-sweepers, come to dust." Then Imogen opens her eyes and comes back to life.

DECLINE AND FALL (I)

If you could live forever in good health at a particular age, what age would you be? As people get older, their ideal age gets higher. For eighteen- to twenty-four-year-olds, it's age twenty-seven; for twenty-five- to twenty-nine-year-olds, it's thirty-one; for thirty- to thirty-nine-year-olds, it's thirty-seven; for forty- to forty-nine-year-olds, it's forty; for fifty- to sixty-four-year-olds, it's forty-four; and for people over sixty-four, it's fifty-nine.

Your IQ is highest between ages eighteen and twenty-five. Once your brain peaks in size—at age twenty-five—it starts shrinking, losing weight, and filling with fluid. In a letter to his father, Carlyle wrote that his brother, Jack, "decides, as a worthy fellow of twenty always will decide, that mere external rank and convenience are nothing; the dignity of mind is all in all. I argue, as every reasonable man of twenty-eight, that this is poetry in part, which a few years will mix pretty largely with prose." Goethe said, "Whoever is not famous at twenty-eight must give up any dreams of glory."

When I was thirty-one, I was informed that someone had written, in a stall in a women's bathroom in a bookstore, "David Shields is a great writer and a babe to boot." This was pretty much the high point of my life, when my acne was long gone and I still had hair and was thin without dieting and could still wear contacts and thought I was going to become famous; it's all been downhill since. Sir William

Osler said, "The effective, moving, vitalizing work of the world is done between the ages of twenty-five and forty," which is in fact true: creativity peaks in the thirties, then declines rapidly; most creative achievements occur when people are in their thirties. Degas said, "Everyone has talent at twenty-five; the difficulty is to have it at fifty." The consolation of the library: when you're forty-five, your vocabulary is three times as large as it is at twenty. When you're sixty, your brain possesses four times the information that it does at twenty.

Your strength and coordination peak at nineteen. Your body is the most flexible until age twenty; after that, joint function steadily declines. World-class sprinters are almost always in their late teens or early twenties. Your stamina peaks in your late twenties or early thirties; marathon records are invariably held by twenty-five to thirty-five-year-olds.

When you're young, your lungs have a huge reserve capacity; even world-class athletes rarely push their lungs to the limit. But as you age, your lungs get less elastic: you can't fill them as full or empty them as completely of stale air. Aerobic capacity decreases one percent per year between ages twenty and sixty.

"It isn't sex that causes trouble for young ballplayers," Casey Stengel said. "It's staying up all night looking for it."

Benjamin Franklin said, "At twenty years of age, the will reigns; at thirty, the wit; and at forty, the judgment."

Arteriosclerosis can begin as early as age twenty.

As you age, your responses to stimuli of all kinds become slower and more inaccurate, especially in more complex tasks. From ages twenty to sixty, your reaction time to noise slows twenty percent. At sixty, you make more errors in verbal learning tasks. People age seventy show a decline in their ability to detect small changes, such as the movement of a clock hand.

Given a list of twenty-four words, an average twenty-year-old remembers fourteen of the words, a forty-year-old remembers eleven, a sixty-year-old remembers nine, and a seventy-year-old remembers seven.

Most people reach skeletal maturity by their early twenties. At thirty, you reach peak bone mass. Your bones are as dense and strong as they'll ever be. Human bones, with their astonishing blend of strength and flexibility, can withstand pressure of about twenty-four thousand pounds per square inch—four times that of reinforced concrete—but if you removed the mineral deposits, what you would have left would be flexible enough to tie into knots. In your late thirties, you start losing more bone than you make. At first you lose bone slowly, one percent a year. The older you get, the more you lose.

Beginning in your early twenties, your ability to detect salty or bitter things decreases, as does your ability to identify odors. The amount of ptyalin, an enzyme used to digest starches, in your saliva decreases after age twenty. After age thirty, your digestive tract displays a decrease in the amount of digestive juices. At twenty, in other words, your fluids are fleeing, and by thirty, you're drying up.

Lauren Bacall said, "When a woman reaches twenty-six in America, she's on the slide. It's downhill all the way from then on. It doesn't give you a tremendous feeling of confidence and well-being."

Jimi Hendrix died at age twenty-seven, as did Janis Joplin, Jim Morrison, Kurt Cobain, and bluesman Robert Johnson.

Until you're thirty, your grip strength increases; after forty, it declines precipitously. After age sixty-five, your lower arm and back muscle strength declines. Due to reduced coordination rather than loss of strength, your power output—e.g., your ability to turn a crank over a period of time—falls after age fifty.

At age thirty, men's enthusiasm declines for typically masculine activities such as sports, drinking, and car repairs.

Nicholas Murray Butler said, "Many people's tombstones should read, 'Died at thirty. Buried at sixty.'" The ancient Persians believed that the first thirty years should be spent living life and the last forty years should be spent understanding it. Reversing the time periods, Schopenhauer said, "The first forty years of life furnish the text, while the remaining thirty provide the commentary."

Since your vertebral column continues to grow until you're thirty, you might gain anywhere from three to five millimeters in height between ages twenty and thirty. Starting at thirty, though, you lose one-sixteenth of an inch in height per year. As you age, you lose body water, your organs shrink, and you lose weight. Your body consumes twelve fewer calories per day for each year of age over thirty.

For most people, the ability to hear higher sound frequencies begins to decline in their thirties; men are three and a half times more likely than women to show a decline in their ability to hear high notes. Whatever level of loss is found, it will get, on average, two and a half times worse each decade. The sweat glands that keep the auditory canal moist die off one by one, ear wax becomes drier and crustier, and hard wax builds up to block out sounds. One-third of hearing loss in older people is due to this buildup. Your eardrum becomes thinner and more flaccid, causing the drum to be less easily vibrated by sound waves. You progressively lose your ability to hear sound at all frequencies.

The limbic system—"the seat of emotions"—exists in a part of the brain, the hippocampus, that humans share with lizards. (Your brain has three layers: the brain stem, controlling basic functions and basic emotions, is the reptilian layer; the mammalian layer houses more complex mental functions such as learning and adaptability; and the third layer constitutes most of the human brain—the cerebral cortex and cerebellum, which allow us to use language and perform complex acts of memory.) Beginning at age thirty, parts of the hippocampus die off.

Emerson said, "After thirty, a man wakes up sad every morning, excepting perhaps five or six, until the day of his death."

At thirty-one, Tolstoy said, "At our age, when you have reached, not merely by the process of thought but with your whole being and your whole life, an awareness of the uselessness and impossibility of seeking enjoyment; when you feel that what seemed like torture has become the only substance of life—work and toil—then searchings, anguish, dissatisfaction with yourself, remorse, etc.—the attributes of youth—are inappropriate and useless."

Before being guillotined, Camille Desmoulins, one of the leaders of the French Revolution, when asked how old he was (he was thirty-four), said, "I am thirty-three—the age of the good sansculotte Jesus, an age fatal to revolutionists."

At age thirty-five, everyone shows signs of aging: gray hair, wrinkles, less strength, less speed, stiffening in the walls of the major arteries, degeneration of heart and blood vessels, diminished blood supply to the brain, elevated blood pressure. One out of three Americans has high blood pressure. The maximum rate your heart can attain is your age subtracted from 220 and therefore falls by one beat every year. Your heart is continually becoming a less efficient pumping machine.

Rheumatoid arthritis most frequently begins between ages thirty-five and fifty-five.

In 1907, the French writer Paul Léautaud, at thirty-five, said, "I was asked the other day, 'What are you doing nowadays?' 'I'm busy growing older,' I answered."

In *My Dinner with Andre,* Wallace Shawn says, "I grew up on the Upper East Side, and when I was ten years old I was rich, an aristocrat, riding around in taxis, surrounded by comfort, and all I thought about was art and music. Now I'm thirty-six, and all I think about is money."

Mozart died at thirty-five; Byron, at thirty-six; Raphael and Van Gogh, at thirty-seven.

James Boswell, Samuel Johnson's biographer, said, "I must fairly acknowledge that in my opinion the disagreement between young men and old is owing rather to the fault of the latter than of the former. Young men, though keen and impetuous, are usually very well disposed to receive the counsels of the old, if they are treated with gentleness, but old men forget in a wonderful degree their own feelings in the early part of life." When Boswell wrote this, he was thirty-seven and Samuel Johnson was sixty-nine.

London Symphony Orchestra conductor Colin Davis said, at thirty-eight, "I think that to so many what happens is the death of ambition in the conventional sense. That great driving motor that prods you and exasperates you and brings out the worst qualities in you for about twenty years is beginning to be a bit moth-eaten and tired. I find that I'm altogether much quieter, I think. I don't love music any less, but there's not the excess of energy I used to spend in enthusiasm and in intoxication. I feel much freer than I've ever been in my life."

The oldest person ever to hold a boxing title was thirty-eight. The oldest person ever to play in the NBA was forty-three. The oldest age at which anyone broke a track-and-field record was forty-one, in 1909. The oldest person to win an Olympic gold medal was forty-two, in 1920. In the prologue to *The Canterbury Tales,* Chaucer wrote, "If gold ruste, what shal iren do?"

At age forty, your preference for fast-paced activity declines.

Beginning at age forty, your white blood cells, which fight cancer and infectious diseases, have a lowered capacity.

Jack London died at forty; Elvis Presley, at forty-two.

F. Scott Fitzgerald wrote in his notebook, "Drunk at twenty, wrecked at thirty, dead at forty." He died at forty-four.

Each year, more fat gets deposited in the walls of medium and larger arteries, causing the arterial walls to narrow. The weight of your small intestine decreases; the volume and weight of your kidneys shrink. Total blood flow to the kidneys decreases by ten percent for every decade after the age of forty. Every organ will eventually get less nourishment than it needs to do its job.

Don Marquis, an American newspaper columnist who died at fifty-nine, said, "Forty and forty-five are bad enough; fifty is simply hell to face; fifteen minutes after that you are sixty; and then in ten minutes more you are eighty-five."

"Forty-five," said Joseph Conrad, "is the age of recklessness for many men, as if in defiance of the decay and death waiting with open arms in the sinister valley at the bottom of the inevitable hill." Those clichés of male midlife crisis—having an affair, for instance, or buying a red sports car—are, on a biological level, anyway, profound rebellions of the "rage, rage, against the dying of the light" sort.

Cicero said, "Old age begins at forty-six." He died at fifty-three.

John Kennedy died at forty-six.

Virginia Woolf said, "Control of life is what one should learn now: its economic management. I feel cautious, like a poor person, now I am forty-six."

Victor Hugo said, "Forty is the old age of youth. Fifty is the youth of old age."

DECLINE AND FALL (II)

Samuel Johnson wrote to a younger friend, "When I was as you are now, towering in the confidence of twenty-one, little did I suspect that I should be at forty-nine what I am now."

At age fifty, your ability to perceive vibrations in the lower part of your body is significantly decreased. The nerves that conduct information signals to the brain are also diminished. Every decade after age fifty, your brain loses two percent of its weight. You have difficulty learning things and you remember less and less.

"At fifty, everyone has the face that he deserves," said George Orwell, who died at forty-six.

Virgil, author of *The Aeneid,* died at fifty.

Evelyn Waugh said, "Old people are more interesting than young. One of the particular points of interest is to observe how after fifty

148

they revert to the habits, mannerisms, and opinions of their parents, however wild they were in youth."

As you age, your eye lens clouds over (cataract). The cells of the optic nerve can be damaged by glaucoma or macular degeneration. Forty-two percent of people age fifty-two to sixty-four, seventy-three percent of people sixty-five to seventy-four, and ninety-two percent of people over seventy-five need reading glasses.

Shakespeare died at fifty-two.

John Wayne said, "I'm fifty-three years old and six feet four inches. I've had three wives, five children, and three grandchildren. I love good whiskey. I still don't understand women, and I don't think there is any man who does."

You gain weight until age fifty-five, at which point you begin to shed weight (specifically, lean tissue, muscle mass, water, and bone). More fat now accumulates in your thighs and less in your abdomen. Your extremities become thinner and your trunk thicker. Middle-aged spread isn't the result of increased fatty tissue; it's caused by losing muscle tone.

Dante died at fifty-six.

Between fifty and sixty, your visual memory declines slightly; after seventy, it declines substantially.

Noel Coward, advising a middle-aged friend to stop dieting, said, "This is a foolish vanity. Youth is no longer essential or even becoming. Rapidly approaching fifty-seven, I find health and happiness more important than lissomeness. To be fat is bad and slovenly, unless it is beyond your control, but however slim you get you will still be the age you are and no one will be fooled, so banish this nonsense once and for all. Conserve your vitality by eating enough and enjoying it."

"The years between fifty and fifty-seven are the hardest," said T. S. Eliot. "You are being asked to do things, and yet you are not decrepit enough to turn them down."

In late middle age, the skin in your hands becomes less sensitive to touch. Your skin cells regenerate less often. The skin weakens and dries, the number of sebaceous glands declines dramatically, and all of the tissues of the skin undergo some change: you get wrinkles and gray hair. Wrinkles don't come from age, though. They come from sunlight, which slowly maims the face, causing wrinkles, mottling, and loose skin. Although the skin loses elasticity and heals wounds more slowly with advancing age, it never completely wears out.

At fifty-nine, Neil Young said, "When you're in your twenties, you and your world are the biggest thing, and everything revolves around what you're doing. Now I realize I'm a leaf floating along on the water on top of some river."

Your enzymes are now less able to adapt to changes they encounter in the proteins on which they act. Blood cholesterol rises until age sixty, then falls. The ability of the blood to maintain a normal level of glucose declines with age. At sixty, you've lost twenty-five percent of the volume you normally secrete for food; it becomes more difficult to digest heavy meats.

When you're sixty, you're twenty percent less strong than you were in middle age; at seventy, you're forty percent less strong. You lose more strength in the muscles of your legs than in your hands and arms. You also tend to lose your fast-twitch abilities (rapidly accelerating, powerful contractions) much more rapidly than your slow-twitch abilities (contractions over a long period of time).

Emerson said, "'Tis strange that it is not in vogue to commit hara-kiri, as the Japanese do at sixty. Nature is so insulting in her hints and notices, does not pull you by the sleeve, but pulls out your teeth, tears off your hair in patches, steals your eyesight, twists your face into an ugly mask, in short, puts all contumelies upon you, without in the least abating your zeal to make a good appearance, and all this at the same time that she is moulding the new figures around you into wonderful beauty which of course is only making your plight worse."

The year he died, Zola said, at sixty-two, "I am spending delightful afternoons in my garden, watching everything living around me. As I grow older, I feel everything departing, and I love everything with more passion."

The PR flak Harlan Boll defends his lying about his celebrity clients' ages by saying, "The American public doesn't really forgive people for getting older." Which is of course true. Jackie Kennedy said if she knew she was going to get cancer at sixty-five, she wouldn't have done all those sit-ups. In jail, O. J. Simpson bemoaned to his girlfriend that the once admirable, apple-like shape of his posterior had collapsed into middle-aged decrepitude. Gravity sucks.

By the time you reach sixty-five, you've lost thirty to forty percent of your aerobic power. The wall of your heart thickens, and you're more likely to develop coronary disease. Sixty percent of sixty-year-old men, and the same percentage of eighty-year-old women, have a major narrowing in at least one coronary artery. A stiffening in the walls of the major arteries results in a progressive increase in blood pressure, which imposes an increasing load on the heart. Since the heart has to work harder for each heartbeat and use more energy, the overall efficiency of the cardiovascular system drops significantly. One and a half million Americans suffer a myocardial infarction each year. Seventy percent of heart attacks occur at home. If you survive a heart attack, you're virtually guaranteed to die eventually of a heart-related illness.

At sixty-five, you've lost one ounce of your three-pound brain and one-tenth of your brain cells. The motor area of the frontal cortex loses fifty percent of its neurons, as does the visual area in the back and the physical sensory part on the sides. The gyri—the twisting, raised convolutions in the cortex within which you do much of your thinking—suffer the greatest atrophy. The brain of a ninety-year-old is the same size as that of a three-year-old.

Joints age due to deterioration in cartilage, tendons, and fluid. The fluid in joints that contain liquid begins to thin. More friction is created. Nearly everyone age sixty-five or older shows some abnormality of the joints; one out of two people has moderate to severe abnormality. One-third of American women over sixty-five have collapsed vertebrae as a result of bone thinning or osteoporosis. The more bone you have as an adult, the less likely you are to develop osteoporosis.

When you're a young adult, the reflex that tells you it's time to urinate occurs when your bladder is half full. For people over age sixty-five, the message isn't received until your bladder is nearly full.

Five percent of the U.S. population live in a nursing home. There are now more people in the U.S. over sixty-five than ever before. Only thirty percent of people ages seventy-five to eighty-four report disabilities—the lowest percentage ever reported.

Five to eight percent of people over sixty-five have dementia; half of people in their eighties have it. One of many dementias and the most common, Alzheimer's affects one in ten Americans over sixty-five, one in two people over eighty-five. Alzheimer's patients are more likely to have had a low-stress (i.e., mentally unstimulating) job. The great majority of Alzheimer's patients die of an infection.

According to Noel Coward, "The pleasures that once were heaven / look silly at sixty-seven."

At sixty-eight, Edmund Wilson said, "The knowledge that death is not so far away, that my mind and emotions and vitality will soon disappear like a puff of smoke, has the effect of making earthly affairs seem unimportant and human beings more and more ignoble. It is harder to take human life seriously, including one's own efforts and achievements and passions."

"Tomorrow I shall be sixty-nine," William Dean Howells wrote to Mark Twain, "but I do not seem to care. I did not start the affair, and I have not been consulted about it at any step. I was born to be afraid of dying, but not of getting old. Age has many advantages, and if old men were not so ridiculous, I should not mind being one. But they are ridiculous, and they are ugly. The young do not see this so clearly as we do, but some day they will."

Thomas Pynchon says, "When we speak of 'seriousness' in fiction, ultimately we are talking about an attitude toward death—how characters may act in its presence, for example, or how they handle it when it isn't so immediate. Everybody knows this, but the subject is hardly ever brought up with younger writers, possibly because given to anyone at the apprentice age, such advice is widely felt to be effort wasted."

Recently, a late-middle-aged and strikingly buff man in a black skintight unisuit ran down my block. A school bus of middle-school girls rounded the corner. He puffed out his chest, let out his kick, put himself on display. Rather than ooh or aah or whistle or applaud or ignore him, several girls stuck their heads out the windows in the back of the bus and did the cruelest thing possible: they laughed.

"You're only young," AC/DC sing on *Back in Black*, "but you're gonna die."

In your late sixties, you eat less. Your metabolic rate decreases slightly. Men lose three percent of their skeletal weight per decade; women lose eight percent. Throughout adult life, men lose about fifteen percent of their total mineral density; women, thirty percent. The diameter of your forearm shrinks, as does the diameter of your calves.

The density of your skin's blood-circulating systems—veins, capillaries, arterioles—is reduced, which is why old people feel cold sooner. As you age, your facial skin temperature falls. For older people, a comfortable temperature is ten to fifteen degrees higher than it is for a younger person.

Each day of your adult life, you lose thirty thousand to fifty thousand nerves and one hundred thousand nerve cells. Over time, your heart, lungs, and prostate enlarge. The level of potassium in your body declines. After age seventy, your ability to absorb calcium is dramatically reduced.

Tolstoy wrote to his wife, Sonia, who was sixteen years younger than he was, "The main thing is that just as the Hindus, when they are getting on toward sixty, retire to the forests, and every religious man wants to dedicate the last years of his life to God and not to jokes, puns, gossip, and tennis, so I, who am entering my seventieth year, long with all my heart and soul for this tranquility and solitude." He died at eighty-two when he collapsed in a train station, in flight from Sonia, with whom he'd been quarreling.

At age seventy, the mass of your corneal lens is three times larger than it was when you were twenty, which causes you to be more farsighted; after age seventy, you become more nearsighted. The lens becomes thicker and heavier with age, reducing your ability to focus on close-up objects. As you get older, the corneal hue takes on a yellow tint, reducing your ability to discriminate among green, blue, and violet. Blues will get darker for you and yellows will get less bright. You'll see less violet. As painters age, they use less dark blue and violet.

Sir Francis Chichester, after sailing around the world at age seventy-one, said, "If your try fails, what does that matter? All life is a failure in the end. The thing to do is to get sport out of trying."

Men and women over age seventy-five suffer ten times the incidence of strokes as do those between fifty-five and fifty-nine.

The professionally world-weary Gore Vidal said, apropos having to sell his house on a hill in Ravello, Italy, because he was no longer able to climb the steps, "Everything has its time in life, and in a year, I'll be eighty. I'm not sentimental about anything. Life flows by, and you flow with it or you don't. Move on and move out."

When you're very young, your ability to smell is so intense as to be nearly overwhelming, but by the time you're in your eighties, not only has your ability to smell declined significantly but you yourself no longer even have a distinctive odor. You can stop using deodorants. You're vanishing.

"I think the old need touching," says the social historian Ronald Blythe. "They have reached a stage of life when they need kissing, hugging. And nobody touches them except the doctor." At eighty-two, E. M. Forster said, "I am rather prone to senile lechery just now—want to touch the right person in the right place, in order to shake off bodily loneliness."

Voltaire wrote to a friend, "I beg you not to say that I am only eighty-two; it is a cruel calumny. Even if it be true, according to an accursed baptismal record, that I was born in November 1694, you must always agree with me that I am in my eighty-third year." When you're very old, you want to be thought even older than you actually are: it's an accomplishment.

At eighty-three, Sibelius said, "For the first time I have lately become aware of the fact that the period of our earthly existence is limited. During the whole of my life this idea has never actually come into my mind. It occurred to me very distinctly when I was looking at an old tree there in the garden. When we came it was very small, and I looked at it from above. Now it waves high above my head and seems to say, 'You will soon depart, but I shall stay here for hundreds more years.'"

At eighty-five, Bernard Baruch said, "To me, old age is always fifteen years older than I am."

At age ninety, you've lost half of your kidneys' blood-filtering capacity.

By ninety, one in three women and one in six men suffer a hip fracture, which often triggers a downward spiral leading to death. Half will be unable to walk again without assistance.

After age ninety, you grow increasingly less likely to have cancer; the tissues of an old person don't serve the needs of aggressive, energy-hungry tumors.

At ninety-five, my father's moles are disappearing—a mole typically lasts fifty years—and in their place, a couple of "cherry moles," which look like cherries and the technical name for which is "hemangiomas," have of late appeared on his chest. His doctor professes to find hemangiomas—benign tumors composed of large blood vessels—beautiful. Easy for him to say; he's a whippersnapper of sixty-one. My father finds the cherry moles as distressing as if he were a teenage girl with an array of pimples on her chin.

At ninety-seven, a month before dying, Bertrand Russell said to his wife, "I do so hate to leave this world."

Bernard de Fontanelle, a French scholar, who died at one hundred, said, "I feel nothing except a certain difficulty in continuing to exist."

Aristotle described childhood as hot and moist; youth as hot and dry; and adulthood as cold and dry. He believed aging and death were caused by the body being transformed from one that was hot and moist to one that was cold and dry—a change that he viewed as not only inevitable but desirable.

In *As You Like It,* Jaques says, "And so from hour to hour, we ripe and ripe, / And then from hour to hour, we rot and rot." The Sullivan County (New York) Yellow Pages informs its readers that "the process of living means that we are all temporarily able-bodied persons." The thirty-one-year-old American poet Matthea Harvey writes, "Pity the bathtub its forced embrace of the human form."

CHRONICLE OF DEATH FORETOLD

When you're dying, your central nervous system goes first, and the connective tissue of muscles and fibers goes last. Your heartbeat ends before your brain stops. Your body knows how to produce morphine-like endorphins and how to time their release to coincide with the moment of need. Endorphin elevation is an innate physiological mechanism to protect mammals from emotional and physical dangers; it's a survival mechanism that first appeared during prehistoric times. Your blood often becomes extremely acidic, causing muscles to spasm. The protoplasm is too compromised to sustain life any longer. You may emit a short series of heaving gasps; sometimes your larynx muscles tighten, causing you to bark. Your chest and shoulders may heave once or twice in a brief convulsion. Your eyeballs flatten out because their round plumpness depends on the blood that's no longer there. When you die, you don't—contrary to legend—lose twenty-one grams in weight; if human beings have a soul, it doesn't weigh anything.

Exactly when someone is pronounced dead depends on where he or she dies. In the U.S., some states say that brain activity is the only criterion. In other states, it's respiratory and cardiac activity. In France, the brain has to be silent for forty-eight hours. In the former Soviet Union, patients needed to flatline for five minutes. According to Dr. Henry Beacher, "Whatever level of electrical brain activity we choose, it's an arbitrary decision." Doctors have more personal anxieties about dying than people in any other profession.

For people in the fifty to fifty-nine age group, the death rate is fifty-six percent less than it is for the general population; fifty- to fifty-nine-year-olds are just too busy to die.

In a study of one thousand major league baseball players who played between 1876 and 1973, the players had a death rate twenty-five percent lower than that of men in the general population. A 1986 study of seventeen thousand Harvard graduates, ages thirty-four to seventy-four, found that death rates declined as energy expenditures increased, up to 3,500 calories a week; above that, and death rates increased slightly. (Swimming for an hour burns approximately seven hundred calories.)

Cardiovascular disease kills forty to fifty percent of people in developed countries. Cancer kills thirty to forty percent; car accidents kill two percent; other kinds of accidents kill another two percent. In the U.S., heart disease kills one in forty sixty-five to sixty-nine-year-olds, one in twenty-seven seventy- to seventy-four-year-olds, one in eleven eighty- to eighty-four-year-olds, and one in seven people eighty-five years old and over. In 1949, fifty percent of American deaths occurred in the hospital; in 1958, sixty-one percent; in 1977, seventy percent; now, eighty percent. Septic shock (extremely low blood pressure due to an overwhelming infection in a vital organ) is the leading cause of death in intensive care units in the U.S.: one hundred thousand to two hundred thousand deaths a year. Only thirty-six percent of Americans have living wills. In the U.S., elderly white men commit suicide at a rate five times the national average. One in five doctors receives a request for physician-assisted suicide, and ten percent of those respond by agreeing to assist.

In the Paleolithic age, half of all babies died before reaching their first birthday; mothers often died giving birth. For most of the last 130,000 years, life expectancy for human beings was twenty years or less. The overwhelming majority of people ever born have died from an infectious or parasitic disease early in their life. In the second century AD, the average life span was twenty-five; at least one-third of babies born died before reaching their first birthday. Two hundred years ago, the average life span for an American woman was thirty-five; one hundred years ago, it was forty-eight; it's now eighty—the largest, most rapid rise ever.

In 1900, seventy-five percent of people in the U.S. died before they reached age sixty-five; now, seventy percent of people die after age sixty-five. From 1900 to 1960, life expectancy for a sixty-five-year-old American increased by 2.4 years; from 1960 to 1990, it increased

David Shields

three years. In England in 1815, life expectancy at birth was thirty-nine years. In Europe during the Middle Ages, life expectancy at birth was thirty-three years, which is approximately the life expectancy now for people in the least developed countries.

Very old age in antiquity would still be very old age now. In the sixth century BC, Pythagoras lived to be ninety-one. Heraclitus of Ephesus died at ninety-six. The Athenian orator Isocrates died at ninety-eight. The average life span has increased since the industrial revolution, but primarily from decreasing childhood mortality. In Sweden during the 1860s, the oldest age at death was usually around 106. In the 1990s, it was around 108.

In developed countries, one in ten thousand people lives beyond the age of one hundred. In the U.S., there were thirty-seven thousand centenarians in 1990. There are now around seventy thousand. The majority of American centenarians are female, white, widowed, and institutionalized, were born in the U.S. of Western European ancestry, and have less than a ninth-grade education. Ninety percent of current American centenarians have an annual income of less than $5,000 (excluding food stamps, federal payments to nursing homes, and support from family and friends); they often say they were never able to afford to indulge in bad habits.

On his hundredth birthday—five days after which he died—Eubie Blake said, "These docs, they always ask you how you live so long. I tell 'em, 'If I'd known I was gonna live this long, I'd have taken better care of myself.'"

"Who wants to be a hundred?" asked Henry Miller, who died at eighty-nine. "What's the point of it? A short life and a merry one is far better than a long one sustained by fear, caution, and perpetual medical surveillance."

Woody Allen, on the other hand, has said, "I don't want to achieve immortality through my work. I want to achieve immortality through not dying. I don't want to live on in the hearts of my countrymen. I would rather live on in my apartment."

A priest, a minister, and a rabbi are discussing what they'd like people to say after they die and their bodies are on display in open caskets.

The priest says, "I'd like someone to say, 'He was a righteous man, an honest man, and very generous.'"

The minister says, "I'd like someone to say, 'He was very kind and fair, and he was good to his parishioners.'"

The rabbi says, "I'd want someone to say, 'Look, he's moving.'"

Eighty-eight percent of Americans say that religion is important to them; eighty-two percent of Americans believe that prayer can heal. Ninety-six percent of Americans say they believe in God or some form of universal consciousness; seventy-two percent believe in angels; sixty-five percent believe in the devil. In one study of three thousand American men and women over age sixty-five, people who attended church were half as likely to have strokes as those who never or almost never attended services. In another study of four hundred American men and women in the cardiac care unit at a hospital, patients were far more likely to recover and go home if their families and friends prayed for them. Those on the receiving end of prayers were less likely to require antibiotics. In a survey of ninety-two thousand American men and women, people who attended church more than once a week were far less likely to get certain diseases than those who attended infrequently. Over a five-year period, the death rate from heart disease was twice as high among those who didn't go to church very often as it was for those who frequently attended. During a three-year period, infrequent attendees were twice as likely to die of emphysema and four times as likely to die of cirrhosis of the liver as were frequent attendees. In a study of 230 older American men and women who had just had cardiac surgery, people who said they received strength and comfort from practicing their faith were three times more likely to survive than those who didn't. No data were available on how Americans who believed in the Easter bunny fared.

Propertius said, "Among the dead are thousands of beautiful women."

Charles de Gaulle said, "The cemeteries of the world are full of indispensable men"—one of my father's very favorite quotations, and mine as well. It's consolation, of a sort: everybody tries, no one wins, everybody dies.

I remember being mesmerized by a neighbor's tattoo of a death's head, underneath which were the words, "As I am, you shall someday be."

Juvenal: "Weigh the dust of Alexander the Great and the village drunkard, and they'll weigh the same."

Schopenhauer: "We are all lambs led to slaughter."

At fifty-one, Tchaikovsky said, "I am aging fast, I am tired of life, I thirst for quietness and a rest from all these vanities, emotions, disappointments, etc. etc. It is natural for an old man to think of a prospective dirty hole called a grave."

Freud said, "What lives, wants to die again. Originating in dust, it wants to be dust again. Not only the life-drive is in them, but the death-drive as well."

In 44 BC, Cicero said, "No one is so old that he does not think he could live another year"; he died in 43 BC. On his deathbed, William Saroyan said, "Everybody has got to die, but I always believed an exception would be made in my case." Edward Young wrote, "All men think all men mortal but themselves." The ancient epic Indian poem *Mahabharata*, written in Sanskrit, asks, "Of all the world's wonders, which is the most wonderful? That no man, though he sees others dying all around him, believes that he himself will die."

Cormac McCarthy: "Death is the major issue in the world. For you, for me, for all of us. It just is. To not be able to talk about it is very odd."

"Life," said Damon Runyon, "is 6 to 5 against."

HOW TO LIVE FOREVER (I)

In 1600 BC, the Egyptian papyrus *Book for Transformation of an Old Man into a Youth of Twenty* recommended a potion involving herbs and animal parts. In ancient Greece, old men were advised to lie down with beautiful virgins. Castration—believed to extend the life span a few years—was popular in the Middle Ages. Eunuchs do live longer than uncastrated men. A sterilized dog or cat, male or female, will live, on average, two years longer than unsterilized dogs and cats. In the early sixteenth century, Ponce de Leon, age fifty-five, searched for the Fountain of Youth because he was unable to satisfy his much younger wife. Later in the sixteenth century, Francis Bacon thought that if repair processes, such as tissue regeneration, healing of wounds, and the capacity of the body to recover from disease, were perfected, aging could be overcome.

In the nineteenth century, the French physiologist Charles-Édouard Brown-Séquard removed and crushed the testicles of domesticated animals, extracted vital substances from them, then used this concoction to inoculate older people, who reported improved alertness and vitality. When Brown-Séquard, at age seventy-two, injected himself with the extract, he claimed to have better control over his bladder and bowels. He died at seventy-six. Eugen Steinach, a professor of physiology in Vienna in the 1920s, convinced older men that they would be rejuvenated by a vasectomy or by having the testicles of younger men grafted onto their own. Rejuvenation clinics sprang up around the world: surgeons devised a number of antiaging therapies, including the application of electricity to the testicles and doses of X-rays and radium to the sex organs.

According to Dr. Michael Jazwinski, a molecular biologist at Louisiana State University: "Possibly in thirty years we will have in hand the major genes that determine longevity, and will be in a position to double, triple, even quadruple our current maximum life span of 120 years. It's possible that some people alive now may still be alive four hundred years from now."

Dr. William Regelson, professor of medicine at Virginia Commonwealth University, says, "As we learn to control the genes involved in aging, the possibilities of lengthening life appear practically unlimited."

Michael Rose, an evolutionary biologist at the University of California-Irvine, permitted only those fruit flies that produced eggs later in their life span to contribute eggs to the next generation. (This is equivalent to selecting women aged twenty-five and older to be mothers and then only permitting the daughters who were fertile after age twenty-six to reproduce, and so on for many generations.) Each generation of fruit flies lived a little longer than the previous one. The fruit flies from this ongoing program of selective breeding continue to live progressively longer than their ancestors. Rose believes that if a similar experiment could be performed on humans, a measurable increase in life expectancy would be observed within ten generations.

Fruit flies given resveratol, an antioxidant found in red wine, live significantly longer than other flies. Molecules in resveratol called sirtuins mimic the life-extending effects of caloric restriction, which slows aging in mammals. Living creatures are hard-wired to reproduce; a low-calorie diet sends a message throughout the body that conditions aren't optimal for reproduction. Cellular defense systems arise and aging slows, preserving the body for better, more reproduction-friendly times. Caloric restriction triggers a release of stored fat, which tells the body it's time to hunker down for survival.

Two thousand people belong to the Calorie Restriction Society, and ten percent of those two thousand have cut their consumption by at least thirty percent. The greatest life extension, as much as fifty percent, comes from starting a severely restricted diet in young adulthood and continuing it throughout life. Starting in midlife and cutting calories ten to twenty percent yields a smaller benefit. Fasting every other day (while otherwise eating normally in between) also increases average lifespan.

A near-starvation diet dramatically reduces the incidence of most age-related disease: tumor and kidney problems, brain-deficit problems such as Alzheimer's, and degenerative problems such as Parkinson's and epilepsy. Rats on a forty percent reduced-calorie diet have a thirty percent longer life span. Monkeys on a reduced-calorie diet—thirty percent less for fifteen years—live longer and avoid many age-related diseases. In humans, Parkinson's and Alzheimer's are closely correlated with increased caloric intake. Is cutting forty to fifty percent in calories worth the extra years and protection from disease, though? You might abstain from cheesecake for twenty years, then get hit by a bus at fifty-seven. So, too, a major new study of body weight and health risks by the Centers for Disease Control and Prevention and the National Cancer Institute concluded that the very thin (a person with a body mass index below 18.5—for instance, a man who is six feet and weighs 136 pounds or a woman who is five foot six and weighs 114) run the same risk of early death as the very fat: very thin people have no reserves to tap if they fall ill.

Vegetarians tend to live longer, healthier lives than meat eaters. The Japanese diet is high in vegetables and soy products. A Japanese person lives three years longer, on average, than an American or Briton. (One-quarter of vegetables eaten in America are french fries.) Okinawans consume eighty percent as many calories as the average Japanese does. Okinawa has the highest proportion of centenarians in the world (six hundred of its 1.3 million people), four times as many as the rest of the world. A vegetarian diet contains large amounts of foods good for longevity, such as tofu and fish. Fish oils, for instance, are rich in omega-3 fatty acids that, compared with the saturated fats found in meats, don't harden as easily and stick less to artery walls—which has a protective effect against heart disease and stroke. As Satchel Paige advised, "Avoid red meats, which angry up the blood."

Early humans apparently had diets containing vegetables, fruits, nuts, and berries, and large quantities of meat that was naturally low in fat. Isolated tribes in remote parts of the world still eat a Paleolithic diet. A recent study of diet, fitness, and disease compared fifty-eight traditional societies with industrialized populations:

hunter-gatherers suffer less cardiovascular disease and cancer than do people living in "developed" nations; the more your diet diverges from that of hunter-gatherers, the worse your health is likely to be. The contemporary American diet contains twice the fat and one-third the protein of diets maintained by indigenous populations. When you eat animal fats and processed sugar, you increase your risk of disease. When you eat soybeans, cooked tomatoes, and fiber, you reduce your risk for, respectively, breast cancer, prostate cancer, and colon cancer. The major diseases in the industrialized world are caused by departures from the diet to which our early ancestors were adapted.

There's a direct relationship between the percentage of fat in your diet and your risk of cancer. The average Chinese diet contains less than fifteen percent fat. The average American diet contains thirty-nine percent fat. The average Chinese has a cholesterol level of 127, compared to 212 for the average American. In China, there are very low rates of heart disease, colon cancer, breast cancer, prostate cancer, and ovarian cancer. What little heart disease and cancer do exist in China are found overwhelmingly in those regions where people eat the highest amount of fat and cholesterol.

Taoists developed diets that would starve "evil beings"—the Three Worms—which were thought to inhabit the body and hasten its demise by causing disease. Battling the evil beings took the form of denying them the grains, such as wheat and rice, thought to be responsible for their existence, and eating magical foods such as licorice, cinnamon, and ginseng that would kill them. Other approved medicines included herbs, roots, minerals, and animal and plant products such as eggs, turtles, peaches, and parts of trees.

If you want to live longer, you should—in addition to the obvious: eating less and losing weight—move to the country, not take work home, do what you enjoy and feel good about yourself, get a pet, learn to relax, live in the moment, laugh, listen to music, sleep six to seven hours a night; be blessed with long-lived parents and grandparents (thirty-five percent of your longevity is due to genetic factors); be married, hug, hold hands, have sex regularly, have a lot of children, get along with your mother, accept your children, nurture your grandchildren; be well educated, stimulate your brain, learn new things; be optimistic, channel your anger in a positive way, not always have to be right; not smoke; eat less salt, eat moderate amounts of chocolate, eat a Mediterranean diet of fruits, vegetables, olive oils, fish, and poultry, drink green tea and moderate amounts of

162

red wine; exercise; have goals, take risks; confide in a friend, not be afraid to seek psychological counseling; be a volunteer, have a role in the community; attend church, find God.

Researchers studied a group of people, ages sixty-six to 101, who had outlived their siblings by an average of seven years. One personality characteristic stood out: the longer-lived sibling had a "better sense of humor." On average, married people outlive single people (here's a shocker: the benefit for married men is greater); older siblings outlive younger ones; mothers outlive childless women (by a slight margin); people with higher education live six years longer than high-school dropouts; Oscar winners outlive unsuccessful nominees by four years; CEOs outlive corporate vice presidents; religious people outlive atheists; tall people (men over six feet, women over five feet seven) outlive short people by three years; nonsmokers live ten years longer than smokers; thin people live seven years longer than obese people; American immigrants live three years longer than natives; Japanese have the longest life expectancy (eighty-one years) and Zambians have the briefest (thirty-three years). Centenarians tend to be assertive, suspicious, and practical. Natalie's former daycare teacher, now a manager for the outpatient clinic of a cancer-care center, says, "It's the assholes who always get better."

Gavin Polone, a thirty-nine-year-old television and movie producer, works six-day weeks and eighteen-hour days and has rejected marriage and children as antiquated nuisances. Polone views kids as unpredictable clutter that leads to "personal drama." His girlfriend, Elizabeth Oreck, who's thirty-eight, says, "People often have children to fulfill some kind of twisted, egocentric reflection of themselves. The truth is, we both prefer animals to people." Polone and Oreck have three dogs and five cats, all rescued from animal shelters or the neighborhood (the mean streets of Beverly Hills). Polone arises at 4:45 a.m., has a waking pulse of forty-eight, eats eight ounces of dry cereal and drinks thirty-two ounces of cold green tea for breakfast, and subsists on eighteen hundred calories a day, primarily protein powder and egg whites. He is six feet one and weights 160 pounds. One of his clients, Conan O'Brien, says, "When I met Gavin, he was an assistant to an agent. In time, he became an agent, then a manager. Now he's a producer/bodybuilder/race-car driver. In nine weeks I think he'll be in the space program. I really do. He's evolving into some kind of superbeing. Or a great Bond villain. Whenever I talk to him, I picture him making demands on a big video screen to the United Nations." By consuming less food, Polone hopes to reduce the physical stress that causes aging, extending his life indefinitely. Another client, the director Jon Turteltaub, says about Polone, "He believes that by being really skinny he'll live long enough for stem-cell research to catch up and create new organs for him, and then he can live for eternity."

The Gerontology Research Group—a loose organization of demographers, gerontologists, and epidemiologists who study very old age—believes there's an invisible barrier at age 115. There are only twelve undisputed cases of people ever reaching 115. Very few people who reach age 114 reach 115; since 2001, a dozen 114-year-olds have died before turning 115. Right now there are, according to the GRG, fifty-five women and six men over age 110 worldwide. The oldest age ever reached was 122, in 1997, by a French woman. No matter how little you eat, how much you exercise, and how healthily you live, you apparently can't live longer than 125 years. In five thousand years of recorded history, there's been no change in the maximum life span. Lucretius, who died in 55 BC, wrote:

> Man, by living on, fulfill
> As many generations as thou may
> Eternal death shall be waiting still
> And he who died with light of yesterday
> Shall be no briefer time in death's no-more
> Than he who perished months or years before.

HOW TO LIVE FOREVER (II)

There are now thousands of people worldwide in the "longevity movement" who believe it's possible to live for hundreds of years, perhaps forever. Very nearly everyone in the longevity movement is male. Because they give birth, women seem to feel far less craving for literal immortality.

Ray Kurzweil, who has won a National Medal of Technology Award, been inducted into the Inventors Hall of Fame, and is the author of *Fantastic Voyage: Live Long Enough to Live Forever*— and has been working on the problem of artificial intelligence since he was a teenager in the sixties—believes that human immortality is no more than twenty years away. In order to make sure he lives long enough in order to be around, first, for the biotech revolution, when

David Shields

we'll be able to control how our genes express themselves and ultimately change the genes, and, second, for nanotechnology and the artificial-intelligence revolution, Kurzweil takes 250 supplements a day, drinks ten glasses of alkaline water and ten cups of green tea a day, and periodically tracks forty to fifty fitness indicators, including "tactile sensitivity."

Millions of robots—"nanobots," the size of blood cells—will keep people forever young by swarming through the body, repairing bones, muscles, arteries, and brain cells. These nanobots will work like repaving crews in our bloodstreams and brains, destroying diseases, rebuilding organs, and obliterating known limits on the human intellect. Improvements to genetic coding will be downloaded from the Internet.

Kurzweil says, "No more than a hundred genes are involved in the aging process. By manipulating these genes, radical life extension has already been achieved in simpler animals. We are not another animal, subject to nature's whim. Biological evolution passed the baton of progress to human cultural and technological development." He also says that all thirty thousand of our genes "are little software programs." We'll be able to block disease-causing genes and introduce new ones that would slow or stop the aging process.

"Life is chemistry," says Brian Wowk, a physicist with 21st Century Medicine. "When the chemistry of life is preserved, so is life."

Aubrey de Grey, a geneticist at the University of Cambridge, says, "In principle, a copy of a living person's brain—all trillion cells of it—could be constructed from scratch, purely by in vitro manipulation of neurons into a synaptic network previously scanned from that brain."

João Pedro de Magalhães, a research fellow in genetics at Harvard Medical School, says, "Aging is a sexually transmitted disease that can be defined as a number of time-dependent changes in the body that lead to discomfort, pain, and eventually death. Maybe our grandchildren will be born without aging."

Robert Freitas Jr., a senior research fellow at the Institute for Molecular Manufacturing, says, "Using annual checkups and clean outs, and some occasional major repairs, your biological age could be restored once a year to the more or less constant physiological age that you select. I see little reason not to go for optimal youth, though trying to maintain your body at the ideal physiological age of ten years old might be difficult and undesirable for other reasons. A rollback to the robust physiology of your late teens or early twen-

165

ties would be easier to maintain and much more fun." Tee-hee. "That would push your expected age of death up to around seven hundred to nine hundred calendar years. You might still eventually die of accidental causes, but you'll live ten times longer than we do now.

"How far can we go with this? If we can eliminate ninety-nine percent of all medically preventable conditions that lead to natural death, your healthy life span, or health span, should increase to about 1,100 years. It may be that you'll find it hard to coax more than a millennium or two out of your original biological body, because deaths from suicides and accidents have remained stubbornly high for the last hundred years, falling by only one-third during that time. But our final victory over the scourge of natural death, which we shall achieve later in this century, should extend the health spans of normal human beings by at least ten- or twenty-fold beyond its current maximum length."

Would life get intolerably boring if you lived for a couple of millennia? In the first century BC, Pliny the Elder, the Roman encyclopedist, wrote of people in previous times who, exhausted by life at age eight hundred, leaped into the sea.

Marc Geddes, a New Zealand writer on artificial intelligence and mathematics, suggests the possibility of "brain refresher drugs," which will prevent "brains from becoming too inflexible. The people living in the far future might be able to alter their bodies and personalities as easily as the people of today change their clothes. The fact that some people living today get tired of life is more likely to be a practical, biological problem than a philosophical one."

Sherwin Nuland, the author of *How We Die*, says about Kurzweil and his fellow fantasists, "They've forgotten that they're acting on the basic biological fear of death and extinction, and it distorts their rational approach to the human condition."

In Tennyson's *Tithonus*, the eponymous protagonist, who is granted his wish of immortality without realizing he'd be aging forever, decides he wants to die:

> . . . Let me go: take back thy gift.
> Why should a man desire in any way
> to vary from the kindly race of men,
> Or pass beyond the goal of ordinance
> Where all should pause, as is most meet for all?
> Release me, and restore me to the ground.

166

THE STORY TOLD ONE LAST TIME,
FROM BEGINNING TO END

As soon as your reproductive role has been accomplished, you're disposable.

After sexual maturation, deterioration in peak efficiency occurs, because, as Harold Morowitz, a professor of biology at George Mason University, says, "perfect order requires infinite work." Also, deterioration builds on itself.

In the late nineteenth century, August Weismann, a German biologist, made a distinction between "the immortality of reproductive cells, the cells in the body that carry genes forward to the next generation, and the mortality of the rest, which will age and die." Death takes place, he said, "because a worn-out tissue cannot forever renew itself, and because a capacity for increase by means of cell division is not everlasting but finite."

Once a body's mission is accomplished, nature has little interest in what happens next. Reproductive life spans of members of a species work as perfectly as possible to match the time an individual of that species might expect to survive before dying. In other words, physiological resources go into reproduction, not into prolonging life thereafter.

The force of natural selection declines with age. Natural selection has shaped human biology in such a way that aging and death become increasingly likely by the time you reach your forties. If a disaster strikes a person who has passed the age of reproductive fitness, the consequences are by and large unimportant to the survival of the rest of the species.

Nature favors the accumulation of genes that do beneficial things early in life, even though they might do harmful things late in life, because—under normal conditions—most animals do not live long enough for the harmful effects to cause a problem. The same general mechanism that protects against cancer protects against aging. Long-lived species, with their better cellular protection, get cancer later than short-lived species.

The pineal gland is your internal clock. It knows how old you are, and it knows when you're past your reproductive prime. As soon as it senses that you're too old to reproduce effectively—around age forty-five—it begins to produce far lower levels of melatonin, which signals all of your other systems to break down and the aging process to begin. (Women's larger pineal gland is another reason women age more slowly than men, and it may be why they live longer.)

Low levels of melatonin signal your immune system to shut down and your endocrine system to produce fewer sex hormones. Lower levels of sex hormones in turn lead to the atrophy of sexual organs in both men and women, to a decrease as well in sexual interest and the ability to perform. Mice given melatonin undergo a sexual transformation: they have renewed interest and vigor, and their sex organs undergo repair and rejuvenation.

In the late stages of adulthood, moths mimic the movements of juvenile moths, leading predators away from young moths and sacrificing their own lives, in order to benefit the species.

Your body has a hundred thousand billion cells, all of which have the potential to commit suicide. However much you may suffer if one of these cells breaks free from the normal controls on its growth and replicates without restraint, the cell is doing nothing more than following the imperative of natural selection acting at the cellular level. The individual doesn't matter. You don't matter. You're a vector on the grid of cellular life. You carry ten to twelve genes with mutations that are potentially lethal; these mutations will be passed on to your children. Aging followed by death is the price you pay for the immortality of your genes.

Pigs of Gold
Forrest Gander

I HAVE MISREAD the invitation. It does not say Join us in Andacollo for the Festival of Cerdos de Oro, pigs of gold, but for the Festival of Cerros de Oro, hills of gold.

And how do you get to Andacollo, Chile? You fly all day to Santiago and when you land, you rush to catch another flight straight up the coast to La Serena. Built by the Indian-killer Francisco de Aguirre in 1549 (just ten years before even more notorious Lope de Aguirre launched his ill-fated expedition for El Dorado), La Serena is a handsome neocolonial town of churches and convents. Your *regular taxi* takes you from the airport through streets flanked with white houses to the corner of Calle Domeiko and Avenida Francisco, where you get out and wait, slumped on the curb across from a muffler repair shop, until the *collective taxi* driver—this is his corner—can rustle up two more passengers for Andacollo.

It's a tight squeeze and a long ride through cactus plains and semidesert mountain roads from which we can sometimes glimpse the snowcapped Andes. At last we descend into a gorge with a town flung into the bottom of it. (The only corollary in my experience is the brake-smoking arrival into the paranormal abyss of Guanajuato, Mexico.)

When the taxi lets us out at the Church of La Virgen del Rosario de Andacollo, I meet K, the other poet from the U.S. We are magnetized to the wall of prayer plaques perimeterizing the church. Made of marble and iron and sandstone, they're shaped like hearts, shields, and open books. Hundreds of Thanks to the Virgin *"por haber escuchado mis oraciones"*—for having heard my prayers, *"por salvar nuestro hijo"*—for saving our child, *"por el milagro concedido"*—for the granted miracle. In an unusually specific *retablo*, a mother thanks the Virgin for helping her daughter turn from the demon of drugs. In another, the only one in English, Miriam, who trekked to Andacollo from Australia, offers plaintively: "Thanks for Forgive My Fault."

Forrest Gander

ANDACOLLO

The bordering river is dry, a depository of bulging green plastic trash bags and strewn litter.

Andacollo, like Juan Rulfo's mythic Paramo, is haunted by the ghosts of miners and dusted with tailings that blow steadily from the denuded, buzz-cut, and beveled mountains, one behind the other into the horizon. An apocalyptic landscape with microavalanches of dark sand pouring in slow motion down sun-baked hills. In the cratered flats, black, orange-fringed pools glisten like tar pits.

A hatbox of a room. A pocket of a room. Our room for the week is no bigger than a pickup truck. I sleep with my suitcase on the bed with me. Two feet away, K snores like Unferth.

Waking at 4 a.m., I step out to the street to check the stars and a man bicycles past me. He is on his way, I will be told later, to the gold mine to break stones all day. At dark, he will bicycle home again. Month after month, for a few dollars a week.

Listen. The three thousand dog nights of Andacollo.

When I sit across from her at dinner, she turns away because I'm from the U.S. Although there is no one else close enough to engage in conversation, she lights up a Derby cigarette and sullenly blows smoke, looking down the table.

Toward the end of the third day of the festival, after many papers, a consensus emerges that there are no longer *regions* of poetry, but there are *zones*. Tarkovsky is mentioned. In his own talk, K critiques the presumptions of urban vanguard poetry in relation to rural and regional practices.

On the final night, a Mexican poet aggressively accuses the organizer of avoiding the issue of regionality altogether, of talking around it with language games when, in fact, some people's lives are at risk because of their writing's relation to the places where they live.

Another poet shouts that vanguard poetry doesn't speak to him at all, that it is elitist, that the tone of the whole conference is elitist.

And so the last evening dissolves into tensions, wounded feelings, a dinner table balanced like a barbell, with partisan drinkers clustered around either end.

I am *rendido*, rent by the effort of constant attentiveness to even the most casual conversation with someone who, were language more exchangeable, might be a friend.

The gift of books cannot be refused, although there is no space for them in our suitcases. *Arigato-meiwaku.* That's what Basho said as he hiked around Japan accumulating gifts he could not carry. *Thanks, but no thanks.*

Between three shopkeepers, an accord is reached regarding the best wine in the shop and the bottle I should buy.

Walking beside his young wife, the husband, considerably older, tries to steer, with a menacing glare, the eyes of passing men from the perk of her breasts.

Before the Virgin's room, a hall of offerings from various countries. Samurai armor. Spoons. A red robe from a church in Kenya. Chinese banners praising, so say instructive note cards, the Virgin of Andacollo.

The last daylight spiders down from a small ring of stained glass in the ceiling. According to legend, a peasant found a wooden statue of the Virgin in Brazil and lugged it back to Andacollo, where it became known for the miracles it bestowed on the faithful.

The Virgin of Andacollo stands about three feet high. But all we can see when we enter the upstairs chapel is her back. Behind a wrought-iron grate, she stands on a small platform looking down into the nave of the church a floor below us. When we press ourselves to the grate, we share her perspective of the empty pews, but her countenance remains invisible to us. Then, just before we leave, we notice a dark rope tied to one rail. Its other end seems to attach, like a crude umbilical cord, below the skirt of the Virgin. I kneel and tug the rope and slowly, without creaking, the Virgin turns around to face us.

Her white, silken, perfectly isosceles gown, strung with loops of amethyst, covers her from neck to feet. The short brown hair on her wooden head is topped with a gold crown. From her ears, slightly outturned, two leaf-shaped earrings dangle. One of her brown eyes looks sleepy and the other focuses intently downward.

When fog covers the town, says the barkeep, it is understood that someone is about to die.

171

Cigarette butts around the bare twig in the sand of the flower pot.

And what are those things that look like white stupas on the hills around Andacollo, we ask him. He hints that he has a story to tell, that it involves a cult of Tibetan monks, but we are too hung-over to return the next day for the revelation.

Even were it in English, and perhaps more so, I would find these long conversations exhausting.

Nervous, I bluff fluency with a convincing accent and speedy sentences that lead to stupid grammatical mistakes that, like the gambler's martingale, redouble my nervousness and compensatory speed, leading to more goofs, clumsy pauses, and overwhelming disappointment. I feel myself falling in slow motion—like James Stewart in *Vertigo*—into a well of silence below the world of human voices.

One night we take a bus to La Silla (The Saddle), one of the famous observatories bordering the southern extremity of the Atacama Desert. After a tour of the facilities, we trundle out into the high, cold desert night to look at a constellation named for a parrot. When my turn comes to cup my eye to the lens, I can make out only two little points of light. There are *cuernos de cabra* in bloom around the observatory, and the air is so still I can smell the nighttime sweetness. A low hum of conversation is all the harder to track because I can't see anyone's lips shaping the words. Shivering, I go inside with the others to the auditorium where our hosts have planned an evening of readings by twenty poets. The first to read decides it would be unfair to skip any section of his book-length poem based on Melville's Ishmael and so, already drunk on free pisco sours in the lobby, he throws his serape over his shoulder and declaims for a solid hour and twenty minutes. It's a little after midnight. Nineteen poets to go.

When the large companies pulled out, some local miners stayed and continued to dig for whatever might have been left behind. Then they, too, thinned out. The exodus continued. The town began to crumble. This small mining operation—four or five men—must have been failing as well, and so the owner, his gums mottled and brown, flecks of saliva at the corner of his mouth—a sign of mercury poisoning—is glad to show us around. In the severe afternoon sun, one man is crushing stone, another scooping the pieces into a crude wooden sieve. The owner leads us below a tin roof where the sieved gravel is swirled into large washtubs. Here he takes a vial and pours into his hand several beads of quicksilver that roll like marbles across the grooved life lines of his palm. He smears the quicksilver against a tin plate that he inserts into a rack at the side of the washtub. After he swishes the muddy water with a paddle and takes out the metal plate, we see a patina of gold adhering to it. This he wipes into a cloth filter, again with his bare hand.

SANTIAGO

Raúl Zurita says he doesn't like abstract poetry. A door is a door. I imagine that being tortured would incline a surviving poet toward the tangible world.

He says that in those days of brutality and distrust and terror, the reign of Pinochet, he began to imagine writing poems in the sky, on the faces of cliffs, in the desert. A city poet nearly all his life, he began to dream of nature. He started to imagine that he might fight sadistic force with poems as insubstantial as contrails in the air over a city. His words *Neither Suffering Nor Fear*, bulldozed into the sand at the skirt of a mountain, are gradually fading away, joining thousands of men, women, and children who disappeared in fear and pain during the Pinochet years. But schoolchildren in the closest desert pueblo come with shovels and turn over the ground inside the letters, refreshing them. And so new editions of the poem are published *in situ*, invigorating the relationship between republic and republication.

Zurita has a remarkable face. His nose, expressive as a collie's, marks him for melancholy. His grandmother was Italian and he talks with his hands—they stretch out behind him or reach over to touch me on the leg, the shoulder. His face, tense with gravitas, suddenly zooms toward me, releasing itself into a smile, a laugh that issues now from the whole of him, not only the eyes and mouth. He talks of the *acantilado* project, his plan to inscribe a poem into the cliff face on Chile's coast. Of his recent kidney operation—he still has four stones. The operation, *it was nothing*, but he doesn't look comfortable on the hard wooden seat at the small breakfast table in the Orly Hotel.

More than anything, Zurita emits warmth. As if there were honeysuckle under his skin. We embrace good-bye and I turn down the invitation to lunch at his house. I am at the end of my capacity to concentrate.

In the Plaza de Armas, the cannon sends shock waves through my shirt; the pigeons whoosh into the air like a spadeful of exploding fists. A little girl with a balloon giraffe grips her mother's hand.

ISLA NEGRA

The bus lets us off. Classic comic scene: two travel-bedraggled strangers on a dusty road looking in either direction for a sign. K miraculously spots a restaurant and we drag our luggage through the tawny dirt toward Restaurante Veinte Poemas de Amor. How, now that we've come all this way without his address or any contact information, are we going to find Nicanor Parra, the ninety-year-old poet? We order lunch and glance idly at the folk art on the wall. One painting, decorated with shells, is a simplified map of Isla Negra. Below a square house on the main road, the artist has written *Neruda.* At the end of the road that curves along the boundary river, another house is labeled *Parra.*

We are the only guests at a hostel called La Casa Azul. The owner is gone, but her friend, an Argentinian painter, shows us to our room and gives us a cursory tour of the kitchen, where we can make coffee and find oranges. Yes, yes, he knows Parra. In fact, Parra's writing studio is just up the road, he can show us. But Parra doesn't stay in Isla Negra. He lives in a house two towns away. With flagging energy, we trudge down to the main street to bargain with a taxi driver. Yes, yes, he knows Parra, too, knows the town where he lives, sure. It's only a twenty-minute ride. When we get there, the taxi driver slows down to ask the first person he sees where Nicanor Parra lives. With fresh directions, he takes us straight to the house, butted against the sea. We leap out with books we hope Parra will sign, with a T-shirt from New Directions, his U.S. publisher, and with a note, in case he isn't there, explaining that we are admirers who have come this long way hoping just to meet him briefly and that if he wants to see us, he can leave a message at La Casa Azul in Isla Negra. The girl who answers my knock sticks her head out from behind the door and tells me that no, we cannot see Parra. Is she sure? Yes, she is sure. I ask if we can leave our gifts and the note. She takes them, closing the door in the same fluid gesture, and we go back to the taxi and wait, hoping that Parra, whom K thinks he glimpsed as the door cracked open, might read the note and step out. No luck. The taxi driver, commiserating, takes us back to Isla Negra. At La Casa Azul, we tell the

174

painter we are expecting a call from Nicanor Parra. A call, he says, perplexed. We don't have a phone here.

Finally abandoning all hope, as it has been written, we decide that we might as well have a look at Neruda's house before it closes, and we walk there and take the tour. The rooms of ships' figureheads, the collections of shells, the enormous narwhale tusk, the African masks, the stunning hand-carved furniture, the broad rafters carved with the names of his dead friends. It's all museum quality. *Lived well for a communist,* I think. When we get back to La Casa Azul, darkness is condensing. The painter sees us making for our room. Oh, he says in Spanish, Parra came to see you. He drove here by himself in his orange Volkswagen and came to the door with some books.

Did he leave the books, a message, anything?

He just said, Tell them that I came.

There is a wonderful poem by Walter de la Mare about a man who gallops his horse to a ramshackle mansion on a dark night and, when no one responds to his pounding, shouts up at the windows, *Tell them that I came.* I wonder if Parra, who knows English poetry well, was quoting that poem. There are Chinese poems, too, written by disciples who hiked into the mountains to visit a master and waited and finally left without making contact. None of the literary precedents, which K and I recall to each other from our bunk beds in the cold, dark room, comforts us.

At last we take ourselves to the good restaurant. A dish of chilled shellfish, called *locos,* tastes like thumbs.

K mistakes the waiter's strange, serious manner for contempt, although as the night goes on, it becomes clear that he's merely trying to impress us with an exaggerated professionalism.

The next day we are waiting with our luggage on the dusty street for the bus. A pitiful, matted dog with a swollen rat tail slinks up to K and nudges his calf. K reaches down to pet it, thinks again, and freezes, still bent over. The dog has rolled onto its back, offering its belly. At the same time, K and I see its black testicular tumor, the size of a tennis ball. It has been chewed wide open, exposing dark pink tissue deep within.

The image is so horrifying, such a fast-pitched memento mori, that we remain silent, next to each other, most of the way to Valparaiso.

175

Forrest Gander

VALPARAISO

We are seated across from the bar within a little parenthesis in the wall, an alcove just capacious enough for the tiny table and two chairs. Neruda was a denizen here. The bartender tells us to be careful not to hit our heads when we stand. I nod *Of course* and half an hour later, needing the men's room, I stand and all but knock myself out.

K takes me to another bar he has reconnoitered while I was sleeping. The proprietor has convinced him, with a few details and several beers, that Neruda was a regular patron here, too. The walls are swarming with murals of jazz musicians and Creole dancers. K says, *I'd like you to meet the bartender: Mr. Primitivo, this is Forrest Gander. Forrest, Señor Primitivo.*

Valparaiso, a pastel city of hills with narrow cobblestone streets spooling down them. Jungled gullies hemmed by colorful houses of tin, of wood, of native stone. Burned ruins and lovely two-story *casitas* with views of the bay, side by side.

We serve Viña Tarapacá, he tells us proudly. Ex Zavala, a 2002 Cabernet Sauvignon. It's the third-best wine in Chile.

The guitar player, whose dream is to live in the United States, stops by our table to strum a song written by Violeta Parra, Nicanor's sister: *Gracias a la vida que me ha dado tanto.* My thanks to this life, which has given me so much. The refrain cuts through my self-concern and sends shivers up my neck.

Chocolate condoms in the men's-room dispenser.

Smell of cat urine in the dirt yard. Each time I pass this alley I think of the Washington zoo.

At another of Neruda's houses, here in Valparaiso, I examine the cylinders of music behind the player next to his writing desk. They are labeled Polka, The Barber of Seville, L'Angelus de la Mer, Las Tribulaciones d'un Pipelet.

Drinking half a bottle of Santa Emiliana Cabernet Sauvignon 2004. That crappy U.S. movie about tornadoes playing in the corner of the restaurant opposite me but not so far off that I can't read the subtitles.

In a back-alley cantina that we find by accident, names have been scribbled with markers and pens across everything—the walls, the cabinets of antiques, the glass windows—and innumerable small photos of visitors have been stuck into every picture frame and mirror, obscuring whatever once appeared there. We are in a shrine celebrating the human desperation to be remembered. I order wine; K orders beer.

A vaguely simian man in a baggy suit stares at us, leaves, returns, smiles, approaches us, leaves again, returns, and mimes clapping his hands. And then from a shelf of antiques, he plucks two gourds I hadn't noticed. An accordionist emerges from the back room and sits by the door and begins to play, swaying, and the crazy man shakes the gourds and breaks into song—something about butterflies coming out of your mouth and end words that rhyme, in Spanish, *Valparaiso* and *I adore you.* We order another round. More people come in.

At the table next to us, two young lovers, eating the traditional dish of steak over French fries, clap when the last song in the set ends. We all join in the clapping.

Putting down the gourds, the singer drops an old envelope on their table and on ours, and winds his way around to every table, greeting those he knows with boisterous exclamations. The air is smoky, the voices loud, the envelope says, *Gracias por su valiosa cooperacion.* We put in a few bills and K asks in a low shout for a tango—the man cups his hand to his ear—K shouts again. The man nods to the accordionist, three generations of a family file in through the door, the musicians launch into a song called "El Indio Vigaro," more people keep coming, bottles appear and disappear from our table, the room is packed, the thousands of hand-scrawled names are pulsing on the walls, the multitude of photographs staring fixedly into the shadowy room, I take off my jacket, K's eyes are slanted, unblinking, reptilian, I stand, wobbling, to try to make my way toward the toilet, the space in the room contracts then expands and we are outside in the alley kneeling on the cobblestones while behind us, within the throbbing cantina, the Valparaisan night copies our faces and signs our names to the wall.

Elements: Two Essays
Rosamond Purcell

GENERATION

Horse from the Sea

Hero

Rosamond Purcell

Balance

Prince

Rosamond Purcell

Owl

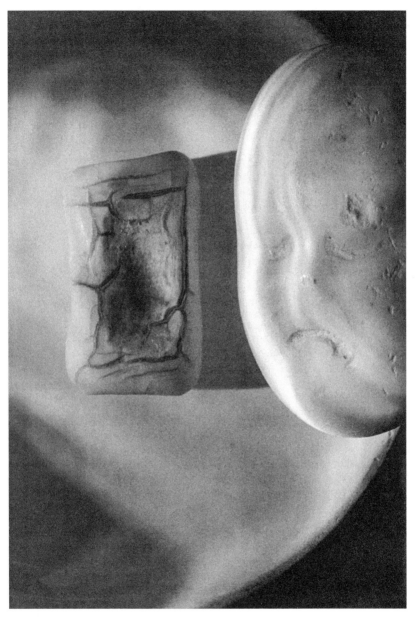

Moon Face

Rosamond Purcell

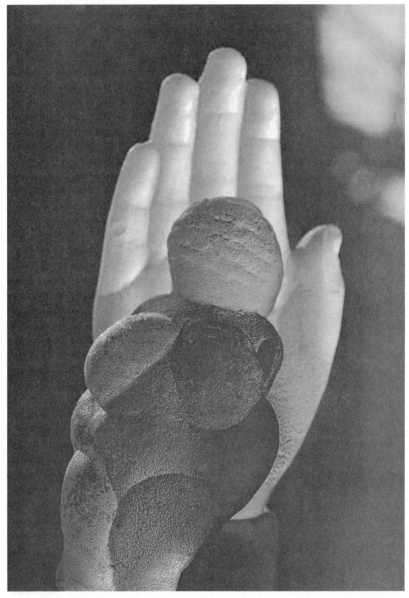

Goddess in Hand

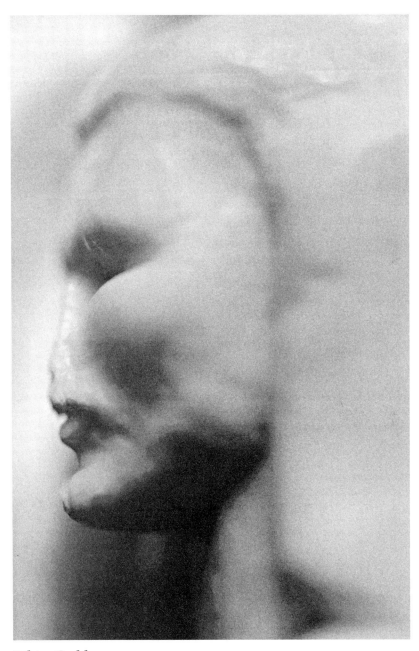

White Goddess

Ephemera

SHADOWS

Mailman

Rosamond Purcell

Sleep

Rosamond Purcell

For Francis Bacon

Rosamond Purcell

Half Cowboy

Boy with Hooked Hand

Mimesis
William H. Gass

IF GREEK THEATER HAD deep religious implications, as some think, and often functioned as a ritual would, then the actor on the stage, his features obscured by a mask and robe, might be thought to be a mouthpiece for the gods. If the play was significant enough, the words powerful and rich and wise, a moment could occur in his impersonation during which the divine spirit entered him; the soul of the actor who, a moment before, had been reciting the playwright's words might, so to speak, stand aside, and his speech take on an imprimatur its actual author could not lay claim to—its metamorphosis would be obvious to every ear—for (in a switch no different than Zeus's frequent changes of form to further an amorous prank or political ploy) these words would be severed from their source of utterance in the actor and from the hand of their author as well; they would participate in the divine; while the audience heard the speech of nature as they had in former times when leaves whispered and torrents roared and the world, more than words, was alive.

Nothing has changed. When the text sings, the reader listens, and soon her soul sings, too; she reenacts thought and passion's passage, adopts Chaucer's, Shakespeare's, Milton's tone, her head echoes with sounds no longer made by Henry James, who is but a portly poor old bachelor after all, and she is not the she of household worry either, or lawyer at her legal tomes, but these words are the words of Sophocles, then, of Oedipus just now blind, and the world is the world it once was when the world was alive.

Like most words, "mimesis" is a nest of meanings. Shadings fly from it like fledgling birds: imitation, representation, replication, impersonation, or portrayal do for Plato; nowadays we could add copy, counterfeit, dupe. Grammatically different forms of what is called "the mimesis group" designate the action of mimicry—or the actor, mime, or mockingbird that performs the tune—while others aim at either the subject of imitation or its result, or sometimes indicate the arena of representation itself: the agora, law courts, or the stage. Mimesis calls the theater home, some say; it is derived from the dance; it belongs to mockery and mime, not always silent, and is often concerned with events and situations in daily life; no, it is the creation of effigies—statues, scarecrows, voodoo dolls—it is the means by which we call upon the gods. But did these meanings of mimesis really compete, or is the competition to be found in the disputatious pages of contemporary scholars, who prefer one meaning (theirs) over others, much as if, in a mulligan stew, one conferred honor and dominance to six pearl onions.

For Plato and Aristotle, I think, the word is still a wardrobe, but it is stashed backstage where the masks are kept and the chorus instructed. The actor becomes his role, we sometimes say; but what does the role become? I remember that Shakespeare says very little about Hamlet's weight, nor does he give Iago thin lips and an evil nose, as Dickens would be sure to. How can I impersonate a creature whose visible form is unknown? Merely claim to be him or her? Zeus dons and doffs bodies the way we do clothes. Clouds are camels one minute, streaming hair the next. Some things, like Proteus, have no fixed form, so I could claim I was, while in my workaday togs, one of the sea's moods. In many paintings Jesus is as blond and blue-eyed as a Nazi.

If Socrates has a snub nose and thyroid eyes, his portrait should have the same painted nose put in the same painted place, and the same swollen eyes painted as protruding—paint for point and point for paint over the whole head. But what good is a likeness *when it is the reality of the thing that should be realized*—should be, yet can't be—not in another medium. Once, when the world was young and still alive as liquor, the soul itself might slide from fern or face into the leaves that covered Eve and Adam, or love pass from the lover's adoration into the heart of the adored. But now, when the gods were called upon to come from their own play into ours, how could the transfer be effected?

A god enters, but speaks Sophocles anyway, having, as some say, no mind of his own. In the theater it is only the words that can achieve the change. The music, the moving limbs, the spectacle from painted drop to gaudy robe and dancing lads, add their emphasis, their rhythm, their emotion to the speech, but what, when Apollo approaches . . . what will . . . what will the god say? And the gods will have the character the poets give them; the gods will wear whatever raiment can be sewn; the gods will do as they are told. . . . But a person that the audience knows well, such as Socrates in Aristophanes' satires, will have to have at least the demeanor Athenians are used to. Certainly this is true of Plato's own challenge to the dramatists. *The Dialogues* are nothing less than the theater of reason where Plato's Socrates plays the role of the real one. There is an irony in this that has not gone unnoticed . . . by Gunter Gebauer and Christoph Wulf, for instance, who write: "There is an element of contradiction in the fact that Plato criticizes art as mimesis in principle but at the same time works mimetically in producing dialogues in which artistic elements are present."

In the early dialogues, Plato may be considered to be presenting Socrates to us in his full historical reality, in which case the philosopher's mimetic skills are governed by historical concerns; whereas, in dialogues of the so-called middle period, Plato's interests are more and more "artistic" and "fictional." But I suspect that Socrates' great speech that concludes the *Apology* is about as faithfully mimetic as Pericles' funeral oration in the imaginative reenactment of Thucydides. Nevertheless, Pericles must sound Periclean, and speak as the occasion demanded, just as Socrates must press his case for suicide in the *Crito* because so many are alive who know he did so.

But if the features of the person to be represented have to be created, the chances are they will replicate the characteristics chosen by the first imitator who undertook the task and did Buddha fat and Hamlet thin, Desdemona blonde because Othello's black, Jesus fair with a light beard and wavy hair, handsome as heaven—as if he'd been there; because the audience has attended these plays, too, and knows what Apollo came arrayed in apart from light, and what suited the Furies and Clytemnestra's moods. Although each author interprets the myths in his own way, what Electra says has to be in harmony with what Electra was in her last show, her previously recounted story, her rap sheet. Otherwise she'll not be she, and fool nobody. The operatic custom that permits a fat Carmen to shake the flats when she dances the seguidilla will not travel any better than the local wine. The success you might have in making yourself similar to somebody else will depend upon the ignorance of the audience you intend to fool, and the success, in creating a tradition, of any previous proponents of your scam. Plato knows there are no gods, that the gods are merely Hesiod's manner of speaking. How much of Homer did he honor as the truth, or were the poets liars in every rhyme and line?

I bring this unpleasantness up because it may help us to understand the relation appearance has to reality. If reality remains unknown, then Punch is Punch and Judy Judy, both as real as the husbands and wives in Devon or Westphalia they might have been used to represent, or as present in the world as the warring forces of good and evil. Furthermore, bowing before a curtain of ignorance, any appearance may choose its cause and claim it. I can be said to resemble my uncle Fred only by those who know both of us. If no one knows, no one can gainsay it. If no one knows, no one will care.

Plato became convinced that Parmenides was too quick to dismiss this world of incessant change, too eager to move on (itself an act of deception) from its illusions to the eternal unshakable plenum that Being really was. These fleeting appearances had to be saved, yet they could be accounted for only if they were explained; and they could be explained perfectly provided this world were indeed a play, much as Shakespeare and others would describe it. It could be saved if the mime it made were as successful as the speeches of Aeschylus and Sophocles, and the world was understood to participate in the Forms through its acts of so eloquently copying them, reality descending to touch our lives like the gods once inhabited the speech of Prometheus, perhaps, or Athena as she made her vows.

And doesn't Plato say in the *Laws* [817b], when the playwrights clamor to be allowed to ply their trade in his second best State, that

> we also according to our ability are tragic poets, and our tragedy is the best and noblest; for our whole state is an imitation of the best and noblest life, which we affirm to be indeed the very truth of tragedy. You are poets and we are poets, both makers of the same strains, rivals, and antagonists in the noblest of dramas, which true law can alone perfect, as our hope is. Do not then suppose that we shall all in a moment allow you to erect your stage in the agora, or introduce the fair voices of your actors, speaking above our own, and permit you to harangue our women and children, and the common people, about our institutions, in language other than our own, and very often the opposite of our own. For a state would be mad which gave you this licence, until the magistrates had determined whether your poetry might be recited, and was fit for publication or not.

Appearances are to be saved by being explained, not improved. It is important to the psyche that this world not be understood to be a deliberate lie, rather just a necessary one. Poets, it is true, do not make things up out of whole cloth. There *was* a Troy. It *was* destroyed. But they are song stitchers of low employ. They make quilts out of scraps and tatters, castoffs, rags, and misfitting sweaters,

195

William H. Gass

which warm as well as the purest wool—a good that frugality might celebrate—if warming were the reason for the sheep.

Plato was of course aware, as many now who peruse these texts or attend these tragedies are not, that committees chose the plays that would compete; that money had to be raised for their performance, much as we squeeze uniforms from our local merchants to doll up our children's soccer teams; that politics was always an issue; that religious implications were rife; and that the aim of the citizens who performed these tasks was principally the reaffirmation of common ideals, and the strengthening of community spirit and purpose. It was important then that the dramas appeal to the public, cause the right sort of stir, and be accounted successes.

In the Athens of this time there was another contest: that between the poets, priests, philosophers, and politicians, for the power that the approval—the applause of the people—might give them. So that they might lead, they claimed to bear the solemn burden of the truth, a burden that many liars are eager to say they carry like an Olympic torch to light the public way. Plato's complaints about the poets—in this context where the truth of things is at stake—are, I think, entirely appropriate and right, because the truth, in the politician's oratory, arrives arrayed in rhetoric fit to the public's fears and wants, while in a poet's mouth, such truth becomes the sweet taste of the line, not the hard design of science or the rigor of philosophical argument. Rhyme, of the sort I have just employed, might be sugar to the ear and thus agreeable to the mind. Although Sophists like Gorgias might make a public show of their rhetorical gifts, it was the mimesis of the drama that most frequently encouraged passion and desire to rule the soul. In the arena of the theater, people sometimes charged the stage, shouted angrily, and even fainted. None of this was known to be a reaction to the premises of an argument.

Plato is critical of the mimesis of the poets and the painters because he has made Truth and Beauty predicates of the Good as every puritan has since. But he has plenty of positive use for mimesis in his own great contribution to aesthetics (in addition to the *Symposium*, of course), namely the cosmological dialogue, the *Timaeus*. This dialogue, cast in meaningful mythological terms, is a description of the making (the poesis) of the sensible universe. The Demiurge of the dialogue is a creator par excellence—the best, in fact, that could be imagined—and he will be responsible for the existence of appearance as well as its relation to reality.

196

From the Beginning there existed Being, Nonbeing, and the great Receptacle, Space. Being is understood as the realm of Forms, and these are formulas, as I prefer to see them, expressible in mathematical terms. The epistemological essence of Platonism (I shall foolhardily say) is that we shall recognize that we have knowledge in any sphere to the degree we can express it mathematically. In any case, these Forms are arranged in a hierarchy topped by the Good that contains them all. It does not, however, contain them the way Aristotle's idea of Being contains all that really is, for Aristotle's formulation is always in terms of genus and species expressed in extensional language—as spaces, or classes, or sets. For Aristotle, the widest, the most embracing class is the least informative one, and to say of anything that it has Being is to say the least possible about it; whereas, for Plato, the Good is an integration of other Forms the way flavors blend or colors mix, and we can find in this intentional interpretation remnants of animistic and naively realistic thinking, because Plato's daring formulae are like recipes interested in the qualitative flavor of ideas rather than classes that can enter a large sphere as dogs might join cats in the realm of pets without altering either their own nature or habits, those of cats, or even the defining properties of the class of pets. You can't mix paint with that expectation.

The realm of Forms has Being but it is not alive. Only the soul is alive. It is the moving principle, an intermediary between Being and the created world that it will animate. The Forms are the Demiurge's model. His palette is the chaos of sensible qualities Plato calls Nonbeing, though it is scarcely nothing. It is called Nonbeing because it is a mess, because without order there can be no Being. And what are these qualities? colors, noises, feelings, I suspect, flavors, pains probably? aches wandering around without knees or any other place to inflict? smells that have never known noses, sours apart from their whiskeys, and every adjective as it would be if bereft of its noun—unattached, meaningless, waiting to modify. They are adrift like seawrack in the Great Receptacle, as Plato calls it. In the womb of things to be. Time will be created as the moving image of eternity, but emptiness has always been, and here it serves as the canvas for the artist, the place the pigments will finally find their regal robes and handsome face.

With every element prepared, the Demiurge makes the Pythagoreans look smart by fashioning the frame of the universe from such simplicities as their treasured right triangle, whose figured image, when flipped so that one shape lies provocatively upon another, causes a rectangle to appear, and when spun creates a cone, and by various whirls around its hypotenuse produces whatever geometry requires, since spheres are cones rolled the right way.

Three important factors in creativity are singled out, and these three remain as resolutely present now as they were then. The Demiurge must suffer some things to come about through sheer Necessity: space is what it is, the qualities are what they are, the mural's wall is but ten feet high, and there is an oval window in it; the words of any language, its grammar, its historical contexts, are as given as a flaw in the sculptor's marble, or as the nubble of the canvas that requires it to be sized, or the fact that the blond the studio has cast in the lead has a lisp more prominent than her notorious chest. On the other hand, many things come about through reason alone, when the Demiurge's intentions are nowhere impeded. Finally, for most effects, the Demiurge must "persuade necessity," as Plato puts it. Here the artist's skill is at its utmost: that flaw in the marble becomes the center of the composition; necessity is not merely the mother but it is the entire household of invention; and what could not be helped is made a help, or as the formula would later be: for the artist, the arbitrary is a gift to form.

Reality is not alive. It is the Pythagorean world of number and as still as the plenum of Parmenides. But think of the plight of the Forms. Put yourself in their place. You are a law of motion yet you do not move, nothing moves, there is no performance. You are the way things would change if anything did but it does not—a falling body would go splat if there were bodies and if they fell, but they do not; or you are the definition of a species extinct before knowing life and have only imaginary members; and though you are an object of knowledge, you will never know what knowing is, or like a castled virgin—flaxen-haired Beauty herself—what it is like to be seen, longed for, touched, loved.

Plato never tells us why the Demiurge felt that need . . . to create an inferior realm, a necessarily imperfect copy of the Forms, a realm of Becoming . . . but I think I have suggested a reason. The Forms have what Aristotle would later call "second-grade actuality"—the kind that things made for a function possess while waiting for that function to be realized: the tool in the box, the book on the shelf, the manuscript at the bottom of a drawer, a talent not yet discovered, young men at puberty before being killed in a war. The realm of Forms will not be perfect if it remains as pure as Plato at first imagines it to be. So its image is required. The forms have implicit denotations. What does it mean to say that there are theories, laws, explanations, definitions without the heat, movement, makeup, character, or morals they delimit, regulate, and rule. Reality needs appearance to complete it.

The world needs souls if the world would be moved, and souls need poets to move them. Pythagorean formulae that resemble those for the harmonic mean are mixed like ingredients for a Christmas loaf by the Demiurge, and out of these numerals soul stuff is rolled into orbits and raised into spheres: the passage of the planets and the ceiling of the sky with all its stars becomes the soul of the world, now understood, in purely animistic terms, to be a living, breathing animal within one of whose countless furrows we live like mites, mostly ignored. Such an amazing dream.

The movement of the planets is rational, therefore it is circular, another bit of animistic logic that prefers cycles: the daily sun, those of human generations, the phases of the moon, the periodicity of women, the revivals of the seasons, and the return of past times like comets from a long journey. And while such perfection the circle has suits the planets, who resemble real gods—unolympian, unanthropomorphic, undeterrable—it will not do for man or any other living things whose perfection falls far short of even the circulations of the hula hoop. Now comes a moment in Plato's account that is straight out of the atelier. The Demiurge may not make man more rational than he is, yet his touch will do just that, so, having created reason, fashioning the lower parts of the soul is left to the planetary gods, subordinate workmen, and from them our vegetable lives and our animal instincts are made, as if the background of a mural were left to the master's best pupils to practice on. Frank Gehry cannot be expected to have designed everything he signs his name to.

These identical three-part souls are sown throughout the universe and bring to life the bodies they enter, with the curious consequence that a carrot will possess as full a soul as the rabbit who fancies it or the hunter who snares, and it will be the inadequacies of their respective bodies that will determine individuality. Souls have no more individuality than a plastic drinking cup. So if you are smarter than I am, it is because your body (hence the lower orders of the soul) has less influence on your thoughts and actions than mine has.

That is to say: you are better ruled. This is another mimetic element in the Platonic system, and develops from a proportional metaphor: the soul resides in the person as the person resides in the state. The soul, it seems, is a little kingdom that may be run well or badly depending on whether it is governed by reason or by passions and desires. The political entity that Plato calls the Republic has a soul as well. It is composed of the three classes of citizens in the state: guardians, functionaries, and workers. Of the cardinal virtues, three are particularly appropriate to the structure of the soul and the ruling organization of the commonwealth: temperance suits the workers who are mastered by their appetites, as fruits and vegetables are—breeding and feeding—next, two kinds of courage, of body and spirit, are appropriate to the soldiers and administrators, while wisdom, of course, is special to the guardians. Justice, the final virtue of the four, is the harmony in each soul that is reflected in an analogous harmony in the state, each element performing its proper task.

Using this scheme it is possible to describe governments in terms of the balance of the classes in them, and whether the citizens have been properly sorted out. Tyrants, who were as plentiful then as they apparently always are, furnished examples of city states ruled by the worst rather than the best, and democracy (by which Plato understood a government largely run by tribes or demes, with officials chosen from them somewhat at random) to be little better run than if they were not run at all.

We have not yet passed through the entire mimetic chain. If the Forms are definitions—definitions of functions—they are also instructions, and the world of appearance participates in the Forms (one meaning of mimesis) by carrying out these instructions, though how specifically Plato never makes clear. Any bed, for instance, will exhibit the physical laws that make its structure suitable for sleep, a need that human beings have, according to a Form's program for us. But we do not dwell in this world the way trees or stones or beds do, unconscious of their surroundings. Is what we see when we see, and feel when we touch, a copy, too?

It would be too much to expect that a culture that has just discovered the self, just made the distinction between appearance and reality, located abstract ideas as if they were stars from another hemisphere, and begun the foundations of logic as well as the entire remaining table of contents for philosophy, to have driven their epistemology so quickly into subjectivity as later the Enlightenment would; but in the *Theaetetus* Plato has put his pedal to the metal. He fashions for us another amazing sexual metaphor. Such images appear to be his specialty.

He conjectures that when we see, rays emanating from the eyes encounter, as a searchlight might, other rays reflected by or sent forth from objects. These rays intermingle like passionate limbs and from their intercourse are born twins (which, as we know, are a sign their mother has suffered trespass as well as the owner's tread over his rightful property). Then the eye *sees*. That is one child. And the object *becomes* white. That is the other. After all, what has Plato's favorite word for our world been but that of Becoming. Perhaps Plato has imagined one too many rays, though today we wallow in frequencies. Still, if I blow the dog's whistle, his ears hear, and the whistle grows loud. We would probably say: for him; but the Greeks don't doubt the public nature of appearances. The world is as external, as objective, as the facade of the palace at Thebes. And Oedipus enters for all to see.

In Plato's day, art was becoming more mimetic by the minute. And that meant: more faithful to appearances. Figures were now individualized, not so hieratic, symbolic, and formal; casts were being taken from the bodies of athletes to the scandal of the connoisseurs; decoration was looser and less geometrical; paintings that deceived the eye were marveled at (Plato was not pleased that painters were proud when birds pecked at their painted grapes); drama was undergoing the same slow transformation: had not Agathon—the writer whose victory in the theatrical competitions the *Symposium* celebrates— introduced, for the first time, nonmythological elements? and what was one to say about Euripides' sensationalism, and his vulgar pandering to the passions of the populace? Aristophanes had made fun of the saintly Socrates before the Athenians murdered him. Artists were in cahoots with the priests who looked after the numerous sanctuaries that had sprung up as if piles of rock had been watered into bloom, and votive objects and other offerings to the gods had collected in the precincts of the shrines like leaves in a windless corner. The politicians, moreover, had led the people into an ill-favored, unfortunate, and lengthy war. Plato's attitude would become a familiar one. Mass culture has been eating away at high culture's cookie for as long as baking has been a business. Sculptors were manufacturing huge heavily bedizened statues for the public to marvel at, and countless pretty boys in marble toes or ladies dressed in plump breasts and long thighs that Roman pillagers would later resell to the Latin bourgeois, received the ardent admiration of the masses—not just then, but, in the guise of Roman copies, since.

What a pleasure it was to produce reasons why copying was so detrimental to the rational spirit, and put painters in their place, because the people and scenes they painted were already artifacts, already appearances, already removed from reality by at least one degree. Falsehoods follow falsehoods like pilgrims to their shrine. The world loves the flattery that all likeness intends.

However, that very character of mimesis is essential to the educational process, much of which must take place before the age of reason, and therefore very often by means of imitation. The youth must be provided with proper role models—to employ one of our popular euphemisms. Plato has still another use for his proportional metaphor of the divisions of the soul and state, because when we are infants, we are also as vegetables, we eat and excrete, cry and kick, and our parents are expected to supply the moderation that would otherwise be lacking. As youths we are controlled by our passions, and we must be taught to bleed for peace instead of oil, to direct our feelings to their appropriate objects, to love the good and hate the ill informed. When adults, we rule ourselves. This is an ideal, of course, because when the State is badly managed, its citizens remain children; they fire their guns into the sky; they die for the wrong causes; they allow their passions to be stirred by raucous music; they read only one book.

Alas, for consistency, if we tell only nice things about Zeus and his fellow loungers on Mount Olympus, so that the youth will have something to be devout about, we shall have to tell lies, for the gods are as wicked as you and I, and don't rule the way guardians are supposed to. Lying is not a seemly exercise, nevertheless Plato recommends a shield of lies to protect the innocence of the people and enable them to be more easily managed.

Yet one more proportion can be lined up alongside Plato's controlling metaphor, namely parallel levels of knowledge. When the appetitive portion dominates, the soul lives in a state of ignorance, is psychologically a child, and should be allowed only a workman's productive role in the ideal Republic. He or she depends upon successful praxis to make do, and learns a trade by imitating those who already have it. Skills, like casting bronze, are passed down from a master to his sons like recipes for stews, and may include good, bad, or irrelevant advice, often a surprising mingling of superstition and good sense. Administrators are allowed doxa—opinions—beliefs that, whether right or wrong, are not supported by satisfactory reasons. Only guardians possess the logos, theoretical knowledge, the justification that makes some opinions sound.

These three levels of "knowledge and education"—praxis, doxa,

William H. Gass

logos—match up with the parts of the soul, and those with the stages of human growth and psychological types, and those with the classification of citizens along with their appropriate virtues, to form the soul of the State; and in every case the connection is established through mimesis—mimesis as either impersonation, participation, or copy—and one in which Form is made manifest through the order it lends to illusion.

If Plato is prepared to put every meaning of mimesis to use, and make it a modest philosophical jack-of-all-trades, Aristotle appears inclined to confine it to more purely aesthetic contexts. Either because of the fragmentary character of the *Poetics*, its sketchy lecture-note quality, or its immense concision, there seem to be more flagrant misrepresentations of its contents than most early tracts have had to suffer. As Stephen Halliwell points out in *The Aesthetics of Mimesis*, "The philosopher's concept of mimesis has played a vital role in the long story of Western attitudes to artistic representation, [but] that role has often been mediated through the reworking and misrepresentation of his ideas, especially those found in the *Poetics*." I would suggest that the philosopher's concept has not played a vital role, after all, but only misconstruals of it have, much in the same way that the Bible has suffered from its readers, so that what it has been taken to mean, not what it means, matters. Falsehood and error have played a far larger role in history than truth and correctness, for falsehoods always find a way to be convenient and of use.

Even if Aristotle had said, "Art is an imitation of nature," the words he would have used—*techné, mimesis, physis*—would have given the game away for each of these terms has considerable philosophical significance in Aristotle's work, and understood in that context, make the formula one I, at least, might love, instead of this infamous sentence's historic meanings, all of which are vulgar and abhorrent. Aristotle says he is going to investigate one of the productive arts—the craft of making poems—and that investigation will involve distinguishing poetry's genres and their particular effects, defining the elements that constitute the craft, especially how to turn traditional plots into decent drama, as well as whatever else proves to be pertinent during the course of his study. And he will begin, as he customarily does, with first principles.

He could have said he was going to study the skill of a pilot of ships, whose aim is a safe arrival in harbor, or that of a physician, whose purpose is healing; but neither is a part of poiesis—the productive arts. He could have made his subject the sandal maker's art: what kinds of sandals there were, what end each was designed to serve, and how you went about making them: the tools you would need, the materials you might choose, and so forth. But, you might say, in that case where does mimesis come in? Some animals have padded paws, some have hooves, some skins as leathery as gloves. But we have no such protection from the sharp stones of the road, so the cobbler remedies that lack, not by imitating hooves but by following the hints thrown out by nature, and bringing shoes into being mechanically without any thought of resemblance, only one of function. The principle of change lies in the cobbler, and is clearly external to its object. When the artisan goes to work, he makes things by *following the pattern of nature* (that is the right rendering of "mimesis" here): it makes lava, he manufactures plastics; it grows talons, he invents corkscrews; it encourages eagles, he runs after rats with baited traps.

There are some things in nature that need to be fixed, and there are others that aren't there at all, but ought to be. The physician mends, the cobbler adds. Potions that physicians might need, our chemists sometimes supply. It will be like that with the craft of poetry. Tragedy, it will turn out, is a purgative, and good for the body politic—an analogy that has its origins in Plato, but one which Aristotle is happy to continue. He was the son of a physician, after all.

There is another consequence of Aristotle's treatment of poetry as a craft. As Gerald Else remarks in *Aristotle's Poetics: The Argument,* ". . . there is not a word anywhere in the *Poetics* about the persons Homer and Sophocles. The artist does not produce *qua* man, person, individual, but *qua* artist; or as Aristotle says, with his special brand of vividness, 'it is accidental to the sculptor that he is Polyclitus.'" Another example, updated from Plato: the art of medicine is a body of knowledge that the physician internalizes. Then when Dr. Weisenheimer cures my gout, it is the art of medicine that does it. When he botches the job, he does so as old Joe Weisenheimer of Louisa Alcott Lane. When the Romantic poets fly their kites, it is the wind that keeps them airborne. They just think is it their own hot air.

So poetry is placed among the productive arts. In the most businesslike fashion possible. I don't think one can stress this placement too strongly. As Gerald Else concludes, "His treatise is not a discussion of 'poetry' in either, or any, sense of the English term; it is, in all sadness and sobriety, an analysis of the nature and functioning of the *art* of poetry and of its species."

It is not *about* Sophocles' *Oedipus Rex*. And those species: what are they? They are the epic (which is recited), tragedy and comedy (which are performed), and dithyrambic poetry (which is sung by a chorus). Flute and lyre music are also deemed imitations. Aristotle goes on to say that some arts use color and shape, but all the others employ the voice, or are at least audible.

Aristotle resides in an oral culture still. Moreover, he knows that the written word can resemble only other written words. "The cat sat on the mat" in no way imitates its situation. When Creon enters in a snit, however, his words enable the actor to impersonate his character, mimic his tone of voice, and say what he might say under the circumstances. We also know that he won't talk American, though he does in this translation.

> Citizens, I have come because I heard
> deadly words spread about me, that the king
> accuses me. I cannot take that from him.
> —*Oedipus the King*, David Grene translation

The stage direction "Creon enters" does not imitate an action, it orders it. The words Creon speaks do not imitate his state of mind, they express it. However, Creon's speaking them—his tone of voice, his choice of the Americanism "cannot take that from him"—do help the actor impersonate Creon's character and consequently could be said to be an imitation.

In the case of music, both Plato and Aristotle seem to find it especially infectious—that martial music makes one martial, that lullabies lull, and so on—that is, they encourage participation, but it is the dynamics of music, more than anything else, that is transferable, and it is music, too, that achieves its harmony through the formal relations of its sounds and the manner of their production, since the Pythagoreans had presumably discovered a connection between tones and the length of a lyre string. Its harmonies and disharmonies affect the morally important emotions; indeed, as Stephen Halliwell puts it in *The Aesthetics of Mimesis*, "They are enacted by the qualities of the artwork. That these qualities are 'in' the (musically organized) sounds themselves is inferred from music's capacity to convey emotional-cum-ethical feelings to the audience."

Previously I observed how Plato had argued for a division between the realm of Being and the world of Becoming that could only be crossed on a bridge of mimesis. The Demiurge uses sensory qualities to imitate the Forms: the things of this world impersonate their real counterparts, and gain their secondary and only reality by participating in them. Aristotle, with so much common sense it seems daring, does not have a gulf he must cross because his Forms exist in every instance of their kinds. They are sunk in their particulars like posts. If all the members of a species are there, in that species, because they have "the same form," then might it not be possible to imagine a situation in which a form customarily found in one place was found in another as well? A musical score possesses a note structure that the performer follows and reproduces in the piece he plays; moreover, the auditory waves that microphones capture and transfer to digital tapes can boast that structure, too, as have a disc's grooves. It might only be a metaphor, but music's moods and the emotional coloration of our consciousness could share similar dynamic relationships without in the least having the same content.

Ultimately, Aristotle interprets the form/content connection first as a structure/function relation and finally as one of potency and act. To understand this we have to remind ourselves of Aristotle's classification of causes into four kinds, because they apply to the sources of action in a tragedy, and to the course of mimesis there, as surely as they do to nature and life generally. Every event has a material cause. It is made of something, sometimes several different kinds of things, and this matter must be considered, when confined to artistry, as canvas and pigment, words in a language, sounds from a flute, stone from a quarry. Every material will have its own actuality (the idea of something that is pure potentiality—prime matter—is entirely conceptual); that is, marble will have that stone's qualities and forms. These, however, will be the basis for the many things it might do or become. The efficient cause is simply the work done in order to realize those potentialities; it is energy enabled by tools and directed by skills, in the sculptor's case, so that out of the marble a marble fawn emerges.

The formal cause is what will be later called the object's essence, and like the material cause is a combination of what the thing actually is and what it can become because of what it actually is; however, the formal cause is its definition, and determines what a thing is destined to become or do if allowed to express its nature. In the case of a work of art, the formal cause, as I've said, lies outside the thing itself and resides in the artist. Nothing grows into a marble fawn on its own, though fawns do. Those principles of change that

206

reside within an object or event are said to be its entelechy—its direction of self-realization. The final cause is, of course, the end at which a course of action aims, the fully realized deer, or statue, or polished skill.

All this is elementary Aristotle. What scholars seem less inclined to do is to apply Aristotle's physics and metaphysics (even his ethics and his logic) to the principles of the *Poetics*. If we do that, many obscurities become immediately clear and the concision of the text understandable. For instance, a tragedy, Aristotle says, is the imitation of a morally serious action—clearly one that has taken place, or might take place, in the ordinary life of extraordinary people—in such a way as to show how its consequences follow inevitably from its nature. These consequences invariably involve the loss of eudaemonia, well-being, or self-fulfillment, not merely for the individual but for the society. So often catastrophe is the result of excess: of success, as if a vine choked the tree it twined upon; or certainty, as if you bet your life on your ability to guess right; or duty, pursuing what you think proper against every advice; or of innocence, or loyalty, or honesty itself, so often not the best policy because virtue is the way to ruin.

Aristotle advises the plot maker to concentrate upon a single unified action, and therefore one that is definable and has a beginning, middle, and an end. His advice is not as simpleminded as it sounds. It has to do, as he says later, with raveling and unraveling, tying the knot, and untying it.

The beginning of a play is complete when the dramatist has established a situation that implicitly contains the conclusion. It is the planted seed. Henry James used to feel that his beginnings always needed more material put in them to support the story, consequently they grew too large, so he studied various methods of foreshortening. For Aristotle, the play's course—the object of its mimesis—must resemble an entelechy. The play's middle occurs at that point in the arc of an arrow's flight when its rise weakens and the course of its return becomes inevitable. This is often seen as a reversal of fortune, since the action was initially regarded as a good and wise one, and prospers in that guise, before showing its true self, and reversing its direction. The conclusion is the completed actualization of what was there to be realized from the beginning. When there are many subordinate plot lines, the trick is to find one fulfillment that will satisfy them all.

The infamous unities of one place/one day are suggested only because such a confinement makes far easier the disclosure of consequences. A tragedy should move like a syllogism from premises to conclusion. The fewer premises the better. The ordinary world rarely offers us such a sight because there are too many competing courses of action. The seed of a tree must not only cope with the earth it finds itself in and employ the moisture and nutrients that are there, but it must compete with other plants for its light and food, avoid being munched into oblivion by a deer, and stand up eventually against the elements, dodge disease, the sawmill, and the forest's fires. History is an account of accidents, collisions of causes, and its results are always maimed. Thousands are throwing their basketballs at the same basket. History hears only the din of disappointed ends. There is no song that isn't interrupted almost the moment it's begun. History is wreckage. Whereas the tragic action grows like a plant in a nursery or a bacterium in a laboratory. No one is permitted to knock it from its stand; no diseases darken its leaves, no worms chew its blooms. We can therefore see what it will be; what it is in its inner self—a complete action as rounded as a racecourse. Who better than Kant to warn us against actions with unintended consequences, advice that, given early, nevertheless comes to our politicians too late. Tragedy drops one small smooth pebble into a calm, pure pond and then measures, whereas history tosses a handful of gravel into a raging sea on a foggy day. That is why poetry is more philosophical than history. History's universals are all dead or dismembered.

Oedipus sees his own tragedy unfold and is the best spectator for his own blinding. He learns that what he never intended to happen fate has seen to. The play that so fascinated the Philosopher does not imitate our world. Nor do Galileo's mechanics. When has a kid slid down a slide the way a kid would if the kid were an imaginary kid computing the rate of his passage along geometry's inclined plane? Utopias, like Plato's Republic, attempt to control causes and consequences, generally with ludicrous results. Better a plausible impossibility, Artistotle remarks, to the consternation of countless commentators, than an implausible possibility; because history is nothing but the implausible, the unpredictable, the incredible concatenation. A good play's movement is inexorable. It is, in that sense, the equal of any argument. In real life, people recover from incurable cancers—occasionally. And nearly always in bad movies. We complain of such conclusions. We blame them on Hollywood.

Aristotle wants his action to be performed by a powerful person so that the consequences will escape their agent and implicate the State. All of Thebes is suffering, the chorus is quick to tell us. Tragedy is a massive loss of opportunity. Right or wrong, Aristotle always makes sense.

The artist brings things into being the way nature brings things into being. Art adds realities to the world that were missing from it, and that well might belong here. That is Aristotle's sense of mimesis: it does not make copies of things. It does not end with a likeness. It is, instead, an investigation, an argument, a realization.

Beuyskreuz
Anne Carson

BEUYSLUCK
How happy[1] it made Beuys that his name rhymed
with Joyce.

BEUYSCUT
During one concert
Beuys took out the heart of a hare. The hare was already dead
and connected by electrical wires to his piano. Which reality?
is a question he liked to ask. He did not want an answer,
he wanted a synonym.

BEUYSCHOICE
Symbols are not his way. To analogize, to interpret, no.
You are in mortal danger. Get onto the sled.

BEUYSWOUND
His actions are a kind of speculation. They are hard work to
figure out. The shaman worries about you every minute of your
life except during the ritual. Then you are on your own.

BEUYSJOYCE
They are two people not the only two people who believe
the first moment after Babel was silent. A silence repository.
Beuys made his belief into a butter pot.

---

[1]To celebrate he cooked a sheep's kidney on a stove in his room.

BEUYSEND I

A. told me Beuys's last work was a forty-foot ladder suspended
up to the ceiling by two huge iron balls. K. told me it was a room
in Venice empty but for twelve canvases painted gold.

BEUYSEND II

Stack these stories against death.

BEUYSEND III

Now bloom your head and ride it six more chapters.

BEUYSTOLL

Democracy is merry!
he used to say.
His eyes
would slightly cross.
Hard to reach into such a person. Humor. Obsession.
Hat. Headwound. To accommodate three tons of tallow he once
persuaded the Guggenheim Museum it should remove part of
its facade! To any question involving the adverb *why* he answered
Take your silly hammer with you.
Now those happy
days are gone, pray
the angels keep Beuys
from all harm.

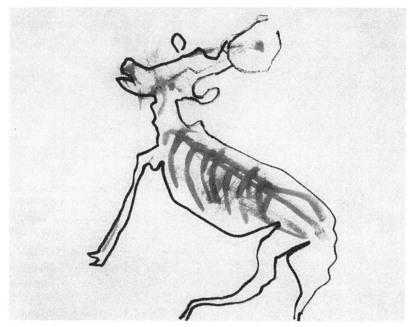

Beuyshammer. 2005. 5 x 7 inches. Pen, ink, and crayon by Anne Carson.

Practicing the Arts of Peace
John Crowley

THE NOTION OF THE ARTS of peace (the term itself is, I suppose, not original with me) first arose for me spontaneously a year or more ago, when I received a letter—well, an e-mail, I mean, naturally—from an MFA candidate in writing at the University of Massachusetts, near where I live. I knew Andre slightly from parties and as a clerk in the best bookstore in Amherst. I can place the time of the letter by his first reference:

"I've been bummed since Susan Sontag died," he wrote. "For me, she is the most important intellectual. . . . It's weird trying to mourn for someone who you didn't know but who changed you so much (and the world, for that matter). So—I don't know, how do you mourn Susan Sontag? Read a novel by someone from eastern Europe? Watch a German film? Go to the ballet? Go to Iraq? It seems so stupid to even try."

He continues then: "I wonder—if you don't mind me asking such a dreadful question—where you think your work fits in the world. And I don't mean 'the world of letters'—I mean the world. . . . What do you think it's doing out there, set adrift? What do you hope it's doing? You don't have to answer—I know people always feel so odd answering stuff like this—I know I would. . . . Maybe you don't hope it's doing anything, really—but I would guess that you do. Anyway, back to other things—hope all is well. Andre."

I didn't write back for some time, and when I did it was without much thought, or maybe with the distillation of a lot of thought that had been going on below the level of even mental speech: "Andre— I'm sorry not to have replied to this letter. There's a beautiful— almost sweet—picture of Susan Sontag in the new *NYRB*. . . . My work and the world: I was asked by somebody back at the time of the invasion of Iraq how we could all just go on writing our funny little stories, especially we fantasists, and I said that in my opinion what we were doing was practicing the arts of peace. What we want is a world in which funny fantastical stories are possible and are valued. In which there is nothing so dreadful or urgent that it causes the

213

writing of such things to stop or to be stopped. Worlds where the arts of peace can't be practiced are wounded worlds, and that's why we have to go on practicing those arts, so that our worlds don't die. Bruno Schulz in the Poland of World War II practiced the arts of peace in his fantastic stories—until he was killed. No one's likely to kill me for being a practitioner, but it's what I do."

This reply now seems to me so compressed as to be not entirely intelligible, and yet it is the answer I meant to give. I would like to explicate it somewhat if I can.

First of all, what did I mean by "the arts of peace"? I didn't mean artworks that plead for or promote peace, or denounce injustice or hatred or violence. I meant something like the opposite of that, or at least ninety degrees from it. I was thinking of works that have no designs upon us, that do not aim to convince or convert or instruct us; works that follow their own aesthetic imperatives and no others, works that are good but can't really be said to do good, that are superfluous to the economics and politics of utility, though they may be commodities, even popular ones in high demand. The arts of peace flourish in times of peace, and their flourishing marks an age of peace or at least a space or a hope or an assumption of peace, maybe only a nostalgia for such a space or time: they assert the possibility of a space of peace by their existence. That's their only utility, though not their value.

Of all the arts of peace, music has the least need to justify the production of works that have only their own aesthetic demands to meet, which is why Walter Pater said that all art aspires to the condition of music. Bach's cantatas and masses are intended to promote or intensify religious feeling, but—unlike religious tracts or religious novels—they have very similar effects on those who are not religious, and his secular or nonutilitarian music has no reference at all except itself. Operas, from those of Verdi to John Adams and Philip Glass, may have designs on us, and be concerned with liberty, injustice, tyranny, and violence, but they all need words and narrative to make their points, as do songs—the indifference of music to import can be shown by the way the same melody can support words of widely varied meaning. Rossini used the same overture for different operas, serious and comic.

Narrative arts, though—stories, dramas, films—are never free of connections to our lived lives, the human predicament, the age, or the social moment; they have to tell stories *about* something, and it's been shown now by a century of experiment that they die if they don't. Most people would agree that bringing us news, or instruction, or descriptions of our own or other social structures, or explication of our dilemmas and moral challenges, is a big part of what stories do and should do. Those that are effective at this work need to have no other power, and some of them have had great power: they really do make things happen. Fictions that have had such power in the world tend to lose it when the world changes, and they cease to be read much, like Upton Sinclair's *The Jungle,* which altered the meat-packing industry and made Spam safe both to make and to eat. Cher-nyshevsky's *What Is to Be Done?* (wonderfully spoofed by Vladimir Nabokov in *The Gift*) inspired a generation of Russian reformers, but couldn't now. *1984* is an exception, maybe, somehow still horribly powerful as parable though its particular lessons are outdated. But *Les Misérables* doesn't send us to the barricades now, any more than *Gone with the Wind* makes us supporters of white supremacy, as it surely was meant to do. If they are still read, they are read for a different reason, and hold the attention in a different way. They die as social power and flow into the sea of stories; they join the great majority—those many, many works that merely build worlds of words, set imaginary people off on adventures, resolve pretend dilemmas in unlikely ways that we find strangely gratifying and always have: we need them, though we can't perhaps say why or what good they are; and the making of them, the making of them well on their own terms and according to their own imperatives, is one of the arts of peace. It's the one I try to practice.

My earliest master was Vladimir Nabokov; that is to say, I had always been a consumer of tales in many forms, was from an early age enamored of the *Alice* books, Sherlock Holmes, EC comics, and John Wayne films, and also biographies of assorted people and nature stories; I was always someone who, as André Gide said of himself, tended to be more moved by the representations of things than by things themselves. I also always wrote or tried to write stories myself; the first I remember writing was when I was probably nine or ten, in collaboration with a younger sister. It was called *The Bloody Knife.* In a great city an apparition sometimes appears in the night sky: a huge knife dripping blood. The next morning dreadful things are found to have happened throughout the city. (I drew a fine illustration of the dark city and the knife in the sky, but I couldn't think where to go with this terrific premise, and gave it up.) I discovered or maybe rather uncovered Nabokov when I was fifteen or sixteen and read *Lolita* in secret, thinking it was a dirty book, which of course it is, and certainly was for a boy not much older than Lolita; but what took me and shook me was the language artifact that it was, the thing of words, the scheme of puns and jokes and cross-references and delicate put-downs and anagrams, many of which I could sense but not get, but that somehow could rise into an agonizing delight. I knew that the entire book was not about a perverse love affair but entirely about itself, the shocking subject matter really just a way of raising the bar of difficulty, though when my father came upon the brown paper–wrapped book in my room he wouldn't have accepted that argument even if I could have made it.

Nabokov is a great writer, and his books are an education, but he may be a bad mentor, especially for a young and almost wholly inexperienced writer. Once within the portals of his new and glittering world I adopted eagerly and without hesitation the credo he expressed in the afterword to that book. With him I learned to hold in contempt teachers who asked, "What is the author's purpose?" or worse, "What is this guy trying to say?" and to despise symbols and allegories and "Freudian voodooism." With him I rejected the Literature of Ideas, and (without having read anything of any of them) rejoiced in dismissing Balzac, Gorki, and Thomas Mann, as well as the "hopelessly banal and enormous novels typed out by the thumbs of tense mediocrities and called 'powerful' and 'stark' by reviewing hacks" that he also mocks. (I did later come to admire Faulkner, whom Nabokov labeled a "corncob humorist.") "For me," he says, "a novel exists only insofar as it affords me what I shall bluntly call aesthetic bliss, that is a sense of being somehow, somewhere connected with other states of being where art (curiosity, tenderness, kindness, ecstasy) is the norm." This sentence, which I read with a shiver of fascinated incomprehension in 1958, could form my definition today of what the arts of peace in their highest manifestations strive to effect.

I'm not certain of the chronology, but it's possible that Nabokov's champagne cocktail of word and Eros drew me out of the imagined worlds I then lived in, the puppet theater, the lesser Elizabethans, the narrative poems of Swinburne, the romantic tragedies whose contents I imagined more than I actually read. If that's so then the germ lay dormant in me a long time. I buried my otherworldly urges and read Camus and Sartre and other Literature of Ideas books and planned to make movies; I wrote parts of a science-fiction novel and a historical novel; not until I was in my midtwenties did I begin on an enterprise of a different kind and far removed (as I thought) from any kind of literature. It was about the distant future, a kind of melancholy autumnal Eden, where there were no arts of peace or any arts at all because there was peace itself instead, perpetual peace. There were stories, though; in fact stories were this society's history, religion, amusement, and truth; the highest ambition in a world almost without ambition was to be a teller of true stories, indeed finally to become the stories you tell: which is what happens to the teller of my story. That book (when it eventually appeared as a book, much chastened, years later) was called *Engine Summer*. It had less to do with Nabokov's austere aestheticism than with 1960s Edenic longings and willed detachment from history.

Even before it was entirely finished I had begun thinking of another book, different again from anything I'd heard about or read but different in a different way. Nabokov says somewhere that the great novels of the realist tradition—*Madame Bovary, Anna Karenina*—are actually great fairy tales. What I conceived of writing was a fairy tale that was actually a long novel in the realist tradition, a family chronicle like *Buddenbrooks* or *The Wapshot Chronicle*. Unlike the usual family chronicle, it would begin in the present and go on into the future, as the world evolved in strange ways I would devise, where—as a great magnate would sadly admit—"there is no power on earth found stronger than love." I say it was conceived as a fairy tale, but in fact the idea that it would contain actual fairies themselves came rather late in my thinking—a way of raising the bar, to see if I could make readers take the little fairies of Victorian and Elizabethan imaginings seriously. I wanted to make an imaginary garden with real fairies at the bottom of it.

The original title of the book was *Little, Big; or, The Fairies' Parliament*, which I thought was expressive of its nature, but the publisher who first issued it objected; this was to be a book for general readers. "If we put fairies on the cover," she said, "this book's going right down the toilet." Whether she was right or not I'll never know; the book did not do very well in its initial fairyless appearance as a general-fiction title. Later it was reissued, with fairies, and migrated to the back of the bookstore, where the kinds of books are kept for readers who read no other kind. It has lately returned to the general-reader shelves for people to find who rarely or never read that kind.

What kind?

It was when I was in the midst of writing it that I myself discovered what kind of book or story mine was, and why it worked as it did, and to what course or stream of the human imaginative enterprise it belonged and had poured from, and that was when I read the great Canadian critic Northrop Frye's book *The Secular Scripture: A Study of the Structure of Romance.*

Frye asserts that as far back as there has been a narrative, there have been two strands: those stories we deem to be true, among which are sacred scriptures and tales that can also be described as myths, that tell us how the world came to be, why we die and what comes after, why there are men and women, and so on; and another strand, a *secular* scripture equally important to us and perhaps primitively not different from the sacred, but whose truth is not important—stories told for their own sakes, to amuse, amaze, and thrill. There is a naive and a sentimental variety of these, in Schiller's terms. The naive is the mass of fable and folktale passed at first orally. Those tales intertwine with the sentimental, that is, stories consciously composed and written down, whose origins Frye traces to the late Greeks. All these tales collectively Frye calls *romances*, a family of stories that (like any family) can't be defined but only characterized, and whose characteristic story shapes and structures, devices, and outcomes are so many that works within the family can share none at all, and yet we sense that they belong together. Heroes with hidden parentage, journeys to win treasure or redeem honor, often leading into dark underworlds of entrapment and repetition, labyrinths and prisons; lovers separated and united, boy meets girl, boy loses girl, boy gets girl; twins, doubles, mistaken identities resolved; weddings that turn winter into spring, talking animals, riddles and prophecies; supernatural agencies good and bad. Stories not all with happy endings yet in which somehow the algebra of imagining comes out right, balancing the dark world we fear and don't want with the good world we do want—the world (as Frye puts it) that our gods would want for us if they were worth worshipping.

What I had written was a romance; those books in the back of the store and on the special-tastes shelves were romances, for sale to those who knew just what they were looking for; but so were many of those in the front of the store, bought by unwitting readers who knew what they wanted when they got it but maybe not before. They are the kinds of stories that Plato would have none of in his Republic. They were lies. Plato's strictures descend into Western Christendom, which is faced with what to do about the vast mass of story, folklore, and fable that interpenetrates its own teachings. The Renaissance rediscovering the great body of ancient romance also reestablished Plato's neat idea that these thrilling wonder stories about the doings of gods and heroes and lovers could be understood *allegorically,* containing hidden morals that can be teased out (*what is this guy trying to say?*) and so be made acceptable to serious people. The head would—as it should—take charge of the heart and show how the tales the heart loves can also improve us: at least some of them can. When the narrative tradition divided again, into romantic and realistic (never completely and in some ways not at all), the same division into imaginary stories that are instructive and those that are not persists: trash is trash, but some good stories are also good for you. Recent serious readers in this tradition have preferred mystery stories—especially the hard-boiled kind—to other kinds of romances, as containing more information about real life.

I would certainly not claim the status of disciplined self-conscious art for all romances. My own tolerance for the romances of others is actually pretty low. I'm with Robert Louis Stevenson, one of the most successful of all writers of romance—in every sense of success—when he wrote, "What the public likes is work (of any kind) a little loosely executed; so long as it is a little wordy, a little slack, a little dim and knotless, the dear public likes it; it should (if possible) be a little dull into the bargain. I know that good work sometimes hits; but, with my hand upon my heart, I think it is by accident." Our culture is stuffed with fantasy and romances in potent new media not invented when Plato fretted over the question of the utility of stories, and most are not good by the Stevenson standard or any other. Cultural critics, uncomfortable about the uselessness of such masses of imagined worlds with no goal or purpose but delight, and unused to making discriminations among the works they encounter into better and lesser according to a Nabokovian aesthetic, tend to rank them instead by their truth-telling qualities. Those most disconnected from our shared social universe and its physics and politics, and most frank in their deployment of the tropes of romance, are classed as *escapist,* a word that implies that those who spend too much time within them are evading or forswearing the duty we all have to work for justice or betterment or at least survival.

There is a case to be made, too: the old Irish Celts, who have been conceived of as dreamy and romantic, perceived a danger in the attraction to other worlds, worlds of delight, excitement, and gratified desire, and represented the danger in the many tales about what becomes of careless wanderers who allow themselves to be drawn into the land of the fairies within the earth: they emerge years later, pale and empty eyed, no older or more mature than when they went in and having gained nothing except a permanent dissatisfaction with the everyday world that their coevals have been all along struggling with—sort of like young people emerging from years of obsession with *Star Wars* or video games or, well, *fairies,* reading tome upon huge tome of news from Neverland and never growing any older—I see them in the conventions and gatherings to which they come, clutching copies of my books among others. So the arts of peace I practice may not only be said to be no help to the world, they may be open to condemnation as inducements to abandon it. To picture worlds that are either Edenic and impossible, or lawless and in ruins, might be to weaken a reader's allegiance to the world as it is and the possibilities it really contains, particularly for those whose connection to it is tenuous to begin with.

A more serious charge can be made against worlds made of words and stories, worlds that have innocence at their hearts or centers because they are incapable of harm. Works that have not done good can be implicated in the doing of evil. In the Platonic high/low critique, those works that don't teach us about real life, directly or allegorically, are simply useless, ignorable; modern Platonists, though, using the tools of deconstruction and the New Historicism, discover that works that seem to connect us to realms where curiosity, tenderness, and ecstasy are the norm are at their core simply coded illustrations of their societies' actual power relationships—"who whom," in Lenin's formulation: who has done harm to, or stolen from, whom; who has despised whom, or defined whom as lesser for reasons of gain, or obliterated from sight in order to retain power. It can all be discovered, in the romances, ghost stories, melodramas, and revels that seem like merely ephemeral fun. This clear-sighted watchfulness is the opposite of the response of the helpless escapist, now seen as not only ineffectual but complicit in wrongs that are merely masked by the works he tries to escape into.

Well, how can the making of romances as an art of peace refute this charge, supposing we want to refute it, without saying well we don't care, we like it, and it makes us feel good to create and "consume" it and the knowers-better can go elsewhere, or rather *we* can, we can escape into the hills of Gondor and the pathetic fallacies of fantasy; but that's only to become the charge we want to meet. My own work in romance genres has often been more *about* romance and its attraction than actually performing the work of romance, I think, and salted with irony; but this sophistication (in the literal sense) doesn't get me off the hook of inconsequence. "Better is the sight of the eye than the wanderings of desire," says Ecclesiastes. Hamlet says that the business of art, of theater art anyway, is to hold the mirror up to nature, to "show Virtue her own feature, scorn her own image, and the very age and body of the time his form and pressure." But of course the most important thing about the image in any mirror is that it's reversed, as Lewis Carroll knew, and the opposite of what it reflects. So perhaps this can point us to an escape, from escapism as well as from Knowing Better: couldn't it be that those works (like Shakespeare's comedies, or the pastorals of Watteau, or the fantasies of Ronald Firbank) are not evasive encodings of social power, inauthentic assertions of freedom canceled out by the very contradictions they are created to hide, but are actually conscious mirror reversals of those dilemmas that we suffer—social, cultural, political, maybe biological or mammalian even? That could be instructive in itself, a revelation, like that famous map you can buy that shows the Western Hemisphere upside down, with Tierra del Fuego and the South Pole at the top, and our own weirdly diminished country looking rather insignificant toward the bottom. Creating a world where power has no power, where only love has power—does it refresh our senses somehow, so we can see more clearly our life on earth, where (as we all know very well) power indeed has power, and love is often, maybe usually, not enough?

Well, I don't know. I think this reversal effect really does describe some of the pull that romances and allied arts have on us, like the hilarious reversals of a joke, or the train wrecks and car crashes impossibly escaped or avoided in a Buster Keaton film that would never be escaped in life. Whether experiencing such gratifying reversals of our actual condition really does us good or makes us better is not indicated by what I know of world history. We have all heard of the death-camp commandant moved to tears by Mozart and Beethoven in his spare time; Saddam Hussein is the author of a couple of tender romances about love and honor. I recently read a profile of the Defense Department undersecretary Douglas Feith, a leading enthusiast for the war in Iraq and one of the neocons committed to using military force to bring democracy to other lands; Feith is the one whom General Tommy Franks famously called "the fucking stupidest guy on the face of the earth." The profile described Feith as, among other things, an ardent lover of books, which he kept in specially built basement bookshelves; among his favorite authors, it was noted, was Vladimir Nabokov. I was forcibly reminded of a moment in Stella Gibbons's *Cold Comfort Farm* when Flora discovers that a vulgarian shares her love for a rarefied author: "It gave one a curious feeling," she says. "It was like seeing a drunken stranger wrapped in one's dressing-gown." Well, Feith seems not to have grown less stupid from reading Nabokov, whose solipsistic cosmocrats have at least a saving (or damning) intimation of their own self-entrapment.

So I don't really want to state that the arts of peace can oppose strong evil and by their cunning innocence neutralize that caustic energy. The arts of peace can't save the world; it's more the case that the world must save them. They are like the proverbial miner's canary: when we see it dead, when the arts of peace have declined, or been corrupted, or are despised or co-opted, as they can so easily be, then we should think about backing out and heading for the upper air.

And yet I still can't help believing that to *practice* the arts of peace, these small and seemingly futile arts without effect, is to create—or help to keep in existence—or at the very least to assert the possibility of—the world we want: a world in which not all our time is spent in vigilance, or in fending off danger, or in struggle with corruption or stupidity, or in the education of the heart by the head so that we can do those tasks. In fact I'll assert more than that: I think that in the darkest of worlds that have arisen in this and in other centuries, to practice the arts of peace as I have tried to describe them may well be heroic, and salvific, too. I have a few stories that I think of as illustrations, or maybe parables. Perhaps you've heard them, though maybe not in this context.

The Cuban poet and journalist Raúl Rivero became a dissident and critic of the Castro regime after working for a long time as a dutiful foreign correspondent. After 1991 he began to campaign for reforms like those that had altered Eastern Europe and Russia; he was a signatory of the famed "Carta de los Dies," and began sending out accounts of life in Cuba to foreign presses. He was growing well known throughout the Latin American world, but he was jobless, without resources, living on the odd check that made its way to him. Whenever a foreign journalist came to interview or visit him and asked, "What can I do for you?" Rivero would answer, "Leave me your pen."

Arrested at last, Rivero was sentenced to twenty years in prison. He was afraid, he said, and even more he was afraid of his own fear. "I was afraid of not being able to stand it," he wrote later.

"Everything is programmed to undo you as a human being." Even his jailers understood his stature as poet and critic, and with an almost Kafkaesque ingenuity, they permitted him to go on writing—with the condition that he could write only love poems.

He didn't find it easy at first. But he began to write, and as he did so, he began, he says, to remember the many, many women he had loved, married, hadn't married, lost, or left; and every time he finished a poem, he felt that his captors had not defeated him. His jailers read through the poems each week, confiscating those that they thought had a secret message or were somehow inflammatory—though Rivero said he had no idea what in any poem might excite their suspicion. He only wrote on.

International pressure on the Cuban government finally freed Rivero, who lives now in Spain. His prison love poems have been published to some acclaim—a rarity, he says, a book of love poems edited by the police. The name of the volume is *Corazón sin furia*—heart without rage.

By himself and in the face of his fears he projected, in that cold cell, a world where power has no power: where love has power. With luck and some genius it may outlast the world of his jailers.

Another prison story: Gregory Pasko, a military reporter and captain in the Russian Navy's Pacific Fleet, observed Russian Navy tankers dumping nuclear wastes in the sea off Vladivostok near the Japanese islands. Pasko filmed the violations and wrote about them, passing his film to Japanese television. The Russian government arrested and tried Pasko in secret and sent him to prison. After nearly two years during which Pasko continued to assert his innocence, the Russian government became embarrassed enough to grant him amnesty, reducing his charge to misuse of office and letting him go. Pasko, however, rejected the offered pardon. "No one could convince me I broke the law," he said.

The Russian government brought new charges against the uncooperative Pasko, and after another secret treason trial (he was supposed to have been a Japanese spy) Pasko was given a four-year sentence at Prison Colony No. 41, a labor prison near the town of Ussuriisk. "Gray, black, and dirty brown," he remembers the place being: that colorless place that I can guess few or none of my readers have ever been condemned to but which we all know, which we all have dreamed of, the gray places of the gray Gulag that snakes across our history. Amnesty International took up Pasko's case, calling it "a clear breach of national and international norms protecting freedom of expression that the Russian state is obliged to uphold." Amnesty International members began sending Pasko letters of support and picture postcards from around the world—some twenty-four thousand in all. He says he has saved them all. The letters were encouraging but the pictures on the postcards were just as helpful: "Many of them were beautiful and bright," he remembers. "The sky, the sea, water, green grass. All the prisoners would come over and look at these postcards from Amnesty International." He put many of them up on his gray wall, a shifting gallery, maybe the Rockies or the Alps at sunset, the Eiffel Tower lit up, castles and countrysides and beaches, the fabulous unreal worlds within postcards that make all of us smile and long without pain—sometimes even those of us who live amid those very scenes. Pasko was released from prison in January 2003, but it was for good behavior and not a reversal of his conviction. His name has still not been cleared.

A third story: There was in Japan once—it is said—a famous master of the tea ceremony or *chado*, which ranks among the arts of peace if anything does. One day, an unscrupulous *ronin* or outlaw samurai challenged the *chado* master to a duel, knowing full well that the *chado* master had no skill in martial arts, perhaps hoping for a bribe or merely indulging a love of bullying. The *chado* master accepted the challenge and agreed to meet the *ronin* the next day. He then went to the house of a well-known samurai to ask for help. I know, he told the warrior, that I will be quickly killed by this fellow, but I would like to be able at least to die with dignity and not look a fool before the world. Could the samurai give him some basic instructions, a stance to take, a lesson in holding a weapon properly? The samurai said that perhaps he could do so, if the *chado* master wished, and then he requested that, since the man was to die tomorrow, he make tea for him, perhaps for the last time in his life. That evening then, the *chado* master made tea for the samurai with all the composure and perfection of his decades of practice. The samurai, having observed the *chado* master's absorption and calm, told him that the only advice he had for him was this: he should engage in his battle with the *ronin* as though the man were a guest for whom he was making tea. He gave the *chado* master a sword he could use, and said that he thought all would be well. The next day at the appointed time the *ronin* appeared, ready to fight. The *chado* master said that he was ready, too. He began his preparations for battle just as he would his preparations for tea. He made his bow, he took off his outer garment, and folded it with care in the prescribed

manner, without hurry or fuss. He laid his fan upon it with the practiced gesture. The *ronin*, observing his complete self-possession,
began to be afraid: what did this fellow know that made him so cool?
The *chado* master reached to take up the borrowed sword with the
same calmness of mind and full attention as he would have the
implements of his art, and at that the *ronin* began to lose his nerve—
surely no one about to die could be so unafraid—perhaps he was a
secret martial arts master as well—and suddenly convinced he could
never defeat the man, the *ronin* fled.

This story is, obviously, different from the other two. The prison
stories are true, though the telling of them may bring forth a point or
a vision that they didn't have when they were *simply* true, that is,
before they were stories. The story of the *chado* master who defeated
brutal power with the arts of peace may be nothing *but* a story: not
a distilled incident from the world's life but merely a hopeful parable—one of those that assert such an impossible, Utopian success for
the arts of peace that on hearing it all we can do is smile. But that's
all it needs to do. It is in itself an example of the thing it teaches.

To the same point I would like to offer a story or a part of one without any claims to being true. It's a passage from an as-yet-unpub-
lished book of my own, the fourth volume of a four-volume novel
with the overall title *Ægypt*. In it a novelist named Fellowes Kraft,
in his sixties and unwell, has come to Europe, funded by a foundation whose eccentric director hopes that Kraft will search for evidence that the life-extending medicines imagined by Renaissance
alchemists have a basis in fact. Kraft is the author of many historical
romances that have turned on such possibilities, and he has hinted
that he may believe that he can find that evidence, that wonder-
working thing; but all he really intends on his journey is to revisit
once more the places he knew in youth. It should be noted that Kraft
was raised in a small Gnostic sect whose mystical teachings about
maleficent Powers and the journey of the soul he retains though he
has rejected their truth. In this selection Kraft is in Prague, a city to
which he first came in 1937; he has returned now in the spring of
1968.

> Prague was restless, almost atremble in that early spring,
> like a March tree about to put out buds. Public places were
> crowded with people, young people talking and smoking and
> hugging each other. Kraft's guide, a young student assigned
> him as a courtesy or for some less openhanded reason by the

Writers' Union, seemed almost to have a fever; his eyes were bright and he quivered inside his leather coat from something other than cold.

He was first put in a taxi, an old Russian Volga—could that really be a picture of Tomáš Masaryk stuck on the dashboard? He didn't dare ask—and was taken to his hotel. It was a wonderful Baroque building that he thought he remembered: but surely it had not been a hotel thirty years ago. No, a nunnery. Where were the nuns? His guide made a gesture like shooing chickens. All sent away, long ago, 1950. Reactionary elements. But now: now they were returning, they were being, what was the word?

Rehabilitated?

New time, the boy said, smiling. Now all old things come back again. And now what would he like to see? The Charles Bridge? The Jewish Quarter?

No, he knew those places well.

Eat? Writers' Union restaurant best in the city. Meet many writers. All new.

No, he didn't want to eat, and yes, certainly, he wanted to meet writers, but not there, or not yet, if that wouldn't be interpreted as an insult? For some reason he knew he could be frank with this unlovely lean young man, tense and somehow twisted, like a hank of wire, smoking more or less continuously and tapping his black pointed shoes. He would, though, like a drink—an easy and apparently welcome request, though he was taken a long way to fill it, to parts of town that seemed to unfold as though right out of Kraft's own jogged memory. The bars and the caves—*spelunka*—were the very ones he remembered, oh yes, remembered well; in his guidebook (still with him here in the Faraways!) he had used to mark with a tiny, innocent star the places where he had *got lucky* as the boys now said; girls, too, for all he knew. They went into Slavie, the café on the corner opposite the National Theater, a long L-shaped room, a fog of smoke and talk. His guide translated what he heard. Rumors of a Soviet army amassing just over the border in the GDR.

"And what new book do you work on now?" his guide asked. Move on, or away, from that subject.

"Oh none," Kraft said. "I would say I have no more to write. None that I think worth writing."

The boy studied him, smiling, as though trying to guess how his guest would like him to react.

"I mean they're all not true, you know," Kraft said. "Not a word of any of them. All made up, you know? Even the parts that are true aren't true. And finally you get tired, and just don't want to play anymore."

The lad laughed, still eyeing him, pretty sure Kraft meant this blasphemy as a joke. And what could his weary abnegation mean here, where descriptions of actuality had for so long been made up, and the only hope lay in the imaginary? He felt a pang of shame, but really it was true what he'd said, there was no help for it, he had lived too long, through too many fictions, he couldn't feature multiplying them anymore.

The lad was not to be shaken. Next day he took Kraft up to the Hradêany Castle, climbing, climbing up the palace district like Pilgrim on his way to the Celestial City. The steps to the castle were crowded, too, not with the prostitutes and young men with collars turned up and shacks where red kerosene lamps were lit and Gypsy children plucked at your sleeve—all that was gone, cleaned away by socialism; instead there were more talkers, young and old, studying newspapers mistrustfully or gathered around transistor radios. His guide wasn't forthcoming about what might be happening, a government employee himself after all, but amid his shrugs and terse replies his eyes looked at his American in hope and supplication.

He took Kraft through the castle, beneath the astonishing vaulting ribbed like celery stalks and exfoliating in unfollowable complexity, the stairs up which armed knights once rode their horses, clattering and slipping. It was hard to get the boy to slow down; there was so much Kraft wanted to see, though less on display than when he had been here years before. When another huge army, he thought, had been massed in Germany, watching and waiting.

They climbed the spiral stair to the room in the palace where in 1618 representatives of the Holy Roman emperor met with the Bohemian Protestant nobles who had determined to break with the empire. When the emperor's people made threats and demands, the Bohemians threw them one by one from the window—that window, there, his guide pointed to it. The high, cold room was crowded today with Czechs old and young, looking around hungrily, touching the table where the meeting had happened, the window's deep embrasure.

Taking Kraft back down through the castle district to his lodging at the Infantines, the young man made a sudden decision, pulled at the sleeve of Kraft's overcoat, and led him at a quick pace another way, smiling but unwilling to give away his surprise, and he led Kraft to the square where the candy-box Loreto church stands next to a Capuchin convent (all the nuns and priests gone from them, too, scattered), and across to a gloomy Baroque palace Kraft didn't remember. A ministry of some sort now. Palace guards in blue caps and rifles at the wide gates to the courtyard, looking uncomfortable, for a little crowd had gathered there, peering into the courtyard within.

John Crowley

His guide pointed to a window above, overlooking the courtyard. Others pointed, too. It was the window of what had been the apartment of Jan Masaryk, Tomáš's son, the one from which he had fallen to his death—pushed, yes, certainly, pushed, the young man made violent motions as he spoke— the night after the Communist coup in the spring of 1948.

Kraft looked from the window to the courtyard pavement to the window again. The guide's face shone with wonder and expectation. This very month, this day maybe, twenty years before.

But Kraft knew that Jan Masaryk had only been the latest, and the poor officials of 1618 not the first, of an age-old series of such ejections in Bohemia. Change here seemed to require a man or men hustled out a high window, looking down shrieking in terror, fingers clinging to the jambs.

Defenestration. Kraft looked up with the others. It was as though the sources of certain events lay not in their antecedent causes but in mirror or shadow events that lay far in the past or in the future; as though by chance a secret lever on a clockwork could be pressed that made it go after being long still, or as though a wind blowing up in one age could tear leaves from trees and bring down steeples in another.

He thought—looking now out the window of his cell in the converted convent, the illusory castle alight and apparently afloat high up—you have to be on their side, you have to be. On their way into the actual future, still surrounded by brutal utopians. He thought: if I knew the secret laws by which history worked, I could reveal them, whisper them in the ears of this people in their peril, and they would know what to do, and what not to do. But the secret laws can't be known, and if known can't be told. You can only pretend to know them.

Yes! A simple clarity that had escaped him or not visited him in 1937, when he had needed it, was now his, as though an egg he'd thought was stone had now cracked, and a fledgling emerged.

You get power over history, he saw, by uncovering and learning its laws, formulating them, teaching them to others, who get thereby a share of the power you have. You form up your followers into an army, which can impose these irrefutable laws on Time's body; you have earned the power, by your grasp of History's Laws, to eliminate or hide away anything that confounds or flouts them. It is thus that in any age the Archons rule; the rule of the Archons in heaven being continuous with that of their epigones on earth.

So the way to defeat power is to propose new laws, laws conceived in the secrecy of the heart and enacted by the will's fiat: laws of desire and hope, which are not fixed but endlessly mutable, and unimposable on anyone else. They are the laws of another history of the world, one's own.

228

It was just what his mother had known so simply, as
though it was obvious. The Archons who made the world,
and whose shadows continue to rule in it, would have us
believe that its laws are immutable, eternal, self-generated,
necessary. Perhaps they themselves believe it to be so. Very
well: then we confound them by a counterknowing: we know
that in fact we have ourselves conceived the laws that make
the world as it is, and can change them if we will.

And didn't he, Fellowes Kraft, know very well how to build
such a history? He did. He did it for a living. He had the tools
and ingredients, and he knew how you used them: with
heart's need you mixed pretend conversations, purported
facts out of books, likely seeming actions, the light of other
days.

Build a new world in the face of power, and make it go;
show them how easy it is. His own could of course only be a
fiction; so was theirs; but his would appear humbly between
covers, unarmed, acknowledged to be false; that was the
difference.

Oh my God, he thought, overcome momentarily with a
familiar giddiness, an anticipatory exhaustion. He had come
all this way, paid to find fabulous treasure or at least the
rumor of it, and what had he discovered instead but another
novel.

My friend Andre, maybe dissatisfied with my answer to him about
the arts of peace, sent a follow-up note: "I think when I asked you
that question—where you think your writing fits in—I was asking
about what you hope or anticipate its specific effects to be. Is it
possible to anticipate its effects at all? Do you feel responsible
for them?"

Northrop Frye, in his study of Shakespearean comedy, defines the
effects of different modes of narrative in a way that I think is crucial.
In watching tragedy, he says—and within tragedy I would include all
that is serious, critical, alerting in fiction from *Middlemarch* to *1984*
and the stories of Alice Munro—we are impressed by the *reality of
the illusion:* we feel that the blinding of Gloucester in *King Lear* is
not really happening, but it is the kind of thing that can and does
happen, and this is what it would be like to witness it. Our response
to comedy is different—and within comedy I would include all tales
of Eden restored, of the lineaments of gratified desire, glittering gay
serpents with their tails in their mouths, happy though not all with
happy endings. In comedy, Frye says, we are impressed with the
illusion of reality: this is the sort of thing that just doesn't happen;

229

and yet here it is, happening. I will believe such experiences are not escapist, that seeing before us the world we *want* can give us heart to bring the world we *have* closer to it, or keep it from impossibility at least—I believe it, but I won't assert it. I will assert this: the arts of peace may make nothing happen, but a world that cannot afford the arts of peace, or despises them as trivial or inauthentic, corrupts them or makes their practice impossible, is not a world of unfooled hardworking realists, but a counterworld where the real ambiguity and multiplicity and unfinishable endlessness of real things can't be seen.

So, Andre, this is what I hope the effect of my work will be, and I will take responsibility for it, though I anticipate its actual effect to be general indifference. I want to open to my readers a realm where curiosity, tenderness, and ecstasy are the norm, or at the very least a realm where they seem possible: the lost child saved, the lovers who find each other at last; the world evolving, out of the past we know, a present different from the one we have; the triumph of love over power; and say to my readers, "Look! This can't happen—but here it is, happening."

Muhammad
Eliot Weinberger

I.

FOUR HUNDRED AND TWENTY-FOUR thousand years before the creation of the heavens or the earth or the empyrean or the throne or the
table of decrees or the pen divine or paradise or hell, God created
the Light of Muhammad. The Light passed through twenty seas of
light, each containing the sciences that no one understands but God
himself, and when it emerged from the last sea, the seas fell in adoration and formed one hundred and twenty-four thousand drops of
light, each drop a prophet in the great procession that circled the
Light.

God then formed a gem from that Light and split it in two. One half
became the waters and he placed the other half on those waters and
it became the empyrean. Then he created the throne that beamed
from the empyrean, and from the throne the tablet of decrees, and
from the tablet the pen divine.

He commanded the pen to write, but the pen lay confounded for a
thousand years.
    "What should I write?"
    " 'There is no God but God; Muhammad is the Apostle of God.' "
    "Who is this Muhammad that you speak his name with yours?"
    "Oh, pen, if he had not existed I would not have created you."

Then God created paradise, and the angels, and from the vapor that
rose from the water of the sundered gem, the seven heavens, and
from the foam of the water, the seven earths. But this world rocked
like a ship at sea, so God placed mountains upon it to keep it steady.
He created an angel to hold up the earth and a rock without measure
for the angel to stand on and a bull on whose back the rock rested
and a fish to support the bull. The fish rests on water, the water rests

on air, the air rests on darkness, but what the darkness rests on only God himself knows.

Then he created the souls of the faithful, the sun and moon and stars, night and day, light and darkness, and further hosts of angels. The Light of Muhammad dwelt for seventy-three thousand years in the empyrean, then seventy thousand years in paradise, and then another seventy thousand years in Sidret al-Muntaha, the tree in the seventh heaven beyond which none may pass, where the Light remained until God willed the creation of Adam, the father of mankind.

The angel Izrail gathered dust from all parts of the earth—white, black, and red dirt, soft and hard, which is why the complexions of the children of Adam are so varied, and why the prophet said all the sons of Adam are the same, like teeth in a comb—and the angel Jibril carried it to the place decreed to be the site of Muhammad's tomb, kneading it with water to form a man. God commanded Adam's spirit to enter his body, but the spirit complained that the entrance was too narrow, so God decreed that forever with aversion would it enter and with aversion leave its mortal abode.

When the spirit entered his eyes, and he saw his own form and the angels singing his praises, Adam sneezed. So God gave Adam speech, and he cried out, "Alhamdulillah," "Thanks to God."

The Light of Muhammad radiated from the index finger of Adam and from the forehead of his wife, Hawwa, and from their son Shays, and from his wife, the beautiful Houri Mohavela, and from their son, Anush. It was with Ibrahim when he was cast into the furnace of Nimrod, with Nuh on the ark, with Yunus in the stomach of the fish, and on through the generations, until it reached Abd al-Muttalib, and his son, Abdallah, whose radiance gave him the name Lamp of the Sacred City, and his wife, Amina, pearl-shell of the jewel of prophecy.

Amina said that on the day the prophet was born, she heard innumerable voices, unlike anything human, and saw a banner of the silk of paradise, mounted on a ruby staff, filling all the space between heaven and earth. She somehow saw the palaces of Damascus, gleaming like flames, and countless birds flocked about her. A youth appeared, taller and more handsome and more elegantly dressed than any she had ever seen, who took her baby and dropped some saliva from his own mouth into the baby's mouth. He cut open the baby's breast and took out his heart and cut it open and extracted from it a single black drop. He then took a purse of green silk containing an unknown herb and placed it in the baby's breast and drew his hand over it. The youth and the baby spoke together in a language she could not understand. Then he took a signet ring from a white purse and pressed it between the shoulders of the child and gave the baby a shirt to protect him from the calamities of the world.

On the night Muhammad was born, every idol toppled over. The palace of Kesry, emperor of Persia, trembled, its dome split in two, and fourteen towers collapsed. Lake Sawwa, which had been worshipped as a god, disappeared, and became a salt plain. The sacred fires of Fars, which had burned for a thousand years, went out. Seventy columns of light appeared between heaven and earth, each a different color, and the Kaaba lifted up and hovered over Mecca. The next morning, all the kings of the world found their thrones facing backward.

On that night, the great fish Tamusa, chief of all that swim the sea, with seven hundred thousand tails and seven hundred thousand oxen who walk up and down on his back, each with seventy thousand horns of emerald—cattle of which Tamusa is unaware, for they are like flies on his immensity—on that night the great fish was shaking with joy and had not God calmed him down, the earth would have turned over.

The prophet was born circumcised.

For the first few days after Muhammad's birth, his mother, Amina, could supply no milk, so his uncle Abu Talib put the baby to his own breast and milk flowed abundantly. A wet nurse, Halima, from the tribe of Banu Saad was hired. Muhammad would only drink from her right breast, leaving the left for Halima's own son.

At four months, his mother, Amina, died, leaving him an orphan, for his father, Abdallah, had died a few months before he was born.

He never soiled his clothes; whatever passed naturally from him was instantly received and concealed by the earth. He never smelled disagreeably, but gave off a fragrance of camphor and musk. At three months, he sat up; at nine months, he walked; at ten months, he went out with his foster brothers to pasture the sheep; at fifteen months, he was practicing archery and all who saw him thought he was five years old.

As a boy, he slept in a room with his uncle, but changed his clothes in secret. At night he could be heard uttering prayers. Often, a beautiful man would appear by his bed, stroke his head, and disappear. He was usually alone, with a light beaming from his head to heaven. He rarely laughed and neither played with others nor watched them play.

He could not read or write. Some say that because he knew all things by divine inspiration, he must have had his reasons. On his deathbed, he called for an inkwell and the shoulder blade of a sheep that he might write his last instructions, and people thought this was a sign of his final delirium.

He had three caps, one of which was white. He leaned on a slender staff while addressing the people. He had a walking stick named Memshuq, a tent named Akan, a cup named Matba, and a vessel named Rayy. Two horses: Erbaz and Sekeb. Two mules: Duldul and Shaba. Two she-camels: Ghasba and Jedan. A donkey named Yafur, and a pack camel named Dibaj. He had four swords—Zulfakar, Aun,

Mejzim, and Rasun—a helmet named Asad, a coat of mail named Zat al-Fazul, a banner named Akab, and a flag named Malum. His turban was named Sahab. He owned two red doors.

When Yafur the donkey was captured by Muhammad, he suddenly acquired speech and said that he came from a line of sixty generations that had only been ridden by prophets. He said he was the last of his lineage, for Muhammad was the last of the prophets, and that he had been waiting for him and had allowed no one else to mount him. At the prophet's death, Yafur was so overwhelmed he threw himself into a pit that became his grave.

He was somewhat tall, but not very tall. His head was large. His hair was neither curly nor straight, and he parted it in the middle. His face was very white, his forehead broad, with a vein that became prominent when he was angry. His eyebrows narrow, long, and arching; some say they were a single brow. His nose was thin and aquiline; light shone from it. It was so long that when he drank it nearly touched the water. His beard was large and full, with seventeen white hairs that gleamed like the sun; his lips were not thick. He had a mole on his chin. His teeth were broad and white, his neck smooth and erect, like a statue. His shoulders were broad, his joints strong and hollow, his limbs symmetrical. His breast and stomach formed a perpendicular line, with a narrow line of fine black hair down the center. He had no hair in his armpits. Some say the seal of God between his shoulders was a fleshy growth, others that it was a mat of hair. His fingers were long, his palm broad, his hands and feet large. The sole of his foot was deeply hollowed, the top of it smooth and soft, so that if a drop of water fell on his foot it immediately rolled off. His steps were long, leisured, and dignified; he always walked as though he was going downhill. He held his head bowed, for sorrow weighed on his mind.

Light beamed from his forehead, and at night it looked like moonlight. He used amber, musk, and civet as perfumes, and spent more money on perfume than on food; days later, people would know from the lingering fragrance that he had passed by. He cast no shadow when standing in the sun. No matter how tall a man was, when he

235

stood beside Muhammad he appeared an arrow's length shorter. No
bird ever flew over his head. He could see behind without turning
around. He could hear everything while he was sleeping. Water
flowed from between his fingers and nine pebbles in his hand sang
praises. He never had a wet dream. An animal he had ridden never
grew old. No insect landed on him. On soft ground he left no tracks,
but his footprints could be seen on hard rock.

He said there were five things he would never abandon: eating on the
ground with his servants, riding a donkey with a blanket instead of
a saddle, milking goats with his own hands, wearing woolen garments, and greeting children.

Once he found a crumb of bread on the floor and picked it up and ate
it, saying we must value the favors that God bestows upon us.

He mainly ate water and dates, or milk and dates. Among the fresh
fruits, he preferred watermelons and grapes. He ate meat, but did not
hunt. He dipped his bread in oil and vinegar. After eating, he licked
the dish and licked his fingers, and then washed. People dining with
Muhammad heard voices from the food.

He once persuaded a group of nonbelievers by summoning the remains of the food they had eaten. Dishes descended from the sky.
Muhammad asked the food to relate who had eaten what, and each
morsel responded: my master so-and-so ate so much, his servants
another portion, and what you see is the remnant. He asked the food
who he was, and the food answered: "You are the prophet of God."

At night, when his disciples were leaving his house, he put his hand
outside the door and the light from his hand lit their way home.

A famous doctor came to treat Muhammad for insanity:
"Why am I insane?"
"Because you say you are a prophet."

"You are the one who is insane because you say I am not a prophet."

Muhammad beckoned, and an enormous palm tree in the distance uprooted itself, approached, bowed down, and said: "What do you command me to do, o prophet of God?"

He split the moon in two and put it back together again. He made the sun rise just after it had set. He put a small stone in the middle of the road that no person or animal ever accidentally kicked.

Another stone, lying on the mouth of a well in a garden, saluted him, and asked that it not become a stone in hell, and Muhammad prayed on its behalf.

A camel complained to the prophet that he worked hard but was given little to eat. Muhammad summoned the camel's owner, who admitted it was true.

A wolf agreed to watch over a flock of sheep, so that the shepherd could join Muhammad.

Muhammad believed that wolves should be allowed to eat a few of the sheep at the edge of a flock. He forbade the killing of spiders, for once he hid in a cave, escaping enemies, and a spider wove a huge web across its entrance. When the enemies came, they saw the web and assumed no one had been there.

He touched the ears of some sheep and they turned white, and all their offspring had white ears.

He said that there are angels who protect fruit trees, for otherwise wild beasts would eat all the fruit. He forbade his followers to perform natural acts beneath the fruit trees, for they would offend the angels.

An infidel said, "I will believe you when this lizard does," and pulled a green lizard from his sleeve. The lizard with great eloquence spoke: "O ornament of all to be assembled at the judgment, thou wilt lead the pure to paradise. . . ."

A man came to Muhammad and said that, years ago, before he had found the faith, he had taken his young daughter out into the desert and exposed her there. Muhammad said, "Come, show me the place." There, he called the girl's name and she appeared, returned to life. Muhammad said, "Your mother and father have become Muslims. If you wish, I will restore you to them," but the girl replied: "I have no need of them. God is better to me than they were."

He made hair grow on the head of a bald man.

When asked what determined the resemblance of a child to its father or mother, he said, "An excess of seed." Bones, veins, and sinews derived from the father; flesh, blood, nails, and hair from the mother.

He would not shake hands with a woman, so in order to make a pact, he would put his hand in a jar of water and then the woman would put her hand in the jar.

He said that good dreams come from God and bad dreams from Satan, and thus good dreams may be told to others but the bad should never be recounted. He said that he who plays chess is like one who has dyed his hand in the blood of a pig.

He was ambivalent about poetry: he gave a mantle, which still exists, to the poet Kab ibn Zuhayr as a reward for a panegyric. But he also said that filling the stomach with pus is better than stuffing the brain with poetry.

At the time it was believed that the soul of a slain man took the form of a bird that kept crying until the slayer was slain. Muhammad said this was not true. He said there were no stars that promise rain.

II.

At twenty-five, Muhammad married a wealthy widow, Khadija, who was forty. She bore seven of his eight children: three sons who died, and four daughters. For twenty-four years and a month, until her death, he married no others, and his future wives had to accommodate themselves to his nostalgia and grief.

His second wife, Sawda, was sixty-five and a widow. Afraid of being divorced, she turned over her regular allotted night with Muhammad to his third wife, Aisha. She said that although she did not enjoy relations with a man, she wanted to be resurrected with the prophet's wives.

He married Aisha, known for her learning and wit, when she was six, and consummated the marriage when she was nine; she was the only virgin among his wives. When she was accused of adultery, Muhammad received a verse that proved her innocence. They took baths together; he prayed lying in her arms; he received verses lying in her arms; he died in her arms when she was eighteen, and was buried in her house. Muhammad was once asked who was his favorite person. "Aisha." "No, I mean among men." "Her father," Muhammad replied. He said that Aisha, compared to other women, was like *tarid*, a dish of meat and bread, to mere food.

When he considered marrying, he would send a woman to smell the neck of the intended. He said that if the neck was fragrant, so was the whole person. The instep of the foot was also examined for if that was plump, so was the whole person.

Umm Shuraik from the tribe of Azd gave herself to the prophet as a "free gift," and he received a verse saying that this was acceptable. Hafsa was a widow at eighteen, beautiful, literate, but short-tempered. The first husband of Umm Habiba, despite his wife's warnings, became a Christian, took to wine, died, and went to hell. Umm Salama was a widow with two children, whose husband had died in the Battle of Uhud. She was asked whether the embrace of the prophet was like that of other men, and she said yes. So Jibril brought Muhammad a dish prepared by the Houris of paradise, which gave him the conjugal power of forty men, and he visited all of his wives on a single night.

Zaynab, daughter of Jahsh, was married to Zayd, a slave Muhammad freed and adopted as his son. Muhammad came to visit Zayd and inadvertently saw Zaynab in a state of dishevelment; he fell in love. Zayd offered to divorce her but Muhammad refused until he received a verse stating that the two were already married in heaven. Thus God himself gave her in marriage.

The husband of Zaynab, daughter of Khuzayma, had also fallen in the Battle of Uhud; she died after eight months of marriage. Maymuna had been divorced, but little is said about her. Juwayriyya, daughter of the chief of Khuzaa, had been taken prisoner with her tribe, the Banu Mustaliq; her husband had been killed in the fighting. Since the prophet could not have in-laws who were slaves, he freed her entire tribe. Safiyya, daughter of Huyay, was seventeen and Jewish, and had been captured in Khaybar, after her husband died in the battle. Rayhana was also Jewish, captured from her husband's tribe, the Banu Qurayza.

There was Aulia, whom he divorced before the marriage was consummated. At his marriage to Fatima, daughter of Dhahhaak, he received a verse directing him to make his wives choose between God and worldly possessions. Fatima chose the world, left Muhammad, and in the end was gathering camel dung in the streets, bewailing her fate.

The prophet died before Shinya could be brought to him. Asma was tricked by the jealousy of Aisha and Hafsa: they told her she must act coy with Muhammad and refuse his favors. He sent her back to her tribe. To assuage Muhammad's anger, a disciple offered his sister Qutaila in Yemen; they sent for the woman, but Muhammad died before she arrived. Malika was also deceived by Aisha, refused the prophet, and was sent back. Amra, daughter of Yazid, was discovered to be leprous. He married Sana, but she died before she could reach him.

One day, when Muhammad sat with his back facing the sun, Layla tapped him on the shoulder. He said, "Who's that? May the lions eat him," which was a joke he often made. She replied: "I am the daughter of the one who feeds the birds and competes with the wind." She offered to marry him. He accepted and sent her back to her village to await his instructions. Her friends told her it was a mistake: Layla was a jealous woman and Muhammad had many wives. She returned to Muhammad and asked to be released. He did so, but later she was indeed eaten by a lion. It is said that she was ill-mannered and rode her donkey in an obscene manner.

He proposed to Umm Hani, but she married his uncle instead and had many children. When his uncle died, she offered herself to Muhammad, but it was too late. Dhaba's first husband died and left her extremely wealthy; her second husband was impotent and she divorced him; her third husband died. Her beauty was legendary: when she sat down she would occupy a great part of the carpet and her body would be covered with her long hair. Muhammad offered to marry her, but changed his mind when he discovered she had grown old.

The tribe of Safiyya, daughter of Bashshama, was captured and Muhammad tried to persuade her to divorce her husband, but she refused and was cursed. Khawla, daughter of Hakim, offered herself but was refused. Umama, the daughter of his wet nurse, wanted to marry him, but she was his sister by nursing, and this was forbidden. Khawla, daughter of Hudsail, married Muhammad, but died before she reached him. Shurafa of the tribe of Kalb had a beautiful mole on

241

her cheek, and it is not known why Muhammad, after his proposal, did not marry her. There was another, name now forgotten, whose father did not want her to marry Muhammad, so he claimed she was leprous, and the disease was immediately inflicted on her.

Beside his wives there were two servants he visited regularly: Mariyaa the Copt and Kihana, both of whom had been sent to Muhammad by Mukawkis, the governor of Alexandria. He spent twenty-nine nights in a row with Mariyaa the Copt, and would appear at the door dripping with perspiration, to the fury of his other wives; the scandal was such he threatened to divorce them all. She was the only woman besides Khadija who bore him a child: a boy who died.

Muhammad said that on the Day of Judgment, the people would be assembled barefoot, naked, and uncircumcised. His wife Aisha asked: "O Messenger of Allah, will men and women be together on that day, and will they be looking at each other?" The prophet replied: "Aisha, the matter will be too serious for them to look."

III.

Buraq was an animal of paradise, larger than a donkey and smaller than a camel, with a human face, hooves like a horse, and a tail like an ox. His mane was made of pearls, his ears of emeralds, his eyes sparkled like the planet Venus, and between his eyes was inscribed, "There is no God but God and Muhammad is his prophet." He was possessed of reason. On a certain night, guided by the angel Jibril, Muhammad rode Buraq from Mecca to the temple in Jerusalem, to the heavens and hell and the empyrean and Bayt al-Mamur, the mosque in the sky directly above the Kaaba.

As they traveled, Muhammad heard a voice on his right, which he ignored, and a voice on his left, which he ignored. He saw a woman with bare arms, adorned with all the ornaments of this world, who called out, "Look at me! Let me speak with you!" but Muhammad ignored her. Then he heard an enormous crash that filled him with terror.

They stopped on Mount Sina, where God had spoken with Musa, and in Baytlakhem, where Issa was born. They entered the mosque in Jerusalem. Muhammad was brought three vessels, of wine, water, and milk. He heard a voice directing him to drink the milk, and Jibril told him that he and his followers had found guidance.

Jibril asked what Muhammad had seen along the way, and explained that the voice on his right was that of the Jews; had he listened, he and his followers would have become Jews. The voice on the left was that of the Nazarenes; had he listened, they would have become Christians. The woman was the world; had he spoken with her, they would have preferred this world to the future. The huge crash was the sound of a rock that had been hurled into hell seventy years before and had just then reached the bottom of the abyss.

Jibril took Muhammad to the first heaven and introduced him to Ismail, lord of the meteors and regent of that place, who opened the gates. They met a man with a wheaten complexion, who looked at his right hand and laughed, then looked at his left hand and wept. This was Adam, who rejoiced at his children who would enter paradise and was afflicted by the thought of those who were doomed to hell. He saw an angel sitting with the world on his knees and a tablet of light in his hand, which the angel stared at with unrelenting melancholy. This was the angel of death, who told Muhammad that there is not a house on earth whose inhabitants he does not observe five times a day, and when relatives weep for the departure of a loved one, he tells them to hold their tears, for he will visit them again and again until none are left.

He saw a company of men sitting at a table heaped with the most delicious foods and the most putrid meat, devouring the putrid. He saw an angel of immense size, and half his body was snow and half fire, but the fire did not melt the snow and the snow did not quench the fire. This angel was crying: "Holy holy holy is the Lord who preserves entire the conflicting element of my being."

243

He saw men who had lips like a camel, and the angels cut the flesh off their sides with scissors and threw the chunks of meat in their mouths. He saw men beating their heads with stones. He saw the angels pouring fire into the mouths of another group of men, and the fire passed through their bodies. He saw men whose mouths were sewn with needles and threads of fire. There were people who could not rise because of their enormous stomachs.

There were women suspended by their breasts, and women suspended by their hair. There were women suspended by their tongues, and melted copper from a fountain in hell was poured down their mouths. There were women roasting over a fire and eating their own flesh; women, bound hand and foot, tormented by scorpions. There was a blind, deaf, and dumb woman encased in a coffin of fire, and her brains dripped out of her nostrils. There were women devouring their own entrails; women with the heads of hogs and the bodies of donkeys; women in the shape of dogs, beaten by angels with maces of fire.

Everywhere in the heavens Muhammad saw angels who stared fixedly in awe and fear, never moving their heads, never speaking to one another, uttering praises to God.

They rose to the second heaven, where they met Issa, and his cousin Yahyah, who had baptized him. In the third heaven they met a man whose beauty exceeded all others, as the moon exceeds the stars, and that was Yusuf, of the many-colored coat, the interpreter of dreams. In the fourth was Idris; in the fifth Harun, brother of Musa, an old man with huge eyes; in the sixth was Musa himself, with pale skin and very long hair.

In the seventh heaven he saw seas of glittering light, seas of darkness, and seas of snow. Every angel they passed told Muhammad to use leeches for healing, and instruct his followers to do the same. He met an old man with white hair and beard who sat under a tree that

244

had udders like a cow, and on each udder an infant nursed. Whenever an udder slipped out of a baby's mouth, the old man would get up and restore it. Jibril told him that was his father, Ibrahim, and the babies the future prophets who were first tasting the fruits of paradise.

He saw a rooster whose feet stood on the lowest earth and whose head reached the empyrean; its wings were white, and when it spread its wings, they reached the limits of east and west and the feathers underneath were green. Each morning this rooster would sing the praises of God, and when it did all the roosters on earth would join in singing.

They came to Bayt al-Mamur, the mosque directly above the Kaaba, and saw two crowds of people, one in beautiful white garments and the others in rags, and only those in white were allowed to enter. He saw the four rivers of paradise—one of crystal water, one of milk, one of wine, one of limpid honey—and the palaces along the banks where Muhammad and his family would ultimately live. The soil was pure musk; there were birds as large as camels and pomegranates the size of buckets. He saw Tuba, the tree of paradise, whose trunk is so great it would take a bird seven hundred years to fly around it, and whose branches extend to shade every house and are hung with a hundred thousand different fruits and baskets filled with brocade and satin robes. He saw what he thought was his cousin Ali, but it was an angel made by God in the likeness of Ali.

Jibril gave Muhammad a quince, which he opened, and a Houri with long black eyelashes appeared, wearing seventy green robes and seventy yellow robes of so fine a texture, and she herself was so transparent that the marrow of her ankles could be seen like a flame in a glass lamp. "Who are you?" he asked. "My name is Happiness. The upper part of my body is made of camphor, the middle of amber, the lower of musk. I was kneaded in the waters of life. God told me to be, and I was."

Eliot Weinberger

They came to a river of light, where Jibril said he bathed every day, and each drop that fell created an angel who spoke a language unintelligible to the rest. Beyond the river were five hundred curtains of light, and between each curtain a journey of five hundred years, and beyond the last curtain was God. Jibril said that he himself could not go a finger's length further, but that Muhammad must cross the river and travel on.

AUTHOR'S NOTE: All of the information in this essay is derived from the canonical non-Quranic writings, the Hadith; from *The History of Prophets and Kings* (*Ta'rikh al-rusul wa'l-muluk*) by the great Baghdad historian of the late ninth and early tenth centuries, Abu Ja'far Muhammad ibn Jarir al-Tabari; and from the second volume of *The Life of Hearts* (*Hiyat al-Qulub*) by the eighteenth-century Persian cleric Allama Muhammad Baqir al-Majlisi. Spellings conform to the *Oxford Dictionary of Islam*.

The Mental Traveler
Robert Harbison

CAN IT REALLY BE Zola who wrote that strange novel about someone who moves to a cathedral town and sets himself up in a house right across from the cathedral? Now his whole life begins to revolve around this building, circling it by moonlight, dipping in at different times of day, observing services from afar. Was the plot of this relatively long book really founded on the relation between a character and a building?

I keep reverting to that idea. There can't be many people to whom it would appeal, but I love the prospect of having all the time in the world to absorb a great Gothic building from a base directly opposite. I think we once stayed in a room—part of some church foundation—from which you could see the long south side of Lincoln Cathedral, but then, as I remember, it wasn't so simple to get there, the route not long but mildly circuitous.

My most recent experience of going back and back to absorb more and more of an endlessly diverting Gothic building occurred a couple of years ago in Reims. I have a book, a set of books, that catalogs the series of over five hundred figures with which the cathedral at Reims is dotted, a book that diverts me from, as well as connects me to, this building. Through its pages I become fixated on the scheme underlying all the separate sculptures. The person who put this book together had a strange tower constructed, which was built onto a van or flat-bottomed truck so that he could move it around until he brought many figures that were almost out of reach of the eyes to eye level, in order to study and—more important—photograph them one by one, from this angle and that as if they were freestanding works in a gallery.

His procedure makes me think of Ruskin, organizing scaffolds to get near part of a fresco in order to spend all morning in a cold church copying a figure by Luini or Botticelli. Actually I agree with Tim Hilton (in his biography of Ruskin) that Ruskin's drawings of sculpture are much more interesting. The details of doorways or gables at Abbeville, for instance, give a wonderful idea of how he spent half a day, focusing on this and not that, interested in how some things disappear and some stand out, so that although the eye and hand are here recording instruments, they don't function like a camera, faithful as a camera, but always selecting, dutifully following, and at the same time imperiously omitting more than they include. It's the empty spaces, always so prominent in Ruskin's drawings, that give the great sense of freedom.

Still, it's a problem I haven't solved, my helpless attraction to the idea of devoting years to one building or one place—maybe I could write *The Stones of Verona* that Ruskin imagined but never pursued very far, or the massive expansion of the *Buildings of England* for the North Riding that I for one feel a desperate need of.

Of course I can't even keep on the track for a whole sentence or a whole paragraph, so how am I going to catalog methodically every settlement in the largest county in England, not omitting the ones on which I think there's virtually nothing to say, unless I uncover in them an unexpected (and perhaps nonexistent) strangeness that their inhabitants will not thank me for bringing into unsuitable prominence.

I become more and more addicted to the most detailed topographical treatments I can find, until I am literally and figuratively and mentally and spiritually and practically and almost continually weighed down by guidebooks to places I am not going to, or have already returned from for the last foreseeable time. So I immerse myself rapturously in the iconographical index (twenty-three pages long!) to an architectural catalog of that part of one Austrian province that lies south of the Danube. How did I wind up here? By a circuitous route indeed, starting with the new-book shelf in the London Library. This is what a lot of my travel comes down to these days—a form of study stuck in one place.

If I do ever actually go anywhere—five days in Rome with fifty students—then for months after, I am reading about the place in a topographical dictionary, most of whose entries refer to features that have disappeared, and in guides to individual churches that are hundreds of pages long, churches I spent ten minutes going round on a walk that included four or five others.

The proportions are absurd and make it seem that the person who behaves this way would always rather be somewhere else. According to something I read downstairs last night in order to use up the warmth of a dying fire, Henry James didn't really know where he belonged or felt less and less attached to any place as home. I wouldn't have put it so categorically, rather that he had chosen his attachment rather carefully. I thought he took about as much pleasure in London as it's possible to take, just regarding it in itself. But the person arguing this is starting from the major fact that HJ seems to have no main attachment, that he lives by himself, not literally, of course: he has servants and a comfortable flat in the middle of a city where he knows a great many people. James gave the cue, I think, by what he said about the loneliness of the writer. Does Dickens, who (at one period anyway) used to write at a table full of noisily conversing people, ever talk about the loneliness of the writer?

To me it feels unlucky to talk about yourself as a writer. Who knows, you might have stopped being someone who has anything left to say just at the minute you begin to pontificate on the subject, or just as you set yourself up in a well-equipped study from which nothing interesting will ever emerge. Anyway, traveling is more lonely than writing, in my experience. As the time to set out approaches, I invariably think the whole plan is a mistake.

How can you give up all the comforts of home—knowing where to find things and having all the old detritus of your life to hand—for this complete and threatening blank? My wife is always moving plants around in the garden as if they were pieces of furniture or pictures on the wall. On the verge of departure I feel like one of those delphiniums, teetery, helpless, out of place. Whatever made me think that I enjoy being transported to arbitrarily selected cities where I have no business and no place?

Without a trip impending, I am a person who loves traveling. And I've only found out by accident how much I value home. For years I functioned without a desk or a work space. There simply wasn't room for one. Then we began to rent a converted farm building that had a little room that became my study. Our landlord lent us a desk full of compartments like a house, and I began the encrustation of this space with books picked up in boot sales, strange ornaments from similar sources, feathers, bits of moss, pock-marked stones from our early walks, until it gave me a very complete sense of being at home.

I think I'll be barking up the wrong tree if I try to say that in traveling you're just making homes for yourself in unlikely places, that the whole enterprise is a kind of settling in. I've never shared Esther's interest in the rooms we stay in in foreign places. She takes pictures of them and notices positive and negative features that pass me by, but, instructed by her, I now check to see if there's a light to read by and a table of some sort to write at.

For I have an absolutely fixed idea that I must record my travels, getting down impressions soon after seeing things. I remember a trip to Gravesend with a novelist friend, chasing Pocahontas, whose grave is there, on which he surprised me by carrying a notebook and stumbling over the graves, making notes on the experience at the very moment in which it was taking place. Later when he put this trip in a novel, did taking notes form part of the experience? I could check on this by going downstairs. Gravesend appears near the beginning of a very long work and there I am, a character (extremely fleeting) in a book.

One writes it down in order to make the chaotic experience of travel meaningful, or one travels in order to have subjects to write about. Writing adjusts all the foreignness to the texture of your thought, and returning time and again to the same destination converts it into a second home. It's a contradictory concept. In some sense there can't be such a thing as a second home, or one is only pretending and being diverted by the idea of setting up a second parallel existence in another place.

There's a famous example—a writer or collector—of someone driven out of his original living space by a silting up of memories and possessions that eventually becomes so dense he has no room to move. And in fact don't collectors often abandon one collection and start over on something entirely different?

Instead of a wide variety of models, I keep recurring to Ruskin. Instead of visiting new ones, he went back to a small number of old spots that could be quickly listed. Doubtless someone's done a statistical study of how much time he spent in each of his main centers of study. Occasionally he shows he isn't entirely happy to be pinned down so easily and says irritably that Abbeville has meant just as much to him as Venice.

The reason my friend's notebook annoyed me may be that it showed him blatantly communing with himself. When Ruskin returns to Lucca, he's paying a visit to some part of himself. Already the first time we meet him there, he's revisiting. And revisiting. He tells his father he follows the same regimen every day, practical necessities, work, private rituals, with the latter bunched toward or saved for the end of the day. I can't recite the whole program here, but it remains a forlorn beacon to me of the satisfactions and dissatisfactions of a life devoted to and used up in art. Every day ends with

250

a session by the bedside of a marble maiden stretched out on her tomb, followed by a walk on the ramparts.

If, as I'm coming to think, the second homes of travel are ways of outwitting death, but temporarily, so the process needs repeating, here Ruskin blatantly reads an end as a suspension (death is interpreted as sleep) but has to wake up from this delusion every day at the same time. Like other motifs in his life this one took on increasingly urgent form, lurching from the realm of art into more pressing actuality.

Ruskin also seems to exaggerate the importance of finding himself in the same hotel room he had occupied on an earlier visit. I've spent many fruitless hours searching for the places where I stayed in far distant years, a dingy courtyard in Florence, a web of little streets near the Winter Circus in Paris. The exact location of the entrance, the entire route to my room—my interest doesn't end when these are established. I want to reconstruct all my nearby walks and journeys as if I had really belonged to this neighborhood or it had belonged to me. All the while it seems ridiculous that your most intense interest in Florence is directed to what it retains in its street pattern of a certain old self of your own. But perhaps you are lonely for a time when travel really worked, when real fusion occurred between a place and the self. For the revisitor this takes the form of thinking you've left something of yourself behind here, which by proceeding carefully enough, you might recover.

I regard knowing a city as something like putting together a puzzle, whose pieces exist in different times and arrive from odd places. Yesterday I collected two bits I need to fit into my collage of Rome, from a friend's lecture and a student paper. The first: in a large sacristy I didn't know lay behind a Roman church I've passed hundreds of times, a huge sloping tube runs through the external wall to bring a shaft of light to bear on a dark corner, like bringing an elephant to crack a walnut or using elaborate but simple means to achieve the impossible. The second: the famous silver image of St. Ignatius in the Gesù, one of the world's most repellent artworks, apparently represents a particular moment in his life—on the road to La Storta, where he was irradiated by a vision until he glowed with it. That wizard Pozzo, who designed the altar, made a little window just behind it that would cast a mysterious beam on the saint's silver head, which would then glow with otherworldly radiance.

You would think that extra pieces for a puzzle already too big and taking too much space might be unwelcome. But it doesn't work like

251

that. It's important that in a simple literal way they fit into space that was already there, somewhat underused in spite of the apparent plenitude, we now see. One continues adding to one's own approximation of that kind of star map that intrigued and baffled me as a teenager walking home down a completely dark street and comforted by the sight of Orion overhead when I wasn't scared out of my wits by the thought of interstellar distances. I suppose I knew even then that these "maps," which leveled things in vastly different planes, showed a pattern that was only visible and thus meaningful from spots like the one I was standing in, a pattern whose point was to locate me, not the stars.

When I go back to that town in Pennsylvania, now a ghost of itself, hollowed out from within by Wal-Mart, the store compared by a writer in *The New York Times* to the universe, I am sad and angry that by changing the place it is in, that town has deprived a large number of my memories of their roosting places in reality.

The Cyborg Suite
Martine Bellen

ASTRO BOY'S FATHER

OSAMU TEZUKA (BORN 1928 in Osaka, Japan) is heralded for having brought cinematic art and narratives to the manga form. His early "comic books" were graphic novels (way before the term was coined in America), two hundred pages of zooming, panning, and complicated plots. He defined the popular style that we recognize today as an emblem of contemporary Japanese culture. Notwithstanding his penchant for visual and narrative movement, what's so arresting about Tezuka's work is his capacity to freeze a moment, to capture its emotion and tension—one instant of our fleeting life on its way to the next. It's no wonder that Tezuka is known as "The God of the Manga."

I've read that manga is an outgrowth of American comics. Joseph Pulitzer, the late-nineteenth-century proprietor of the failing *New York World* newspaper, published the first comic strips and their popularity reverberated all the way to Japan. Although Tezuka has recognized Disney as his principal influence, Peter Carey writes in his memoir, *Wrong About Japan,* that manga is derived from a source other than our cartoons and comic strips. During one of Carey's visits to Japan he was told that manga and anime hearken back to "kamishibai" or "paper theater," which is a kind of Japanese visual storytelling that was popular in the 1920s. The kamishibai storyteller would ride his bicycle to a village or city, strike two wooden clappers to attract the attention of neighborhood kids, and then he'd pull out pictures mounted on cards. He'd narrate elaborate, dramatic tales with cliffhanger endings that left the audience of kids hungering for his return. They would also hunger for his candy—a sideline that brought in profits. According to Carey, after the war many of these kamishibai storytellers became manga artists and the more popular kamishibai characters made their way into print.

In 1949, the young Tezuka created the manga *Metropolis.* Tezuka admits to having never seen the Fritz Lang film; he based his story on a poster that hung at the local cinema. In 1957 Tezuka's *Astro Boy* (*Mighty Atom*) began airing on Tokyo TV. It aired in this country from 1963 to 1966. Astro Boy is Tezuka's most popular character. Recently I attended an anime festival at the Museum of Modern Art in New York City and viewed the original and early reels of *Astro Boy*.

Astro's background is complicated. The robot Astro was commissioned by the head of the Institute of Science, Dr. Boyton, who lost his boy Toby in a car accident. Boyton's neglect of Toby was what instigated Toby's reckless driving. Boyton ordered his greatest scientists to use all their skill and brilliance to create for him a perfect son. Finally Astro Boy was completed and ready to "live." Dr. Boyton told Astro that he'd love him forever. Boyton spent his free time with Astro, teaching him everything he knew and being the father he never was to Toby. He hired tutors for Astro Boy and strived to give him "the best of everything." Sadly, after not too long, Dr. Boyton realized Astro was never going to grow. He'd always be a boy (his one fault).

Dr. Boyton banished Astro and this rejection broke the boy bot's heart. After all, Boyton had promised his eternal love. Boyton sold Astro to a robot circus so he'd never have to look at his disappointment again. This transaction takes place before the emancipation of robots, before we were forbidden to trade them like sex slaves. Dr. Elefun saves Astro Boy from his life of indentured servitude (in fact, he emancipates all the robots) and comes to be known as Astro's "real" father.

As a kid, I loved watching *Astro Boy* and now I know why—Astro the misfit, Astro the abandoned alien—I identified the robot in myself. Astro lived within robot law. He was propelled by his rocket-fueled legs and he protected the weak and vulnerable with his laser gun. The story of Astro Boy was set in the far, far future—the year 2000, or six years ago. We have passed the future. We have surpassed robots.

Donna Haraway in her *Cyborg Manifesto* investigates our bond with technology. She claims that we are "theorized and fabricated hybrids of machine and organism; in short, we are cyborgs." Haraway studies our cyborgness in relation to feminist and Marxist theory, in terms of sex and power relationships. We've ingested the future, which is now our past. Astro Boy, his pain and potential, is of our loin. We are of him. Astro, or Mighty Atom, as he is called in Japan, is our Adam.

OUR CYBORGS, OURSELVES

Our skin is an organ, the same as a heart and kidney. The epidermis, the outer layer of our skin, is 0.1 to 1.5 millimeters thick. Our epidermis interfaces with the operating environment in which we live. The platform that an epidermis interfaces with on personal computers might be Windows 2000 or OS X. (Check to see which platform you're compatible with. By the way, this is personal information to be shared only with an intimate. And even then, consider wisely!) Recently, concern has been expressed about the rate at which the epidermis has been expanding. First we heard random reports from news organizations (note the word "organ" cloaked innocently in a Latinate wolf in sheep's clothing) expressing warnings about our consumption of trans fats that were causing weight gain. Next, wireless solutions began to augment us beyond our expanding flesh. We are bionic cyborgs—enhanced by electromechanical devices. We have surpassed the twentieth-century futuristic imagination, though are unable to see, accept the hybrid machine that we have become. We are in Freudian denial of our intimacy with, and our dependency on, e-mail, handhelds, iPods, etc. They have become us.

What makes us human? Are we biotic systems? Communication devices? Septic tanks to cleanse our planet? A self-propagating virus to infect our planet? When we confront an operating manual are we reading our creation myth?

As our flesh extends to the outer limits, as we embark on face transplants, cloning, etc., as we lose more pieces of our bodies while living longer lives, the question of what makes us us becomes increasingly prevalent. A dominant argument in Cartesian philosophy is that the brain is the seat of humanity. Thought, not limb, makes a person. And as our bodies are wasting away and being replaced by enhanced simulacra, we are becoming aware that we are not our heart, not our leg, not our face. Have you heard Descartes traveled with a life-size female mechanical doll, a replacement for his dead illegitimate daughter—Descartes' Astro Girl? According to the Buddhist concept "not-self," everything is impermanent: "This is not mine, this I am not, this is not my self."

My PC is me (though not me, too; next year I upgrade). My better half. The half with extended memory and an external drive. I am weary. My blood pressure lowers when it's near. Tail wags. Sits on my lap. Warm. Gods and Dolls and Cyborgs. The question of how information enters us, melds, or a soul inhabits the body, shell, machine, ghost, the only part left of us that is human. Donne called it ecstasy. Enter computer data and see what computes, what exits. Exists, still. See. [X]

And what if I am a robot? A goddess? A monster?

*

[*Prize inside
Dictionary around back]

METROPOLIS
By Fritz Lang and Osamu Tezuka

The following strip tells the tale of a world in the near future. Just a few yards away. A factitious citadel—Our Postmodern Tower of Babel whose lexiconal roots penetrate deep down Metropolis's unsavory bowels. In scatology our story begins:

Zone three:

We enter with anteriograde amnesia (the memory of tomorrow
Deleted from the brain's analphabetic Bible)

In Zone three there's a shift change

Imagine not understanding this:

    1. Lowercase night workers
    2. Title case graveyard

Shift / Return

Worker 11811 enters the gates of work / of hell / holding the arms of time in his arms as he dreams night after night of time in Yoshiwara, the Japanese section of his life in which he peers off at a speck of frost that will melt when lifted from the bamboo leaf.

What we call "end" is a misnomer

To face all versions of one instrument / oneself / software
                             She shifts / changes her mind
to satisfy a power not understood

"Contact" means the exchange of knowledge; for instance, she uploads song upon another's system

Our future depends on the ocean's intension and CGI effects

As he does his day, he senses the song she has inserted into him

From on high, far from Workers' City, far from the depths of female robot, while Worker 11811 dreams of swelling plums, the following voices are heard:

Son: Where are the hands that built your city?
Father: Where they belong—in hell.

Son: Father, do you know what it means to be dismissed by you? It means: "Go below to the depths where Worker 11811 is stricken with Wollust and Zorn."

Martine Bellen

Regardless which **METROPOLIS** you enter, there is always a female robot. One never knows if she's human, part human, or 100% bot. She herself has no idea. She is always powerful and sexy. That's a visual.

A lamp illuminates the vector between the female body and its structural design

Although a jar, she is also a building

In the unbreakable halls she hides—hallucinations

A stunning young girl—hair, incandescent light—bereft of memory and speech. What could be sexier? (Consider this question mightily, and come up with three answers!)

The following are voices heard in your head:
Kenichi (voice):
Ham and Egg (English version voice):
Astro Boy (English) and Mighty Atom (Japanese) Voice:

One of these answers is a wish.

Zone two:

The house welcomes him, a door swings open, then another, more; he doesn't have a handle on it

    Some of him likes some of the doors—their trickery and humor

When neon, fluorescent, chrome, candle, movie, church, star, moon,
meaningful and meaningless light fall . . .

When night after night you find yourself in Yoshiwara, the Japanese
section of life

HM 2 [Heart Machine two]

Your heart generates heartlight / your hands palmlight

How did you get inside me? Who gave you clearance
To allow me to feel / know your thighlight, your headlight?

The problem started with sunspots on earth

Then the digging

What information do I need in order to understand
                           this manga?
                      This anime of mine? my saga?

Related work: None
Background: None
Lineage: None

What zone are you allowed in?

Zone won

Zone too

Zone tree

A cool life is waiting for all who finish, so give it a shot!

259

Martine Bellen

THE BIRTH OF FEMALE ROBOT

This is a story of a robot girl constructed by a mad scientist on orders from the master of the city,

The sunspots, the exploited city workers, the disappointed father and son are excuses to draw closer to the female robot, to probe into the incomprehensible that has no lineage, background, or prior works that are related to her. The unknowable.

A quarter of the film is lost
Three quarters of my life gone
Rotwang the Inventor
The Thin Man
The Guardian of the Heart Machine
Creative Man
Death
Seven Deadly Men sinning
        These I've met.

[The external drive with source memory *lost!* Never backed up! When I pass from one world to the next, one zone to another . . . nothing is permitted through the firewall / war zone / hallucination]

Zone one:

Her creation rests in the ambitions of a powerful man
A city planner who lives in a tower far above the masses of the undercity

The Human studies the Bot,
Observes the metal epidermis at sunset in ocean light
Its battered, pitted mirror
Mental abrasions
[The mirror is a technology for distortion, not illumination]

In bodybuilding, striations are tiny grooves of muscle
In geology—tracks inscribed by the process of time
Crystal twinning, glacial flow
In love—tears [rips] in faith that generate fault lines
Tears [geysers] tinkling across a hilly cheek
Arcadia

"I am in Zone one. I suspect I've visited Zone two and three but retain no memory of who I was then; my present system is incompatible with undated materials

"As a human I feel sorry for the bot,
                    her lack of recurring characters,
themes, dreams, seasons, payments, pen pals, birthdays, births, days
& days, cancer & canker, hoopla, meteors,
          as though her hand is my hand, as though a stronger one
is reaching up through me."

The Arcadian escape

Imagine not understanding this.

Dictionary
CGI—Computer Generated Image; denoting that computers will
     generate full imagery and a Worker is, for the time being,
     relieved of imaginary duty.
Factitious—Produced artificially; not related to fictitious (produced
     through imagination); not related to fact (that which is
     based on truth, not fiction). Though in many instances,
     "fact" can be produced "factitiously."

261

Martine Bellen

Anteriograde Amnesia—Pothole of the brain. Inability to remember there's tomorrow. Halcyon. Overly successful Buddhist.

End—A domino with two "ends" and a dividing line. Similar to an inning in baseball. A period of uncertainty in one's day. A word often and religiously used by those suffering from anteriograde amnesia.

Hypnagogic Hallucinations—Mental images that occur just before sleep and cannot be categorized at the moment of inception. (This is when our poem takes place.)

Analphabetic—An analphabetic arrangement of letters or a writing system that is not alphabetic—not literate.

Scatology—The chemical analysis of excrement; the study of dirty language and obscenity.

Heart Machine—A pump that propels feelings and intuitions through the body's blood vessels and vases.

Zorn, Wollust—(German) Anger, lechery (Sins).

Bot—Short for "robot." Artificial or factitious intelligence [AI] masquerading as a human user. An interface we refuse to acknowledge because of cultural / ethnic prejudice. Our inner child.

Thighlight—A charged sexuality that emits ultraviolet rays. Glows in the dark. Often mistaken for twilight.

Osamu Tezuka—A comic creator, heralded the "God of Manga." Best known for *Astro Boy*. He has said his *Metropolis* manga (later made into anime after his death) was inspired by a poster of the Fritz Lang movie, which he had never seen.

Hypnopompic Hallucinations—Images viewed in dreams that persist on awakening; have been known to walk off the dream screen and gain control over one's day / life.

The Ghost of Electricity: The Dylan Face
Sven Birkerts

I REMEMBER HOW I used to shake my head when the literary theorists of the seventies and eighties started in on their semiotic analyses, all that business about "signs" and "referents." I found it such a strange way of looking at the world, but I could also see a kind of sense in it. And for a time I did my best to follow along. It was the intellectual order of the day, after all. Everything was a language, a millrace of competing codes. I drew the line, though, at the "transcendent signifier," that anchoring entity that supposedly gave meaning to everything else in the relativistic slipstream, but which for me toppled straight into absurdity when Lacan, I think it was Lacan, linked it to the primacy of the phallus, that symbolically vertical entity that could be seen to preside over certain discourse like a conductor's baton, with everything falling in behind it. Find that phallus and arrest the chaotic flow. I'm sure it was more nuanced than that.

Fashions fade, of course. Years have now passed without anyone using the words "transcendent signifier" in my hearing. It arrived of its own accord the other day, hard on the heels of my first of several viewings of Martin Scorsese's recent documentary *No Direction Home.* I know how ridiculous that sounds, but isn't a great deal of our thinking absurd at the point of germination? I was trying to get clear from a blue tangle that I'd managed to wrap myself in—I'd gone from wanting to write some simple responses to Scorsese's portrait to experiencing a total mental saturation. And how not? The whole of my affective interior is crosshatched with Bob Dylan. I was sixteen when I was first bowled over by "Don't Think Twice, It's Alright," and I'm fifty-four now. Though there have been gaps of attention and devotion, I've never strayed far from the music or the lore. Lines from his songs are woven through my whole memory grid. There was, I realized, no standing to one side to make an assessment. Nor has there ever been a clear emblem figure to make an assessment *of.* From the first, Dylan's career has been a procession of masquerades, brilliant stylized poses, reversals—in fact, the very *point* of Dylan at some level has been this mercurial game.

Sven Birkerts

What I had with Dylan—I sensed this watching—was a teeming swirl of signifiers overlaying a veritable jungle of signifieds, the whole great mass of images and words sliding around, as signifiers are said to do, with my own identifications everywhere adding to the complication. I saw no way to find purchase and address the whole business directly. Not that I didn't try—I scribbled pages of notes, doing everything I could to boil chaos down to some version of "first principles." But nothing firmed up, nothing clicked together like I like things to click. And then, suddenly, ironically, I got that phrase in my ear, and for the first time I was able to step to the side of my own fussing. Enough, at least to realize that all along I'd been asking myself, the mind's needle skipping in a circular groove, why I was so interested, so *compelled*, by one particular aspect of Scorsese's film, by the intercut segments of "present-day" footage of Dylan responding to questions.

The obvious answer was that deep down I'm a rubbernecker who is drawn to all sites where time has been doing its work. *Of course* I would be fascinated to study the man as he looks now, to move my loupe over the features of Joan Baez's "original vagabond." But absorbing as I found the aging face, its lines and pouches, its repertoire of expressions, it was not the spectacle of change and continuity that held me so much as the startling realization that here, for once, through design or happy chance, I felt like I was seeing the face behind the mask—unadorned, without its thousand protective feints, sans its veils of sarcasm, its obfuscation, its deliberated elusiveness. Just a man talking, unless, of course, and I thought of this right away, this was the ultimate performance of them all. But I don't think so. I've seen the film three times now and the shock of those segments is still acute. They are nothing in themselves, simple head shots of a famous artist talking, pausing, fumbling to articulate his responses. Absolutely everything is found in the contrast. And it is when I watch these recent segments that I get, profoundly, what I've always sensed: that from his first filmed appearances Dylan was never that. Never not posing. Not even in his most "authentic," unwashed, scraggly "troubadour" days. He was—obviously I theorize—always Robert Zimmerman, trick-or-treating, donning the garb of the wanderer, the hard-luck Woody Guthrie, or the lyric surrealist—those myriad identities that Scorsese has soldered together. This, for me, is the disturbing draw of the film. Without these cut-in segments I would be watching just another well-done documentary, following the familiar hagiographic trail that starts with the early still photo images of childhood and family then moves to interviews with aging survivors—friends, fellow musicians—everything held together with generous lengths of concert footage. An interesting portrait in itself, but nothing like the revealing artifact Scorsese has put together.

From the first, Dylan's core dynamic—the dynamic established and certified by his decision to change from being five-syllable Robert Zimmerman to plain Bob Dylan—has been his exuberant will to impersonation, the creation and maintenance of a public self that is not only seen as ever changing but is at the same time always at a slant to any expectations his listeners might have. Naturally, this is just the outward play of guises, his mock-serious theater, a vastly heightened version of what many of us do at certain times in our lives. Something more than impersonations, but less than incarnations, these shifts of presentation would be merely interesting if it were not for the music, which is so often, so obviously profound—is arguably the most important musical oeuvre of our time. I don't think I have to list songs, quote phrases and lines and verses to make my case.

Normally I run on two tracks with Dylan. Listening to the music I tend to forget the shape-shifting of the public phenomenon. Almost any one of his great lyrics goes straight to the inner man, giving me an artistic connection that renders the idea of such gamesmanship almost incidental. Only on the other track, watching the film, do I confront the icon and feel the palpable tension between levels. This tension expresses itself as fascination. As one of the many listeners who heeds the man—even if I'm more an intermittent partisan than a tour-list following, tracking aficionado—I remain drawn in, intrigued. Because if the songs lay out a true lyric map of our era, the artist himself appears to be forever skirting the consequentiality of his inspiration, or bracketing it, or refusing overt image-identification with it. He has simply not accepted—indeed has at every point flouted—the expected mapping of appearance to what we like to think of as reality. He has created an uncertain, often agitated—but at other times stony cold—presence that shimmers ectoplasmically in front of the music.

I don't want to overstate. Dylan is by no means a playful showman chameleon, though at points in his career he has tried this on as well—think of the white face of the Rolling Thunder tour. No, the

265

presence is often a calculated distancing, a way of throwing up a wall between performing a song and claiming its emotion—its verbal passion—for his own. Some of this must be self-protective, having to do with his grueling performance schedule, often as many as two hundred shows a year. For whatever reason, Dylan takes his music on the road far more than his reputation or his bank account would presumably require. But this in itself is part of the disjunction, a feature of the mystery. Why does the man perform so much? Is it a penance? Or, as he has sometimes claimed, a way of vocally revising the songs? I don't know. But certainly he keeps himself publicly removed and changeful in a way that makes me think that there might be a mysterious third narrative unfolding between what we hear and what we consume as image.

This brings me back to that unfortunate semiotic phrase and the idea behind it, which is that that whole elaborate ballet of shifting public personae changes its nature the moment we isolate the idea of the actual—that which has always lain implicitly behind the changing faces as enigma, but which now, for whatever reason, seems to be revealing itself. Revealing itself not only in Dylan's decision to appear without masks, *as himself,* for Scorsese's film, but also more or less concurrently on the larger time line, by writing his memoir, *Chronicles* (2004) in a voice purged of obfuscations and posturings. The prose is marked by its unvarnished casualness, its overt refusal to be straining for effect. Of course, as I said before, both self-presentations, on screen and page, could be instances of the most insidious put-on of all—putting on a self that appears, for once, to not be putting itself on—but I prefer to think not. I'd rather have it that the man has reached a point in his life where he feels free—emboldened—to risk being himself. Why this should be the case—now, in late middle age—is anybody's guess.

It is not, I imagine, an easy or natural shift, not a simple matter of turning off the artifice switch. Artifice is not assumed quite that readily or directly, not in this case; artifice is more like a personality style, a way of being that develops out of a compelling inner need. Dylan's dropping of facades, in other words, is not the same as an actor's letting go of a part, though I would add that seeing him "unplugged" in the Scorsese film has some of the feel of seeing a character-identified actor answering questions about his craft.

But with this comparison things get more complicated. For an

266

actor, interviewed in shirtsleeves, will reflect on his work, his roles, his inhabiting of, say, Hannibal Lecter. But Dylan, to my knowledge, has not closed the circle; he has never really gone public about the relentless metamorphoses that have defined his public career. Rather, in showing himself for who he is, he has simply stopped being who he's not, bringing forward the "natural sign" (another semiotic concept, as I recall), almost as if this face were simply the latest in the ongoing sequence. But no, after this, after the shedding of all masks and with them the idea of pretense, there is no going back; no later return to masked performances.

While I think of this self-exposure as being bold or risky, my feeling as I watch those sections is also of a strange kind of flattening. The shock is in the *fact* of the difference more than in the presentation itself. That Dylan, talking, answering questions, should have to fumble for phrases like the rest of us. That Dylan, so lyrical and strange in his songs (many of them), should write a simple, straight, matter-of-fact prose: "Topical songs weren't protest songs. The term 'protest singer' didn't exist any more than the term 'singer-songwriter.' You were a performer or you weren't, that was about it—a folksinger or not one."

The contrast not only tells on Dylan, on our fantasies and projections, but it also deepens the split between the idiom of the artist "inspired" and the artist in day-to-day mode. Dylan coming to us in an ordinary voice underscores like nothing else the otherness of the songwriter. Between the prose and the lyrics is a great gulf.

Studying the face of the sixty-five-year-old man, I'm fixated on the intertwined mysteries of self-making and impersonation. At what moment does a person coin a new name for himself, and when, if ever, does he gain title to it? Seen in the right light, the issue is fascinating. For an emerging performer to change his or her name to something more catchy is a career decision; it makes marketing sense. For a teenaged boy to invent, claim, and then begin to inhabit a name is something else again. The shift from Robert Zimmerman to Bob Dylan is obviously fraught with association and implication. On the one hand, it is a move toward the plainspoken/ casual ("Bob," not "Robert" Dylan), on the other toward the "poetic" (Dylan Thomas); it is also, obviously, a way out of the Jewish identification. Dylan attempted in Hibbing what generations had ventured at Ellis Island, the shedding of racial traces. It makes perfect sense for an American-legend-besotted kid, one who dreamed of hoboes and hard-luck travelers à la Woody Guthrie, to want to lose the Jewish connection, which is simply not suggestive of solitary poetic rambling, the legend of Wandering Jew notwithstanding. The image Dylan was after had a distinctly non-Jewish pedigree—rootless, authentic, American. The very same image Elliot Adnopoz was after when he rechristened himself Ramblin' Jack Elliot. The question, not to be answered here, is how successfully one ever grows into an assumed identity, whether any traces remain at the root, whether wishing is enough to eventually make it so.

Dylan uses a wonderful phrase in the film to describe his younger self. He was, he says several times, "a musical expeditionary." This is not a word I recognize as a noun, and I'm tempted to look it up. But I won't, preferring to think of it as Dylan's ad hoc coinage. "Expeditionary." Meaning what? One who goes on musical expeditions? That would make a certain obvious sense, except that the way Dylan uses it, the context, which is all about the young singer's enormous zeal for absorbing influences from all directions—indeed, borrowing and not returning large quantities of records from friends in Minneapolis (among them Tony "Little Sun" Glover of Koerner, Ray & Glover fame)—makes me wonder if there might not be a hint of "expedience" stirred in. What comes through loud and clear is that the Dylan of those early years was a magpie, a Gypsy, a poacher. Enough years have passed by the time of filming to allow Dave Van Ronk (he has since died) to be bemused, though clearly still nettled, as he recounts how Dylan appropriated his arrangement of "House of the Risin' Sun" for his first album. But stories like Van Ronk's abound. David Hadju's eye-opening *Positively 4th Street* explores at some length how the artist piggybacked on the reputation of the then-far-more-famous Joan Baez.

Dylan never stopped, never let up; his artistic ambition was formidable. Formidable, but also very much at odds with the ethos of the folk scene, which was populist and collective right down to its manifestly radical roots. As was, let's note, Dylan's own image in those early years. He was creating himself as the Woody-inspired ramblin' boy, the work-shirted proletarian, never mind that Woody himself was never on the make, and that his populism was genuinely about helping the poor. Dylan sang "Pretty Boy Floyd," but he did so while elbowing his way to the front of the line.

But it's too easy somehow to call him a phony or a poseur, though both labels are gummy enough to stick. To me it makes more sense to study the contradiction as just that. Not, in other words, a case of a false front laid upon a less attractive reality, but of two drives in tense opposition. What's more, I would argue that this face-off of polarized selves—the idealist and the climber—allowed, even encouraged, the public procession of masks and poses. The more he changed his pitch, the less he was invested in its implications. So long as he was in one of his enigmatic guises, Dylan was free of having to account for the contradiction, either to others or to himself. The image could become an arena of freedom.

Of course this is only a supposition, but it does help me understand why in a movie like D. A. Pennebaker's *Don't Look Back* (Scorsese's title makes an interesting echo), the singer comes across as so impossibly antic, such a tightly compacted bundle of warring energies. On the one hand he is wooing his British audiences, on the other he is snarling and writhing, at every moment trying to shake off the expectation that he *be* this or that. Thrown into the dense sociability of the tour—with Baez, Allen Ginsberg, Donovan, Albert Grossman, or the dozens of hangers-on who haunt his room—he can be seen constantly absenting himself, drawing away to sit at the piano, or at his typewriter. His art, at those moments, seems almost less an avenue of creative expression than a shield against the first breaking waves of his fame. That first movie is remarkable for various reasons, not least for the fact that Dylan does not show himself even once without armor—without sarcasm, silliness, teasing, verbal gamesmanship, nonsensical assertion, or one of his other performing postures.

The same is true of most of the sequences in Scorsese's film, except for the surprise of the present-day interview clips. What makes these last so fascinating, in part, is Dylan's own detachment from his various younger personae. Where he once launched his sardonic, cynical, brooding front at the world, now he comments back with a kind of wry indulgence, almost disavowing, locating his younger self in fondly distanced anecdote. As the young Dylan left Zimmerman behind in Hibbing, so this recent-vintage Dylan puts miles between himself and that former version of himself. Watching the face closely, we can't help but notice that he is constantly at war with his own impulse to smile.

Another night of watching. . . . I'm no longer following the film from start to finish so much as just checking in on it, collaging it like a favorite CD. It doesn't seem to matter that I dip this way—I don't know that there is a binding shape to what Scorsese has done. Or if there is, the intensity of my local absorption and my associative "bleeds" off to this side or that make the idea of a larger documentary unit almost irrelevant. I notice two things. One, that it seems to make no difference to my involvement at what point I enter: I have no interest in the "narrative" beyond what I already know of the basic career evolution. And two, that my appetite for plunging into any particular scene is, at least so far, inexhaustible. Though I know the footage well, I don't get bored or impatient. I look and look, drinking in whatever is before me, zeroing in on different things each time. So it will likely be so long as I regard Dylan as an enigma, a mystery to be solved.

One of these clues is the mouth. The more I watch, the more my eye is drawn to the lips, how they move while Dylan is talking and singing. The mouth is a tell—there is some way in which it doesn't seem comfortable, just isn't right. Tense. I see it as the focused site of Dylan's extreme self-consciousness. When he is talking, especially, the lips seem unnaturally tight, not at ease with the words they are forming. Sometimes he seems at the point of smirking, at other times I see him clamping back on some afterthought or correction.

This tension proposes a rich paradox. For Dylan is one of our bards, one of our truth-telling visionaries, the artist for whom the words are everything. What does it mean that the instrument of his expression is not relaxed—in sync with its expressions—but clenched up? Again, I'm thrown back on the idea of a split, a collision of opposing energies. On one hand, the drive to give voice to a profound, highly charged vision of the world, and on the other a competing impulse to dissimulate, to tell it slant. This has to do with more than just facial discomfort. It somehow also connects with the gulf, the disjunction, between the level of verbal articulation in the songs, and the often halting, obstructed, generalizing speaking self. Romantic as it may sound, I often think that the composition of the music and lyrics originates in a different register of the self—not exactly the muse of former days, but her psychological equivalent. If this is in any degree true, then the performing—and speaking—Dylan must register the split, possibly to the extent of feeling like an impostor in the face of his gift.

I find it interesting, in this light, to watch the clips of the young Dylan singing some of his early protest songs, like "The Lonesome Death of Hattie Carroll" or "Only a Pawn in Their Game." Until you

270

really study him more closely he seems passably earnest—an understated idealist who is muting all stage affect in order to convey the seriousness of his message. Of course that's the style—the pose—of the day. Certainly it's what his folkie public and his influential elders (Pete Seeger, the Weavers) wanted from him. In one sequence, Dylan is singing at Newport, singing "Mr. Tambourine Man"—controversially secular, lyrical, *not* political—and we see a young Pete Seeger squatting on his heels just behind him on the stage, tapping his foot slightly, but as vigilant as a commissar in his facial expressions. Could he be vetting for authenticity? Is he registering the full transgression under way, the turn represented by those "smoke rings" of the mind?

Dylan tried to dissociate himself from protest over and over, but it was as if the supreme folkie committee wouldn't let him go. After all, he had written all the songs—"Blowin' in the Wind," "The Times They Are A-changin'"—how would it look if he stepped away? It's almost as if the man had to go electric just to get their attention, so that he could make it clear to the inside circle, as well as the larger world, that he did not want to be tied to the cause as a spokesman. Not because his artist's heart didn't belong to the oppressed—at the deeper generative level perhaps it did—but because he felt a larger ambition, one that included but also went beyond the sectarian-political. And if we think of it this way, the expression, the sober intensity of those early outings at the mike, can almost be seen as an impersonation by one who knows he is biding his time.

The longer I work at writing, the more I trust and treasure the interventions of serendipity, which is not, of course, some purely divine strike of accident, but rather the happy filling of a need, which only happens when that need has made itself inwardly evident. This does not necessarily mean that it has become *conscious*. In my case, I was writing about the image, what I imagine to be the public and private face of Bob Dylan, but my concept of the masks and the face behind the masks somehow didn't feel rich enough, didn't answer to my sense of mystery. But then—the gods took pity—I went to visit a friend, and this woman, a photographer and writer, asked me right off how my project was going. I naturally vented my frustrations and doubts, brought up my whole fixation with the face, the image. This, in turn, put us on a track; we started speculating, doing what all Dylan fans do, revisiting ourselves by way of favorite songs and lines, remarking the cruel passage of years, only gradually finding our way back to my topic. There was a moment's pause before my friend looked at me and said: "You haven't mentioned the main thing. The main thing is that he was just so beautiful."

Beautiful. That stopped me for a few seconds—two responses were instantly superimposed. One was: "Dylan—beautiful?" The other, possibly faster and more decisive, was "Of course!" I knew exactly what she meant, over and above the first dissenting reflex: "That skinny scraggly-haired kid *beautiful?*" But he was, utterly and absolutely, to the point where—so clear once I admitted it—it was the overwhelming unvoiced recognition of my watching. Bob Dylan was in so many ways arresting, radiant, completely stunning to contemplate. This was the heart of my response to Scorsese's film. This was what allowed me to return to those familiar moments over and over. I had told myself it was because I was being a detective, processing evidence, taking in the subtle dissonance between the performing affect and the contents. And to be sure, there was some of that. But really it was beauty I was staring at. For isn't it the nature of beauty that we want to be in its presence, that we don't—can't—tire of it? We don't—can't—because it communicates not a message but a sense of essence.

But I was also curious. My friend had seen the film. "Do you mean that all of Dylan is beautiful, or—?"

"Oh no—no, I mean that boy, that young boy up on the stage with Joan Baez, all those scenes—"

"So not the present-day Dylan, the one who looks like an embezzler?"

She laughed. "Certainly not—at least not in the way I mean."

Here I knew I'd gotten it all wrong. Or, if not wrong, then at least I was woefully incomplete. Struck by many of the same moments, I had fooled myself. I had dressed my reaction up as nostalgia. The powerful feeling I got watching Dylan in front of a mike with Joan Baez, or singing by himself at the Washington march, or at Newport, or in England—I had told myself it was nostalgia, pure and simple.

Nostalgia: she gave me another word for it. But nostalgia is there, too—nostalgia, the root meaning of which is, from the Greek, "the longing for home." Home, for which there is no direction, for which there is only the desire that grows in proportion to our distance.

I will come back to this idea, but first there is the beauty question. How is it that that thin and bony-faced singer—that boy whom any good Jewish mother would want to stuff with blintzes—is beautiful?

To answer is to move straightaway off the conventional, for this is no paradigmatic pretty boy. If he is beautiful it's because the face, the mobile performing face, even masked as it is, communicates an intensity and clarity that the soul finds irresistible. At least my soul does. Young Dylan singing gives off a pure radiance, not the ghost of electricity, but the real thing. Watching the clips from the early sixties it is obvious as can be that he will become a star. And everyone back then said so, too. Joan Baez can't get enough of recalling what wattage he put out. Is it self-evident—the intensity, the genius, that is also the beauty? How much does it have to do with the fresh power of the songs themselves? Would I feel the same if he didn't have the name "Bob Dylan," if he were singing "C. C. Rider" instead of "Chimes of Freedom"? But also, as important, does this perception square with my prior conviction, that Dylan is never not acting, never not holding up one of his calculated facades?

Face or facade—its strangely glowing familiarity has somehow presided over my life. If not "presided," then been steadily present, intimate and puzzling. And I've spent a good deal of time staring and wondering, trying to figure my way to the root of my connection. Thanks to my friend, I now get that at some level I've been responding to beauty, a realization that pulls me right back into the mysteries of expression. Whether it is a mask or the essential thing, what I see I see as the face of the man who makes the music, who writes and sings the songs. And this can only pull me back to my very earliest listening, that time of peak vulnerability when I was not only moved by what I heard, but I took up a kind of occupancy there. *The Freewheelin' Bob Dylan*—my first—that Columbia album with its red label, spinning at 33 rpm through the afternoons and nights when I was sixteen. There is no way to understand this without wondering just how the floating emotional self inscribes itself, its own obscure sense of fatality, into the scenarios conjured by the lyrics. So little was needed. I took the bare-bones longings of a song like "Girl of the North Country" and I decked them out with everything I knew and imagined about love, loneliness, sacrifice, regret. . . . I don't think I can get much more specific: these events—gaining through endless repetition—happen on the frequency of daydream and desire. They're not fully fledged thoughts, or even scenes. Less substantial, they are inward waxings and wanings that take place around the shift from a major to a minor chord, somehow soaking

273

the available contents of the self in formation.

I had responded deeply to Dylan back then, long before I knew anything more of the look, the image, than what was there to be contemplated on the album cover. But the transfer took, and the proof is undeniably here in the fixation of a fifty-four-year-old man upon the face of a twenty-year-old singer. Nostalgia does play into the response, no question. Complex nostalgia—for a back then, for myself when young, for a raw state of possibility that underlaid everything that would come later, and that maps, imprecisely, to all the possibility that Dylan himself embodied then. For he was himself in his first germination, the enormity of his fame and influence, as well as the extent of his explosive talent, still hidden from him. It is the power of retrospect to infuse what was with what will be—the perspective of the gods.

Alongside the personal nostalgia, the ineffable tropism toward the self *before,* is the collective historical pull. The times, how we all were, the world as we knew it then. And here Dylan has an ensemble role, really. He is there with all the others, his face alongside Ginsberg's, Seeger's, Baez's, Van Ronk's, his physical presence there in the ambushed atmospherics of the times, reminding us that the more vivid, more poignant world was still unfolding in black and white. Dylan at the mike with Baez, Dylan at Club 47 in Cambridge, lifting young Baez off her feet and carrying her. The heart-stopping spectacle of all that youth, with all the erosions and undoings of time still in the wings, not even surmised.

But here is Dylan again, the man as he looks now, that radiance completely effaced, remade, the face turned retrospective, sly, self-deprecating. If there is any beauty now it is the beauty of wisdom, the "heads or tails" of possibility finally settled on the countertop. But I realize that I'm every bit as compelled by this face, if for completely different reasons. The latest Dylan gives off a difficult beauty, but one that fairly vibrates with the ironies of its self-contemplation. It offers a completely different promise. This man is no longer the cipher of possibility, but rather the idea of arrival, possibility having been claimed and lived through, the man on the other side, having come through, having at last dropped the masks that stood guard over the gambles of change. *No Direction Home* is a natural choice for a title—so very Dylan—but I don't know if it is completely accurate. It gets the prodigal's profound restlessness, his outward momentum, yes, but it too readily rules out the return trip—which seems to be the power of those astonishing recent clips.

The Shadow Factory
Paul West

WHEN YOU CROSS from one room of your private domain to another, you expect some continuity. When I did so, to wash my hands, I felt like King Lear on the blasted heath: a savage wind tore at my mouth and cheeks, beginning those three months of lockjaw, and left my face stunted, out of shape, biased leftward. Into the bargain, my right arm lay by my side, useless.

As I emerged, everyone gaped at this, the masterpiece of my parlor tricks (as they all at first thought). Thus began my year of aphasia, eventually enabling me to write what Keats called the spirit ditties of no tone. Here are twelve of them, shaped as they fell.

ERMINE

The heavens still had their music, though a scratchier kind, to which I still listened intently when I could. Added to this, however, was sleek indeterminacy that sent the heavenly bodies off center and made my pilotage pretty much a torment. To this I added a twitchiness of the eyes, as if continually going to see something that I would prefer to bypass. Besides, I had a twitchiness of the limbs that must have counted for something, but only a mild form of Saint Vitus' dance.

There were other phenomena too, from a shaking sound in my head to a noise like tea leaves from somewhere in my lumbar region. Not quite distressing, although these sounds could not help but suggest the multiplicity of sounds there *could* have been. I add to this belfry of quiet sounds the tinkling that roamed around my head, driving me to think I had become one of the elect. Or when the belfry sounds would decrease and drive me mad with delight.

Such sounds and noises belonged presumably to no one else, and in that I could take pride. But it all sounded like too much of a good thing, and I more than once yearned for a quiet world, akin to the

275

world that once blighted me. All the same, I clung to fragments of this world, not least to the taste of something in my mouth, a taste balsamic and crude, that I homed in on with all the rapture of a man touching for the first time his toothache in the night.

I add to this a strange sensation in my good arm. The fingers were not as sensitive as they should have been. Similarly, my fingers felt partially deprived of their quick response to anyone trailing a hair across them or bouncing a balloon on them. It was not the old sensation as before that could easily have been pleasant, so stylish was the touch of those fairy fingers. It was simply a brutalization of those tiny tempi to something not as joyful as before, but duller and more opaque.

If you add the topic of touch to this merry-go-round of the black night, you may find a phenomenon almost impossible to describe: a feeling that my whole body, though not being case hardened, had become more defiant to touch. It was not an unpleasant sensation, but it was as if I had converted to something stiffer. I am aware of sneaking in many surreptitious references to the piano, a glancing reference to my mother the pianist, and here is another one: something starker and more mahogany hued has been added to the mix. And whether it makes it easier to play, whether the keys go down with a firmer punch or lift upward with a genuinely soft touch, I have no idea.

Besides, such divisions approximate only a tenth of an inch, if that. In any case, that is not my initial concern because I am not playing the piano anyway. And in fact never played it after my first stumbling performances at it, much to the initial distress of my mother, who wished she had a pianist and not a novelist in the family.

A sentient observer would find, perhaps will find, that here is a case of a man who has come around from repeated delirium to observe the minute changes in his world. True. I've been overloaded with minute changes, some ever to be ignored as the big bustle of everyday living takes charge. I sense in the complex fabric of my being that I have changed, which is not to say that the changes have been wholesale and discounted, but they have been irrevocable and final.

FLEET

The difference between my own refracted gaze of the world and Diane's is that she sees the world in all its detail, squirming into the needlepoint alleyways that leopards reject. Mine looks on the offered scene as a species of broadcloth identified mainly through its ribbons and tam-o'-shanters. This sharing the load usually means that between us we cover the waterfront, missing a few mouse holes and locked jaws here and there, but getting the plurality right.

It may not happen that the skills of either of us would often be brought into play, cutting us off in different ways from the charming scene about us, but when you are dealing with something that neither of us has ever seen before—not in bulk, anyway—the situation is profoundly different and likely to fall off the universe for not trying hard enough.

One way of trying extra hard is to imagine one dimension of the universe coated in either black velvet or a blue that no one has reported outside the province of Baffinland. This same needling eye one imagines as bringing reports of blancmange, mince pies, jam tarts, cream pies, chocolate éclairs, Odwalla bars, chocolate chip cookies, ice cream, and all manner of other delicacies to the invalid's bed.

However you spell the word *invalid*, you are either invalid because not valid, or invalided out. Or you disentangle the least bit of wiry fluff that has been haunting your tongue for half an hour, and assign it to the unwilling project of the human mess. These rank as contributions in some way or other, but the assorted confectioneries are too massive to eat, and the strand of hen-pecked fluff is too narrow, which makes them both second-rate substitutes and sees them out. What I'm trying to say, in language ever more oblique, is that the human psyche can sometimes see evidence of what is not present to the senses.

"Bosh," one hears you exclaim, "this man is writing about nothing!" But is he? It could be that he is writing about something somebody said to him after he had regained his senses, or that he regained these senses for himself, and detected shreds of rabbit fluff here and there. Imagine a man coming round after five days in the human tank that denatures us all and finding no memory worth talking about. I suspected as much from my ten-day immersion in whatever I was immersed in.

I say this in the most tentative manner because there isn't a great deal of difference between what's roiling and not rolling. You could

Paul West

easily miss it for the whole of the ten-day period. Nonetheless, I think it was there for human consumption, and I am content to identify it—if that is not too canonical a word—as a lump of Lot's wife going nowhere, or what Samuel Beckett, in one of his wilder notions, identifies as Arsene going the unerring rounds on his bicycle, even when he has nothing to deliver.

Clearly we are dealing with shadowland at its bleakest, and should not expect too much. It is not likely to reward us with any vision of something discernible. You always have a chance to say, "I saw nothing." Or "I saw something." And it is not enough to say, "I saw Versed or chloroform," because that would generate far too much reportorial weight. To recognize that we are not dealing with much of the known hardly delights anybody, but just imagine how much of the unknown is out there among the dark clusters of stars and the dark matter of which we know nothing. We may think that we are dealing with the nonstop hodgepodge of daily life, but we are also dealing with the opaque mysteries of the universe itself.

Cabbage served twice means death. So says one of the older Greek proverbs, though it goes no further into the lethal lineage of cabbage. I was becoming accustomed to these devil servings, mainly of the mythic cabbage, as distinct from the real one. But how to divest yourself of the mythic one, when the real thing offers itself up? I long ago decided to opt for both, lest I for some reason lose one or the other, whether bull-rushing into a dead end, or having the real thing played out on my skull for days.

Was it indeed days? Or merely a squawking interim in the full gamut of time, no more than an hour? I settled these and other questions for later on when I had got the better of my bearings. For now, there was the serious business of interpreting my condition, as far as decency would allow. First, was the matter of my jaw, affixed to my head in the certain manner of a Greek wrestler and extending right through my head with no give in it at all. Some things were happening not for the first time, and I experienced serious reluctance to pursue the matter further. If a locked jaw was any indication, things had already gone from bad to worse and could not be trusted.

I addressed myself next to my temple, which, seeming in no way to have enlarged, felt for the first time brittle and temporary. Could it be that some of it was missing, obliged by some demented operator with a fretsaw to have given doughty service? Certainly it didn't feel right, and slowly I cruised the surface area, waiting for a mishap or the plain bald gap where something had been and was no longer. So

278

let us say that between one jaw null and void and the other, there was a temple that was highly suspicious and would remain so for the duration.

I turned my thoughts next to the ghostly hand that dangled uselessly at my side, paler than it had been, and with an odd look of failure about it that I had not noticed before. Could it have withered during the process? Stranger things have happened to a victim of a stroke. It was the same inert apparatus, but somehow more useless, as if it had been ratcheted down a peg or two. In the tremendous lusting ovation of the stroke proper, I rapidly formed an adverse view of my jaw, temple, and hand, wishing them all far away and put to the good uses of someone else who was not too proud of what he brought to the human encounter.

Rapidly turning my attention to my whereabouts, I very soon wished I had not, for there, as I imagined it, lay a whole suite of uncoordinated rooms, from the one in which I had waited in vain to be called to the lecture platform to deliver a talk my mouth would never emit, and the second-floor suite in which I spent one night arguing with two nurses about tax returns I would have to fill in before going anywhere. Also there in this bewildering array were the two redheaded ladies who insisted on bidding me farewell and hoping I would get back to the writing of books very soon.

Most antique of all, there was the strangest impression of noise from the other room—a chipping sound or the recital of a mandolin beautifully played, and several other noises I could not identify. I stepped across the lintel to check, but both noises had ceased, yet the room had somehow walked with me, and the chipping sound and the sound of the mandolin began again. These noises have made a reasonable facsimile of haunting me ever since, so that I often wake at night and go outside, finding the noise has stopped, only to recommence once I step back into the room. I now interpret them as benign, and a little taken for granted, but all I need is a new noise to get my suspicions up again.

On the whole, the ghostly workplace, as I dub it, though fragmented and in its way supremely desolate, was mine alone, and parts of it began to recede as I became used to my new role of silent artificer. It might be said that my whereabouts remain peculiar, part of a museum set that shuffled according to my mood and would cease this activity when, finally, I was cured and galloped up the hill to where Triphammer crossed onto Texas Lane, and all the joys abounding awaited me.

279

There was a bewildering assortment of false starts and incomplete sentences for the mind only. I no sooner thought of something to say to myself than I forgot it, and I was lucky to get beyond the second or third imagined word. Of course, no one in his right mind overheard any of this, the dumb speaking to the silent in a reverse image, so no one was upset. But if this happens fifty or sixty times, one wants a little revenge of some sort. Of course, one was in all probability speaking no kind of written English, so this meant that whatever you said was relevant and you could not say anything irrelevant.

I formed the habit of forcing language back on itself, beyond even its failure to communicate anything at all, to see what was there. Language, at least as we know it, had ended, and I was left there on countless occasions with something like a white sheet of dental floss or a carnivorous absence. There was nothing beyond. So I cheered myself up by taking as my starting point the notion that all I had to do was pass the zone of no known language and automatically be speaking English once again. These are mental compensations to be sure, but they serve superbly in times of need. And it isn't a matter of some old Oriental asking another, "What happens when two elephants meet?" The answer is the grass suffers. It is more complicated than that, but not complicatedly so.

So, groggy, weak, and famished, I take my plight on the chin. Milling around me there are all sorts of verbal alternatives both nonsensical and full of meaning, to some of which I have permanent access without speaking. I wonder if one can safely execute a lifetime using the language of dumb show. I know of one woman in New York who has successfully done it for years. It is a matter of the breaks. I would, of course, prefer to speak the English that I know and revere, but I think I can see past gobbledygook to a pure and vivid English, instead of starting every sentence five or six times, writing sentences that lose heart halfway through a futile clutter of grossly amalgamated syllables.

PLAINBALL

Others have told me how I raced through several doorways in pursuit of an exit. Either I sidled through or worked the door in a long blast of would-be freedom. For, remember, I was still the owner of a good pair of legs, thinned out as you would expect. Sometimes I caught the two auburn-haired sisters who officiated as guardians off guard, and managed to go all the way. Sometimes, thanks to these same sisters, I was trapped before I had begun. Sometimes, on at least one or two occasions, I penetrated the major hallways and then spent the few minutes of my precious freedom looking in vain for a door that would lead down into the outside world. The sisters quickly got used to my midnight forays, and became adept at cutting me off before I reached the outer anteroom, either trapping me with a palliasse or running me to ground in one of the lavatories. It was a jaunt for the full body. In one way I looked forward to being captured and restored to my bed and told for the umpteenth time to stay there or they would not be responsible for my safety.

One day, I continued on my vagrant ways, and suddenly found that somebody had removed all of my clothes. I was a naked runner and maybe gained an extra inch or two of speed from that as I saw it. I was fit enough to run, although naked, and in good enough condition to escape with a military salute, the next destination all the way home where my books and other treasures awaited me. Clearly some renegade part of me was still tinged with lunacy: I saw the problem as only extending between the way out and the way home. There were many hurdles in between that I would have to learn one by one. The mad dasher over the parquet floor was to become the sagacious intellect of floor B7. I am sure now that the impulse to dash madly about was inspired by the lull between five o'clock AM and breakfast time when there was nothing to do and all kinds of forces were arrayed against you. Had that not been the explanation, I would not have risked all those incomplete early morning adventures, either sliding to a gliding halt or cannoning to a stop above either sister's iron-hard bosom. They never caught me anyway. I did not find the entrance to the way out, and always they returned me, with wagging fingers and nagging expressions, to my bed.

It was vain to point out to me the dangers of it all. I had certainly not been blank during any of this, but there were all kinds of things going on in my system, and these the staff pointed out to me. I was mute still, and had no business scooting around the halls, either naked or clad. And I was further reminded of the eleven or thirteen chemicals that wandered about in my breast, some of them impervious to what I put them through in my nightly excursions, some definitely not. I decided to be a good boy, and work my passage outward as good boys do.

281

Paul West

MIST

Something grounded. Something stabilized. Something marked even for my own consumption. That was how I faced up to my new fate, sensing in the air about me a flavor like mint. I could not be wrong this time—after all those other times of relenting, shameful fastidiousness. It was no longer a matter of something firmer and trustworthy beneath my feet. It was not that simple at all; indeed, the emanation that came from my head had a lilt about it that could not in any way be attributed to my head.

If life was going to be as simple as that, things would be certain to improve. It might take a year or more, but something bold in my head would one day urge me to speak. It's easy to form an obsession, making up in passionate addiction what we lack in concentration.

This is to say, to hell with prosy statements about numbness, or about anything else, for that matter. It's all about what the self-sufficient man assembles to keep himself awake, and as far out as possible from the range of the cur who roams the hinterland looking for food, or the equally mangy cur who confidently haunts the bright, sunlit avenues of our city, scalpel in hand. Sometimes the constant waiting and brisk incertitude tire me out and provoke me. I grow hostile, to any form of life. You let the shriek out and double up on it until it is a goner and is quietly put to bed again, beneath the latest down comforter.

I often wonder why the mind does not go blank more often. You would think that with so much to do, it would welcome any respite that lies at hand. But no, my own experience shuttles back and forth between oblivion and talk, and the oblivion part is unfairly dropped. What gets you eventually is the waiting: after the initial period of waiting, there is more waiting and still more, until waiting suffers a sea change into something opaque and gruesome, not like the original forms of waiting at all, but delicate to touch. I think within my heartiest of hearts that something has changed: a little flick of time's chronometer, or even an upward movement in time itself. Such things may easily defraud us into thinking something positive is afoot, whereas of course it could be the first stage in a downward cycle that promises the end.

I have no ulterior knowledge, though I have reasonably happy memories of Robert Browning's character Pippa Passes, whom I remember, vaguely, was an expert on optimism. But you do not have to read Browning to glean something of his mood. You can get it from

282

almost anywhere because people don't know, much of the time, what is happening to them anyway; they advance from darkness to darkness, from half suspension to something stronger, from ecstasy to nightmare, seen as a flash, until they emerge quite mesmerized by the changing scene and circumstances, to lose heart. Yet I know what I know, as the big bloated commissioner once familiar from German movies said, all bustle and bristle of the mustache. But now lost. Not much, almost enough to tide me through until the next.

LAST DRAGON

Always I have told myself, "Dream the hospital dream" but it be-came the paradise of the lost sunglasses. In my case, it was no longer a dream, as of things that at first glance didn't have the heft. I was comparing, in this instance, number, time, and intervals with those aforesaid heavy hitters. The strange thing was that my dream of clocks was backward, otherwise perfect. My dream of number was also confused; whenever I sought to indicate the time of day, I got it wrong, in maybe three separate ways. It may be said that I was still referring to clocks, but that's all that could be said, and I roamed in a maze of miscalculated times, back to front statements, and a pro-found disinclination to tell the right time to anybody. Half the time (no pun) I didn't know whether I was operating on American time or Continental time, and my ventures to tell it right were skewed and loutish. I had also contracted the habit of skipping words from my misjudged sentences, so that mythical persons idly seeking out infor-mation found themselves amidst chop-logic formulations that only intermittently made sense. Ah, the time, the money, the vision, the clocks, the checks, the words. Ah, the whole lamebrained formula-tion of it all.

My main related exploit was to, in the language of the dumb, in-dulge in sequences of utterly incomprehensible pseudo words. I was saying baffling things in the language of the dumb, only very occa-sionally breaking into what I recognized in my delirium as rational speech. But this was a language of silence that now and then prom-ised also to be a language of shadows and dumb show. You cannot ask too much of the babbling dumb, but you must if we are going to get anywhere at all. My habitual pseudo language of "Pell pell pell" led nowhere at all and, clearly, when I managed to propel my mouth into the ugly grimace that accompanied these sounds, it would prof-it from some kind of restoration to the straight and narrow. How often was it that I retained enough motor control to utter nonsense for half an hour, which does not make for an interesting conversa-tion, especially among those who have been accustomed to the high jinks of intellectual performance.

I also had insoluble problems with money. The mere sight of a check bouncing on my horizon gave me the jitters, for I knew full well that I was not equal to the demands of well-aimed and pru-dently inspected integers, as the prescribed mission demanded. I only several times attempted to write a check, floundering amid a quag-mire of lost vowels, consonants, and little signs I had no compre-hension of. I jabbed at the paper only to produce signs where I had not intended them to go, and I reduced my signature to a one-line fiasco. My attempts at penmanship were utterly bizarre and bore no resemblance to a piece of documentary worth. What was to be done with me? The faster I trod into the outside world, be it of checks, time, or beef, the deeper I got into the mire, and could now be said to be a person of much reduced intelligence, liable for even a police station's remote cell.

This was what I had always dreaded, to watch my brain slowly decompose until I reached the status of vagrant. How far I was from this final tumult I did not know, but it could not be far away. The question remained of what irked worse—having no sensation in my mouth and being unable to speak the language of man, or being deprived of what I must call, in my elegiac way, the means of iden-tification at the humdrum level. I realized that I had already chosen both, for I was dumb as well as inexpert. Especially at such things as counting and reading clocks. Surely there must be, lurking some-where, a third member of this ghoulish trio ready to pounce on what I had left, say my legs and almost salient arm, or the other half of my head or my heart.

So far, no show, but it required only a little intelligence to see that when Drs. Costello and Vohra met for one of their little secret con-ferences, they were talking about me in the most explicit sotto voce way and of what would be done with me when at last I achieved the status of candidate for straitjacket, then onward up to the moon.

Reading, at which I used to be no slouch, now gave me the most incredible, disheveled experiences of my print-bound life. Now print jigged toward me, then it hung back. The one part of it that was read-able swam backward or forward to render the reading experience at best incomplete, or subject to the vilest, maddest vagaries of a proof-reader's nightmare. When would it end? The list of possible insults to my body, already some thirty-five pounds lighter than usual, was extending to mop me up, and I could see the day not-so-distant when West, against all his better judgment in aesthetic affairs, would be lowlier than a bagman. I would become the Ratman of Paris I had invented for a novel!

My sight would get worse, either waning away altogether or producing those scintillates of light that give hope to the persons blinded in the wars and prompt visions of something or other where there is no vision at all. I declined to enter the subject further. Morbidity is usually its own reward, and I could not for the life of me see how things could get better.

Whatever was being done to me behind my back, and under my front, it amazed me that so much attention was being paid to respective parts of my body, so much energy being applied in different ways. To be sure, they had left a great deal out, but they had also left a great deal in. Once again I felt the shady conundrum of life as we know it, first producing a PEM-umbra of what you have and then producing the penumbra of what you have not.

Some kind of trumps to be sure, but which is which? I never reconciled myself to this idyllic-evil switch, knowing in my heart that I would choose neither and so be left with nothing at all. It was like having to choose between the Hound of the Baskervilles and Jack the Ripper, or some other combination playing into one another's hands. I can never get over the way in which the relevant pieces appropriate to each body come piping through, and I look forward to the day when the miracles of nature, such as stem cells, will officiate as the guardians of our composite bodies. All you would have to do is choose.

STREET

It begins abruptly with a loss in the zone peculiar to Broca's brain. You expect not to be without it. You are. It goes on, it begins, as far as I remember, with a distorted vision stretching on the right side of my face and jaw, a closed space where nothing seems to enter. Whether people find this apparition offensive, I don't know. But of course the air is breathing in all the time. It felt like a weight perched on my brain. And it was no good my saying anything else. Unless you pass out.

There is more to add to this record. The right side of my ear felt florid, which is to say that a dozen times a day the tympanum would release a dissonance that sounded ten times louder than mere sound and effectively cut off communication with the trenches. I found this change even more disconcerting than my local outer swelling. It was like being half a man with a nagging habit of probing his ear in full view in the hope of snagging the offending portion. Whatever it was persisted.

Many people would be forgiven, I think, for relegating such an individual to the trash heap of history as someone who had failed and been found wanting, or who had achieved a brief prominence and then sank into the ruck. Who is this? they would utter, who once was so demure and now is so dreadful. Is he human at all with his crossbow eyes and his elephantine stance? Is he deserving of pity or some other outlandish emotion, or should we pass him by? Not exactly an Elephant Man, he goes some small way to being one. What is wrong with him? We would prefer not to know. Despite whatever agony he feels, we would seek the company of happy convivial people rather than molder in his crude animal sedan.

I'm proud to relate my legs were almost intact, and I walked on them with brittle ease. No doubt they would break down at the first sound of the trumpet. I walked on them notwithstanding, proud for them because they were proud of me. I would one day soon be deprived of these hostages to fortune, but not yet.

One nurse, professing to want me to shave, made such a fumble of the toothbrush, razor, hairbrush, and lather that she had me in and out of there before I even got to the brush. These encounters in the toilet reminded me of an antique civilization in which nothing was to be complete. Whether your destination was the toilet or the toilette, you always had the sense someone was overlooking you with maximum disapproval and urging you on to complete whatever you were doing before you finished. Here the doings of the Rehab Unit remained in permanent disarray, nurses being the nourishers of life's feast.

I should perhaps explain that for days I was incognizant of what was happening, but I was at one point consigned to the geriatric floor, and then as suddenly removed. I was unaware of this shift, or of any other, to my knowledge. This made me a nocturnal visitant in both places.

The voices. There is a voice of rhetorical artifice in which I can say just about anything I want without fear of contradiction and another voice that I fear is much of a blur. When I'm on form, the two, while staying separate, overlap.

When I am out of control, and should be asleep, there is this out-of-control voice that savages anything I want to say. In almost every circumstance it provides the wrong words and even exerts a deadly compulsion to say them incessantly. And nothing you can do will correct it, so you might as well shut up shop and go to sleep because you are not communicable on the human level at all. For me there still remains the voice of rhetorical artifice, which enables me to make slow but intelligent conversation with my coevals. This enables those who are lucky enough to be writers to survive. I feel very grateful for it because I don't think it's a unique gift, but it's precious as rubies to me.

Do you see the difference? It's bowlegged but it's legible, whereas the other is mostly nonsense.

The second day in the Rehab Unit I heard the voice of pellucid, articulate reason droning on in the absence of any sound and I knew at once that I was going to be all right even then, in spite of the evil-seeming things that had been happening to me. I mean that though I hadn't tried to speak yet and the whole world was some kind of abstract fanfare waiting to be fed on or off, I would be all right because I could still think language even though it led to an immensely private universe decorated with the full panoply of speech.

So that side of him remains! I can turn it on whenever I want to speak. It's very eerie. You might say: It is almost like having a second language forced upon one—one the lackadaisical, partly formal voice of the BBC announcer; the other, the rapscallion Calibanesque language of a substitute. No need to say which one I prefer.

Three voices really. One, the faint intellectual voice of the speaker who didn't know whether he existed or not. The second, the somersault-executing virtuoso of my three hours daily, if I'm lucky, of joyous harmony. The third is that speaker you already know too well for his far-flung, defiant nonsense.

A TOUCH OF SLEEP

It begins with a rotten start, by which I mean a start that begins well but turns you down part way with an assortment of misnomers. For instance, you can get well away with such references as "moon" but then find it abruptly *changing* into such a word as "doubloon." Such swerves are all right for what I was then, totally unnerving and leading nowhere at all. How would you like it if five times a second you managed to entertain the beginnings of certain thoughts, agreeable at the start, that threw curves at you as soon as you got beyond the first or second word?

Actually I didn't manage to get beyond the first word because what passed for a word in my neck of the woods usually formed three or four. For instance, the sample would run: the letter I, the letter M, the letters EJ, and possibly the letters AFFB. With such a workload it would be impossible to complete anything, especially if your mental repertoire extended to a gallimaufry of phonemes such as would render the head of any responsible person inane. It is a far cry from those rounded sentences beginning with "I am" and "He sits" to this kind of thing when no one knows what someone is trying to say so volubly.

It isn't a matter of people not knowing, it's a matter of people knowing you can't hear them in any case: for you are deaf, to the spirit ditties of no tone, which echo in your ears time and again. You are deaf in the broadest sense imaginable. You are deaf and they cannot hear you. So what is all the fuss about? They can pass you by without hating you, but fortunately many do not, trying to make sense of your silence. The attempt, of course, is futile and many people rush away from this ignoramus of the woods, thankful they have normal people to return to. I, on the other hand, am left with the illusion of thinking I've communicated something whereas in all likelihood I've communicated nothing at all and am left with the sad roundelay of all those impossible conversations, firm in my shaky conviction that I've said something useful, but increasingly devoid of sense. I suppose this is merely one of the many changes humans may expect in the course of their seventy years, from heart attack and stroke to AIDS and tuberculosis. Sooner or later, something attacks everybody, and with that I should rest content, I suppose. One does not change about eventualities.

Let me be more specific. For instance, a typical member of the tribe called stroke may not remember his own name or remember the names of his intimates and friends, instead remembering those names as a shadow factory, just in the wombs of memory, but unable to reach the surface of thought. That is why you often see the stroke victim babbling away, attempting to pronounce all the names simultaneously with the word hoard at his command, but failing dismally. Or consider the predicament of the stroke person who is commanded to raise the right hand and reluctantly raises the left or raises none at all. Consider the fate of someone who is asked to rise from a chair and doesn't know how to do it, or commanded to rise from his bed of undoing and doesn't know how to do that either. The catalogue of can't do this and can't do that rises sky high, and I always thought I was profoundly lucky to have two good legs to stride about on, although the rest of me was subject to this or that assortment of ills. Rehab facilities are fairly full of people who have lost their hearing in spite of losing wits. Or of people who can pucker without being able to swallow and swallow without being able to pucker.

Many a sufferer is subject to clocks seen in reverse or clocks not seen at all or only the right half of the clock face. Newspapers are alien to most of them, for different reasons, including an inability to read print sequentially and the rival inability to make the print stay in position and not go wobbling about from one corner to the other. Many a poor soul doesn't even know where he is, in China or La La Land, in the eighteenth century or the time of the Schneider Trophy Races held in the twenties. Many don't even know which parts of their bodies belong to themselves and which belong to someone else by miraculous sleight of hand. A good many sufferers know no one's name at all, or they try fiendishly to secure it, often going to elaborate lengths to rescue it from some elaborate rodeo game that always produces nothing. How to spell also evades many of them. At one sight a stroke victim's penmanship is fit to drive a supporter of holy penmanship into madness. I once wrote "Poop"—P-o-o-p—for "Paul" after performing mightily for five minutes on the transliteration, not even noticing the ambiguity of my response. So many stroke victims make a point without getting anywhere at all, piling up errors in language and metatheses. Their end is their undoing.

Most of the stroke victims you will meet will strike you as agitated beings in whom the very slightest setback will produce explosions of rage and shock that the poor innocent in the outside world has again failed to understand them. This takes many forms, but the most usual, I've found, is a rapidly rising crescendo of abuse when one syllable is pronounced with increasing loudness. Example: PEM.

PEM. PEM. PEM. This, of course, is no use to anybody, but it is the best they can do, especially in the early stages, when language seems to enact a signal or a mesmeric function, to the distress of the signaler or mesmerist, and to the increasing despair of their company. This usually grows into something else, either a whirligig of elaborately produced language or even, in some cases, a return of total aphasia. God knows why. When I graduated from my first weeks in speech school, exchanging the null response of a genuine aphasic for the jabber-jabber of English all around the clock, first words meant nothing. When Diane reported my first sentence to my guide, philosopher, and friend Dr. Ann Costello, downtown in the holy of holies, at going-home time, they both burst into tears as if I had quoted Cicero's Latin without any of Cicero's graces.

VACANT SHUTTLES WEAVE THE WIND

Every time I settled on an idea that would give me courage, it flew from me at top speed and left me floundering in its wake like a rodeo dancer. I could trump up a noun or an adjective, you see, often to an embellished extent, but no sooner had I uttered it, spiritual leper that I was, than it skipped away from me to the paradise of lost birds. It may be that someday all these evanescent ideas will come together, generating beautiful harmonies of well-wrought gold, but for now they serve only to puzzle and confuse me as I try to make my way through the whirligig world of other men.

I had hopes of what-had-happened-to-me being in some way a constructive, although chastening, experience, but it was coming out like nothing of the sort, and I would cheerfully have surrendered these startling, incomplete images to nothing at all.

LAST

For the first time in what had seemed to pass for my life, I felt I could breathe. No one was there, I confirmed this, and what a charm it was to credit the bright, joyous aroma of that place. Soon, no doubt, it would be overrun by people bearing IV poles, syringes, and sandwiches. That Battle of Hastings all over again. What a battle that had been. Although my fate was far from clear, some signal had gone up about me, no doubt from Dr. Ann Costello, saying that I was at least trustworthy for the next few minutes and was to be allowed some of the delights of human society again.

Although I still felt blurry, it was a kinder blur, and one in which a few objects managed to stay in consort. The best and the brightest may have seemed only the slackest and the dullest; but the whole thing was the beginning of a meal to me.

I was looking for something bell-like or the flavor of an old tobacco, but nothing of that came my way, and I was beginning to lose hope. It began when I noticed a noise, somehow brighter and denied to all civilized people, and in my semiconscious way I asked myself if this was an effect of too much light, or was it the light rays bending together to produce an effect denied to most civilized people? In other words, I didn't believe it.

But the noise persisted. And I began to realize that my misshapen nose and my withered arm apart, things were sounding louder. The sounds, time and again, had me reaching to protect my ears and abandoning the effort halfway. I felt like some poor soul who had been to the doctor to have his ears reamed out, and then stood in shock in the street, hearing the first pure noise in ages.

There was another facet to this auditory compulsion. Now and then, as if in some brief reciprocity to my loud noises, the hearing in one ear or the other weakened by a good half, thus guaranteeing a muffled higher-pitched noise that continued for as little as an hour or as much as two days. The Lord giveth and also taketh away. You cannot have Santa Claus all the time. I was to have an augmented noise backed by a deficient ear and I was once again suspicious of any arrangement that both cancelled and restored. Those twin armchairs were taking their toll on me once again.

There was another aspect, too, to this renewed increment of the physical world. I did not notice at first, but several flashings later I remarked that things seemed impossibly brighter, more dazzling. I blinked and recoiled more than I'd ever done in the bright, lofted sunlight of the rehabilitation room. I doubted if this was an overcharge from my eyes, though I would not have put it past them. More things seemed to be touched by daylight. There were just more things waking up. This could be one of the severer diapasons of sunlight, after all; I was only recently in my own kind of murk, and was not entitled to swap sunlights.

An even more insidious event took place when Diane, lying

opposite me in some comforting position or other that took no account of my moldy face and paralyzed vocal cords, sensed something out of the ordinary. "I felt your eyelashes. They must have grown." "All hail to diabetes," I would have said, if I'd had the vocal power to do so. All was not lost even yet. My eyelashes had grown!

Other strange phenomena followed in the fullness of time. I flinched more when I got into the open vault of Ann Costello's and Vohra's external world. It seemed to me that I blinked more and had watery eyes to boot. When I started eating again, which was not for some time, my taste buds had altered; whereas I used to feast on all kinds of salmon and jars of salmon paste, I now made a fetish of mashed potatoes and the meats. I could imagine that taste bud changes were temporary, doomed to fall away. I resumed a normal enough diet, but what was I to make of the aversion to fish and the compulsion for meats?

One is at the behest of the machine, and the machine changes its mind more often than we like to think.

HELMET

I want to revisit the topic of my arm, lolling in its passive socket. A dollop of an arm, you might call it, with fingers, wrist, hands, all useless and with its future all bright before it, with my imagination resurrecting it, stage by stage, into the ziggurat it was once. Reconstruction work has not gone very far since all the attention has been given to my jaw. Obediently it rises when I tow it up with the other hand, and then it crashes down again with a noise like festering eels. To have such an appendage attached to you is no joke. I am right-handed, or I was, and now have to face the workmanlike plight of one who has to begin working with the other hand. The sooner this arm of mine resorts to its regained status, the sooner I'll be able to get back to work, a chore and a delight that awaits me several years from now.

Several experts have counseled me on how to begin, reckoning that a man who is mute deserves all the help he can get. First, I am to work on the fingers, three of which look as if they still feel the stirrings of an old clutch, two of which seem to have given up the ghost entirely, and emit slight creaking noises when I squeeze my hand under a certain amount of pain. Shall I throw over the whole job and concentrate on getting the left arm back in training, for I once was ambidextrous, or shall I see what the defunct arm will bring me by way of peace offering? My vote goes to the right arm as the one-time tenant of all he surveyed. In addition, I was slightly fascinated by the idea of a withered arm rising from the dead and resuming its normal place in the world.

First go the three fingers in which there is still a sign of life, creaky and arthritic as it is. Sometimes stroke issues you a little pardon, saying if you work hard at this, a little life will return and off you go not in the least daunted by the fifty thousand flexings that you have to do before any of the vital spark returns. Taunted and daunted, you head for the last of many roundups, afraid you will lose count in a short while, and so two fingers as well.

I call this the surplus of the stroke, meaning that you almost have enough before you begin, and then you have the stroke proper, which pulverizes the life out of you, in many instances not to return. I would have called it excessive, but it goes on and on, and I wonder in my more cerebral moments if one day we will have strokes to start with, and take it from there. A monstrous vision to be sure, but one not so distant from the wilder improvisations of Joseph Conrad.

EIGHTY-PLUS EXPERIMENTS

When Carl Sagan told Diane he'd heard that "out of sight, out of mind" translated into Chinese and back again produced "invisible idiot," she laughed, and wouldn't again for a few months. My later volubilities included the one I am proudest of, and this was "I can speak good coffee." This I distinctly remember bracing Diane for, as if I were about to speak one of the noblest prose anthems, and ended up speaking these three or four little words instead.

Sometime later when I was in full flow, I addressed a remark to the limping little kitten Diane had recently acquired. "Limping little kitten," I said, which pleased her, because she had heard little of that sentimental side of myself for the past month.

I suppose in some way I can be thought lucky; I have a good pair of legs and an almost perfect left arm, which is a hell of a lot better than many patients. I can safely be left alone with my fate, mute and of disheveled intellect (I cannot count, read the telephone book, or sign checks, for instance, because my penmanship wanders all over

the place and never comes back to the place it first thought of).
Maybe these minor flaws can be put right one day by an enterprising
physician or speech therapist.

I now turn my attention to what happened when the full flagrante
of my handicap came to the fore after being subdued by stroke,
unconsciousness, and a big violet rose, shaped like a spider, that
hung fast to my gut.

The truth came about in a most unusual and terrifying way when
I went next door to wash my face and stared at the face confronting
me. As far as I could tell, it was a normal face, perhaps a little pale
and thinner than usual. As I stared again, something began to move.
Was this an optical illusion sired by long exposure to milk and
oxygen? The face moved swiftly in a downward direction, dragging
with it the corresponding jaw. The jaw seemed to collapse downward
until it seemed to set up a new satellite where it should have been,
and the teeth went with it. What I had to do in this circumstance
was what all recipients of flummery have to do, and that was blink.
This did not work. Again I blinked and this did not work either. In
fact, this seemed to tug my jaw farther than before past any line
decreed by man or beast. So I kept my eyes open as long as I could,
hoping to make the jaw shifting stop. It did, but left me with an in-
opportune fraction of what my face had been. While attending to my
newfound facial hideousness, I noticed something else: my right arm
fell uselessly by my side and refused all efforts to pick it up.

The rest is a blur. I felt that each subsequent facial was worsening
my appearance. Besides, I couldn't speak to explain. There Diane was
confronted with the apology for an elephant man who was worsening in his condition. The sooner they came, the better, thus depriv-
ing her of any further opportunity to do any further harm to the neat
outlines of the human face. As I said, things became a blur and I had
strange memories of being buried under a groundsheet, being up-
chucked again into the mouth of raging torrent, and then being
secreted under a lime-like torrent of earth. What were these to do
with the changing of my face and arm? If nothing, why had the combination sought me out? One was surely enough. Now there were
three. I had dim, opaque visions of people bending over me, bending
around me, but they never lasted long enough to assume cogency. It
was like being buried in a world of fragments, but surely some of me
persisted in the world above long enough to give me harness on identity, but that, too, in all probability, had changed and was now the
face of Shelley's Ozymandias or amounting to a rift of clouds. This

at least could be said for phantoms. They were supplying me with rich disordered fragments of a world I thought I knew, but in each case I found I was wrong: each shape was the beginning shape of a shape I thought I knew but then had mutated into a bolus indivisible that I had never seen before and in all probability would never see again. My sequestered life was becoming a disrupted scherzo.

What was uncanny about the arm, in all its grandeur, was the way it seemed to collapse upon itself, falling in sequence from fingers, knuckles, wrist, and the body of the arm, to rest in a not unlikable pirouette by my armpit. I could even, for a few seconds, hold it out and have it obey some as yet unwritten law of gravity and perch there on a pilgrimage to the Tudor forts. Of course it collapsed as soon as viewed.

I quite a few times thought that an interesting art form could be made by having the left arm ascend and collapse, and the right arm ascend only a few seconds after it refused to collapse. I kept all such thoughts to myself until now, convinced that such rumors distributed along the Rialto might dissuade some clever person from abandoning his lifetime's deformity. But I'm not so sure now, feeling that any attempt at wholeness is worthwhile, not least to the persons with this or that deficiency to their name. I leave it to you, the experienced connoisseurs of human frailty, to set the matter right.

SMOKING GUN

One can easily and pleasurably be consumed by an organ, as was the neuroanatomist Alf Brodal, by the hippocampus in 1947. Such absorbing labor can take year upon year out of a life, and I don't have that in mind at all. Instead, for a change, I choose to observe the wonderful behavior of tissue or blood about me, noting second by second the regularity and consistency of its metronome-like beat. Although I do not pretend to be any kind of authority, I marvel at the steady way the organism keeps things going, beating and measuring till the cows come home.

It is possible to see them dancing together in elegant concert as if the whole universe depended on their unanimity or fidelity. And when I say these things, I mean fidelity to us, a living species that nonetheless would go its own way to a quite different destiny if its mechanism suddenly failed. I remember a piece of jargon from my days in the air force, which described human condition as "flapless," by which we meant not easily perturbed. I can see it now, the bare splendor of tissue, blood, and saliva with blood for the uppermost, and one day caving in, as it must; the blood just follows its track in another direction, and the three tissues fade away into the forest dim until yet another pathologist heaves into view.

"No trouble at all," say the organs and tissues. Just doing what comes naturally. And what delights me, when I am so disposed, is the way the human organism keeps going—the larger part of it— when single things like the jawbone may be breaking down. One does not have to be a neuroscientist to single out these relationships, multiple or singly, only an observant one. They are part of life's unconscious flow to a very narrow destination and will keep going until time cries, "Stop." You would think, therefore, that on the one side you have an organ that's malfunctioning, and on the other side all the rest chiming in in perfect order. But reality is not like that at all, and we resent anything, even in the slightest, that does not do its duty. I try nonetheless to heap the good on the bad, saying it's only the jawbone of a pixilated ass and shouldn't be made too much of.

This bright moment of virtual seizure lasts only five minutes, and then I am back at the grumbling game, arguing why the offending organ does not fall into place with the rest. You can't win them all. Another way of gleaning some comfort from natural surroundings is to take a flower or natural perfume and inhale it deeply if you happen to have either on the premises; some recently arrived flower child will have the one, and some recently arrived lady still caparisoned in patchouli or eau de cologne will have the other.

"Oh," you can say to the flowers, real and artificial, "you smell more than life itself is worth." Or you, going further afield, making your apt oblation felt where it counts, "What a nice structure for a harebell! And you beautiful crocus, spread out winter dares you to get no nearer!" Or you address the nasturtium, "You valiant creature with sails like a yacht in autumn, do you never get weary of crowding out the crocus?" Such fanciful eloquence is not to everybody's taste, but I resort to it occasionally when I run out of steam and patience with the lackeys who support the various varieties of our sickness.

For this is a sick man's account, although I have been out among the hay fields and the oats. I sometimes get the yearning to be merely out somewhere, commanded to return in fifteen minutes by the stern voice of the day nurse.

DATA IS LOST

Things sped up. Time's tinny trumpet achieved a few plangent notes and swiftly swallowed them up. Anhedonia cracked in. There was a quickening in the afternoon as my verbal attempts continued. I had graduated, by now, from "Mem, mem, mem," which was nearly language, to "Men, men, men," which was language right and proper. There followed on these nonsensical exaggerations not exactly a host of words, but a series of reminders. "No" would not shake the timbers of an old man's dream, but "It's simple, stupid," might disturb any person looking for a topic.

To have been responsible for such elocution was amazing. With me, traipsing through the thicket of language to achieve a final effect of racy jingoism was capital. How I did it exactly would remain a mystery, but I suppose it could be said that I had been preparing for several months to combine phonemes and vowels to just such an extent. Such an outlandish phrase may not come my way again (it had better not), but for the moment it was a triumph of self-mastery and ironic verbal control. Crows have shrieked nobler orisons than that one.

My next venture was of the series that I referred to as semiautomatic, faintly offending the stories of H. G. Wells in the use of parrot language. It said, "Invisible idiot," a triumph of a different kind, calculated to bring into play complexities of thought beyond the average man, and certainly beyond the kind of man we had on the premises in that drab quasimilitary room. I must confess, of all my phrases, this was the one that lingered longest, maybe because it echoed a fine mot of a Chinese scientist who once upon a time outfoxed the wits of Peking with a similar saying. If he continues to outwit them now, good Chinese luck to him. We have moved on.

My major effort in this mode was a phrase that had been haunting me for at least a month, but I couldn't get it. On a triumphant note it said to all and sundry, "I talk good coffee," a passing reference to my old skills as the coffee maker, now lost in the sands of time along with Ozymandias. I must have used it, once having explored its accreditation with humbling nervousness, several times until I had it right. First stumbling all about the phrase, it was my first four-word exploit, then stumbling further as I worked each word in turn through the mazes of my corrupt language.

I knew Diane would come within moments and I once again rehearsed the phrase, all complete, as the French say, pending her arrival. I mumbled, "Boy, do I have a surprise for you!" She glowed with a nervous sheen, and I began speaking as slowly as common sense would permit until I had it all there: four words masquerading as four postage stamps a million miles apart, for it seemed that long to get it out. Hearing this, this highly imaginative woman said, "What? Say again please." I did, advancing my individual words off the scale of temerity until I had nothing more to say and closed my mouth. Now she was speechless, for to her I had turned the corner from my putative best and my most lyrical utterance to something that had a structure and a name. I had, as it were, declared war by making that very pronouncement on all the other coffee makers in the world, and I was not about to retreat from my position. "Good coffee" is exciting, but it hardly resembles the language of Beckett or Nabokov. Still, it is language, after all, and one that pleases me by going on as it seems determined to, from strength to strength. And my jaw has not resumed its shape, still bulging outward like a bit of Mars, and my passion for relief by water continues unabated.

I suppose that the weary expert, tracing his route from stroke to Broca's brain and back again may avidly recite his best lines until he can stand them no more. I have no such troubles, reciting my best lines by heart almost as soon as having had them, because few of them there are. I would like to somehow purloin the best lines of my favorite authors, but that is not allowed: common sense forbids it, and I am left with, at the very most, a dozen lines of narrow prose, and a million words of utterances in three languages, half of them making no sense at all.

If I did not have the median voice that speaks to me in more or less the idiom of every day, and the BBC man who fills in for me whenever I run into trouble, I would be left with three hours of exact talk, which is not much. Not when you consider it in the round. But when you take it word by word, it amounts to quite a lot. And who's to say that three hours of discipline may be all that one requires daily, and all the rest is mere silence.

PAUL WEST HANDWRITING SAMPLES
MAY 2004

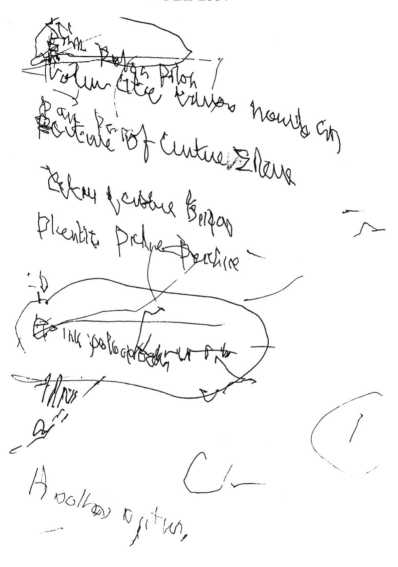

June 2004

chasc a ca[illegible] chelmr back & ~~Ask~~
Chuumie ~~Eckbes~~ and Bockle
Cl[illegible] w[illegible] ri'kes to ~~Kett~~ and back.
Cherman belleter back + back
Hawkin Brillig [illegible] to back to back
[illegible] [illegible] free frisbee Seesdon

October 2004

The bright wind of
an early ~~[illegible]~~ brought
Dr. Sanjeev ~~from the below~~
with a flash. ~~Decreed~~ by
~~Dr.~~ Silver concumba ~~or~~,
~~a junior~~, he ~~dead~~ explained me posted
~~12 only seconds~~; and only the wan
~~standards~~, Sanjeev was
conducting the art of the
art murmuring: We dot cut
so there is no pain. I
felt wonderful, and appied
my privates ~~flowers~~ but
thought out. We were in
for another session of the
the Foley, and ~~[illegible]~~,
red out red and sodden.

and coupled with it,
in what 'happened only
yesterday. Lost for a word,
however briefly, she u'
turned to me (an unlikely
source for this) and
returned fast as a tennis - ball
" meconium"; darkly recessive
from I new not where,
Things were looking up
again.

One Night in Weimar: An Essay
Fanny Howe

SNOW AND IRON

Late January 2003. Close the lights!

Snowlight on top of a crust of it, made a plated meadow.
Trees are like poles, leafless and unposted, but branches begin high
up, except for some blackthorn.
A mighty view through mist over a plateau to low mountains.
Entrance long and gloomy along the Road of Blood.
One enormous beige building houses a museum of artifacts and
upstairs documents.
A few rooms, where people were washed, is now a gallery of art
done in and after, on yellow parchment with pencil.
A sculpture gallery. Destroyed stuff. Photographs.

Outside the barracks have disappeared, stones mark where they
stood, and the infirmary has been reconstructed. The crematorium
with baths, doctors' instruments, and ovens still are primitive,
ashy, unswept.
The hill is high. A brick smokestack and then the slope goes down,
down through barbed wire into the forest.

Not cold on hands but on feet. This was the men's part.
The women's *hasag* was farther away. No train tracks but a little
brick station beside the car park. The cells where people were
tortured (iron doors, tiny windows, a wooden bench), inside some
a photo of the one killed there, including one of a priest, small
and real.

Time Lane is a path through the forest to the place where materials
were produced by inmates.

"Despair kept him going," they said of Goethe, who sat under a tree often in the center of it all before it happened.

*

Jedem Das Seine: these are the words inscribed on the gate into Buchenwald.

I ask a foreigner there: *What does that mean?*
We are standing on snow and iron.
To each his own, is his reply.

To each his own?
I still don't understand. I snap a photo of part of the words to study later.

What did they have in mind when they thought of those three words? The motto sounds like a democratic ideal.

To each his own.
His own what?
Choice of a home, a partner, a nation, a perversion?

Because the motto is inscribed on the gate to a forced labor camp, I am sure its intention is cruel and cold rather than genial and philosophical.

To any prisoner—Polish, for instance—who happens to be on the outer side of the gate and doesn't speak German, it must look like a description of the arrangement inside, like "This Is Jail."

The assumption behind most prison signs is that the prisoners will only see those words once. But the guards will see them every morning and be reminded of an attitude they must sustain. It is like a road sign that is useful to people heading in one direction only. *To each his own.*

No. I have nothing to say. It is beyond my understanding. Perhaps if I heard the words aloud, I would understand them.

For instance, if someone shrugged his shoulders and muttered, *To each his own,* referring to an unpleasant fact about human

303

behavior, I would see that his shrug intended the tolerance that is really indifference.

In that case, the statement would be a familiar gesture rather than a threat or an economic projection.

Somehow a shrug seems like the most convincing expression of those words so far.
If I think of this shrug as a bitter jerk following an observation about something unpleasant, it suddenly makes sense.
To each his own.
Maybe an ironworker was given the job at the last minute. He was told he could put whatever he wanted on that gate. So he shrugged and wrote it.

But wait. *Jedem Das Seine.* It is a slogan with a specific cultural meaning. I have to remember that. Maybe it doesn't say at all what it seems to be saying in English and the guy who was Russian had it wrong.
Because now I suddenly get it from the original point of view.
What these words mean is: "Everyone gets what he deserves."

IRONY AND SNOW

Let's say three words come out of one mouth in a sequence. They go into two ears, which receive the words as they are uttered one at a time.

Because the ear and the mind have to hear the entire sequence before they can understand it, they have to listen backward while the words enter forward. The listener must listen as a mirror would listen.

The speaker in the meantime pushes out a sequence of syllables that plan to conclude in a complete sentence before forgetting where they began.
For instance, the nasty phrase *"Jedem Das Seine."*

It is strangely hard to explain this phenomenon without a diagram. Each word rushes into the air after the word *Jedem*. But look at them! They are in the opposite order!

If the three words were visible, the speaker would see *Jedem* rushing away to the right, while the others ran after.

In a poet's mind, the first word in the line is also the last. The poet's head is like everybody's, but it works as if there were no outside ears. It is as if the poet's head's ears are too near its mouth and so the sound of its own thoughts vibrate as if in a spiral shell between breath, throat, and ear. This sets the poet apart as someone lost in thought.

With a person constructing a gate, words usually thought or breathed are forged in iron, where they have no ears or mouth. They have been taken out of a context of breath and away from two speaking with one mind, away from one mind speaking to itself, and have been burned into a gate that functions like a book cover with the title *To Each His Own*. (There was such a book.)

Are written letters shadows of thoughts?
To be a ghost on the snow is to own nothing but naked intellect. Ashes, rock, solid soil, voices stopped midlife. When you visit this place, you are a shadow. The snow is paper.

Abandon hope, all ye who enter here, Dante wrote on the Gate of Hell.

The Nazis could have just used that sign. But I guess someone wanted to be inventive and think up a new one: *Jedem Das Seine.* I guess they didn't want to admit that they had created hell by appropriating Dante's gate sign. They wanted to be ironic.

The creation of hell is not exclusive to Nazis. Names of places over the years have come to stand, worldwide, for massacres.

One of the identifiable factors of a massacre is that the victims can't believe what is happening to them, since they have nothing to do with the idea behind it.
They are not soldiers but civilians in the middle of their hopes.

305

Fanny Howe

They simply can't believe it. It is like coming to understand the full meaning of the five words:

Everyone gets what he deserves.

To understand what these words mean takes as long as it lasts to get back to the day when someone said them for the first time. Listen backward long enough and you will get there. But try and stay with the present tense.

On Reading the Bodies of Fathers
Matthew Kirby

AT THE MOST BASIC LEVEL, a father's body can be understood as a testimony that something has gone out from him—his seed; for this sending, this putting forth into the world, is the prerequisite of fatherhood. Unlike the mother, whose pregnancy and period of nursing span time and articulate the arc of a complete narrative, the father's fathering always exists in an unknown and mythologized moment—as the crack of generative lightning that has struck somewhere in an irretrievable past. His body, then, is like the trunk of an old tree, which, having been blackened and split, records the power that once struck the spot. The old tree has its secrets, yet, in order to tease out the manifold narratives embedded in the mysterious, paternal body, we must first separate it into its three component signifiers, which work together to represent the various forms of fatherly outwardness: the unruly beard, the glorious paunch, and the ghostly, receding hairline.

The fatherly beard suggests dissemination, both in the sense of lost possibility and as a kind of bounteous Abrahamic diaspora. Its multifarious tendrils, reaching out delicately into the world that hovers, dreamlike, before the gaze of the father, symbolize the infinite possibilities of his seed—doctor, lawyer, equestrian, entrepreneur, vagabond, tramp, schoolteacher, raconteur, etc. Yet, at the same time, these wispy follicles represent the lost possibilities of the father himself, which he perceives as relating dialectically to the life choices of his offspring, so that whatever is accomplished by the child justifies, yet never fully compensates for, fatherly losses. Thus the paternal sacrifice must be retold again and again at countless family gatherings.

The second way in which the father's body communicates its characteristic outwardness is by means of the magnificent paunch preceding the stride of the approaching father into unknown territories. This paunch, because it vanquishes the austere abdominal muscles with an effusion of tender fat, has often been interpreted to suggest both the outward journey of the inner realm of the psyche—a kind of protuberant vulnerability—and the repose appropriate to one who has invested his genetic currency and is waiting idly on a return. Yet, in a deeper sense, the paternal belly signifies a kind of ontological confusion about parenthood and is a mock approximation of the pregnant female abdomen. Like the domes of mosques and churches, it is an imitation of the divine, built not on transcendent life, but on wealth—in the case of many fathers, on the caloric wealth of alcohol and midnight samplings of a variety of cold cuts.

The third and perhaps most touching component of the patristic figure, the receding hairline of the father, signifies the tide that has just gone out, leaving the beaches strewn with the building blocks of newer, more evolutionarily complex life, but which has itself returned to the vast, primordial formlessness of the sea. This illustrates how the father engenders life of which he himself will never attain comprehension, a life that evolves into consciousness with a profound suspicion of its own origins. The father stands in contemplation of his offspring as primitive man might were he faced with the devices of modern technology, judging them based on the old paradigms of wizardry and the direct intervention of divine beings. Thus the cryptic utterances of the father often concern hazy, otherworldly concepts such as "quality time" or "character." When pressed regarding the specific, material criteria these concepts imply, the father will often lapse into a kind of spectral jargon, gesturing hermetically with his hands as he attempts to reconcile conflicting cosmologies in an effort to communicate with the inscrutable, trackless beings whom he has supposedly engendered.

These three components of the fatherly symbology also correspond to actors from the mythic realm in which the father is rooted. The beard, with its mass of jagged, lightninglike protuberances and its spatially contiguous relationship to the head, represents Zeus, governor of the gods and issuer of divine judgment. The hairline, then, is the mark of Poseidon, connoting the fleeting attention and unpredictability of the oceanic depths. Thirdly, there can be little doubt that the protruding stomach of the father corresponds to Hephaestus, the god of fabrication and of the forge, for it is, as noted above, a sign of artifice—an approximation of the pregnant female abdomen. Furthermore, in deriving its origins from the realm of woman, the paunch is a doubly apt mark of Hephaestus, who was born of the goddess Hera without the help of Zeus in competition with his cephalogenesis of Athena.

Under the conditions of modernity, the Hephaestian belly of the father is pitted against his Zeusean head, for the beard, signifying wisdom, is undermined by the appetite for foods high in cholesterol and other unhealthy vices—such as tobacco, which connotes the industrious glow of the Hephaestian forge—that lead to the premature death of the father and the resulting abandonment of the family. Hephaestus, thus challenging Zeus, calls the beard into question as a signifier of masculinity.* Thus, the paradoxical Hephaestian desires to consume and to forge, to sculpt and control the shape of the family mock the cerebral, Zeusean restraints of reason, rhetorical debate, and just governance by calling into question their manliness. This conflict drives the father to retreat into the realm of Poseidon, the deep, where he hides himself from his family for fear that his Hephaestian, controlling element will destroy them, or that his logical, Zeusean capacity for just governance will leave him vulnerable to usurpers through reasoned argument.**

As a result of this internal struggle, the expressions and gestures typical of the father often consist of two mutually contravening components that occur simultaneously or in close proximity:

> Frustration (Hephaestian): anger that no indelible mark can be left on the world. The father's efforts to simulate the generative act of the mother through the imposition of an external order upon the substance of life are ultimately impermanent, slouching toward entropy.

> Resignation (Zeusean): realization that the consolidation of power necessary to make such an indelible mark has no ultimate justification. The act of shaping

---

*The ambiguity of the beard dates back to the conquering of philosophically and artistically oriented Greece by the military hierarchy of Rome, where soldiers were forbidden facial hair. In this context, the beard was associated with the pacifism, effeminacy, and homosexuality attributed to the conquered Greeks.

**The thought process behind the latter trepidation goes like this: if the father employs a consistent logical measure in his implementation of order—for example, punishing the same offense to the same degree regardless of persons—then his children will begin to distinguish forms of justice existing independently of the semidivine identity of the father, attributing them either to other gods or to nature. The realization of the natural existence of these forms gives rise, in the minds of the children, to an awareness of the possibility of alternate models of government, which, over a long enough timeline, can devolve into voting on family policy, cries of "It's not fair," and the application for legal emancipation.

future generations is fundamentally violent and lawless, and the order that it establishes and presupposes is
an illusion. All is chaos.

Thus, the following are some typical utterances of the father:

"Why are you wasting your life? It doesn't bother *me* if you turn
out to be a ditchdigger!"

"How can you expect to learn if you won't take the time to . . .
Fine, I can't *make* you a person of character."

"I've told you a thousand times—not that you ever listen to anything I say anyway."

In each instance, the vexed father alternately asserts and effaces
his power over the child, undermining the edifice of his credibility
even as he builds it to new heights. Similarly, "Because I said so" is
an expression characteristic of the Zeuso-Hephaestian split in that
it asserts a patriarchal right while simultaneously revealing that
fatherly authority lacks any basis in reason. Occasionally, rather
than being verbal, this irreconcilable contradiction manifests as a
kind of inarticulate, self-pitying groan of halfhearted rage that replicates the form of the father's body: at once protruding, receding, and
going to seed.

If there is any hope for the father, it lies in the Poseidonic realm of
darkness and myth, to which he must frequently retreat in order to
reestablish equilibrium between his Zeusean and Hephaestian elements. This endeavor, however, is difficult and plagued by the danger of permanent separation from the family, as it consists of the
father entering a brooding and noncommunicative state and often
retreating to some dark, cave-like structure such as a garage, study,
or broom closet, depending on his socioeconomic resources. It is
here, publicly claiming to be at work on some vaguely utilitarian
or intellectual project, that the father engages in a titanic, internal
struggle in an attempt to create a bridge between the fiery, Hephaestian realm of fabrication and mimesis and the ethereal, Zeusean
arena of justice and governance.

Failure to arrive at such an accord can result in the dissolution of
the father's identity and his reduction to a kind of nomadic, wayward
state, exiled within the self. Fathers unfortunate enough to experience such a dislocation of their mythic elements often develop a
waxy, sunken appearance. They take up shuffleboard and can be seen
pacing median strips, empty baseball diamonds, and the parking lots
of bait-and-tackle stores, the melancholy deserts of their foreheads

reflecting the pale glow of the moon as they make fumbling attempts to piece together the psychic shards of a fatherhood lost.

Worse still, a victory for one side over the other forebodes the degeneration into either a fascistic or a nihilistic/anarchic condition—either the repression and ultimate destruction of the family in the name of unity and creative genesis or a flight from the basic responsibilities of fatherhood brought on by a failure to reconcile the tautological nature of patriarchy with the mores of the liberal democratic milieu. The former, authoritarian decline typically begins innocently enough with the imposition of some sort of music or language lessons, but can end in a terrifying regime of classical or alternative education (depending on the father's political and cultural identifications). Children in such situations have been forced to make their own clothes, memorize passages from Mill or the Heidelberg Catechism, cultivate herb gardens, and play solely with wooden toys, embarrassingly crafted by the father himself. Equally disheartening, the latter and opposite outcome can leave children fatherless, or worse, faced with a large, bearded man who, abnegating all station of parentage, really just wants to be "pals." The perennial task of the father, then, is the cultivation and maintenance of the Poseidonic realm in which his true identity is hidden—not as mere escapism, but to ensure that the family continues to navigate safely between the Scylla and Charybdis of reductive and destructive absolutes.

This reliance on the Poseidonic reveals a startling truth: the father is ontologically rooted in myth, his identity hidden in the dark, primordial night when lightning struck and life was engendered, a moment always having occurred outside history, before sonograms and baby registries and the incessant photographic documentation of the child's progress. It is from the realm of the story and of the fairy tale that he derives his authority—his being *as* "father"—and his judgments are those corresponding to the narrativity of myth rather than the causality of the material world. Though the shattering of the father's fragile claims regarding his supernatural identity and supreme authority may result in independence, it is always accomplished at the cost of exile from the mythic, from the story of the father himself. Yet where, one might ask, is this mythic realm and in what sense can it be said to exist? Does it occur in the psyche of the father alone? To this we must respond emphatically that the mythic realm of the father is not solely a mental construct but has its material reality in the physical body of the father himself.

To discover it, we have only to reorient the body of the father horizontally, so that he lies supine with his back to the floor. Now we see that his three component signifiers—the thicket of beard, the magnificent paunch, and the ghostly, receding hairline—are radically and mysteriously transformed and no longer denote mythic actors or correspondent psychological processes but formations of a geographical nature. The multifarious tendrils of the protuberant beard are changed into the innumerable, twisted trees of a vast primeval forest, dark and teeming with creatures of varying disposition toward the weary traveler. The magnificent paunch has become a treacherous, windswept mountain—its foreboding slopes tower ever upward, treeless but covered in hearty, weather-beaten undergrowth. At its peak, the lip of a dormant volcano heaves and rumbles ominously. It is rumored to contain strange treasures, a reward for those bold enough to make the formidable trek. Of the three signifiers, the forehead of the supine father retains the most meaning from its prior context in the vertically oriented father: it is a bleak and rocky shore, strewn with the shipwrecks of years of worry, connoted by the father's deeply furrowed brow. Standing amid these salty hulks, one can look out, past the gently lapping waves to the distant, gray horizon of the realm of myth where the leviathan leaps and twists in the crisp, bracing air.

Any small child fortunate enough to come upon a sleeping father knows the delightful and dangerous adventures to be had upon this misty continent. Indeed, many grown children continue to possess fond if hazy memories of the battles once fought there—of exploding projectiles hurled from the mountaintop onto the beach, of an army of trolls routed from the dark confines of the primeval forest, chased by thundering steeds out across the great plains and trapped at the foot of the mountain. Yet, as we grow older still, the memories become hazier, and the magic of the father's body wanes. The great mountain is subjected to a barrage of fad diets and the mysterious forest clear-cut in the name of respectability. There arises the danger that the father himself will become alienated from the essence of his own body and come to consider it as a mere vehicle for walking around, eating, speaking, working, or fiddling at some hobby. This senseless tragedy must not be allowed to take place. Setting aside our professional concern for objectivity, we must always endeavor to remind him that he is, in fact, no mere mortal, but an entire *continent*, a sprawling landmass with a long and illustrious history dating back to the time when the first tiny ships arrived, unloading small wayfarers upon his far-flung shores.

The Blackened Puppet
Kenneth Gross

IN HIS NOVEL *Riddley Walker*, Russell Hobban describes the unearthing of a puppet. Pulled out of the mud on a rain-soaked hillside, the figure has a great curved nose almost touching its chin, small wooden hands, a pointed hat, and the remnants of a cloth hump on its back. The puppet has been turned uniformly black, blacker than earth. Inside it is the hand of the puppeteer.

It is miraculous that such a thing has survived at all. And a puppet is not what the twelve-year-old narrator, Riddley Walker, has been looking for. Hobban's book describes a future Britain, "Inland," that an atomic catastrophe has reduced to a kind of primitive, authoritarian society. It is an earth of deserted, unproductive landscapes, full of ruined cities, empty highways, and wasted fields, roamed over by packs of vicious dogs. The humans who remain support themselves by poor farming, charcoal burning, or scavenging in the desolate ground for scraps of metal, often breaking up huge, rusted machines, monsters of an uncertain past. The diffused system of rule that oversees their work is sustained by thuggish violence and also by a curious religion. This faith is based around a myth of ancient catastrophe and possible future redemption in which we can glimpse the truth of the historical destruction combined with pieces of the stories of the fall, the crucifixion, and the medieval legend of Saint Eustace (a ruthless hunter who is converted by a vision of the suffering Christ that he sees between the antlers of a stag he is chasing). These legends of "Eusa" and "the shining Addom" and his horrific splitting are presented to the people of Hobban's world by itinerant puppeteers, quasipriestly authorities whose shows are in turn interpreted to the communities by a shamanlike figure, a "connexion man." This is a vocation that Riddley Walker himself has inherited from his father, who has shortly before been killed under the weight of a vast machine that he and his fellows had been ordered to remove, unbroken, from a pit of mud.

The blackened puppet resembles nothing in the official shows. "This here figger tho it wernt like no other figger I ever seen," says

313

Riddley in the peculiar idiom Hobban invented in his novel to suggest how English survives in the unmeasured centuries after the catastrophe, an English made more crude, broken, childish, and yet also dreamlike. The chance find somehow answers the loss of his father even as it isolates him. A suspicious overseer wants to take it from him, and Riddley's violent insistence on keeping hold of this "crookit figger" is what prompts his flight from his village and his wanderings in the wasteland, where he tries to solve the riddle of the ancient myths and to find the buried truth about a form of power that both creates and destroys. It is never quite clear what part of the world the puppet is.

I remember seeing in a provincial museum in Denmark the head of a bog man, dated to the fourth century BC. The man's body had not been preserved, or was in too bad shape to show. He was an old man with a rope around his neck—he had been ritually strangled, the guidebook said, though the rope looked more like a necklace. The head rested on its side, somewhat flattened and dented, and was much smaller than a normal head, as I recall. How could an old man be so small, like a child? It was not like an Egyptian mummy, since its perfect preservation was an accident, not art, the result of the chemicals in the peat bog where he was buried. The head looked not so much dead as asleep, in a kind of dreamy reverie. Each whisker, each eyelash, each wrinkle and fold of skin was visible, as were the cloth of the cap and the hemp of the rope. The time in the bog had left the head a uniform, shiny, almost iridescent black, vivid in its darkness. It was like a glaze of some dark paint spread over the surface and at the same time the real substance of which it had been formed or made, in that sense belonging to a different kind of death or sleep, casual but resistant to time.

> As if he had been poured
> in tar, he lies
> on a pillow of turf
> and seems to weep
>
> the black river of himself . . .
>
> Who will say "corpse"
> to his vivid cast?

> Who will say "body"
> to his opaque repose?
>
> —Seamus Heaney, "The Grauballe Man"

It is this sort of blackness that I imagine in the puppet Riddley finds.

Hobban probably counted on readers recognizing the uncovered puppet as Punch, the ur-puppet of European tradition. At one point during his travels, Riddley is held captive by one of the official puppeteers named Goodparley, who, with the sly malice of Dostoyevsky's Grand Inquisitor, tells Riddley the hidden truth of the ancient Punch show, more potent and more subversive than any pious "Eusa show." Indeed, Goodparley puts on for Riddley his own version of a Punch-and-Judy performance with brightly painted figures he has kept secretly to himself, and whose use he'd been taught by a strange old man in his childhood. Punch, he tells Riddley, "hes the oldes figure there is. He wer old time back way way back long befor Eusa ever ben thot of. Hes so old he cant dy." The puppet speaks, as the traditional Punch does, in an unearthly squeak that distorts words and penetrates the ear, produced by the use of a small reed or "swazzle" held in the puppeteer's mouth. "It wernt a voyce Id every heard befor yet it wer a voyce I knowit some how it wernt no stranger to me." And the show itself, more violent and obscene, more full of murder, rape, cannibalism, ghosts, and devils than even the traditional Punch-and-Judy show, is like something he'd always known; indeed, a reminder of the darker truths and more troubling questions concealed by the anodyne forms of the official spectacle."I never seen that show befor nor never heard the names of Punch and Mr On The Levvil and that goast befor yet now as I seen them and heard what they had to say it seamt like I musve all ways knowit about them. Seamt like I knowit mor about them nor I knowit I knowit."

The novelist wants to tell his story, but he is also thinking hard about what a puppet is, the kind of hold it has on our imagination, the strange form of life it creates. Here the figure of the blackened puppet, or the blackness of the puppet, suggests that the puppet's life—its pathos and power—has something to do with survival, with an earliness that is wrought up with things suffered, destroyed, yet strangely preserved, alive in the present. It shows the strength of fragile things, the humanity of inhuman things, a knowledge that precedes knowledge.

In the traditional Punch-and-Judy show the spirit of Punch lies as much in his energy of survival, his refusal to be killed, as in his violence. If he dispatches other puppets with anarchic glee—wife, neighbor, doctor, servant, policeman—it is because they are representatives of forces that would constrain him to speak and act according to conventional terms. (Those puppets that represent a dog, crocodile, or clown Punch will not kill.) It is the child's revenge against rules of obedience, decorum, silence, and sympathy, also the puppet's revenge against any more respectable version of theatrical artifice. His mode of violence indeed speaks for the object's vengeful insistence on its remaining an object, as Punch seems to demonstrate when he keeps time to the music by knocking his wooden head repeatedly against the play board. The puppet's shrill voice, at once visceral and artificial, the tongue's habits of the swazzle, breaks through all other, more intelligible forms of speech, and can even become independent of the puppet itself when it speaks from below the stage, as often happens. The story of the Punch play works not just as a reflection of human impulses, conscious or unconscious, but as a story about the puppet, a way of giving shape to the peculiar kind of activity and being that the puppet allows, what it means to live in a world where puppets are possible. The poet-puppeteer Dennis Silk spoke of puppets as "things made of things," needing to possess the impersonal force "of a thinking billiard ball."

The deformed yet haunting language of Hobban's novel itself recalls something of Punch's talent for a nonsense of survival, a way of refusing all ordinary names or words addressed to him by the world. Here is one example of Punch's language games from a nineteenth-century transcription of a Punch-and-Judy show. It is a piece of the puppet's dialogue with the hangman who wants to script Punch's last public words (an agent of law whom Punch eventually tricks into hanging himself):

JACK KETCH: I want you to say, "Ladies and gentlemen, I have been a wicked man—"

PUNCH: I want some bread and jam—

JACK KETCH: Not you "want some bread and jam"—"I've been a wicked man and the law has found me guilty—"

PUNCH: And the floor is jolly dirty—

316

JACK KETCH: Not "the floor is jolly dirty"—"the law has found me guilty and I must hang by the neck until I am dead, dead, dead."

PUNCH: Bread, bread, bread.

The public language of law is blackened here, made to show its violence even as it is reduced to nonsense, made opaque and infantile (from *infans,* speechless), thinglike; it is replaced by a language of gleeful indifference, deforming official command or prayer, which also evokes the cry of the child and the beggar. That is simply the kind of language that puppets have, or that they need, that we need to lend to them.

Hobban's narrator eventually takes up Goodparley's more intact puppets to use in his wanderings through the ruined landscape of his world, where he becomes both suspect entertainer and itinerant shaman. But he always keeps the blackened puppet with him as a kind of talisman or guardian; he always has it in his mind and in his hand. It suggests to me that within or alongside all working, moving, and painted puppets there is always a blackened puppet. This is an image of the puppet's fate and origin, a reminder of how powerful and fragile its life is, how blunt yet hard to read; it marks the interiority of things that have no interior. It suggests why puppets are so unsettling, since they are at once more ancient and more childlike than human beings. ("Puppet" derives from the Latin *pupus,* boy, also the root of "pupil.") I am here reminded of Rainer Maria Rilke's description of dolls or puppets that have outlived their human masters, outlived the sentimentality and violence of the children who first owned them—he seeks in them a "thing-soul" that outlives both our skepticism and our endlessly sentimental, narcissistic projections, a soul that gains its strongest hold on us at the moment when these puppets throw themselves into the fire, and we are intoxicated by the very smell of their burning. The puppet's life lies partly in its being abandoned or about to be abandoned, in its patience, its power to wait to be taken up, always knowing its fate as a mere piece of matter, yet the stronger for that. The face of the working Punch puppet is almost always a ruin, hollowed out, split, battered, stained, smudged, and scarred, always requiring repair, recarving, and repainting. Through the blackened puppet Riddley Walker pursues the buried life of the world, that which is at once dead and unborn, that which is visible everywhere and yet hidden, at once an object of desire and an object of suspicion, dangerous to release. He indeed starts to see in the face of Punch a reflection of "every face," the faces of Christ, the devil, the dogs and boars he has killed, his father, an eyeless child, and his thuggish taunters. That face is mirrored as well in a battered carving he finds in the ruined stone forest of Canterbury cathedral, a face with curling leaves and branches that spring from its mouth, eyes, nose, and ears. Looking at that visage, he thinks to himself, "The living stoan will all ways have the living wood in it I know that. With the hart of the chyld in it which that hart of the chyld is in that same and very thing that lives inside us and afeart of being beartht."

In the Holocaust Museum in Washington, DC, one can see a tiny figure of a marionette preserved behind glass. The control mechanism and most of the threads suspending the puppet are lost. Only the body survives, with bits of string trailing from its arms, legs, and head. Its black, crudely formed, and segmented limbs were sculpted by a camp inmate out of pressed and hardened bread. It is breathtaking, that sacrifice of scant food to create a form of play among the living and the dead, among those who are reduced to walking corpses at the mercy of a machinery of murder. What kind of sustenance and survival is this, what kind of will to making and playing survives in such a figure? Who made it? What are the plays that it performed in, and for whom? What form of love did it give or demand? *Dead, dead, dead. Bread, bread, bread.*

Along with its mode of survival, the fascination and power of the puppet's life lie in its being at once a part and a whole, at once dependent and independent. Puppets are not automata, self-moving things or robots with a will of their own. They always imply the collaborative work of another body and will behind them and before them. Their life depends on a human talent for lending motion, intention, and self to inanimate things, even as the puppeteer—as Heinrich von Kleist wrote so well—must yield himself to the specific gravity of the puppet itself, to the weight and density of matter, the alien or inhuman life that is waiting in lifeless things, a process that in turn gives to humans a different vision of their life and death. The movement such yielding allows, at once contingent and willed, is the puppet's soul, says Kleist. That is another part of the blackness of the puppet—its blankness and opacity, and how we yield ourselves to this. What belongs to the puppet? How do we imagine our own complicity with these made things?

In his parable "The Cares of a Householder," Franz Kafka describes a being named Odradek. It is at once a creature, a piece of the living world, and a purely made thing, an object of human manufacture:

> At first glance it looks like a flat star-shaped spool for thread,
> and indeed it does seem to have thread wound upon it; to be
> sure, they are only old, broken-off bits of thread, knotted and
> tangled together, of the most various sorts and colors. But it
> is not only a spool, for a small wooden crossbar sticks out of
> the middle of the star, and another small rod is joined to that
> at a right angle. By means of this latter rod on one side and
> one of the points of the star on the other, the whole thing is
> able to stand upright as if on two legs. One is tempted to
> believe that the creature once had some sort of intelligible
> shape and is now only a broken-down remnant. Yet this does
> not seem to be the case; at least there is no sign of it; nowhere
> is there an unfinished or unbroken surface to suggest any-
> thing of the kind; the whole thing looks senseless enough,
> but in its own way perfectly finished.

Unowned, nimble, impossible to lay hold of, Odradek is part of the
narrator's household and yet something of "no fixed abode." It refuses like a child to answer even the simple questions put to it, and
its laughter has a sound like dead leaves, with no lungs behind it.
Can this material ghost possibly die, the narrator asks, like something with a human (or even divine) purpose that can wear out? And
if he does not, what does his continued existence betoken? "He does
no harm to anyone that one can see; yet the idea that he is likely to
survive me I find almost painful."

The broken threads might indicate that Odradek is the remnant of
a skeletal marionette body, but Kafka's description suggests that he
is rather some piece of the marionette's otherwise hidden control
mechanism—often just two crossed pieces of wood, or something
with various extensions, handles, and bars added, depending on how
many strings and how complex the movements required. It is such a
control, rather than the marionette body itself, with which the puppeteer is most intimate. He cradles those wooden sticks in his hands,
stained with the sweat of endless work, tugging, hooking, sliding,
grasping them with strength and delicacy, for these are the means by
which the hand's myriad gestures and meanings are transferred down
the cords to the heavy, mobile body of the puppet. This is the instrument of the puppeteer's mastery, but also that by which he registers
the impulses of movement, momentum, and weight that ride up to
the human hand from the puppet hanging below, the place where the
puppeteer must feel and put to use the weight and momentum of

319

the puppet, translate its direction or indirection. In Odradek we see the control assuming an uncanny life cut off from the human hand, or else retaining within itself the remnants of the hand's and the puppet's life, a control with nothing to control, unheld itself.

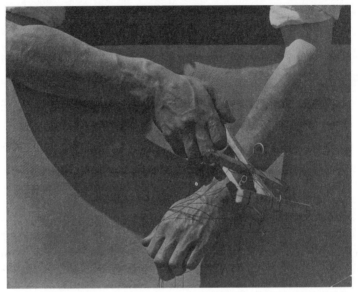

Hands of a Marionette Player. 1929. Photograph by Tina Modotti.

The story of puppets becomes the story of embodied souls and ensouled objects. Gaining power from the human capacity to yield up power to something else, its life is bound to curious collaborations and displacements of life, unions and divisions of life and object. The puppet insists that our souls are never our own, our bodies are never our own. They are entities smaller and larger than any selves we think we own—so puppets are always larger and smaller than we are, less and more than we are or than we suppose we are, more ugly and more beautiful, faster and slower, lighter and heavier. Little big, old young, dead living.

What I have called the blackness of the puppet belongs as well to the puppeteer. He or she is so often concealed from view, hidden in the space below or above the stage, a space whose inhabitants we surmise through the visible strings, rods, sleeves, or hands that enter, by design or accident, into the stage space. It is an unknown, generative, yet dreamlike space, a refuge for the puppeteer yet also a space of fierce work. It is an offstage space different from the backstage or flies inhabited by living actors, because we know at once that so much of what we see on stage is made possible there, in the movements and voices of the hidden players. The puppets entering the stage from below or above have crossed a metaphysical threshold different from that of any human actor, and leaving the stage they lose their life more radically, yet they survive there *in potentia*, even if we see them in our minds' eyes hung up on hooks. That is perhaps why Punch's shrill voice calling from offstage, which often begins the traditional show, has such uncanny force.

An anonymous nineteenth-century Punch player whose words are transcribed in the pages of Henry Mayhew's *London Labour and the London Poor* (1861) evokes the fascination of this offstage space. He is explaining to Mayhew the genealogy of one of Punch's more exotic victims, the blackface puppet he calls "Shallaballah" or "the Grand Turk of Sinoa" (a figure who in some versions of the spectacle takes on the identity of the minstrel-show clown, Jim Crow). In ungrammatical yet eerily eloquent English, an idiom that speaks from inside the puppet world, the Punchman declares that "Sinoa is nowhere, for he's only a substance yer know. I can't find Sinoa, although I've tried, and think it's at the bottom of the sea where the black fish lays." The space of the puppet and the puppet stage that we cannot see is like the bottom of the sea, and like the blackness of the unknown fish that lies in wait there.

Though it must often peek above the surface of this sea, the hand of the puppeteer inside the visible glove puppet is itself always blackened, hidden in the dark, always cut off and yet strangely alive. It is the most remarkable thing, that power of the puppet player to lend an autonomous, sufficient, yet also alien and unpredictable life to one part of the body, to make the hand the source of gestures that appertain to tinier hands and heads and bodies and persons. It extends the limits of the hand's life and motion, allows the hand to discover itself in a new whole. The Punch-and-Judy show must always be staged by a single person, since its wars are the wars of a left hand with a right hand, hands that find themselves yet collaborating in a dance of affection, trickery, rebellion, treachery, and murder, as if to suggest the multiple souls we have within our bodies, souls that in turn are given up to the audience. The great Russian puppeteer Sergei Obraztsov (1901–92) famously used his bare hands along with mere wooden balls on his fingers to create puppets in courtship and conflict, puppet-creatures who lost and gained their heads in the unfolding of the drama. Even Obraztsov's naked, visible hands were themselves invisible, opaque, cut off from the puppeteer in giving life to the ball-headed entities, creatures whose heads could so quickly, even mercifully, revert to being mere things when one hand removed a wooden ball from the other hand.

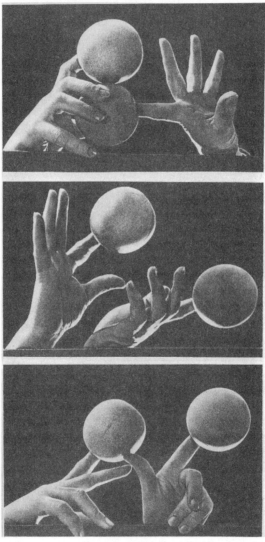

Photographs from Sergei Obraztsov.
My Profession (Moscow, 1950).

In the Japanese tradition of puppet theater, the Bunraku, there is no concealing screen, no backstage; the puppeteers are always visible to those who watch. Three persons are required to manipulate each of the half-life-size puppets, a master and two apprentices, the puppets' voices being supplied by an offstage reader, the *joruri*. The vividly stylized movements of the puppets, by turns violent and delicate, so grab the eye that one is mostly, but never completely, oblivious to the visible persons who collaborate to give them life. There is the master in full kimono and uncovered face, who operates the head and the right arm; impassive in concentration, he is trained to give up no emotion that would take away from what is shown in the puppet's gestures. The two apprentices, one moving the left arm and one moving the feet that walk only on air, by contrast ask us *not* to see them: they wear black suits and their heads are covered with domed black hoods. In the visible fiction of their invisibility, the blackened, shrouded apprentices are like split-off pieces of some larger darkness, a darkness not necessarily absolute or deathly, some abysmal background to the visible world, yet still a solid, embodied opacity that represents those hidden spaces and those uncontrolled, neglected impulses that shape our lives, that make up our selves and the world we move in, at once within and beyond our merely human selves. It is hard to describe the pathos of a puppet-hero on the Bunraku stage who labors to kill himself for love or honor through the skilled, loving collaboration of the three manipulators, such that the puppet's death, however solitary, is immediately larger than itself, bound to the motions of the puppeteers, and also no death at all, since what is killed cannot really be killed.

In 1999, in London, I saw a play titled *Mnemonic,* conceived and performed by the British company Theatre de Complicite. At the center of this work of interwoven stories—a work about searchers, survivors, and immigrants—is the life and death of a mummy, the body of a man preserved in ice some five thousand years and discovered in the Italian Alps in 1991. At intervals this figure is given substance by an actor lying naked on stage, miming the posture in which the Iceman was found frozen, or by a silhouette of the mummy itself projected on the back of the stage. The dead man also takes form in the conversations of scientists who speculate wildly about his life and death, drawing on evidence of his body— signs of disease, violence, age—and the few objects found with him: "A broken stick. Splinters of wood. Scraps of leather. Fur. Tufts of twisted grass. Strips of hide. Fragments of birch bark . . . two round objects on a piece of twine" (words repeated like a mantra in the play). Was he a hunter, a shepherd, a trader, a shaman, or a refugee, a man in search or a man in flight? The uncertain identity of the Iceman also merges in our minds with that of a person who figures in another thread of the plot, a lost father being searched for by his daughter, who has never met him and had thought him dead. Toward the close of the play, however, there is a startling moment of transformation. It begins when the actors take up a chair on stage, a piece of furniture that, we have learned, belonged to the director's grandfather—the director also being the actor who both mimes the Iceman and plays the searching woman's lover. This carefully engineered prop is tugged at, shifted, yanked, allowed to collapse, until it reveals itself as a curiously hinged clump of boards that in turn becomes, in the hands of the actors, the torso and limbs of a crude, skeletal (if still chairlike) manikin. The jointed figure is held by four members of the cast, supported visibly like a collapsing body, while a fifth holds a gathered clump of clothes above its shoulders to represent a head. Slowly, most slowly, with stunning care and a kind of arcane sympathy, as the illumination dims and the lighting creates an impression of storm, the five actors collaboratively animate the bits of wood and cloth. They show us the Iceman's last moments of wandering, his collapse to the ground, his last breaths, his falling into sleep and death—and into the stillness and duration of ice. The chair is brought to life most vividly in showing us an ancient, solitary, unknown death, showing us the strangest version of the work of memory in this play that is so much about memory. The object is left on stage at the close, and as the audience files past it we become mourners, not just for the dead Iceman but for the abandoned puppet and even the chair of which it is composed.

The blackened puppet represents a mode of speech that includes its own meaninglessness; it is a pathology as much as an innocence, both a putting together and stripping away, a loss or fragmentation of self combined with a collaboration and jointure of selves, the gaining of power through the loss or yielding of power. The blackness of the puppet is a blackness of the spirit that is also a blackness of matter, dead preserving molded mold unlighted earth, the blackness of our interior selves, the black hole that is inside our skulls yet made part of the outside world.

The blackness of the puppet emerges most literally and most strangely in the case of shadow puppets—"*les pupazzi noirs, ombres animées,*" as a French study from 1896 calls them. Here the dark, displaced, complicit life of the puppet belongs not to what one might call the puppet figures, the thin cut-out forms of paper, parchment, wood, leather, or plastic; rather that life belongs to the shadows these forms cast on a translucent screen that conceals both the forms themselves and the puppeteer who moves them. We see a blackness that resides not in things more solid, dense, hard-headed, and material, but in entities too light and fragile to be mummified, rapid, flickering, and quick as a flame. They belong to a world always out of reach, an alien, two-dimensional world—and yet never quite two-dimensional, since in almost all shadow shows part of the pleasure comes from the play of intermittently sharper and vaguer shadows formed as the cut-out figures that cast them move closer to or away from the screen. The very space between figures on the shadow-puppet screen cannot be read as ordinary space, but as something that has the materiality of dream. The shadows are also like ghosts. There is a Japanese legend that the puppet theater took its origins from the device of a sympathetic magician who persuades an emperor into thinking his dead wife has returned to life by showing him her silhouette behind a screen, conversing with him by imitating her voice.

In the great shadow puppet tradition of Java and Bali, the Wayang Kulit, the elegantly shaped pieces of stiff, opaque buffalo hide that must cast the shadows, filigreed with holes throughout their length, are also brightly painted in tints of red, gold, blue, and black. These colors, however, are principally a way of pleasing the eye of the puppet-maker, or else the eye of the puppeteer, the *dalang*, who sits cross-legged behind the screen, moving the vast population of shadows and providing all their voices in an ancient, barely comprehensible argot, whose idioms range from heroic to clownish. Or perhaps the colors are a means of honoring the gods, demigods, heroes, monsters, and clowns whose stories the puppets make visible. For, with the exception of a few curious, often uninvited guests who gather behind the screen, none of those watching the show see the colors at all. The shadows the figures cast have no color, save for a slight yellowish tint that they are lent by the oil lamp behind the screen, whose bright flickering is always dimly visible. There are otherwise just endless shades of gray and black. As I've suggested, it is these shadows rather than the leather figures that cast them that we must call the puppets, or else the dance of complicity between hidden substance and visible shadow. The fluttering yet potent life of these puppets is shown at the very opening of each show, as the *dalang* rolls in a wide arc across the cotton screen a great pierced leaf form, the *kayon*, that represents the shape of the world, its elemental forces of fire, water, and air. Following this comes a procession of puppet figures that brings onto the screen the whole cast of personages and powers, hundreds in all, whose stories we will see.

Wayang Kulit shows are performed over the course of an entire night, the *dalang* improvising with astonishing art and endurance on a frame story that is taken, most frequently, from the ancient texts like the *Mahabharata*, accompanied by the percussive, metallic music of a *gamelan* orchestra. If the illuminated screen defeats the darkness, the shadows that move across that screen yet recover

Wayang Kulit, Bali. 2002. Photograph by Otto Stadler.

and redeem the dark; they take pieces of the night and make them speak for older stories and myths. The *dalang*, always alone at his work, is the master of shadows and yet also their servant, the voice of all of them, shaman and clown at once. Part of the power of the shows, again, is that the shadows the figures cast on the screen are never perfectly clear. The screen is like the surface of a muddy pond or an aquarium filled with green water, through which we glimpse the movement of fishes dimly at first, and only clearly when they are just at the surface (though these shadows never can break the surface as a fish might, leaping at an insect or pulled up by an angler's line). So there is always a sense of mysterious depth, a third dimension of motion and substance and time that yet doesn't belong to a world that we as fully rounded bodies can inhabit. A figure is lifted a little from the screen, then pressed closely against it along part of its length, passing, crossing, moving, and out of view. This process gives the bodiless shadows a life and history of their own, gives them a flickering body of a sort, created in collaboration with flat cutouts and the operating hands we cannot see, yet know are there. The shadows are like writing that has gained a life of its own, lifting above or burying itself more deeply in soft, white paper; that writing traces ancient histories, a story cycle always known yet always varied in each performance, the stuff of the audience's shared memory and present understanding of the world, embedding those watching in a larger substance that is already inside them.

A traditional gloss on this theater suggests a dualistic map, the idea that "from the *dalang* side the *wayang* figures show their bodies, their outside, but from the shadow side they show their souls, their inside." But such shadows seem to me at once the spirits of bodies and embodied spirits, witness of a dream that is at once permanent and always changing. It is a density that is also a lightness, a blackness bound up with light.

The Original Death & Burial of Cock Robin
Shelley Jackson

EXEMPLARY SCENES

A KITTEN IN A VEIL is being married to a kitten in a suit by a kitten in priest's robes with a miniature book sewn to his paw. Gentleman squirrels pack their pipes before a painted fire, while athletic frogs roll hoops, their feet stapled to painted turf. Bunnies study sums, guinea pigs mouth miniature French horns at a cricket match, rats spring their own traps, and ninety-six British birds weep tears of glass at the death of Cock Robin.

MR. POTTER'S MUSEUM OF CURIOSITIES

On September 23 and 24, 2003, on the great flat bruise-colored Cornish moors, at Jamaica Inn (which is a real place, not invented by Daphne du Maurier), the holdings of Mr. Potter's Museum of Curiosities were sold in lots to the highest bidders, and one of the wonders of Victorian England passed into private hands and out of the public view.

The collection included many objects that seemed to have gone through the distorting lens of dream: a church made of white feathers; Tom Thumb's tiny calling card; two pipe-smoking gents, a Squire and a Parson, made from lobster parts; and a number of unusual taxidermy tableaux.

It also included a book of nursery rhymes. This book, not obviously "curious," had belonged to Walter Potter's sister Jane, and contained the rhyme "The Death of Cock Robin."

THE DEATH OF COCK ROBIN

Who killed Cock Robin?
I, said the Sparrow,
With my bow and arrow,
I killed Cock Robin.

Who saw him die?
I, said the Fly,
With my little eye,
I saw him die.

Who caught his blood?
I, said the Fish,
With my little dish,
I caught his blood.

Who'll make the shroud?
I, said the Beetle,
With my thread and needle,
I'll make the shroud.

Who'll dig his grave?
I, said the Owl,
With my pick and shovel,
I'll dig his grave.

Who'll be the parson?
I, said the Rook,
With my little book,
I'll be the parson.

Who'll be the clerk?
I, said the Lark,
If it's not in the dark,
I'll be the clerk.

Who'll carry the link?
I, said the Linnet,
I'll fetch it in a minute,
I'll carry the link.

Who'll be chief mourner?
I, said the Dove,
I mourn for my love,
I'll be chief mourner.

Who'll carry the coffin?
I, said the Kite,
If it's not through the night,
I'll carry the coffin.

Who'll bear the pall?
We, said the Wren,
Both the cock and the hen,
We'll bear the pall.

Who'll sing a psalm?
I, said the Thrush,
As she sat on a bush,
I'll sing a psalm.

Who'll toll the bell?
I, said the bull,
Because I can pull,
I'll toll the bell.

All the birds of the air
Fell a-sighing and a-sobbing,
When they heard the bell toll
For poor Cock Robin.

WALTER POTTER'S BIG IDEA

Walter spent a lot of time with dead birds—peeling off their feathered skins like gloves, pulling them over little fists made of tallow and twine, wiring their claws to twigs. (He was a taxidermist.) So "The Death of Cock Robin" was real to him. Writing can sometimes do that: it can make imaginary robins fly. Then it can let them fall, and make the world mourn the death of what never lived.

Maybe Walter took a professional interest in the trick that makes us see life where there is none. That was his job, too: making twine and feathers seem poised for flight. But the birds in "Cock Robin" didn't just *fly*. The owl used a trowel; the sparrow shot an arrow; the rook read a book. That gave Walter an idea.

It took him seven years to realize it.

Shelley Jackson

THE ORIGINAL DEATH & BURIAL OF COCK ROBIN

The little blue coffin is borne by four birds in black tie through an orderly graveyard with flocked grass in front of a painted backdrop depicting a small country church with five painted birds flying above it. An open grave waits in the foreground, some diminutive bones heaped beside it, as if thrown up by the gravedigger, an owl. A rook in a ribbon holds an open book. The book is real, though tiny. The bull is not real, of course—he's less than a foot tall—though his wooden body is covered with real hide. (Whether cowhide or not, nobody could tell me. It looks improbably *fuzzy* to me, and I wonder, though I find the idea somehow disturbing, whether it might be cat.) Tied to his nose ring is a cord that arcs up to the painted bell tower of the painted church and disappears through a small square hole cut in the backdrop. Birds perch in the mossy branches, real, that protrude from painted trees. Like the supernumerary birds in the separate compartment under the gabled roof, these take more birdlike poses than the mourners below. They could be specimens from a museum of natural history, were it not for the glass beads glued to their cheeks.

The entire poem is painted in gold on the wooden frame. A button beside each stanza lights up the corresponding part of the scene. (As Edison did not invent the lightbulb until 1879, this feature must have been added later.)

THE LIFE OF WALTER POTTER

Walter was born July 2, 1835, in the small town of Bramber, where his father kept the White Lion Inn. He taught himself the art of taxidermy, practicing on rats and chicks and kittens the local farmers gave him. He wasn't much good at it; his mounts were stiff, scrunched, and shapeless. But his ambition was great. In 1861, at the age of twenty-six, he unveiled *The Original Death & Burial of Cock Robin* in the garden of the White Lion, to general amazement.

Gratified by the attention, he made many more tableaux that, like *Cock Robin,* showed animals behaving like men. Some illustrate rhymes or proverbs ("The House that Jack Built," "Babes in the Woods"); others, conventional scenes of daily life—the schoolroom, the gentleman's club, the cricket game. Over time, Walter added

331

many other curiosities, some donated by visitors, to what had become a bona fide museum. He died in 1918, after a stroke.

LOOK, LARK

The Original Death & Burial of Cock Robin is, frankly, kitsch. It's naive about representation and unpleasantly insouciant—to a twenty-first-century eye—about the serious business of death. And yet it gives me the same feeling of beautiful trouble as Cornell's boxes or Nabokov's *Pale Fire* (works also preoccupied with birds and death). The excavating owl seems on the verge of breaking through into a maze of mirrors.

To find my way, I find I need to name each turn, out loud, slowly: real dead birds . . . representing real live birds . . . representing imaginary live birds . . . mourn a real dead bird . . . representing an imaginary dead bird . . . represented by words . . . in a poem. (It is possible that the imaginary dead bird of the poem represents something else again. We'll return to that point.)

Actually, it's even more complicated, because the dead robin, like the "live" owl, is not a real dead robin, since that would quickly decompose, but a semblance made of a robin's skin filled with wax and twine.

To one side of the grave lie the bones of a real dead bird, representing an imaginary bird (Potter's flourish—it's not in the rhyme) that has been dug up to make room for Cock Robin. This bird was itself buried once, and presumably mourned, but has been forgotten; once an individual, it has become nothing but bones. In other words, by an imaginary trajectory it has returned to the place it really occupies: simple, anonymous dead-animalness. It occurs to me as a peculiar wrinkle that those bones were probably taken from one of the other birds in the tableau.

The bull is especially tricky. It's a *fake* dead animal (there is no bull the size of a rook) made of the hide of a *real* dead animal (possibly one of a whole different species) in imitation of a real but much larger dead animal, representing a real live animal, representing an imaginary live animal in a rhyme. Furthermore, the bull is tolling, with a real bellpull, an invisible bell in a painted church tower. The real string feeds through a hole in the backdrop, behind which, for all I know (the docent could not tell me), it may be tied to a small but real bell; if so, this real bell represents the imaginary bell of the poem, and if it tolled, its tinkle would represent the *dong* of the bell in the poem, though because that bell is much bigger, we know it would sound a lower note—if it existed.

What is it about the human mind that believes it is possible to make a distinction between one kind of imaginary sound, that of a bell ringing in a poem, and another, that of an unseen bell that may or may not exist—and believes that the distinction is real, even if neither bell exists? Yet we seem to delight in such distinctions, and in testing them.

Trompe l'œil painting draws on this delight. In a painting depicting a recently slain game bird, the illusion of a dead bird is taken for a real dead bird. In a taxidermy tableau, on the other hand, a real dead bird bodies forth an illusion. Instead of objects replaced by images, images are replaced by objects. The passage between the two might be figured by the cord around the bull's neck—a real cord attached to a painted tower.

But taxidermy is not a simple inversion of trompe l'œil, turning three dimensions back into two. The stuffed bird does not stand for a painted bird, but for an imaginary bird conjured up in a poem. Walter Potter translated words into the objects to which they refer.

This is a weird reversal of the usual order of signification. Words, we commonly think, refer to things. The simplest sentence is a kind of verbal pointing: "Look, lark!" Reference is more complicated in literature: we know that the lark of poetry—Shelley's "blithe spirit," for example—does not exist outside the poem ("bird thou never wert," indeed), so we do not bother to look out the window for it. It's conjured up in our minds by words. Nonetheless, those words, we believe, are signs for things, and a lark is a thing, even if in this case an absent and imaginary one.

In Potter's tableau, the real dead lark signifies the word "lark," which itself signifies another lark, imagined by the anonymous author of the rhyme: a living lark endowed with clerical skills, who therefore must be, to some uncertain degree, human. Potter's lark, which once flew, sang, and ate bugs, folds over upon this clerical lark with its inkwell and quill, both more real than it and, in another sense, a whole step further from real.

How can that be? Surely a stuffed lark is a better representation of a lark than the four shapes we agree to see as letters, spelling a word, "lark," that (assuming we speak English) we agree to understand as meaning that "blithe spirit." Surely the most vivid way to represent a thing is by holding up the thing itself.

But there are problems with taxidermy as an object language: 1. The stuffed lark is dead; the poetic lark is alive. 2. The stuffed lark is a real bird; the poetic lark is an imaginary bird. 3. The stuffed lark is a particular, historical bird; the poetic lark must be reinvented by every reader.

The stuffed lark, for all these reasons, does more than represent the poetic lark; it foists its own, literal presence on the onlooker. So two larks compete for our attention, one of them agile and imaginary; the other stiff, a little dusty, and visibly dead. Our attention splits. One part attends to the story of Cock Robin, the other part to a dead bird.

But doesn't the word "lark" have some of the same problems? Certainly, it interferes much less with the imaginary lark it represents, because it's not as interesting to look at as a dead bird. But it, too, splits our attention. Readers can usually overlook this. Writers, though, can't write without attending to the material of language: the clicks and moos of k's and o's, the lag and lurch of commas and full stops, the black and white of the page. Like Potter, Shelley kept the living lark in mind, but he, too, spent a lot of time fiddling with feathers.

I mean "feathers" figuratively, of course. (Though Shelley did use a quill pen.) Words are not pieces of dead animals. But I sense, all the same, that there is some connection between language and death.

The first bird was a lark, said Aesop, and she was created before the world was. When her father died, she had to bury him inside her own head, for lack of other burial ground. (I'd like to see *that* tableau.) One could read this as an allegory of memory. The mind is a cemetery in which the past is buried, and thought itself is elegiac.

So is taxidermy. Many of Potter's rats were supplied by one industrious dog who wound up in a glass case in his turn, after leaping out of a barn window in pursuit of his last rat. This dog stands alone, which is not characteristic of Potter's style. But this is not just any dog. It's a dog with a *name* (Spot). A dog who was, obviously, loved, and mourned.

Nobody mourned the rats he killed. Still, recall that the first tableau Potter did depicted a funeral—a strange funeral, in which all the guests are also dead. So let's try and figure out: Who is in mourning here? For whose loss?

BUT FIRST, A BRIEF HISTORY OF TAXIDERMY

Like literature, taxidermy has genres.

Most common (as in fiction) are the realists. Carl Akeley, taxidermist to the Museum of Natural History in New York, eschewed crumpets and cravats: let squirrels be squirrels. His tableaux aspire to capture moments from real life, like photographs in three dimensions.

Of course, there's nothing realistic about that. The more successful the illusion of stopped motion, the more uncanny the scene: what could be weirder than a gull stopped midflap, each feather in place? Realism in literature is achieved through highly artificial means, and taxidermy is no different. Nor could a nature photographer hope to seize such iconic scenes—perfect generational groupings posing among characteristic flora. The tableaux are like those shrines in which statues of saints are ringed by the symbols of their martyrdom. Every element signifies: the cactus, the hummingbird, the three-pronged print in the "wet" mud by the "spring." Around the elk or rhino, smaller animals—chipmunks, quail—cavort like cherubs. Their heaven, though, is not cloud-cuckoo-land, but an idealized representation of their native habitat.

It's a world from which the hunter has been erased. We behind the glass are his stand-ins, looking at a world we have kept by killing it. But we are invisible. In sonorous darkness we drift, shadows passing before radiant, unblinking ones whose only purpose now is to be seen. They address themselves to the glass as to a mirror. (Reflect: if they could see, the glass *would* be a mirror. We'd be invisible, offering no chance of the cross-species communion evoked in Julio Cortázar's *Axolotl.*) Like characters in a novel or on stage, even their solitude is public. Like porn stars they strike poses that afford a complete view of what in real life is usually out of sight, and they offer this view as proof of the real, even as the support of the real—as the *realer* real, which both is and represents itself at once. This is realism's paradoxical claim: through artifice, to make the real realer than real itself.

If scientific taxidermy is realism, trophy taxidermy is romance. The snarling tiger tells the story of the perilous courtship between man and beast, which always ends the same way. Trophy taxidermy celebrates man's triumph over nature.

Anthropomorphic taxidermy is the despised genre of fantasy. Few practice it, but Walter Potter wasn't the only one, or even the first.

In 1851, three years before Potter had even started *Cock Robin*, Hermann Ploucquet, a naturalist at the Royal Museum of Stüttgart, Württemberg, displayed over fifteen hundred mounts at the Great Exhibition at the Crystal Palace. Most of these were realistic tableaux, "illustrative of animal life by its characteristic incidents as well as by the preserved specimens themselves." But his "comical groups" caused a bigger stir. These included illustrations of Goethe's fable "Reineke Fuchs"; Ploucquet, too, borrowed from books. (It is uncertain whether Potter was one of the thousands who visited Ploucquet's work at the Great Exhibition, but it seems likely that he had heard of it.)

Scientific and trophy taxidermy, which shade into one another, are boundary establishing. As Donna Haraway has ably demonstrated, the tableaux in the Museum of Natural History introduce the viewer to an order of nature, with clear hierarchies and subdivisions. Man, invisible in these scenes, is present everywhere as the precondition for this ordering, and is ushered into what is made to seem his proper place in that order: the top.

Anthropomorphic taxidermy, on the other hand, is boundary blurring. Rather than reiterating their natural lives, Potter's animals imitate ours. They go to school, get married, play snooker. We are invited to identify with them. True, this is not exactly the call of the wild, or the "becoming-animal" that Deleuze and Guattari invoke. Like cats and dogs, which Deleuze and Guattari declare to be thoroughly Oedipal animals, Potter's mounts are way too implicated in our human neuroses to provide any access to the animal *other*, any more than those "furries" who put on pointy ears and a tail and attend conventions in Holiday Inns.

What they might provide is an encounter with the animal in ourselves.

True, they rely for their effect on the consciousness of difference. One must probably be persuaded that animals never serve tea to find it peculiarly pleasing when they do. Maybe the sight is so preposterous that it confirms our humanity. "I might not be much of a man," the thinking might go, "but compared to a squirrel, I cut a fine figure at the club." But I suspect that inner voice might actually whisper, "Yes, I, too, have felt that way, a little awkward on my hind legs, claws slipping on the pool cue. I, too, have wondered how I wound up here. I, too, have the nagging feeling that I'm on some sort of stage, even if I can't hear the applause." Donna Haraway has said, "We would do well not to anthropomorphize the human, too."

In *Our Mutual Friend*, written only a few years after Potter unveiled his great tableau, Dickens exhibits a rival one: "a pretty little dead bird lying on the counter, with its head drooping on one side against the rim of Mr. Venus's saucer, and a long stiff wire piercing its breast. As if it were Cock Robin, the hero of the ballad, and Mr. Venus were the sparrow with his bow and arrow, and Mr. Wegg were the fly with his little eye." Note that here it is the people who resemble animals, not the other way around.

Dickens may not have known about Potter, but he did visit the Great Exhibition. He must have seen Ploucquet's tableaux, or if not, something very like them. (*Our Mutual Friend* also features "two preserved frogs fighting a small-sword duel.") He understood something about them that Potter may not have: likening works both ways. In Potter's tableaux we find the performing animal in ourselves.

THE LOST WORLD

Children have not yet lost it. To children, adult behavior is a game of pretend: inexplicable rituals in fancy dress. So where we most often meet dressed-up animals is in children's books. But talking animals have a darker, more venerable history. The dinky, impotent birds and bunnies of children's books (I exempt that other Potter, Beatrix, whose rabbits have a bracing dignity) are the sanitized, domesticated revenants of the animist beast-gods of ancient Britain. Potter shows us these gods, murdered, stuffed, and propped up in an artificial Arcadia outside of the reach of time.

That Arcadia, the England of cottage gardens and cricket games, was already under assault in Potter's day. Akeley created the Museum of Natural History tableaux to preserve his vision of unspoiled nature (Haraway points out the tragic irony—of which Akeley was aware—that his campaign to preserve it itself aided a little in the spoiling). Bizarrely, Potter's tableaux preserve a threatened way of life for *humans*. There are no factories in these tableaux, no cities, no slums. Citizens of an agrarian way of life, these rabbits and kittens and squirrels and chicks are preserving a human fantasy of a rural Arcadia. They are the Kinks' "Village Green Preservation Society."

Possibly what we are mourning, then, is our own lost past.

But how can we mourn what we've never known? Already these

tableaux evoke other representations—scenes in books and paintings—more than that Arcadia itself, of which few of us have firsthand knowledge. We can imagine a time when that Arcadia will exist *only* in its representations. When that time comes, the world in Potter's tableaux will seem an original, not a copy—itself something to be imitated.

In Italo Calvino's *Invisible Cities*, the city of Eusapia has an identical copy underground, peopled only by corpses. Every change in the city above is reflected in the city below. However, the city below also seems to change subtly from time to time; the city aboveground has taken to imitating it. In fact, "[t]hey say that this has not just now begun to happen: actually it was the dead who built the upper Eusapia, in the image of their city. They say that in the twin cities there is no longer any way of knowing who is alive and who is dead."

BEING DEAD

If I am right that we identify with the animals in these frozen tableaux, we are not just "becoming animal." We are also becoming *dead*.

The animals are not just dead, of course. Like dolls, they must look alive enough to support our fantasies. Really they are indeterminate, neither quite dead nor fully alive. In fact, it is this in-between status that makes them tools to dream with. If they were really alive they would not act out our fantasies; if they were purely fantastic they would have no material presence. Their substantiality helps body forth the dream. But it also resists it: the doll has a body, which makes it realer than a daydream, and yet it's a *doll's* body. The squirrel with the snooker cue is real, but it's really *dead*. The fantasy must coexist with this knowledge.

I would argue that this knowledge does not necessarily damage the fantasy. It might even provide part of its pleasure.

A modern American life, broadly speaking, is deficient in gunk. We are cleaner than any age before us, and the surfaces we touch are smoother. We know more about how the world works but less about how it feels. Our hands are, I think, a little starved for the touch of the world—for its nap, its grain, its *tooth*. What's more, in employing our hands as instruments, we forget they are also objects. Recently, I visited what I call "the two-headed calf store" in the East

Village, New York (its real name is Obscura Antiques and Oddities). In its narrow, cluttered space one can find two stuffed Mexican toads tippling tequila, a wax model of a leprotic nose, or a blackened, tiny human hand in a box. The hand appears dense, gummy, like an ancient dried apricot. That it was once human is a distant abstraction. It is a *thing*.

And it is a reminder. The dead do not depart. They don't "pass on." They stick around, and join the material world.

The Victorians knew this better than we do, because they knew death better—so many of their friends were dead. They created memorial art from the intricately coiled and braided hair of the departed: a hair angel hoisting a hair soul up out of an open hair tomb near weeping willows of hair; a hair lamb at the foot of a hair cross, a hair dog guarding a hair tomb. These are worlds in which everything—the memorial, the mourners, the landscape itself—is the lost loved one.

To a modern eye, raiding the dead for an arts and crafts project is tasteless and creepy, not to mention unsanitary. Witness the consternation at Gunther von Hagens's exhibitions of Plastinates (specially treated, dissected human bodies). These were volunteers, however. When the dead did not give their consent, our reaction is sharper; there is a special hell, we are convinced, for those Nazis who enjoyed lampshades and letter openers made from those they killed. We fear a vicious killer, but a whimsical one revolts us. This is true even when it comes to animals. Though we see (or eat or wear) dead animals almost every day, Nathalia Edenmont's photographs of severed cat heads bizarrely balanced on vases shock us, and so do Potter's tableaux. I feel this shock. But I suspect that part of it lies in unexamined feelings about our place in the material world. Death, to modern Westerners, is abstract, an almost mathematical operation of subtraction. By custom, by euphemism, by the undertaker's arts, by medical practice, the materiality of the corpse is kept out of view. When we see it openly displayed, it is obscene, but also, if we're honest, a little thrilling.

I said we join the material world when we die. But that is not quite right. We are already part of the material world. We forget it because thinking makes us feel vaporous, unreal, but while we think we gurgle and steam. We are not so different from the dolls we play with: something in us resists the stories we dream up. We are characters, but we are also stuff—bone, meat, goo. This is what we "leave behind" when we die. It's the same thing animals leave. When we look at a taxidermy tableau, we see the stuff a living thing was made of. This resists the fantasy and survives it. "Bunnies at school" fades, but something remains: the dust on a fur coat, the light in the shaft of a whisker.

Now hold a piece of your own hair to the light.

In taxidermy animals, we locate the relic in us, what repels understanding and fellow feeling, the part of us that remains outside our own knowledge.

Maybe the death all the birds of the air are mourning for is ours?

THE EMPTY COFFIN

I have a confession to make. When I explicated the chain of substitutions between Potter's stuffed birds and the birds in the poem, I forgot that Cock Robin doesn't actually appear there. That real dead bird representing an imaginary dead bird? I made it up. What's really there, as I can easily see in the postcard that has been propped up on my desk the whole time I have been writing this, is a little blue coffin, probably empty.

In fact, the one dead bird that *isn't* there is the one named in the poem.

I'm surprised, because Walter is otherwise scrupulous, even slavish in reproducing the poem. Maybe he left it out lest it undermine the illusion. How could he, with his limited skills, make *one* dead bird look deader than the rest?

But no: Walter is right, I'm wrong. In the poem, as in the tableau, Cock Robin is absent. The stage seems to hold everything *but* Cock Robin. At the center is an empty coffin.

"The Death of Cock Robin"—both rhyme and tableau—commemorates a loss. But whose loss? Is Cock Robin just a bird? Many scholars have thought otherwise, seeing the rhyme as allegory, and Cock Robin as, variously, Robin Hood, the Earl of Essex, Jesus, and the Norse god Balder. Freud, however, might propose something closer to home. (*Cock* Robin?)

If allegory works through displacement and substitution, then fetishism is a kind of allegory. As Freud tells it, the little boy (Freud believed all fetishists to be male), on discovering that women have no penis, fears greatly for his own. "Who killed Cock Robin?" the child asks, alarmed, and switches his affections to something less

340

unnerving. An intermediate object, Freud calls it, and he means that quite literally, because often it's something you might find on your way to the vagina (if you were working your way up from the floor, as children do).

The substitute relies for its charge on the repressed desire for (and anxiety about) the genitals, but that is not to say that the shoe is just a disguised vagina. The fetishist *really likes shoes.* He articulates his desire solely in terms of, say, tiny eyelets, the smell of leather, and the glint of light on a polished heel.

Is this so different from what I was saying about taxidermy, dolls, and our own bodies? We relish the stuff. In fact, it seems to me, *pace* Freud, that all objects are fetish objects, including the genitalia: material things that simultaneously possess considerable fascinations of their own, and stand in for something else. That something can never be grasped, because it is a phantasm—the pure object of desire. As Lacan says, it must remain unattainable, or what you want would cease to be what you want, and become what you have. "You can't always get what you want"? Actually, you can't *ever* get what you want.

It may be, then, that the loss mourned in Cock Robin cannot be named. Cock Robin is loss itself. Our lives are, in this sense, one long funeral.

But the coffin is empty, as it has to be, and there are robins everywhere.

Of course, fetishists usually prefer things that are closer to the ground. Common fetishes include shoes, feet, stockings, socks; leather, lace, silk, and fur.

WHICH BRINGS ME TO THE KITTEN WEDDING

The case is stuffed with kittens, in orderly rows and matching lace-trimmed frocks. Much effort went into the tiny dresses with their tinier stitches, but the kittens themselves are Potter's worst work. Their skin is scrunched and awry. Their balding heads are round, as if the skin had been pulled over a balled sock, not a skull, so the eyes goggle like cloves stuck in an orange, and the thin mouths, pulled crooked, have the look of mouths that will be crying soon.

"Do you, death, take death to be your lawfully wedded bride?" Death poses the question before an audience of the dead, who look shocked. "Aren't they a bit young?" they whisper.

The kittens are the only animals in the Potter museum that are fully clothed. This is, I suspect, because they are at a wedding, which means sex is in the offing. Covering it up just advertises it. Victorians are famous for their pudency, which put cart horses in diapers, piano legs in bloomers, but every fig leaf is also a come-on. Putting clothes on a piano leg might in fact be the only thing that could make it sexy.

The museum literature says the kittens have little knickers on, under their skirts. (Someone looked?) Pussies in panties: the fetish is in very weak disguise here. If this savors unpleasantly of necrophilia, remember that the Victorians risked pregnancy with every fuck, death with every pregnancy, and often survived labor only to see their babies die. Child mortality was so high that toddlers were prepared for their own likely fate by books with titles like *Brief Lives* about saintly children who died young. To associate sex with death you didn't have to be perverted, just observant.

Where do you think all those kittens came from? From barn litters, drowned in barrels: the progeny of all-too-many kitten weddings.

THE HAIR OF THE DOG

As with other fetish objects, the sex appeal of dead kittens lies in their specific materiality. That is, in their fur. The fur (and underlying skin, of course) is just about all of the kitten that's *kitten.* Everything else is plastic—or, in Potter's time, straw, twine, sawdust, and wire. Without fur, they would be lawn sculptures. With it, they are, at least in part, real. Real is a slippery notion, but here it has something to do with the fact that that fur was once actually worn by the creature represented here. The taxidermy animal stands for the live one not just because it resembles it, but because it is *part* of it. It is an example of the literary figure of synecdoche. "The hair of the dog that bit you" is a more familiar example, but it works the same way. The hair stands for the whole dog but it isn't just a spoor. It's also part of the dog. Like the relic of a saint, it doesn't just refer to the saint, it is imbued with the saint's own presence. But it works (if it works) because it isn't identical with the dog. It is both part of and distinct from the dog.

The hair of the dog, as hangover cure, is like a vaccine: a manageable dose of poison that steels you against the real threat. The ancient Greeks had a word that meant both poison and cure: pharmakon. Plato, as Derrida observes, called *writing* a pharmakon. But if writing's the hair of the dog, what's the dog?

Maybe the dog is life. Life is a kind of binge, ultimately mortal. It's not particularly good for us, but it provides all we know of joy, so how can we quit it? Still, we sicken. Language treats life homeopathically, in measured doses. It doesn't cure us of living, because it is *part* of living, but it can help us feel better in the morning.

Or maybe the dog is death.

WRITING AND DEATH

We don't need to say, "Look, lark," if we can point. Language becomes necessary when we want to talk about what isn't there. The lark may fly away, but "blithe spirit" stays. The lark might even die, but fly on forever in verse. For this reason, you might say language is haunted. Even if the lark still lives, its death haunts us in advance, through the word.

This is true of all signs. Roland Barthes says, "In front of the photograph of my mother as a child, I tell myself: she is going to die: I shudder . . . *over a catastrophe which has already occurred.* Whether or not the subject is already dead, every photograph is this catastrophe." Likewise, as Derrida observes, though a friend is standing in front of us, her name stands for the possibility of her absence. We can keep calling it, even when she is dead, and so to name her is already to begin to mourn her loss.

Written words call on people who are even farther gone. On Plato, for example, who thought written words were mere husks—you might even say skins—of the living word, the spoken word, still full of breath. ("If only we could make them breathe," sighs a taxidermist of his models.) This makes written words deceptive and a bit macabre. It also makes them permanent. To make words last, the breath must be squeezed out of them. Then they can be arranged into books.

A book is a three-dimensional crystal of words, a solid block that, like mica, separates easily into sheets. It's the reader who turns it into a story. By running our eyes over it from beginning to end, we supply the passage of time, which has been peeled out of the written word like the vein from a prawn. We allow literature to borrow a length of our life-line and string a plot on it, and in this way the words are pulled before our eyes at the pace of living.

The truth of the matter, though, is that written words, at least in books, are stuck in unchanging constellations. Characters are stiff, simplified figures we arrange in fixed positions to suggest stopped motion. They inhabit shallow foregrounds in which water is not wet, grass is an unnatural green, the background is sketchy, and only the main characters possess three dimensions. Like Potter's and Akeley's, these scenes are often slightly too exemplary to be real— the animals are the ones appropriate to the ecosystem, be it the tundra, the steppe, or the parlor. But above all it is their fixity that renders them unreal.

Occasionally, amidst these stiffs, we find something stiffer. The effect is ambiguous: do the quick seem quicker by contrast, or do they betray their close resemblance to the dead? In Robbe-Grillet's *La Maison de Rendezvous,* a stuffed dog is being walked by a mannequin in a shop window: "The animal has been mounted with great skill. And if it were not for its total immobility, its slightly over-emphasized stiffness, its certainly too-shiny glass eyes that are also too fixed, the excessively pink interior, perhaps, of its gaping mouth, its exaggeratedly white teeth, one would think it was about to complete its interrupted movement." A similar dog appears over and over in the novel. Sometimes it is stuffed, sometimes alive, sometimes a painted statue. For Robbe-Grillet they are all equally real— that is, all fake. The living one is no more genuine (and no more alive), since it too is made from words. Indeed, there is a sense in which *all* characters in literature are dead.

Sometimes one of them seems to know it—to open its eyes and see the cracked glass, smell the dust, feel the beetles crepitating under its skin. Try reading a few paragraphs of Beckett's *The Unnamable* as if it were narrated by a stuffed buffalo head. I think this is not altogether to abuse Beckett, whose lifelong work was acknowledging the death in life, the life in death of literature—and of existence itself.

And yet, over and over, we are willingly deceived: we see life where none is. Often it lies in fleeting details: A tiny striated rainbow in eyelashes. Light creaming on a pale breast. The nervous jerk in a red Adam's apple. Where did we get these? Captured them from life, of course. We have, somehow, the capacity to take an impression and fix it in words. I do not mean that we kill the moment by noticing it (though some writers have felt so), or that we hunt human trophies and set them up in fierce poses to show how bold we are (though some writers do). I mean to say only that when we prop up our prize in a novel, it is no longer anything living, but a piece of fixity that depends on the viewer's affectionate familiarity to reanimate it.

Because this is the paradoxical aim: to coax motion out of stasis, life out of dead matter. Like taxidermy, literature traffics in the stuff of death in order to transcend it. It sets itself against the normal decay of evanescent things, the erasure of every gesture, the instant dissipation of every spoken word. As Elaine Scarry demonstrates, it presents precisely what never lasts (transparency, sheen, a gesture), and thereby gives the illusion of life's lightness and lambency. This is fiction's glass eye. It is fake, but it shines on the page like life. Just so, the taxidermist freezes the alarmed flick of a tail, the cocked head, to make this fixed scene seem to last an instant only (because instants are all we ever have, in life, the just-for-an-instant-ness of life is precisely its register, that by which we know it, and yet because we are grabby fetishists we want to hold on to what, like a preserved frog, loses its slipperiness when we preserve it), but an instant to which we can return, magically, forever.

Taxidermy and literature both aspire to keep the living moment. This is true even when the living moment has had its head cut off and mounted on a plaque: synecdoche rules, as in portrait photography. The head is enough to capture a likeness. But it is only by removing what is truly temporal (decaying flesh, the fugitive) that the impression of temporality can be fixed. A dose of death is administered, homeopathically, to arrest death's course.

But only with our help. In Flaubert's story "A Simple Faith," Jesus appears in the figure of a stuffed parrot wired to a cruciform perch. The parrot spreads its wings before a dying woman, offering her a redemption animated by misprision—or, if you prefer, by imagination. Whether this is a real redemption or not depends on your opinion of God. But it is all the redemption literature offers.

Dickens had a pet raven, Grip. Grip died suddenly, and Dickens described the event to his friend and biographer John Forster in almost Potterian terms. "At half-past, or thereabouts, he was heard talking to himself about the horse and Topping's family, and to add some incoherent expressions which are supposed to have been either a foreboding of his approaching dissolution, or some wishes relative to the disposal of his little property: consisting chiefly of half-pence which he had buried in different parts of the garden. On the clock striking twelve he appeared slightly agitated, but he soon recovered, walked twice or thrice along the coach-house, stopped to bark, staggered, exclaimed Halloa old girl! (his favourite expression), and died." Dickens had Grip stuffed. You can find him perched on a rock amidst dried grasses against a painted sky in a wooden box (Dickens's handiwork) in the rare book room of the Philadelphia Free Library. You can also find him in the fiction section, because Grip was the model for the raven of the same name in *Barnaby Rudge*.

You might also find him in poetry. Allegedly, Poe read *Barnaby Rudge* with particular interest. Poe's raven, like both Grips, the real and the fictional, can talk. But like all talking birds, he has a limited vocabulary. In fact, he knows only one word. He repeats it mechanically; he cannot "mean" anything by it, and yet meaning alights upon it and roosts. It does not matter whether or not the raven is the demon he appears to be; he is a "prophet still, if bird or devil," for he gives voice to the knowledge in the listener's own heart.

This is astonishing. If meaning does not lie in words themselves, or in the intentions of the speaker, then the meaning of Poe's poem, too, does not lie in the poem, or Poe. *"The Raven" is a talking raven.* "Nevermore," it repeats. It doesn't know what it's saying, but it might tell the truth all the same. It depends on how we read it.

THE EYE

We have come full circle, and are looking at ourselves looking.

Writing is often compared to a window. Through it, we see a world. But every window can also be a mirror, and show us ourselves looking. It just depends on the light you shine on it.

As *Pale Fire* reflects, the reader reads *himself*—or herself. If she reads well, that reading enriches both the reader and the read. If poorly, both lose. "Mirror, mirror": the magic mirror that tells the truth is always named twice. Maybe that's because every mirror has two sides. If the image in the mirror resembles us, we also resemble it. Like the citizens of Eusapia, mirrored by their dead, we do not know for sure who is imitating whom.

When I look at Potter's tableaux, I see myself, as he intended, but not the way he intended. I do not see the schoolmarm or the student, the bride or the tippler. I see an animal awkwardly attired in human clothes, performing rituals it doesn't completely understand. I see skin, hair, teeth. I see a corpse-to-be.

TEN UNPRODUCED SCENARIOS

The Quay Brothers

PINUS SYLVESTRIS

THE ADVENTURES OF AN AVON LADY

ÜBER VERSCHIEDEN FORMEN DER
LUSTGEWINNUNG AM EIGENEN LEIBE

STILLE NACHT V

STILLE NACHT VI

NIGHTWATCH

LILIUM INTER SPINAS

EROTIK

MIRRHA ELECTA

EX VOTO

PINUS
SYLVESTRIS

§

WITH THE THEATER CURTAIN DOWN, the house lights lower slowly. As the audience settles down, their ears are already perceiving a chorus of crickets behind the curtain. They are heard for another minute before the curtain swiftly rises to reveal a solid wall of tree trunks right to the height of the proscenium. The crickets persist but then we slowly begin to distinguish the sound of chopping. One tree in particular begins to shudder from the assault. Our eyes are now fixed upon this one tree. Then with a start we see it list precariously and begin to fall headlong into the audience. It's stopped halfway, but not before actors in the front row dressed as audience members have already scattered. As they return sheepishly to their seats, a man now appears on stage with an axe and with a supreme effort pushes the tree back up.

The sound of the crickets continues but is gradually displaced by the harsher sound of drilling. For nearly another minute we listen to drilling and only drilling. Then the massive facade of tree trunks lifts slowly to reveal an even more impenetrable wall. Behind this wall there is still the sound of drilling. Occasionally it stops only to begin again.

Suddenly the volume of the drilling increases. Flying down in front of this wall is a duplicate wall only seen from 180° behind. Attached to this quickly descending wall is the man who is doing the actual drilling himself. As the wall and he simultaneously meet the floor, his drilling breaks through to the other side and we see him disappear inside the rubble of this hole.

Then, far off, the sound of chopping is heard again. The front curtain lowers and conceals the wall entirely. Behind it the chopping still continues. Suddenly there is an irregular pause and then the unmistakable creaking sound of a huge tree falling. There is an awesome crash and the front curtain billows out as dust blows from underneath it into the front row of the audience.

AFTER NEARLY ANOTHER MINUTE of dust settling, the curtain rises on a nineteenth-century facade. Through an open window we see the haze of dust still slowly settling. Suddenly this entire facade lifts to reveal an enormous fallen tree that has just demolished a dining table in the middle of a zebra crossing. Off to the right, surrounded by other pieces of furniture, is a woman naked to her waist, seated in profile, holding a teacup in one hand and a saucer in the other. She is observing over her shoulder the tree that has just cloven her table in half a few centimeters from her elbow. A man on his knees between her legs now looks over her thighs to observe the carnage. Farther off in the same direction that the couple are looking is yet another man. He is wearing dark glasses and stands motionless in front of a traffic light. His face is turned in their direction and from all impressions he would appear to be observing *them* and not the *tree*. It is only as the traffic light changes and the sound of high "peeping" is heard that we realize the man is blind. With a stick he slowly taps his way across the stage and carefully steps over the fallen tree. As he passes, he is closely scrutinized by the couple until he disappears offstage. Taking a further sip of tea, she returns her gaze to the fallen tree, and he to the confines of her thighs. Meanwhile the constantly changing traffic light appears to add a further dimension to their dialogue.

SHE:

Not so hard, please.

In the distance we hear the sound of drilling again. She seems almost
oblivious to his ministrations. The traffic light turns red. The drilling stops
immediately. He looks up.

HE:

I didn't think they did that.

She continues to observe the fallen tree. The traffic light turns green.
His head lowers between her opened thighs and the sound of
drilling starts again.

SHE:

You mean entering without knocking.

She takes another sip of tea and places the cup back on the saucer.
The traffic light changes to red. His head withdraws. The drilling stops,
and we hear his voice contained in the hollow of her thighs.

HE:

{Without looking up}

No . . . using that disguise.

His head returns and the sound of drilling continues.
Putting the teacup down, she looks in the direction of the traffic light.

SHE:

But that's why we're here.

HE:

Disguised like this.

The light changes to green. His head is gently consumed by
her thighs again.

SHE:

Yes . . . disguised as people.

G RADUALLY THE STAGE HAS BECOME DARKER.
The drilling is no longer heard and only the traffic light is
visible changing from green to red to green. The sound of
metal scraping against stone is heard. From downstage right two
stonemasons are seen entering backward on hands and knees, alternately

sliding work implements and plastic cups of coffee. They stop and with string begin to measure and prepare laying cobblestones into the floor. Looking around, they both sit back on their legs, light up cigarettes, sip their coffee, and begin chatting expansively. Their lips move but we don't hear a word. Suddenly, from the rear of the stage, a car is heard turning a corner and the sweep of its headlights catches them *in flagrante*. Instantly they are back on their hands and knees laying cobblestones. But no sooner have they laid another one than they are back on their knees smoking, chatting, and drinking coffee again. Once again the sound of a car and the sweep of its headlights exposes them loitering. Immediately they are back on the floor again laying another cobblestone. Then they look at each other, finish their coffee, toss the cups aside, and leave the way they came in. In the distance the traffic light clicks from green to red. As they disappear offstage, the high "peeping" sound is heard. Immediately a car is heard as it brakes to a halt. Its headlights spray harshly across the entire stage and silhouette the couple. We hear a car door open and close. Then, emerging from the shadows along the side, we see a figure creeping downstage casting glances along the way, but utterly oblivious of the couple. As he arrives at the front, we hear him muttering to himself as he crosses to the cobblestones. Kicking aside the two cups, he bends down and tries desperately to pry up the stones. He attacks various ones but to no avail. Standing up again, he starts shouting at them. Finally pulling out a gun and aiming, he fires five shots into the stones. Suddenly the high "peeping" is heard. Turning around in the glare of the car headlights, he runs quickly upstage, pauses at the zebra crossing, waits for the light to turn green, then crosses, steps over the tree, and exits offstage. As the car door is heard closing, it backs up and the headlights swing away. Suddenly there is silence. A light comes up on the couple. In the distance we hear the sound of drilling. The woman takes another sip of tea. The traffic light turns red. The drilling stops. He looks up.

T HE STAGE GROWS STILL DARKER. Toward the front there can be heard the faint shifting of stones grinding against each other. This continues until one of the cobblestones suddenly dislodges and lifts to the surface. A second and third follow and almost immediately they are gently floating in the air. A fourth and fifth also follow in their path. Outlined only by the traffic lights, the couple can be seen gazing at these cobblestones as they rise gracefully toward the theater ceiling. While eyes follow these ascending stones, black cloths along the wings are flown up to reveal, along the entire length of both sides of the stage, facades of village houses facing one another. Suddenly loud rapping on glass is heard. Then, in the farthest upstage window, we see a hand cleaning the inside of the glass with a cloth. This same hand raps on the glass again. The man between the woman's legs rises and approaches. The window is thrust open and this same hand flings a rope into his hand and points to the opposite side. There we see another hand cleaning an identical-looking window. It, too, stops to rap on the glass.

We see him take the line and from this window is pulled all of the woman's washing with the clothes already prepinned to it. As he reaches the far side, the window is thrust open and a hand takes the rope from him. Immediately the next window downstage is thrown open and another line is thrust into his hand by a hand that points to the opposite side. He pulls this line with yet more washing attached to it across the width of the stage, where yet another hand opens a window to receive it. Immediately the next window downstage opens and another hand thrusts out a line that now, when pulled across the stage, half obscures the seated woman. Reaching the other side, a further window opens and another hand grasps the line from him. Immediately a last window explodes open and the final line of washing is flung into his hand. Arriving at the other side, the entire stage is now filled with the village's laundry with only a traffic light and a woman's head visible above it all. As he turns toward the woman, two hands pull his head back inside. There is momentary struggling, then suddenly there erupts from this window the wailing of a baby. The entire village's washing glows luminously as though lit by the moon and the child's wailing. A breeze gently envelops the washing and magically begins to fill out all the clothing with a breathing of its own.

The child's crying turns to gentle cooing. The traffic light is still functioning, and as the washing rises in the rhythm of the breeze, it is only now that we realize the very same man is still between the woman's legs. It is as though he had never left her. The couple are looking in the direction of a man emerging from an open window who once seemed formerly related to them.

PLACATED BY THE BREEZE, the sound of the cooing child is now punctuated by the stirring of the two downstage empty coffee cups by his feet. They now start rolling upstage as though filled by this same sympathetic breeze. The cups continue rolling until they are lost from sight beneath the washing. Although we no longer see them, we hear them. Their progress upstage seems to accord with the sound of all anonymous trash being swept down a street late at night by a cold wind. But slowly these tumbling cups become the sound of horse hooves, more distinctly a horse cantering down a street. This is finally confirmed when the sound of the hooves comes to a halt and we hear boots and spurs dismounting. Heard entirely offstage, these boots approach and then pause, then approach again and stop again. Their rhythm and cadence is deliberately provocative. The sound of the boots and spurs takes another few steps but again we see nothing. Then they are heard even louder and we see emerging from behind the far upstage facade a muscular, hairy, bare-chested man wearing a policeman's hat. Looking straight ahead, he looks more like a cliché policeman from some kind of stud porno magazine. He takes another few steps forward and it is only now that we realize he is entirely naked save for the hat and boots. But another few steps later, we suddenly glimpse an enormous erection through the rising and falling washing. Almost frightening in its stallion length, the potency of both the nudity and the spurs, the hat and the erection make a disturbing combination against the innocently billowing cloth. He takes another few steps and for the first time, he glances over the washing to observe the couple. Distinctly aware of his presence, the woman takes another sip of tea while the man lowers his head between her thighs.

SHE:

Not so hard, please.

The cop, without taking his eyes off them, takes another few steps. The jangling of the spurs adds a flagrant aggression as he basks in the aura of his own phenomenal erectility. There is a distant rumble of thunder. The traffic light turns red. From between her thighs the man looks up.

HE:

I didn't think they did that.

353

The traffic light turns green. The man's head lowers and again distant thunder is heard. The cop has turned the corner and is now proceeding in the opposite direction. Shielded behind the washing, he doesn't take his eyes off them. His rhythm remains demonstrative and provocative.

SHE:
You mean entering without knocking.

Stopping once again, the cop arches his neck backward, aware that his entire body is a walking penis. She takes another sip of tea. There is more thunder and a distant flash of lightning. The traffic light changes to red and the echo of more distant thunder is heard. We hear the man's voice contained in the hollow of her thighs.

HE:
{Without looking up}
No . . . using that disguise.

His head returns and now more urgent thunder is heard. As the woman lowers the cup into the saucer, the cop's head turns toward them. Looking out beyond this provocation, her voice resonates like a whisper.

SHE:
. . . Pinus . . .

SUDDENLY THERE IS A BLINDING FLASH of lightning followed by a massive clap of thunder so awesome that it would appear the theater itself had been struck. Intermittent strobing and dimming give an impression of a massive electrical failure in the theater. At the same time a huge wind envelops the entire stage, swelling and lifting all the clothing on the lines. In all this confusion, we glimpse the clotheslines and village facades being flown out with extraordinary speed. The jangling of spurs has now turned into a soft rain. The cop has mysteriously vanished and a blind man is calmly standing under the traffic light. In this sudden calm we see the tip of his stick, as though in slow motion, falling forward in an arc and striking the zebra crossing. Her voice follows in the same exhorting whisper.

SHE:
. . . Pinus . . .

HE:
{As though gently reminding her}
...Pinus Sylvestris...

SHE:
Only dreams do that.

HE:
Using that disguise.

SHE:
Yes ... but then that's why we're here.

HE:
Because we're pines.

SHE:
Yes ... because we're disguised as pines.

GRADUALLY THE STAGE has become darker. The last rumbles of thunder have disappeared and the couple can now no longer be seen. All that remains is the blind man positioned under the traffic light. The high "peeping" sound is heard and in the darkness we can visibly hear his walking stick blurring across the stage as he carefully navigates the log and disappears from the stage. There is now a complete silence save for the audible clicking of the traffic light from red to green. The original facade of trees now lowers and meets the floor. Not nearly as dense as before, we can still see the traffic light and zebra crossing. Fireflies can now be glimpsed luminously flitting through the trees. Then slowly all sound begins to be sucked away and we hear rushing to the foreground, the closer sound of wind gently buffeting the branches of a tree. As the sound becomes still closer, we begin to feel that we have arrived on the surface of another cosmos. For the first time we hear music, and the voices that are heard are those of the very same couple. Their words are hushed and exalted.

SHE:
You ... Pinus Sylvestris ... here ... wrapped in
the evening breeze.

HE:

With your needles in my face.

SHE:

Pinus Sylvestris. Pinus Linguae.

HE:

You taste of resin.

SHE:

I'm yours made of pine.

HE:

I your restless, roaming fir.

SHE:

And I the firefly under your tongue.

ALMOST IMMEDIATELY a chorus of crickets wells up, but this is instantly obliterated when the traffic light turns red and the high "peeping" can be heard. When the light turns green, the sound of the crickets can be distinguished in the presence of the fireflies. Again the light changes red and the "peeping" sound inundates the forest. The theater curtain drops halfway before slowly lowering to the floor. In the now totally darkened theater, our ears slowly grow accustomed to the lack of sight and we can just now begin to distinguish far off what we imagine to be the sound of chopping—to the degree that we think we are hearing the sound of chopping even when we are still hearing the sound of crickets and the traffic light—even to the degree we think there is now the possibility of two trees being chopped when we are in fact hearing the sound of only crickets and the traffic light. This ambiguity is elaborated for several minutes more before we begin to hear the sound of tapping sticks filling the aisles. Then the house lights are lifted just enough to realize that blind ushers will now make generous attempts to lead people in the direction of the exits. The sound of the chopping increases in volume. The music that we had heard earlier now escorts the people out of the theater.

§

„*TEATR*"

OR SECOND ALTERNATIVE ENDING TO

PINUS SYLVESTRIS

Curtain goes up on a forest. Beautiful smell of pine infiltrates the entire theater. We feel the awesome sanctity and fragrance of a forest tamed inside a theater proscenium. Very slowly one begins to become aware of all the subtleties of sound that a forest can transmit. Suddenly, from out of the rear of the stage, led by a man shouting directions, backs a huge garbage truck with flashing yellow light and the obligatory "beeping" noise of a vehicle backing up. It arrives at the very front of the stage and stops. The engine is turned off. Another man dismounts. There is silence as only their footsteps are heard on the forest floor. One of them presses a button and suddenly the enormous din of another engine shatters the silence, and the rear of the truck laboriously begins to grind the garbage. Slowly an unbearable stench is released and begins to permeate the entire theater. Both men stand by the side of the truck drinking coffee and shouting to one another to make themselves heard. Finally, after what seems like ten minutes, the grinding comes to a halt. The awesome silence and presence of the forest are suddenly restored but it's too late. The stench is simply intolerable. It's like a wall. The two men, now stretching out on the forest floor to nap, are completely unaware of huge portions of the audience slowly filing out holding handkerchiefs over their noses.

✳

357

The Quay Brothers

The Adventures
of an
Avon Lady

COLLECTIVELY MIS-REMEMBERED AS A SCENARIO WRITTEN
IN CIRCA 1957

The camera whips to an interior floor space
showing the lower half of two closed doors. Offscreen we hear
footsteps approaching. A pair of women's high heels enters
the frame and pauses. One foot attempts to negotiate the step
that is in front of these doors but it is too high.
We hear the woman's voice.

SHE:
I'll kill myself one of these days on steps like these.

More footsteps are heard and a pair of men's shoes arrives next to hers.
HE:
*Yeah . . . I remember you promising that only last week. And you were
in the same shoes, too.*

SHE:
But last week I wasn't wearing this skirt.

The camera anticipates her and rises to frame her skirt.
HE:
Here, let me help you.

We see the skirt suddenly fall around her shoes. She steps out of it.
HE:
Everything, darling.

We see the knickers come down, too. She steps out of them as his
hand snatches them from the floor. Stepping up on the door ledge, she
knocks. We see the knickers disappear inside his suit jacket pocket.
SHE:
Don't you think I should put my skirt back on?

HE:
No one will even notice.

The door opens. They enter. We see only the lower halves of people
standing about at a party as her glowing out-of-focus naked thighs are
escorted past the legs of the other partygoers. Arriving in another room,
she immediately sits down at a table and leans into a tiny mirror to
check her makeup. He sits with his back to us on the edge of a table
in the foreground. We see only her eyes in this mirror.
HE:
See . . . I told you no one would notice.

SHE:
OK this time but what about tomorrow?

HE:
Tomorrow! The last time I thought about tomorrow was yesterday.

SHE:
I didn't know you could think in reverse. Here . . . flex a muscle.

She extends a bottle for him to open. In a parody of a weight lifter he
flexes his biceps, then reaches into his pocket, pulls out the knickers,
and drapes them over the top of the bottle, returning both to her.
She unsmilingly opens the top, then promptly throws the knickers back
into his face. Laughingly, he peels them off and stuffs them back into
his pocket. She returns to the mirror. Still grinning, he removes them
once again and threads his hands inside the waistband and ludicrously
stretches them in all directions.

HE:
Say . . . how do you know which is the front?

SHE:
[Still looking at herself in the mirror]
The warm side faces the back.

HE:
[Raising an eyebrow, he leans against the wall]
*Back when I was a kid, I always thought the back door was just where
you took out the garbage. Only the milkman or the neighborhood kids
ever came there . . . or . . . the dog.
Only something really classy would come to the front door . . . and that
was special because only the front door had the doorbell.*

She catches his eye in the mirror.

HE:
[Now twirling her knickers on his index finger]
And guess who I always imagined would ring the doorbell but never did?

SHE:
[Mockingly]
The Avon Lady.

HE:
Hell, honey!!! You know everything, don't you???

The camera now frames her high heels and slowly begins to ascend the entire length of her stockinged legs until it reaches the mirror surface, where we see her fitting on a small hat with a veil.
His dialogue continues.

HE:
It's like whenever the doorbell would ring, I'd peek around the corner hoping it would be her. . . .

SHE:
And . . . ?

HE:
Well . . . she never came.

SHE:
Maybe she was too busy.

HE:
No . . . Not even that.
I just know she never made it to my neck of the woods.

SHE:
And where was that?

HE:
Bethlehem.

SHE:
Never heard of it.

HE:
You never heard of Bethlehem, Pennsylvania?????

Carefully outlining her eyes with a fine pencil, she utterly ignores the question before glancing back into the mirror.

SHE:
Maybe she was a myth?

HE:
Who?

SHE:
Her!

361

HE:

The Avon Lady? No! She wasn't a myth. I even remember seeing pictures of her on TV.

SHE:

Well . . . maybe by the time she got to your block she was already out of makeup.

HE:

She couldn't have. I was waiting for her.

SHE:

[Sarcastically]
She wasn't Santa Claus, you know.

Suddenly looking hard into the depths of her mirror.

HE:

What's that got to do with her?

SHE:

Just that her bag had a bottom.

HE:

And Santa Claus's didn't!!!! Hey!!!! You should talk!!
You never even heard of Bethlehem, Pennsylvania!!
[Returning to his thoughts]
Still . . . I always waited and secretly hoped I'd hear the Avon bells.
I'd imagine she'd be there peering around the edge of the screen door and
it would be like this lush veil covering her face . . . and there I'd be . . .
mouth wide open . . . buck teeth and all . . . looking up at her face getting
closer and closer to mine and . . .

SHE:

[In the mirror we see her eyes turn in his direction]
She was a slut.

HE:

[Thrown from his reverie]
A slut? How would you know?

362

SHE:
[With confident resolve]
How would I know?

We see her face rise from the mirror and turn toward him. The camera slowly dollies back to reveal her nude save only for her stockings and a glimpse of the hat and small veil. The camera comes to a halt behind him just as her thighs arrive and press between his knees. She raises her hand and gently places two fingers on his eyes.
SHE:
How would I know?

As she pushes firmly on both eyes, we hear that distinctive sound of the doorbells.
SHE:
Because I'm her. I'm "Avon Calling."

It is the unmistakable voice of the Avon Lady. The knickers drop from his fingers and fall next to her shoes. We see her fingers delicately pick them up. Without taking her eyes off him, she brings the knickers slowly to her nose, sniffs them gently, then pulls them over his head. Pausing a second, she spins them around another half revolution.
SHE:
There! I've put the warm side to the front.

Exiting swiftly past him, she leaves the frame. The camera now tracks in upon his hooded face as he turns slowly in the direction of her still echoing footsteps. When his face entirely fills the cinemascope frame, her knickers can be seen gently sucking in and out inside his nostrils. The irregular sound of his breathing is all that can be heard.

The Quay Brothers

ÜBER VERSCHIEDEN FORMEN DER LUSTGEWINNUNG AM EIGENEN LEIBE

VARIOUS FORMS OF PLEASURABLE GRATIFICATION UPON ONE'S BODY

THIS CASE HISTORY ORIGINATED IN A SMALL TOWN
THAT LAY BETWEEN THE CARDINAL TOWNS OF
BISTRITZ, KARITSCHEN, HALLENKAU, WSETIN
(MORAVIA), AND UGROCZ (HUNGARY).
THIS TOWN BOASTED MANUFACTURING
WITHOUT GLUE. ONLY ONE OF THEIR SONS
NEEDED REPAIRING. UNFORTUNATELY,
HE REQUIRED THE GLUE.

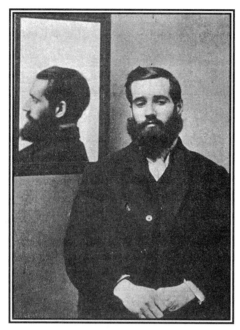

CASE 81. F.K. 1883

A PROVINCIAL AUSTRO-HUNGARIAN DOCTOR'S OFFICE;
a fly is seen crawling over a telephone. A pencil point enters the
frame and tries to distract it. A wider shot reveals a doctor sitting
beside a desk too small for him. He is talking on a telephone to a
colleague as he plays with the fly. Observing opposite him in shadow
is the back of a patient's head. He is distracted by the waiting and
his head occasionally follows the banal activities of an administering
nurse as she busies herself around the office. So bored is he that
should she reach for something, his arms will involuntarily lift.
Simultaneously he will glance at the doctor to see if he has been
noticed. He has been noticed. The entire time on the telephone, the
doctor will not move from his chair and will barely take his eyes off
the patient. Occasionally he will nod his head, agree or disagree with
his invisible colleague. All dialogue will be in Hungarian and
subtitled in English.
The doctor's eyes now follow something invisible in the air.
The patient rises in silhouette and corrects something in his pocket
before seating himself again.

[DOCTOR:]
*Satin...yes....She has repeatedly stolen it
in department stores....For nearly two years now...
and each time it's with the onset of menstruation....
Exactly....
The first time she rolled it up and simply
went off with it between her legs...the next time
she claimed it was at the behest of a vision....*

We see the doctor's eyes still following the flight of the fly. As the patient turns to casually observe the nurse retrieving some fallen documents, he looks back at the doctor, who is now manipulating a partially stunned fly with the tip of his pencil.

[DOCTOR:]
*...Yes...Catholic...thirty-two...slightly neurasthenic....
Apparently she passed it into a large bag beneath
her skirts and then masturbated publicly in the store....
Of course they were onto her like flies....
For her...yes...utter shame....Absolutely...
...Paroxysms of tears....
But the very mention of the word "satin" provoked
sexual ecstasy...and she would experience a
tremendous orgasm if she rubbed the satin against
her parts....*

In silhouette we see the patient insert his finger inside his collar in order to loosen it. The camera now reverses 180° and imperceptibly begins to dolly in on his face. The doctor's voice is heard offscreen.

[DOCTOR:]
*And the poor husband had no inkling whatsoever
of these habits and naturally thought his wife's
"pruritus vulvae"* was due to excessive
intercourse instead of excessive masturbation.*

---

*PRURITUS VULVAE: Itching of the vulva

The patient's eyes are drawn to the tip of the pencil eraser the doctor is absentmindedly tapping. The sound retreats as the camera continues to creep in upon the patient's face. In the background, a woman's distant voice lost in a haze of static is heard. The patient's lips move silently as though responding to these distant exhortations. The doctor's voice and tapping pencil have entirely receded. The patient's eyes close. Music surges and there is a quick insert of a pair of women's empty shoes. His closed eyes open as a man's voice is now heard offscreen. Enunciating tentatively, the offscreen voice and the patient's lips fall into sync. He speaks clinically as though confessing.

⌈PATIENT:⌉
She seemed to have a penchant for treading on things...
things that gave way before her feet...flowers...
grass...fallen fruit...acorns...chestnuts...
and ultimately...yes...
ultimately...me.

The doctor's lips are also seen moving silently over these very same words. The nurse passes through the frame and pauses in front of the doctor, who, putting his hand over the receiver, indicates something in the corner of the room. The patient follows her with his eyes. He looks to the floor as her shoes pass through the frame.
Both shoes come to a halt side by side.
They stretch up on tiptoe.

⌈PATIENT:⌉
She was very much in a position to buy whatever she
wanted...and then she would demand that I lie
down and get the feeling of them for myself.

The patient's eyes follow the shoes back to the doctor. The nurse's body pauses in front of him and places a file on the table. Her face leans into the frame. We see a finger point to a particular line, then, turning slowly, she looks directly into the patient's eyes.

367

⌈PATIENT:⌉
*It was then that she would step up on me and place one
foot on my penis...then the heel would sink into the
root...and the sole would cover the rest of the phallus...
while the other foot would be placed upon my abdomen...
such that I could see and feel her weight shifting...
from one foot to the other.*

Suddenly distracted, he looks up as a woman's hands arrive from
nowhere to gently guide him down. As though obedient, the head of
the patient disappears from the frame. The doctor's eyes glance down
as the back of the patient's head is lowered to the floor. The voice
of the doctor, still on the telephone, breaks through.

⌈DOCTOR:⌉
*Irregular...but not unusual for that type....Yes...
of course...But then if I had an emission for every
moist spot I saw, I'd still be back in...*

⌈NURSE:⌉
Turning to him and smiling.
Ugrocz.

Close-up of her face turning away from the doctor and looking down
in the direction of the floor. In a less identifiable space, a woman's
shoe is seen stepping onto a man's fully clothed abdomen. The
patient's supine head strains to look. A woman's second foot is seen
stepping onto his abdomen. We see his eyes close as he slowly
succumbs to the weight. The back of his head touches the floor.
Behind him are seen the flames from a fireplace. Still looking down,
the doctor continues his conversation.

⌈DOCTOR:⌉
*But it is his persistent disorientation with
respect to the female body...*

Both her feet stand balanced on the man's stomach as the flames
lick her legs. We see her one hand gingerly lift the skirt while the
other reaches for the mantelpiece of a fireplace. Balancing herself on
one leg, she extends the other foot toward the roaring fire. She is
laughing. Again the music surges. The contours of the shoe are
silhouetted by the flames. Looking up at her, his eyes glisten.

[DOCTOR:]
He can never find the "foramen vaginae"*
without the woman's aid...
and this is due to his chronic confusion
of the vagina and the navel....
He always climbs a floor too high.

Suddenly he grasps her foot and kisses it. Bringing it down,
he places it over his penis. His head arches back against the floor.
His ragged breathing suddenly crests as the entire weight of her
body leans forward in the shoe that is now compressing his penis.
The camera is suddenly zooming in on that space under the instep
of her shoe as all sound vanishes into an indefinable white haze.
There is complete stillness. Bending up, with a paper in his hand,
the doctor interrupts the silence. We see the nurse still in the
same identical position in front of the doctor. She is still looking
at the patient intently. Reaching toward him with her hand,
she places a finger under his chin and gently lifts it.
The patient's eyes open and blink.

[DOCTOR:]
And of course further associations
developed when the wet nurse lifted
him another story higher....
... Definitely.... Unmistakable....
...Or that obscure instinct not yet
conscious of its object....

---

*FORAMEN VAGINAE: Vaginal opening

369

With a handkerchief that the nurse offers him, the patient wipes saliva from his chin. In the background the doctor is laughing and saying good-bye. We hear the telephone being put down and papers being handed to the nurse for filing. She then introduces the new patient to the doctor in German.

⌈NURSE:⌉
Kallos Zoltan ... Hungarian....
Twenty-four ... single....
Mother healthy ... father healthy....
Can give no explanation of the
origin of his peculiarity.

Distracted, the patient looks down to see her ankles rocking harmlessly in their shoes. Looking back up, he sees the doctor picking up a pencil and tablet with an air of impenetrable remoteness before leaning toward him. The doctor, now in complete shadow in the foreground, sits with his back toward the camera. We see him brush aside an invisible fly in the air. The patient's lips move but nothing is heard save for the same inexorable music beginning its quiet ascent. Slowly the camera rises above them to reveal shelves of annotated boxes of various objects and clothing. The camera comes to a halt as a hand is seen depositing a pair of women's shoes that look conspicuously like the ones she wore. A little tag is already affixed to the heel. CASE 81. 1883. F.K. The music surges.

*Large tableau of a wall upon which is drawn graffiti of a little girl
jumping rope. In front of this wall we see a couple kissing.
On the graffiti itself, sand is seen draining from two little holes
precisely where the little girl's breasts would be. Directly below the
drawing at the foot of the wall, the sand is forming two little pyramids.
The couple pauses to observe. Together they both move toward the two
draining holes and simultaneously peer through them. From each of
their individual viewpoints, they both see the same identical wall
opposite them showing the same graffiti of a little girl jumping rope.
Immediately passing before their eyes (a little like the blink of a
camera shutter) is the arc of a rope in its ellipse. It grazes this distant*

371

wall opposite them as a little puff of dust shows the point of impact upon her breasts. Still continuing its downward arc, the rope literally passes beneath the very wall they are standing in front of, exits the background just behind their feet, and now passes over the back of their heads and disappears through the wall above them. Again, from their point of view, we see the rope still continuing its downward arc to strike the distant wall opposite them with another puff of dust. A few more revolutions gradually reveal two small holes beginning to bleed sand in fine streams from the little girl's breasts. As the rope repeatedly leaves the ground behind their feet on this side of the wall, we begin to notice that their physical presence is now gradually being erased and slowly being reestablished anew in front of the wall opposite them. The sound of the skipping rope striking both the ground and the wall is now indistinguishable from the new lovers who now notice the same sand draining in two fine streams from the same graffiti on the same wall showing the same little girl jumping rope. They move toward the wall and as they stoop to peer through her breasts, the camera slowly starts to crane up to reveal in the distance yet another wall showing the very same graffiti of the same little girl jumping rope. The scene fades out and only the repeated sound of the rope striking the ground and the wall remains in our ears.

A small Baroque chapel
in a desolate landscape, its single tower now replaced by a portion of a
high-tension wire stanchion, sits inconspicuously connected to these
overhead wires as though electrified to a new perspective. Off to the
side of the chapel is the presence of a parking lot, empty save for a
single car. Almost before we can see it, we hear the methodical thud
of a football being kicked against a wall. Simultaneously our ears
perceive the intermittent sound of a revolving water sprinkler, which is
accosting a small portion of grass. However, in its imprecise orbit,
most of the water is being expended over the chapel wall that the
football is being kicked against. Then, in a graceful arc across the top
of the parking lot, we see one of those very old tour buses. It circles
hesitantly, then returns and descends even more slowly to arrive in
front of the wall. We hear the engine turn off just as the path of the
water sprinkler splashes across its windscreen. As though it was too
much trouble to repark the bus, we see the windscreen wipers turned
on. The doors of the bus thrust open and two women and a child spill
out just as the trajectory of the football is seen striking the wall behind
their heads. Mindful of their vulnerability, they are completely unaware
of the passing spray behind them and are immediately inundated.
Running closer to the side of the bus, we see them urging others to
join them but none do. We see them stretching warily between the arc
of the football now passing noiselessly behind their heads and the
spray across the windscreen now covered by the sound of one long
sustained organ chord.

Inside the chapel on a wall, a sign in a heavy glass frame reads:

MUSEO DELLA CAPPELLA SCONSACRATA
DI SANTA MARIA DEL POPOLO

MUSEUM OF THE DECONSECRATED CHAPEL
OF SANTA MARIA DEL POPOLO

We observe the glass in the frame vibrating intermittently. On the
floor directly beneath it, little pyramids of plaster and dust have
formed beneath the routine accuracy of the football. In one of the
half-lit recesses of the chapel, we see the source of the sound:
an organ loft suspended high up on a wall overlooking a
miniature forest below.

The organ pipes are enveloped in baroque foliage and give the
impression they have escaped the earthly bonds of the forest and
have ascended to the heights of the wall with part of the forest still
attached. Only the music appears to mediate for this apparent
description. From out of this miniature forest a man rises with a
little domed sacristan's hat such that when he is at his full height it
looks as though the forest is clasped around his waist. He looks up at
the organ and cocks his ear as though trying to locate a particular key
in the music. We see him lower through the treetops and immediately
we're inside the forest as he crouches down among the gnarled roots
that penetrate beneath the heavy wooden floorboards. Pointing his
ear once again in the direction of the sound, he brushes his hand over
the forest floor. Suddenly he winces and draws his hand to his face.
A small wooden splinter protrudes from the fourth finger. Looking up
in the direction of the sound, he slowly pulls the splinter out.
Wedged between two organ keys, we see a single pine needle delicately
being dragged down between two depressed keys. Immediately
the music stops.

♣

The sanctity of the forest is returned to the muted thud of the football, and in the distance, the sound of the chapel door opening and cautious feet entering. We see a hand turning on various light switches. Emerging out of the dark is the face of the man with the little domed hat. The heavy sound of boots propels his robe across the floor in the direction of the tourists. We hear more light switches being turned on. The three look up and around, trying to be optimistic in their evident disappointment. His approaching feet elicit an embarrassed offering of coins, deposited through a narrow slot. But the sound of the boots never reaches them. They seem to perpetually echo off into different corners of the chapel. The three visitors take what they believe to be the only logical path through the few pools of light afforded them.

The chapel has become, without the slightest hint or suspicion, an imaginary museum; a collection of artifacts curated by the Devil himself. And in these times when the Devil is really little more than an artifact himself, he has materialized as a kind of sacristan cum custodian—here, in this deconsecrated chapel, where no one is either looking for him or expecting him. And within these walls he has begun forging a hybridized version of the documents surrounding the life of Christ and various saints, enriching and subverting their well-known pageantry with the grain of his own anarchy. Disorientation and confusion will be the key part of the seduction and the unsuspecting will discover and question upon leaving whether this was a real museum or a simulation.

Footsteps are heard and the two women and child are seen arriving in front of one of the glass vitrines. Lowering their faces, they see in the available light two small wooden hands loosely tied together at the wrist. A number of fingers are either broken or missing. An inscription reads: "A nun's bra made of the baby Jesus' cupped hands." There is a hesitation on the faces of the two women before they rise and take the child by the hand. Again distant footsteps are heard approaching, but immediately they vanish the moment the three of them stop. Arriving at another glass case, they inspect what appears to

be a branch set inside a small glass capsule. The inscription reads:
"A segment of the olive tree holding the still visibly moving shadow
of the kneeling Christ rising from the Garden of Gethsemane."
The women look at each other. The shadow clouding both their faces
is transferred to the hand of the child.

Down the length of an aisle, the three are seen crossing. There is a
momentary pause when suddenly the child appears on his own. He
looks back in their direction, then chooses another aisle. We see the
lips of the women silently reading the inscription: "La Virgen del
Apocalipsis—a 13th-century Saint whose thighs liquefy on a certain
Holy Day and for a certain sum of money, the ecstatic can sniff the
effluvia off a thread that her body is wheeled over." We see the
sacristan standing among the shadows as the child runs past.
Both the women's faces disappear behind the visor of an eyepiece as
the child arrives between two vitrines. What he sees is an empty corner
of the chapel walls lit by an overhead street lamp. However, what he
barely notices is that the chapel floor has become an extension of the
parking lot itself; as though, like water, the striping had slipped under
the walls and reestablished the parking lot there in the very depths of
the chapel itself. Suddenly we see one of the women's faces pulling
away and her hand searching for the child's but not finding it. We hear
footsteps echoing in further parts of the chapel as we see the two of
them trying to locate sounds they hope are those of the child. Behind
them a vague light flashes up on a distant wall.

Lights are rippling across the child's face. We hear the sound of an
automobile accelerating out of a corner. Headlights race along the
length of the chapel wall. Tires squeal . . . brake . . . and swerve. There
is the dull bone-breaking sound of a body being thrown from a car and
hitting the ground with a terrific impact. Rolling across the chapel
floor a body slowly comes to rest on the white parking stripes.
There is utter stillness. Painfully, with great effort, the figure rises.
The light is just sufficient enough to outline the glint of a tattered
halo. The face turns . . . it is bruised and bleeding; nevertheless we still
recognize the image of Christ. A rope is hanging from his neck and
his wrists are tied in front of him. He turns and looks up at the street

377

lamp and then in the direction of the child. The child doesn't move.
He simply studies the scene. Flapping wings suddenly turn the Christ
figure's head toward two pigeons already landing on the spot where he
had risen only minutes before. Their pecking barely distinguishes
between scraps of detritus and bits of the broken halo. Christ is
momentarily transfixed until the sound of far-off footsteps turns
his head once again. The footsteps pause. The Christ figure
tries to ascertain their position. He retreats. The sound of his
entering the forest is followed by the sound of pigeons landing
heavily in the trees.

There is total quiet. The worried hands of the women suddenly find
those of the child. Relieved, they look in various directions before
choosing an aisle and disappearing down it. But just prior to leaving,
they will have searched for the sound of a cricket and this will have led
them around a corner to discover the sacristan perched on a stool
chafing his thighs beneath his robe. They will have greeted his smile
with the expectation that they'd been hoodwinked. Their eyes will
have lowered and seen what they believed were hooves beneath his
robe. Their unsmiling smiles would have left the chapel with them.
As they exited, they would have realized it was now dusk. A mist
would have already rolled in under the perspective of the wires. As they
entered the bus, the headlights would have been turned on and have
illuminated that part of the chapel wall that had held the sound of the
football. A single light over the parking lot would convince them that
the sprinkler system was now contained in the windscreen wipers.
The bus would not have moved. The mist would start to envelop the
chapel and slowly consume it. Edging in at the top of the frame,
we would see the headlights of another tour bus sweep across the
parking lot. It would slowly circle and descend toward the facade but
never reach the wall. We would hear the sound of alarm sirens as the
chapel is now entirely consumed by the mist. Inside, thirteen chords
of music redistribute what light is left among all his shadows.

♣

„NIGHTWATCH"

MUSEUM BOIJMANS-VAN BEUNINGEN
THE CARD PLAYERS
BY

BALTHUS

The camera pans across an interior gallery
of the Museum Boijmans-Van Beuningen at night. We observe the
stillness of the paintings trying to sleep under the condition of relative
safety that pin lighting offers them at this hour. Slowly we distinguish
what sounds like a curtain blowing in the wind. The camera lowers
and swiftly tracks across the floor to stop just short of a wall.
Barely noticeable on the floor is a stone. The camera rises to frame
The Card Players by Balthus.

Exterior facade of the Museum Boijmans-Van Beuningen
theatrically painted on canvas. Scaffolding is on both sides.
A curtain billows out of a window and is then violently sucked inside.
From the top of the facade a portion of the stone pediment collapses
and falls to the pavement below. A fragment of stone ricochets through
an open doorway to the left of the facade.

A dark interior space. A couple, the very same ones from the painting,
sit opposite one another at a table. We see a white piece of paper
suddenly dipping across the frame toward the floor. Simultaneously,
we see the trajectory of the stone passing beneath the paper toward a
full-length mirror that reflects the couple and the open doorway from
where the stone entered. The stone bounces off the base of the mirror
and comes to a halt. Slowly their heads turn toward the intruder.
However, even before we are permitted to see their faces, the camera
cuts 180° behind them to see the backs of their heads still turning
toward the stone. We now observe them observing the stone.
There is a complete cessation of sound save only for an insignificant
breeze that redistributes the folds of the tablecloth, the hem of her
skirt, and the edge of the paper that gleams on the floor near
the solitary intruder.

No longer concerned with the stone, the couple turn their gaze back
to one another. However, before their faces are revealed, the camera
cuts to the mirror to see their heads still turning away from us.
Again we are denied their faces and presented only with the backs
of their heads. We see an invisible draft sweep the paper from its
reflection in the mirror. Long fade-out over fine dust particles stirring
in the paper's wake.

Fade in on a front tableau of the couple that presents them with
a solitude of two, as though caught in eclipse. We are prompted to
decipher their conduct. On one hand it would seem that *he* is trying
to elicit something intractable from *her*, but this is only made apparent
by the inscrutability of her demand. Furthermore, everything suggests
that a certain malaise or denouement has already been irrevocably
conferred upon the two people, and that the space between them
has been further contaminated by the intrusion of the stone as an
outside catalyst. He now bends imperceptibly toward her.
From behind, we see a huge close-up of his hand leaning on the table.
Suddenly it slips.

Exterior facade as another portion of the stone pediment collapses.
A fragment ricochets through the doorway.

Interior space: The camera spins wildly across the floor (from the point
of view of the stone itself) and stops just shy of her chair to frame his
face diving to the floor to witness the stone trapping itself in the slender
arch of her heel. He observes the oscillation of the stone back and forth.
His hand moves forward.

Exterior facade: Another portion of
the pediment collapses again.

Interior space: We see him glance out of the corner of his eye to notice
another stone ricochet across the floor and come to a halt close to the
first one. As he returns his gaze to her shoe, his hand approaches and
pauses. From behind, a huge close-up of the space between her heel
and sole as this kinetic blur is gingerly captured between his two
outspread fingers.

Immediately the sound of alarm sirens and choral music fill out the
tablecloth and her skirt. The entire table seems to swell and pitch
forward. We cut to a hazy, indistinct landscape with trees blowing
lugubriously. A tablecloth flaps in the foreground both revealing and
obscuring the same couple. She is on the ground, he above, but it is
difficult to say whether he has thrown her down or whether she
is simply extending her arm to be lifted. The trees continue to blow,
undeterred by their personal drama.

We cut to a close-up of him. The wind that was blowing in his hair
has now entirely subsided. The camera dollies back to reveal that he is
observing a rugby scrum that has materialized in front of him and has
utterly eliminated any trace of her. The sound of the wind has now
become the sound of the scrum. We are no longer in a landscape but
somewhere in the depths of another part of the museum itself. He
cautiously follows the scrum, peering into its depths as it moves toward
the center of the floor. Suddenly it stops and a stone is kicked out.
Grasping it, he looks up and sees a ladder rapidly extending from the
center of the scrum to the height of the wall opposite him. Before
anyone can respond, he is leapfrogging up the ladder as it stretches
toward the upper pediment. Reaching the top, he leaps to the pediment
ledge and, hanging by his fingertips, crawls hand over hand toward a
window, dislodging a shower of pebbles onto the floor. When the last of
the stones falls silent, he pulls himself through the window.

Suddenly, he is on the top of the museum roof, where we discover her standing with her back toward him. He approaches slowly. We realize that she is poised dangerously close to the edge. There is also the hint of expectation. We see her feet creep just a little closer to the edge. His open hands extend slowly toward her back, but hesitate. We see his feet move closer, then he gives a little push. We hear a complicitous giggle from her. She repositions her feet. He pretends a mock push. Her feet remain still, his step still closer. The camera rises behind them such that we see the backs of their bodies and the great height that lies below them. We see him make an even stronger push, followed by an ineffectual one that only makes her giggle more. She steps even closer to the edge. The camera now frames her toes in huge close-up as they extend over the edge. We immediately surmise an attempted push as we see her ankles suddenly tense, followed by another suppressed giggle. She spreads her feet farther apart to disadvantage herself even more. His fingertips are but a few centimeters from her shoulder blades. We see him push still harder. She tips forward but, using her arms to flail, she regains her balance. We hear another giggle. Then she turns to look back at him as though to urge him on. Returning his gaze, she looks down over the edge. Her vulnerable neck reveals fine hairs in the breeze. The camera lowers to the buttons on the back of her dress, which already anticipate his fingers and begin to undo themselves. A bra strap is revealed that just as swiftly is unhooked by his now arriving fingertips. As though relieved of a further restraint, she looks down over the edge again. As she begins to turn toward him, we see a close-up of that slender trace of flesh between the buttons of her dress being flattened by his hands. There's a sudden gasp and we cut to the exterior facade as we see her body fall through the frame and strike the ground in a cloud of dust.

As the dust gently settles around her, she raises herself up on one arm. Dazed, she looks around. Rising slowly to her feet, she dusts herself off, turns, and walks back toward the museum entrance again. We hear footsteps mounting the stairs of the tower. On the roof he is still standing in the same spot. She brushes past him to arrive at the edge again. We see his hands button the back of her dress, then smooth out the small creases. She looks down at her feet to reposition them. She turns to indicate her readiness, then there is a sudden gasp. For a split second we see his hands relaxing where her back had been only an instant before.

384

Exterior facade: She flies past. The curtain sucks in and freezes into a
final position. Inside the interior space the ricocheting stone is now
oscillating before the mirror. In the reflection we can see the couple's
eyes transfixed by its presence. Slowly their faces turn to meet one
another. The table is perilously capsized forward and the tablecloth
and her dress have billowed into one indistinguishable sail. The only
movement is her hand stretching toward his to play a card.

In the ensuing dialogue their faces
never part from the frozen masklike condition they have maintained
throughout the film. All gestures are minimal as they play with their life
like a game of cards from a painting.

SHE:
I like it like that.

HE:
Like what?

SHE:
The way you push.

HE:
Like this?

SHE:
No . . . more like this.

HE:
Does everyone do it like that?

SHE:
Most.

HE:
You mean most like to do it that way.

SHE:
When I say so.

385

HE:
Which is often?

SHE:
Which is always often.

HE:
And is often always enough?

SHE:
Often is never enough.

HE:
Especially when you like it?

SHE:
Especially when they hear me saying I like it.

HE:
And that's always?

SHE:
That's always.

Cut to exterior of the museum tower as we hear two sets of footsteps mounting the stairs. There is a momentary silence. Two swallows fly past. The curtain sucks in and we hear the sound of the pediment crashing to the pavement and a stone ricocheting across the courtyard. In the dark interior space we see reflected in the mirror the stone spinning across the floor beneath playing cards already scattered and frozen in the air just above the now slowly arriving stone.

LILIUM INTER
SPINAS

BEING A SACRILEGIOUS

EX VOT
O

♣ High up on a wall a ladder is leaning precariously ♣
against a painting depicting the dead Christ in the arms of
his mother. A little girl at the top of this ladder is reaching
up to clean out his wounds with cotton wool and a bottle of
disinfectant. We see a close-up of the ladder's weight pressing
heavily into the canvas. Suddenly there is a loud ripping sound. She
and the ladder fall simultaneously and her beautiful porcelain face,
arms, legs, and body all smash as she hits the ground.

Off to the side, three praying spectators who have been silently
observing her begin to laugh. They rise, walk over, and start to pick
up all the pieces. They can't stop laughing as they drop little porcelain fragments into the outstretched apron of one of the other girls.

When they have finished they leave. In the distance we hear the
echo of their continued laughter as the camera now frames Christ's
wound in huge close-up. A single drop of blood begins to form. It
falls to the floor and lands next to one of the little girl's porcelain
eyes. The eye begins to shed a tear. Then from above we hear a
cough followed by a laugh. Then more laughing. The camera rises
up to the wound as blood is seen gently spurting out in rhythm to
his final laughter.

Erotik

NACHTSTÜCK IM STILE VON
E.T.A. HOFFMANN'S
»*DON GIOVANNI*«

A MODERN EIGHTEENTH-CENTURY
ANXIETY DREAM

FÜR

MELANIE SERSCHÖN

(*POLIZEIKOMMISSARIN*)

UND

(*DEM DICHTER*)

RICHARD WEIHE

IN ZURICH

A S H E C A U T I O U S L Y S T E P S
THROUGH the concealed door in the
ivy wallpaper into Loge 23, he immediately steps on her foot. She has been
waiting, or rather not just waiting, she
has figuratively always been waiting for
the real crime against her being. His
mere stepping upon her foot has simply
made him an involuntary accomplice
without his knowing why or how. She
doesn't, however, attempt to draw her foot away. In the darkness
he carefully sits down next to her but still continues to keep gentle
pressure on her foot. She doesn't resist. And now an entire litany
of analogies adds a further pressure to each and every following
image. All movement is now irrevocably caught in its final act of
completion: tram steps are seen folding back into a tram, the tram
is then seen disappearing around the corner of a building, a
window is being closed, a tablecloth gently floats down over a table
and conforms to its final shape just as a dress falls to the floor
around a woman's shoes. At this very moment we hear her voice:
»WEIHE !!RICHARD EMMANUEL!!« and the sudden sound of
a folder being snapped open. There's an insert shot of her foot
suddenly withdrawing from under his foot just as we see his fingers
retract from touching her hand. Immediately she instructs him
to stand. Dressed in eighteenth-century costume, she maneuvers
herself behind him and kicks his feet apart. Quickly frisking him
in modern police style, she forces him to lean over the edge of
the balcony with the entire weight of his body centered on the
palms of his hands. With great precision she starts to undress him.
Pulling his breeches down over his knees, she begins to verbally
interrogate him while at the same time manipulating him until he

is uncontrollably erect. With measured strokes, she literally has him in her hands. On the final question as to his intentions, she holds him so intensely that he ejaculates over the edge of the balcony onto seat L23 down below. Smiling, or only appearing to smile, she continues to hold him as she steps delicately out of her shoes. Returning him limply to himself, she now steps in front of him to take up the same identical position. To the sound of rustling cloth, we see her hands gather up her costume until her naked buttocks are extravagantly revealed beneath layers of eighteenth-century fabric. Also revealed is a holster. Removing the gun from it, she turns and places it between his already moistened lips before withdrawing it. Turning around to look out over the entire theater, she inserts the barrel up her vagina and whispers: "Now if you really love me, Richard, you'll give me the bullet I deserve... before I do." Cocking the pistol with the same hand, her head rolls back onto the side of his face. Closing his eyes, he is already imagining the sound of the pistol shot in his ears as her cheek slides longingly against the sound of his skin. In this deafening pause we see her feet slowly go up *on point* as he desperately tries to become erect to the already multiple echoes of the gunshot that is now resounding throughout the entire theater.

The Quay Brothers

Mirrha Electa

Or How
The Virgin Calms The Infant Jesus'
First Nightmare

THE CAMERA FRAMES A
NAÏVE PAINTING OF THE CHRIST CHILD
in the arms of the Virgin. We hear the child crying and the
voice of the mother trying to console it. Almost invisibly
the camera begins to lower from the painting. It passes
through the tops of trees and down among the leaves.
The sound of the sobbing child is gradually lost to the idyllic
sounds of the forest. From a distance we see a crucifix
standing in a peaceful glade. A certain holiness reigns
supreme. As the camera approaches closer we hear the sound
of flies buzzing. Arriving at the foot of the cross we notice
dried blood heavily congealed at the bottom of his feet.
Then from his rib cage flies and maggots are seen crawling
around the wound and over the mouth a total infestation of
both. There is the immediate horror of vulnerable flesh, even
that of the sacred flesh of Christ. Suddenly the body on the
cross shudders violently . . . then again. Only the peaceful
calm of the forest and the buzzing of flies can be heard.
The camera cuts back to see a bulldozer slamming into
the base of the crucifix. We hear no sound save for the
magisterial calm of the forest. Wearing a yellow hard hat,
the driver is seen holding a handkerchief over his nose. As he
slams into the base again only the flies can be seen scattering.
Off to the side two other men in identical yellow hard hats
confer. They, too, hold handkerchiefs over their noses.

Suddenly the crucifix is seen falling face-first into the underbrush. One of the two men signals to the driver. We see him dismount and stand before the fallen cross. He looks back in their direction and they make a further signal. The driver drags a tangle of underbrush over the cross. Still there is only the sound of the forest at peace. The body under the cross is now barely visible. The driver looks up again and the two men motion a further layer. Looking behind him, the driver reaches down and drags yet another tangle over the cross. As he looks up, the two men in helmets are already walking away. With his foot, the driver makes a halfhearted attempt to flatten the underbrush before leaving. As he mounts the bulldozer, the camera is already beginning to rise through the treetops. It climbs higher and higher until the sounds of the forest disappear. As we emerge through the trees onto the painting again, we are already hearing the last sobbings of the Christ child. Virtually asleep now, the Virgin is singing a lullaby. So sweet is this lullaby that we almost fail to recognize the distant sound of nails being hammered into wood.

A child is asleep in bed bathed in moonlight. A breeze blows through a curtain at the rear of the room. Suddenly a dark figure is standing at the foot of the bed. He leans over the child and exhales deeply into its face. We hear a little cough as the figure disappears into the bureau. The mirror on top tilts down to reflect the child in bed. The coughing continues. Fade out.

•

Fade in. Morning. The coughing continues. From the mirror's position, we see the mother enter to console the child, then leave. Returning to the long shot, the mother now enters with the doctor. He inspects the child. They leave. The coughing worsens.

•

Then three men with a table appear. They erect it in the center of the room. The doctor is consulting with the mother. She sits by the coughing child. The doctor and three men take the child and lay him on the table. The mother leaves the room. Through the mirror on the bureau we see the men hold the child down. The operation begins.

•

The three men tighten their grip on the child as we see the scalpel blurring into the skin. Suddenly the doctor is extracting the windpipe from the child's throat. One of the assistants lays it on the bureau in front of the mirror. The child's open throat is now stitched shut.

•

The operation completed, the mother enters and stands beside the table surrounded by the doctor and his assistants. The doctor hands the child his windpipe. The child blows a little melody on it. They all laugh. Then from the mirror we see the mother returning the windpipe and placing it in huge close-up in front of the mirror.
Fade out.

•

Fade in. Night. The child is peacefully asleep. From the direction of the bureau we hear the same melody that the child played earlier on his windpipe. There is a pause followed by a little cough. The melody is attempted again, but there is another cough. We see the child rustle in bed, then sit up and look around. There is only the breeze from the window. The child lies down and is soon asleep. We hear the melody attempted once again, but interrupted by coughing . . . then a suppressed fit of coughing. The room grows darker as the light in the mirror reflects still further coughing.
Fade out.

•

ACKNOWLEDGMENTS

MARTINE BELLEN. Cartoon images from *Metropolis* by Osamu Tezuka. 2003.

ANNE CARSON. *Beuyshammer* by Anne Carson. Pen, ink, and crayon. 2005. Used by permission.

KENNETH GROSS. *Hands of a Marionette Player* by Tina Modotti (1846–1942). Gelatin silver print, 7¹/₂ x 9¹/₂ inches. 1929. Anonymous gift (349.1965). The Museum of Modern Art, New York, NY. Digital image © The Museum of Modern Art/Licensed by SCALA/Art Resource, NY. Untitled photographs of puppeteer's hands with wooden balls from *My Profession* by Sergei Obraztsov (Moscow, 1950). Photographer unknown. Photograph of Wayang Kulit by Otto Stadler. 2002. Used by permission.

ROBIN HEMLEY. Photograph of dead Confederate soldier by Mathew Brady. Circa 1861. Photograph of the Tasaday in a cave by John Nance. Circa 1972. Used by permission. PANAMIN photo of Elizalde, Mai Tuan, and unknown woman. Photographer unknown. Circa 1971. From the collection of the author and used by permission. Photograph in the Louvre by Dave Munger (www1.davidson.edu/academic/psychology/Munger/Humes). 2004. Used by permission. Vintage photograph of man and boy from *A Postcard Memoir* by Lawrence Sutin. Date and photographer unknown. Used by permission.

MICHAEL LOGAN. Family photographs used by permission of the author.

HONOR MOORE. Vintage Moore family photographs. Circa 1896. Courtesy the Moore family collection. Photograph of Hobart's brushes by Maria Levitsky. 2006. Used by permission.

THE QUAY BROTHERS. *Über Verschieden Formen der Lustgewinnung am Eigenen Leibe.* Photographic image from unknown German medical volume. Circa 1900.
  Stille Nacht V. Original collage by the Quay Brothers. Used by permission.
  Stille Nacht VI. Original collage by the Quay Brothers. From *Le Christ tombant* by Melchor Pérez de Holguín (1660–1732) and an untitled photograph by Norbert Ghisoland (1902–1939). Used by permission. Organ pipe image by Gian Lorenzo Bernini (1598–1680).
  Nightwatch. Les Joueurs de cartes (The Card Players) by Balthus. 1973. Copyright © Artists Rights Society (ARS), New York / ADAGP, Paris. *Projet pour la façade de Saint François d'Assise de São João del Rei. Museú da Inconfidência, Ouro Preto* by Aleijadinho. 1774. *Le démon l'avait saisie par le cheville! (The Devil Has Seized Her Ankle!)* by Balthus. 1933. Copyright © Artists Rights Society, New York / ADAGP, Paris.
  Lilium inter Spinas. Ex Voto image from La Bâtiaz, Valais, Switzerland. 1821.
  Mirrha Electa. Ex Voto image, artist and date unknown.
  Ex Voto. Image by unknown artist. 1853.

NOTES ON CONTRIBUTORS

Award-winning author DIANE ACKERMAN's many books include, most recently, *An Alchemy of Mind* (Scribner) and *Origami Bridges: Poems of Psychoanalysis and Fire* (HarperCollins).

A special edition of MARTINE BELLEN's *Further Adventures of the Monkey God* has recently been published by Spuyten Duyvil. "The Cyborg Suite" is part of a collection of anime poems that she will be working on at the Rockefeller Foundation Bellagio Study and Conference Center.

SVEN BIRKERTS is the author of five books of essays and a memoir, *My Sky Blue Trades* (Viking). He edits the journal *AGNI* at Boston University and is a member of the core faculty of the Bennington Writing Seminars.

ANNE CARSON is currently working on a production of Euripides' *Hippolytos* at the Getty Museum in Los Angeles. Her translation of four Euripidean plays, *Grief Lessons*, is forthcoming from *The New York Review of Books*.

JOHN CROWLEY is the author of *Little, Big* (Harper Perennial) and the Ægypt sequence of novels (Spectra), among other works. "Practicing the Arts of Peace" was first delivered in a slightly different form as a Branigin Lecture at the Institute for Advanced Study at Indiana University on December 1, 2005.

JOHN D'AGATA's new book, a meditation on Yucca Mountain, is forthcoming from Farrar, Straus and Giroux. He teaches creative writing at the University of Iowa.

FORREST GANDER's books of poems, essays, and translations include, most recently, one of poetry, *Eye Against Eye* (New Directions), and one of essays, *A Faithful Existence: Reading, Memory, and Transcendence* (Shoemaker & Hoard). His recent translations include *No Shelter: Selected Poems of Pura López Colomé* (Greywolf) and *Firefly under the Tongue: Selected Poems of Coral Bracho*, forthcoming from New Directions. With Kent Johnson, he has translated *Immanent Visitor: The Selected Poems of Jaime Saenz* (University of California) a PEN Translation Award finalist, and *The Night: A Poem by Jaime Saenz*, forthcoming next year from Princeton University Press.

WILLIAM H. GASS's many books include *Reading Rilke* and *Tests of Time*, and most recently, a collection of essays entitled *A Temple of Texts* (all Knopf).

KENNETH GROSS's books include *The Dream of the Moving Statue* (Cornell, reprint 2006 by Pennsylvania State University), *Shakespeare's Noise* (University of Chicago), and *Shylock Is Shakespeare*, forthcoming from University of

Chicago. His essay in this issue finds some of its roots in an earlier one, "The Puppet's Calling," co-authored with Leslie Katz, published in *Raritan* in 1995. He teaches English at the University of Rochester.

ROBERT HARBISON's books include *Eccentric Spaces* (MIT), *Pharaoh's Dream* (Secker & Warburg, UK), *Reflections on Baroque* (University of Chicago), and *The Daily Telegraph Guide to England's Parish Churches* (Aurum). He is professor of architecture at London Metropolitan University, where he heads a master's program in architectural history, theory, and interpretation.

ROBIN HEMLEY is the author of seven books, including *Invented Eden: The Elusive, Disputed History of the Tasaday* (Farrar, Straus and Giroux) and *Turning Life into Fiction* (Greywolf). He is the director of the Nonfiction Writing Program at the University of Iowa.

FANNY HOWE's most recent books of prose are *Economics* (Flood Editions) and *Lives of a Spirit/Glasstown: Where Something Got Broken* (Nightboat).

SHELLEY JACKSON is the author of the short story collection *The Melancholy of Anatomy* (Anchor), hypertexts including *Patchwork Girl* (Eastgate), several children's books, and *Skin*, a story published in tattoos on the skin of 2,095 volunteers. Her first novel, *Half Life*, is forthcoming from HarperCollins.

MATTHEW KIRBY's fiction has appeared in *AGNI, 3rd Bed, Diagram, Lady Churchill's Rosebud Wristlet,* and *Snow Monkey.*

"Investigation into the Death of Logan" is an excerpt from an unpublished book by MICHAEL LOGAN. This is his first published essay.

RICK MOODY's most recent novel is *The Diviners* (Little, Brown).

HONOR MOORE's recent books of poems are *Red Shoes* (Norton) and *Darling* (Grove). "Hobart's Brushes" is a variation of material from her memoir in progress, *The Bishop's Daughter,* to be published by Norton.

GEOFFREY O'BRIEN's poetry has been collected in *Red Sky Café* and *A View of Buildings and Water* (both Salt), and *Floating City* (Talisman House). His books of prose include *Phantom Empire* (Norton), *Dream Time: Chapters from the Sixties, The Browser's Ecstasy,* and *Sonata for Jukebox* (all Counterpoint). He is editor in chief of the Library of America.

ROSAMOND PURCELL, photographer and installation artist, collaborated with the late paleontologist Stephen Jay Gould on three books including *Finders Keepers: Eight Collectors* (Norton) and with sleight-of-hand artist Ricky Jay on *Dice: Deception, Fate, & Rotten Luck* (Quantuck Lane). Her most recent book, *Owls Head,* is a meditation on the nature of ruined objects. *Bookworm,* Purcell's photographs of constructions and collages, with an introduction by Sven Birkerts, will appear this fall (both from Quantuck Lane).

Masters of stop-motion animation, the identical twins STEPHEN and TIMOTHY QUAY are among the world's most original filmmakers. Their classic 1986 film, *Street of Crocodiles*, was selected by director Terry Gilliam as one of the ten best animated films of all time. They made their first foray into live-action feature-length filmmaking in 1994 with *Institute Benjamenta*. The Quays' work also includes set design for theater and opera, and in 1998 their Tony-nominated set designs for Ionesco's *The Chairs* won great acclaim on Broadway. Their most recent film is the feature-length *The Piano Tuner of Earthquakes* (2005).

A co-founding editor of *Conjunctions*, KENNETH REXROTH (1905–1982) was one of the twentieth century's greatest poets, essayists, translators, and polymaths, as well as an accomplished painter. His centenary year is being celebrated with readings and performances around the world.

Pulitzer Prize–winning composer NED ROREM is also the author of eighteen books, most recently the forthcoming collection *Facing the Night* (Shoemaker & Hoard), in which these two musical essays will appear.

JOANNA SCOTT's most recent novels are *Tourmaline* and *Liberation* (both Little, Brown). Her new collection of stories, *Everybody Loves Somebody*, will be published by Little, Brown in December.

DAVID SHIELDS is the author of eight books, including *Black Planet* (Crown), which was a finalist for the National Book Critics Circle Award and is being reissued by the University of Nebraska this fall, and *Remote* (Knopf), which won the PEN/Revson Award and was recently reissued in paperback by the University of Wisconsin. "The Thing About Life Is That One Day You'll Be Dead" is excerpted from a work in progress.

ELIOT WEINBERGER's latest books are *What Happened Here: Bush Chronicles* (New Directions); *The Stars*, a collaboration with the artist Vija Celmins (Museum of Modern Art); and an anthology, *World Beat: International Poetry Now* from New Directions.

Among PAUL WEST's numerous books is his newest, one of poetry, *Tea with Osiris* (Lumen). His next one, excerpted here, is *The Shadow Factory*, an account of his recent stroke.

DELILLO FIEDLER GASS PYNCHON
University of Delaware Press
Collections on Contemporary Masters

UNDERWORDS
Perspectives on Don DeLillo's *Underworld*

Edited by Joseph Dewey, Steven G. Kellman, and Irving Malin

Essays by Jackson R. Bryer, David Cowart, Kathleen Fitzpatrick, Joanne Gass, Paul Gleason, Donald J. Greiner, Robert McMinn, Thomas Myers, Ira Nadel, Carl Ostrowski, Timothy L. Parrish, Marc Singer, and David Yetter

$39.50

LESLIE FIEDLER AND AMERICAN CULTURE

Edited by Steven G. Kellman and Irving Malin

Essays by John Barth, Robert Boyers, James M. Cox, Joseph Dewey, R.H.W. Dillard, Geoffrey Green, Irving Feldman, Leslie Fiedler, Susan Gubar, Jay L. Halio, Brooke Horvath, David Ketterer, R.W.B. Lewis, Sanford Pinsker, Harold Schechter, Daniel Schwarz, David R. Slavitt, Daniel Walden, and Mark Royden Winchell

$36.50

INTO *THE TUNNEL*
Readings of Gass's Novel

Edited by Steven G. Kellman and Irving Malin

Essays by Rebecca Goldstein, Donald J. Greiner, Brooke Horvath, Marcus Klein, Jerome Klinkowitz, Paul Maliszewski, James McCourt, Arthur Saltzman, Susan Stewart, and Heide Ziegler

$35.00

PYNCHON AND *MASON & DIXON*

Edited by Brooke Horvath and Irving Malin

Essays by Jeff Baker, Joseph Dewey, Bernard Duyfhuizen, David Foreman, Donald J. Greiner, Brian McHale, Clifford S. Mead, Arthur Saltzman, Thomas H. Schaub, David Seed, and Victor Strandberg

$39.50

ORDER FROM ASSOCIATED UNIVERSITY PRESSES
2010 Eastpark Blvd., Cranbury, New Jersey 08512
PH 609-655-4770   FAX 609-655-8366   E-mail AUP440@ aol.com

Waltzing Again

New & Selected Conversations

with **Margaret Atwood**

Edited by Earl G. Ingersoll

"I don't mind being 'interviewed' any more than I mind Viennese waltzing—that is, my response will depend on the agility and grace and attitude and intelligence of the other person. Some do it well, some clumsily, some step on your toes by accident, and some aim for them."

"Time is a fact of life. In some ways, it is *the* fact of life. It might be considered the true hidden subject of all novels."

—**From the Interviews**

April/ $16.95 paperback

Recently Published

The Identity Club

New & Selected Stories and Songs

by Richard Burgin

"The book provides a chance to encounter this powerful writer, whose fiction has won four Pushcart Prizes... Burgin's collection of best stories constitutes a compelling vision of contemporary America."

—*The San Francisco Chronicle*

"Above all, these are city stories, and Burgin gets it all in there: loneliness, homelessness, prostitution and pickup basketball games."

—*The Philadelphia Inquirer*

$24.95 cloth

NOON

NOON

A LITERARY ANNUAL

1369 MADISON AVENUE   PMB 298
NEW YORK   NEW YORK   10128-0711

EDITION PRICE $9 DOMESTIC $14 FOREIGN

Black Clock

Bruce Bauman / Aimee Bender / Francesca Lia Block
Mary Caponegro / Tom Carson / Samuel R. Delany
Don DeLillo / Brian Evenson / Glen David Gold
Rebecca Goldstein / Arielle Greenberg
Maureen Howard / Andrew Hultkrans
Shelley Jackson / Heidi Julavits / Miranda July
Jonathan Lethem / Ben Marcus / Greil Marcus
Joseph McElroy / Rick Moody / Bradford Morrow
Dwayne Moser / Yxta Maya Murray / Geoff Nicholson
Joy Nicholson / Geoffrey O'Brien / Robert Polito
Richard Powers / Jon Savage / Joanna Scott
Lewis Shiner / Darcey Steinke / Susan Straight
Lisa Teasley / David L. Ulin / Michael Ventura
William T. Vollmann / David Foster Wallace
Mary Yukari Waters / Carlos Ruiz Zafon

Spring / Fall

edited by **Steve Erickson**
designed by **Gail Swanlund**

blackclock.org

Published by CalArts in association
with the MFA Writing Program

One-week Writing Intensive

workshops ·· readings ·· seminars ·· panels

FICTION

NONFICTION

POETRY

SCREENWRITING

TIN HOUSE MAGAZINE and
TIN HOUSE BOOKS
Present the 4th Annual

Tin House
Summer Writers
Workshop '06

Faculty and Special Guests

DOROTHY ALLISON ·· STEVE ALMOND ·· AIMEE BENDER

CHARLES D'AMBROSIO ·· NICK FLYNN

MATTHEA HARVEY ·· LEE MONTGOMERY ·· LORRIE MOORE

OREN MOVERMAN ·· ANTONYA NELSON

MICHAEL ONDAATJE ·· D. A. POWELL

ELISSA SCHAPPELL ·· JIM SHEPARD ·· ANTHONY SWOFFORD

Agents ·· Sarah Burnes, Liz Farrell, Betsy Lerner, Ira Silverberg

REED COLLEGE, PORTLAND, OREGON
JULY 9 – JULY 16

SPACE IS LIMITED. For more information and application guidelines visit www.tinhouse.com or call 503-219-0622

Mothers & Other Monsters
Maureen F. McHugh

"Gorgeously crafted stories."
—Nancy Pearl, NPR (*Morning Edition*)

» Story Prize Finalist.
» Book Sense Notable Book.
» Paperback edition includes author interview and essay.

HC · $24 · 1931520135
PB · $16 · 1931520194

Skinny Dipping in the Lake of the Dead
Alan DeNiro

"You can't help but stop and take real notice."
—Jonathan Carroll (*Glass Soup*)

A passionate, poetic, and political debut fiction collection reminiscent of the work of Aimee Bender & George Saunders. Includes stories from *Fence, One Story, Crowd,* and *3rd Bed.*

$16 · 1931520178
July 1, 2006

Magic for Beginners
Kelly Link

» Best Books of the Year: *Time Magazine, Salon, Village Voice.*
» "Stone Animals" reprinted in *Best American Short Stories 2005.*
» Illustrated by Shelley Jackson.

"Advanced alchemy."—*The Believer*

"A class of its own."—*Boldtype*

$24 · 1931520151

Travel Light
Naomi Mitchison

» Peapod Classics No.2

"No one knows better how to spin a fairy tale."—*The Observer*

"A 78-year-old friend staying at my house picked up *Travel Light,* and a few hours later she said, 'Oh, I wish I'd known there were books like this when I was younger!' So, read it now—think of all those wasted years!"
—Ursula K. Le Guin (*Gifts*)

$12 · 1-931520-14-3

Bard FICTION PRIZE

Bard College invites submissions for its annual Fiction Prize for young writers.

The Bard Fiction Prize is awarded annually to a promising, emerging writer who is a United States citizen aged 39 years or younger at the time of application. In addition to a monetary award of $30,000, the winner receives an appointment as writer-in-residence at Bard College for one semester without the expectation that he or she teach traditional courses. The recipient will give at least one public lecture and will meet informally with students.

To apply, candidates should write a cover letter describing the project they plan to work on while at Bard and submit a C.V., along with three copies of the published book they feel best represents their work. No manuscripts will be accepted.

Applications for the 2007 prize must be received by July 15, 2006. For further information about the Bard Fiction Prize, call 845-758-7087, send an e-mail to bfp@bard.edu, or visit www.bard.edu/bfp. Applicants may also request information by writing to the Bard Fiction Prize, Bard College, Annandale-on-Hudson, NY 12504-5000.

Bard College
PO Box 5000, Annandale-on-Hudson, NY 12504-5000

Back issues of
CONJUNCTIONS
25th Anniversary Year!

A limited number of back issues are still available for those who would like to discover for themselves the range of innovative writing published in CONJUNCTIONS during the past twenty-five years.

Conjunctions:32, Eye to Eye: Writers and Artists. William H. Gass and Mary Gass, C.D. Wright and Deborah Luster, Camille Guthrie and Louise Bourgeois, Rikki Ducornet, John Yau and Trevor Winkfield, Diana Michener, Robert Creeley and Archie Rand, Lynne Tillman and Haim Steinbach, Thomas Bernhard, Suzan-Lori Parks, and others. 400 pages.

Conjunctions:33, Crossing Over. Richard Powers, John Ashbery, Reginald Shepherd, Eduardo Galeano, Joyce Carol Oates, Isaac Bashevis Singer, Yoko Tawada, Mark McMorris, Noy Holland, Rosmarie Waldrop, Arthur Sze, Gilbert Sorrentino, and others. First translation of Thomas Bernhard's *Heldenplatz.* 424 pages.

Conjunctions:34, American Fiction: States of the Art. Sandra Cisneros, Julia Alvarez, Paul Auster, Russell Banks, Ann Beattie, Robert Coover, Rikki Ducornet, Steve Erickson, Maureen Howard, Carole Maso, Edwidge Danticat, Rick Moody, A.M. Homes, Leslie Marmon Silko, William T. Vollmann, and others. 488 pages.

Conjunctions:35, American Poetry: States of the Art. Lyn Hejinian, Jorie Graham, Gustaf Sobin, James Tate, Martine Bellen, John Yau, Robert Creeley, Ann Lauterbach, Fanny Howe, Michael Palmer, Forrest Gander, Barbara Guest, Charles Bernstein, Jena Osman, and others. 488 pages.

Conjunctions:36, Dark Laughter. Homero Aridjis, Jonathan Safran Foer, Valerie Martin, Can Xue, Ben Marcus, William T. Vollmann, Robert Coover, Lynne Tillman, George Saunders, Jonathan Ames, Mark McMorris, Alexander Theroux, Gilbert Sorrentino, Sarah Rothenberg, and others. 360 pages.

Conjunctions:37, Twentieth Anniversary Issue. John Barth, Richard Powers, Anne Carson, David Foster Wallace, Rikki Ducornet, Paul Auster, Brian Evenson, Diane Williams, Gilbert Sorrentino, John Edgar Wideman, Walter Abish, C.D. Wright, Mark Z. Danielewski, and others. 464 pages.

Conjunctions:38, Rejoicing Revoicing: The Art of Translation. Vladimir Nabokov, Charles Baudelaire, Miguel de Cervantes, Fyodor Dostoevsky, Octavio Paz, Leo Tolstoy, Marcel Proust, Robert Musil, and others. Also work by Julia Alvarez, Rick Moody, Rikki Ducornet, Paul West, and others. 384 pages.

Conjunctions:39, The New Wave Fabulists. Guest-edited by Peter Straub with original drawings by Gahan Wilson. Neil Gaiman, James Morrow, John Crowley, Kelly Link, M. John Harrison, Elizabeth Hand, Jonathan Lethem, Gene Wolfe, Jonathan Carroll, and others. 2nd printing. 438 pages.

Conjunctions:40, 40x40. Robert Coover, Joy Williams, Lois-Ann Yamanaka, David Shields, John Ashbery, Angela Carter, William T. Vollmann, Han Ong, Donald Revell, Leslie Scalapino, Gustaf Sobin, Mary Caponegro, Robert Kelly, Maureen Howard, William H. Gass, and others. Features a full-color portfolio of paintings by Ilya Kabakov. 498 pages.

Conjunctions:41, Two Kingdoms. Guest-edited by Howard Norman. Don DeLillo, Reginald Shepherd, Siri Hustvedt, Madison Smartt Bell, Eliot Weinberger, Jackson Mac Low, Brian Evenson, Russell Banks, Robert Kelly, Mary Caponegro, Paul Auster, Jonathan Lethem, Honor Moore, Christopher Sorrentino, and others. Includes a Special Tribute to William Gaddis edited by Rick Moody. 432 pages.

Conjunctions:42, Cinema Lingua. Peter Gizzi, Tan Lin, Elizabeth Robinson, Ann Lauterbach, C. D. Wright, Maureen Howard, Gilbert Sorrentino, William H. Gass, Luc Sante, Clark Coolidge, Gerard Malanga, Peter Straub, Eleni Sikelianos, Donald Revell, Alexander Theroux, Joyce Carol Oates, and others. Includes a previously unpublished play by filmmaker John Sayles. 452 pages.

Conjunctions:43, Beyond Arcadia. Kelly Link, John Sayles, T. M. McNally, Rick Moody, Ben Marcus, Can Xue, and others. Features a portfolio of twelve emerging poets selected and introduced by twelve established ones. Includes Christian Hawkey, Frances Richard, Michelle Robinson, Genya Turovskaya, Eve Grubin, Peter O'Leary, Sarah Lang, Justin Lacour, and others. 396 pages.

Conjunctions:44, An Anatomy of Roads. John Barth, Elizabeth Hand, Arthur Sze, Joanna Scott, Rikki Ducornet, Alai, Joyce Carol Oates, Carole Maso, Robert Kelly, William H. Gass, Rachel Blau DuPlessis, Forrest Gander, Frederic Tuten, Joshua Furst, Robert Coover, Jon McGregor, Bradford Morrow, Rae Armantrout, James Grinwis, and others. 404 pages.

Conjunctions:45, Secret Lives of Children. Shelley Jackson, Robert Clark, Howard Norman, Can Xue, Mary Caponegro, Robert Creeley, Paul La Farge, Emily Barton, David Marshall Chan, Lois-Ann Yamanaka, Scott Geiger, Kim Chinquee, and others. Includes a new cartoon strip by Gahan Wilson and new translations of Stéphane Mallarmé by John Ashbery. 404 pages.

Send your order to:
CONJUNCTIONS, Bard College, Annandale-on-Hudson, NY 12504.
Issues are $15.00 each, plus $3.00 shipping.
A small number of copies of certain back issues of *Conjunctions:1-31* are available. Please inquire.